AGAINST NATURE

By Casey Barrett

Against Nature

Under Water

AGAINST NATURE

Casey Barrett

KENSINGTON BOOKS
http://www.kensingtonbooks.com

Library of Congress Card Catalogue Number: 2018932844

ISBN-13: 978-1-4967-0971-4
ISBN-10: 1-4967-0971-3
First Kensington Hardcover Edition: August 2018

eISBN-13: 978-1-4967-0973-8
eISBN-10: 1-4967-0973-X
First Kensington Electronic Edition: August 2018

10 9 8 7 6 5 4 3 2 1

Printed in the United States of America

To Bruder Lars

And

To George, beloved hound, RIP.

There is no passion in nature so demonically impatient as that of him who, shuddering upon the edge of a precipice, thus meditates a plunge.

—Edgar Allan Poe

AGAINST
NATURE

Prologue

It was a beautiful view. The deputy couldn't stop staring at it. Death rested on the rocks below, but his eyes were drawn up and out toward a rolling horizon in a crisp spring sky. The valley was framed in a V by the Kaaterskill Clove, a deep gorge that dove between a pair of green mountains in the northern Catskills. Since the nineteenth century painters had stood on these rocks and tried to capture the absurd beauty.

His boss, the sheriff of Greene County, gazed over the falls at the broken dead figure that had gone over the side. The body appeared to have detonated on impact. Blood splatter covered the rocks and flowed down with the falling water. He sighed, never looked up, immune to the nature gawking. Every season there would be a handful of these, fool city folk who raced up the sides of waterfalls in flip-flops, then took a wrong step on loose rock and down they went. But this wasn't that. He knew the poor bastard down there. He was a local, a writer of faded fame by the name of Victor Wingate.

He went to join a thin man who was crouched off to the side, petting Wingate's orphaned Lab named Filly.

"Whaddya think?" he asked.

The thin man frowned, his eyes moist. They'd been

neighbors. He straightened up, gave Filly a pat on her big brown head. "He's tried it before," he said.

The sheriff nodded. "Few years back, was it?" he asked. "After the wife left him."

"He was doing well," said the thin man. "Better than I've seen him, in a long time."

They glanced over at the apparent reason for this. A frightening beauty dressed in black, smoking and scowling next to a dying ash tree. She was tall, severe, with ink black hair that fell around a pale perfectly symmetrical face. The sheriff approached.

"He didn't kill himself," said the lady. "There's no fucking way."

He backed off without reply. There would be time for questions later. She was giving off a dark energy that threatened to make a bad situation worse. Instead he walked over to his deputy.

"Bother you for a hand?" he asked.

The kid blinked, shook his head, as if waking from hypnosis. "Sure, sure," he stammered. "What do you need?"

"Called the Rescue Squad yet?" he asked. "Gonna need them to climb down there and retrieve Mr. Wingate before dark. Unless you'd like to do it yourself?"

The deputy took a last look at that view, then turned and hiked off through the woods to organize the rescue effort, reflecting as he went that rescue *was a foolish word for the recovery of a successful suicide.*

The sheriff and the thin man looked at each other, then over at the striking woman in their presence. The gulf between Wingate's physical appearance and that of his girlfriend was difficult to fathom. "Perhaps hung down to his knee," the men would say later. Victor was a good six inches shorter than her. Paunchy, almost bald, not much style. A divorced has-been bachelor living like a shy wood-

land animal in his big house on the side of a mountain. Then this woman showed up.

"He didn't kill himself," she said again.

On a flat dry rock, a few feet from the falls, there was a glass of cut crystal. The sheriff pulled a sleeve down over his hand to protect the prints and picked it up and smelled the remains. A last sip of bourbon swirled in the bottom. The angel's share, he thought. He set it back down and leaned against the rock. For the first time he allowed himself a look outward. He noticed that the neighbor and the woman were doing the same. A hawk appeared above the clove, then another, the pair circling in wide graceful arcs against the blue sky, moving lower into the green, preparing to dive for prey in the shallows below.

It really was a lovely view.

Chapter 1

We'd just finished. I was fetching Kleenex after a strenuous round while she lay on her back gathering her breath. My knees buckled as I limped to the bathroom and gave myself silent praise. Well done, Duck. Her response was reward enough, but I couldn't help thinking of the envelope of cash that would be waiting bedside in the morning.

My employment was difficult to define these days, but it had its perks.

I returned to bed, offered her the cleanup Kleenex, and kissed her on salty lips. She returned it with hunger and pulled me closer. I gave slight resistance and she laughed lightly into my mouth. "I'll give you a few minutes to recharge," she said.

My employer slash lover was a catch of considerable status in certain circles. Juliette Cohen: divorced, one child, worth a couple hundred bucks. Art dealers and headmasters and various hat shakers would genuflect in her presence. She was a long-legged blonde, who dressed like the fashion editor she once was. Now in her early forties, money was something to be spent, not earned.

Ostensibly, my job was tutor and swim teacher to her eight-year-old son, Stevie. I had surprised myself with competence. Stevie had responded to me, I'd managed to teach him a few things of value: like how not to drown, and how to play a bit of piano. His mother told me I was the only male he'd ever listened to. Never mind the father, his bitterness at losing a reported 300 million dollars in the divorce left him uninterested in parenting a son produced by that greedy slut. He was off on family number two now, with a pair of daughters and a younger wife who signed a favorable prenup.

I met Juliette in the usual way, on a case, a simple matter of deterring an overeager suitor. Divorcées with that kind of money become a mark. Eyed by rising finance guys, the sort who worship hedge fund managers like A-list celebrities. They keep an eye on ladies like these, tracking the constellations of fortunes like astronomers. This one was a chiseled smiling sack of flesh named Bret, a VP at Fortress. He made the common miscalculation, confusing proximity to wealth to possession of it. He was caught throwing a coke party at her Village apartment, while mother and son were out at their place in Amagansett. When she found out, he took a helicopter out east, and billed it to her account. He told Stevie to shut up when he tried to intervene in an argument. And finally, one high Saturday night, he refused to leave after too much blow prevented him from performing. He did not take the breakup well. He wouldn't leave her alone.

I was referred by a mutual acquaintance, one Margaret McKay, whose life I helped wreck after she hired me to find her missing daughter a year earlier. The search—and eventual horror show of discovery—had shattered both of our lives. I was still a cracked shell; I was surprised she was still alive. In the aftermath I was confident that suicide was inevitable for her. I'd set my own odds at 50/50, and

so far the coin toss was settling on this side of life. I had
Juliette to thank for that.

It didn't take much to deter the determined Bret. The
threat of physical violence tends to backfire with these
sorts. They want to fight back, and if that looks like a losing battle, they'll hire reinforcements. But the threat of
shame is always effective. An email to the boss, a humili-
ating confrontation during a business meal at Per Se, these
things put the fear of the money god into a man. He learns
that it's easier than he thought to be excommunicated
from the church of the Street. He falls in line and learns to
set his sights a bit lower than the Juliette Cohens of his
world.

I should have learned as much.

Instead I filled his bedroom void. It was a subtle arrangement with a noble cause. The night we settled our case,
which ended with an emailed pledge from Bret never to
contact her again, we enjoyed a few bottles of Chateau La-
tour. The conversation was easy and interesting and flirty,
the sort that leads to the inevitable, but that night Stevie
was having a sleepover. With a trio of eight-year-olds and
multiple nannies mulling about, it would have been inele-
gant to stay late. We ended our evening by eleven, with me
agreeing to give Stevie a swim lesson at their building's
rooftop pool the next day.

Eight months later I was a part of her staff. I hadn't
worked a case since. I felt like a rescue dog picked up by
his best-case scenario, only to resent the taming process. I
was healthier than I'd been in years, and trying to keep a
lid on the self-loathing. Juliette helped keep me off the
bourbon and painkillers. Our only indulgence was expensive wine and a bit of weed. It was as close to clean living
as I cared to get.

She was disciplined in all things in her life, but sex. Her

body preserved by a strict regime of yoga, Soul Cycling, and vegan eating. In the evenings she allowed herself a moderate amount of wine, followed by a single small bowl of sativa, inhaled from a one-hitter and exhaled with eyes-shut bliss through a cracked living-room window. She claimed to dislike the high of the healthier trend of vaping; burning fresh weed the old-fashioned way was her one private vice.

Then she would drag me off to the master bedroom, where I would earn my income. Since my teaching rates for her son were never clarified, the arrangement was loose but impossible to misunderstand. The thickness of envelopes bore no relation to Stevie's progress. They were based on the pleasure I provided after he'd gone to bed.

Juliette wiped between her legs and handed me the Kleenex.

"Love, would you mind getting me a glass of water?" she asked.

I swallowed a grumble and moved back toward the bathroom.

"From the kitchen, darling," she said. "You know I can't drink it from the tap."

Another gulp of sleepy pride, then I stepped into a pair of boxers and left to make the walk across the endless apartment. The floors did not creak. No sounds of the city filtered up through the windows. They were hermetically sealed to ensure total silence. The effect of lifeless luxury was unsettling. Large modern art from Gagosian and Zwirner stared down at me through the darkness with incomprehension. The sound of the refrigerator opening felt like an intrusion. On my way back I found myself tiptoeing aware of the slightest disturbance. As I approached the bedroom, I noticed a light shining beneath the door. Inside, Juliette was sitting up in bed, staring at my phone.

"You have a text," she said, icy as Arctic.

"From who?" I offered the water, reached for my cell.

She ignored the glass, looked down at the offending screen.

"From Cassandra Kimball," she said. "It reads, 'Need you. Please call.' "

I snatched the phone from her grip. Ice water splashed from the glass across Juliette's bare chest. "Watch it, asshole!" she said.

She dried herself with the sheets, glared up at me.

"You're fucking her again?" she asked. "How dare you."

I looked at the screen, confirmed the message; I looked down at my snarling lover. "I never was," I said.

"Oh, bullshit. I'm supposed to believe that?" She kicked at the phone in my hands. I dodged the painted toes. Then she flung herself from bed and fled to the bathroom.

I looked back at the text. **Need you . . .**

It had been twenty months since we'd seen each other. Twenty months since I'd almost gotten her killed. At the end of the McKay case, Cass had absconded to the country. The bullet in her gut left a scar, but nothing like the psychic wounds we would both forever nurse. I didn't blame her for going. It was too much for anyone to process. But I blamed her for not coming back. After she left, I did my best to sober up. I rode the wagon like a good boy as I put mind and body back together. But then one day I received a letter from the still-missing girl, Madeline McKay. It brought back all the failures and demons and soon I was reaching for the bottle. I dove into the whiskey abyss, deep as I could go. I would have kept diving until I reached the land without light, if not for Juliette. No, that's not quite right—if not for her eight-year-old kid.

The day I showed up for his swim lesson was the first day I hadn't taken a drink before lunch in months. It was selfishness at first, and greed. Like Bret and plenty of others, I was seeing his mother as a mark, even if I wasn't admitting it to myself. She had overpaid me in the blithe way of wealth for my services with her spurned lover. I figured she was good for another easy payday for teaching her kid. I just had to stay sober until after the class. I did. Then for reasons unclear to me I did not drink to unconsciousness later that night. So began another reluctant limp back to sober-ish living.

And now with a four-word text I was on the cusp of being thrown from this well-paid paradise. The thought made me smile. This was not the facial expression desired by Juliette when she emerged from the bathroom.

"How dare you," she said. "You smile . . ." I watched as she searched for something to throw. She chose an elephant figurine, the trunk used as a ring holder. Juliette grabbed it and flung it, end over end, at my head. I ducked and heard it shatter over the bed.

"Get out," she said.

I scurried for my clothes. She watched as I dressed. Maybe she expected me to plead, to gush out all the perfect words that would soothe her raging ego. I stayed quiet, kept smirking. Then came the slaps. Her fury exceeded the jealousy of an ill-timed text, no matter how threatened she was by Cass. It was my response, my grin. There was no denying it. I couldn't wait to call.

When her blows abated, I tried to explain that there must be something wrong, how long it had been. My lover was not interested. *After all I've done for you* was the prevailing theme. I reached the bedroom door with one shoe on and my t-shirt backward. Tears came next. The untrusting, burned divorcée alone again behind a wall of fortune that prevented basic human bonds. She gathered herself while I lingered, wondering if there was some way to appease her. Juliette wiped at her damp blue eyes and

inhaled a long breath through her nose like her yoga training taught her. She exhaled, tilted her sharp chin up to me.
"Don't come back here," she said. She closed the door.

In the living room I found my keys, wallet. I took some
parting mental snapshots of this gorgeous apartment. From
the open kitchen through the dining and living areas, the
loft stretched some seventy feet across, with a dozen high
windows from end to end. Large silk rugs in an aqua
palate covered the blond hardwood floors. The décor was
Turkish inspired, with exotic lighting and richly patterned
pillows across plush couches and low-slung designer
chairs. Tossed on one was Stevie's backpack. I wondered
for a brief mad second if I should go wake him and bid my
farewell. Then I heard his voice behind me.

"Duck, what's going on?" he asked, rubbing at his eyes.

"Hey, buddy, I'm sorry to wake you," I said. "I need to
head out."

"Why?"

I took a step closer to him, reconsidered and backed up
again. "A friend of mine is in trouble," I told him. "I need
to see if she's okay."

"What happened?" he asked.

"Well, I don't know yet, she just asked me to call."

"You said she was in trouble."

"I think she is, or I'm sure she is, but I don't know
what's happened."

I lowered myself to his eye level, then reached out and
patted his shoulder. "I'm sure everything will be okay. Just
go back to sleep, all right?"

"Are you coming over tomorrow?" he asked.

"I hope so, buddy, but I'm not sure," I said. "Ask your
mom, okay?"

He nodded, understanding. Already the scar tissue of
divorce had built its layers of protection. Stevie turned and
shuffled off toward his bedroom without looking back.

It was one a.m. I stood before the building's private garage next to the lobby doors on 13ᵗʰ Street. Still early to my old way of thinking, the bars would be open for another three hours. I salivated at the thought. When was the last time I'd drunk till closing? When had I last savored the amber on my tongue? Too long. I considered the nearest suitable venues. There was Black & White over on 10ᵗʰ, Old Town up on 18ᵗʰ, an array of others for all ages in between. Then I remembered why I'd been kicked to the curb: Cass. **Please call.** I took out my cell and walked toward University and listened to it ring.

"Thank you," she whispered. "I wasn't sure if you would call back."

"You know that's not true," I said.

"Something terrible's happened, Duck," she said. "I really need your help."

"Tell me."

"My boyfriend," she said. I seized at the word, wanted to hang up and hear no more. "His name was Victor Wingate. It was serious. We were living together. It was the first real relationship of my life. We were . . . I think we were in love."

"What happened, Cass?"

"He's dead."

"How?"

"He fell, from the top of a waterfall near our house. I don't know how. They think he jumped, but I know he didn't. He . . ."

She stopped and I listened to the silence. The gulf between us had never been so wide. There was emotion in her voice I had never heard before. I thought Cass was beyond all notions of romance. This was the woman who worked as a dungeon mistress for years at the Chamber. This was the imperious dominatrix who whipped and tortured men for a couple hundred bucks an hour.

"I'm sorry," I said, without much depth.

"I need to see you," she said. "I need your help."

"Where are you?"

"The Catskills. About three hours on the bus, I can pick you up."

She told me the details and I told her that I'd see her tomorrow.

Then I walked three blocks over to Black & White. The dark bar was playing early White Stripes, "You're Pretty Good Looking (For a Girl)." The tables were filled with rocker types and the girls who like them. There was one seat left at the bar, next to a tattooed couple talking close and ending each sentence with a kiss. They didn't acknowledge me. I motioned to the bartender and ordered a double Bulleit. I roared the whiskey down. Ordered another. He smiled with indulgence, asked if I wanted to open a tab. I handed him a card, looked down into the amber, lifted the glass and took a sip. It never tasted so good.

Chapter 2

I woke early, with the old confusion, to an empty apartment. All senses were blunt and worn, ground down from misuse. My subterranean flat had the stale smell of neglect. Of late it was used for stopovers, a change of clothes, a remembered book. I spent the occasional night when Juliette and Stevie were out in the Hamptons without me, but I'd more or less taken up residence at their eight-figure loft on 13th Street, which was roughly eight times the size of my one-bedroom cave four blocks away.

I rolled over and sought the warmth of the one being I could depend on. All that was left was his ghost.

Elvis died a few months back. He wasn't young, but I thought we had a few more years together. He never quite recovered from the beating on the night of the double murder at my apartment. The night it was almost a triple when Cass flatlined in the ambulance.

The hound healed from his kicked-in ribs and the internal bleeding, and he lay by my side every day as we put ourselves back together again. There were plenty of nights when his loyalty was the only thing that kept me from swallowing down a pint of Drano and being done with it. Instead I'd rub his belly on the couch and turn the pages of another book full of blood and suffering, taking solace in the shared misery. Until one day in September when I woke beside him in bed and he didn't stir. Elvis died peacefully in the night, pressed against my side. There are worse ways to go.

I spent a week on a blow bender, staying at the St. Marks Hotel, afraid to return to my dog-free apartment. When Juliette Cohen contacted me, through none other than Margaret McKay, I took it as an omen. I accepted the case in hopes that the McKay curse would ruin me further. The coke hangover left me a jangled, depressed mess. I took it out on her lover, Bret. At Per Se one night I confronted him in front of a dozen colleagues. I pretended to be the enraged husband of a woman he was screwing. I shoved him across the table and told his dinner companions that he'd given my soon-to-be ex herpes. Threatened castration if he ever came near her again.

If Elvis had been alive, I wouldn't have stayed over at the Cohen apartment quite so often. I would have had the good sense to get away postcoitus and keep my distance. But in my loss home was a space to be avoided, so I accepted her invitations to stay, waking with a romp each morning, until the envelopes fattened and her son grew used to seeing me at breakfast. It was an untenable position, but I can't say I resisted the gilded setting. I always wanted to be rich again.

Those environs, just hours removed, seemed like a lost dream. Reality was my tiny flat on East 17th Street, the basement rental of the elderly Mr. Petit, who would soon be joining Elvis in the ground. I often wondered what would come of his brownstone when he was gone. It was an 1880s Italianate beauty, with all the original accents and crown molding and pocket doors. The kitchen and bathrooms needed an overhaul, but it would be criminal if it fell into the hands of a modernist bastard who gutted the place. I knew my days in the golden handcuffs of below-market rent would soon be coming to an end. Mr. Petit, closeted into his eighties despite the acceptance all around him, had no heirs I knew of. We were friendly enough. I didn't mind when he watched me out in the garden shirtless on hot summer days. And he'd once worked for my father, before the fall, which explained the sympathy rent he charged me. Still, I doubted I'd be making the will. I was just lucky I wasn't evicted after his home turned into a homicide crime scene during the McKay case.

I limped through the waking process, dressed and reached for the leash that still hung on the door side hook. I could smell Elvis's scent on the harness. Thought about heading straight to the closest animal shelter and adopting the first rescue I saw. But it still felt disrespectful to the hound, so I walked around the block by myself, stopping at all his favorite trees, marked forever.

It was a fine spring day, the blossoms bursting, days after the latest Kentucky Derby. Won by a rare filly called Smiling Eyes. Cass would appreciate that. She had a fondness for the ponies that I failed to grasp. Triple Crown season was always her favorite time of year. I thought of her up in the mountains, in love a world away from the urban prison she escaped, and now heartbroken after her man jumped to his death. She didn't believe it could be voluntary, but that was the natural human response. It shattered every narrative. She thought she found peace after all the violence I put her through. Found a man she allowed herself to love. I hated the dead guy already. What was his name again?

Victor Wingate . . . the name rang a faint bell.

When I returned home, I Googled him, found the broad search strokes of his past. Wingate was a writer, a magazine journalist of some renown, with one book to his credit. It was called *Walk Through Fire,* the story of a 1920s boxer named Eddie Finn, a former light-heavyweight champ. The reviews claimed Finn's life was like "an ancient Irish fable" and that Wingate captured his story with "muscular prose suited to the subject." It sold well enough, and then it was adapted into a film of the same name. Earned a handful of Oscar nominations. Dylan provided the theme song, a haunting dirge called "The Bell," which I remembered playing a lot back then. A good book, a better movie, it was enough to set a writer up for a while. It appeared Wingate hadn't worked much since. The most recent byline I could find was from three years ago. It was a *Village Voice* obit of a fellow writer.

I checked the bus schedule and found a five p.m. out of the Port Authority, arriving in a town called Palenville a little after eight. Cass said she lived up the nearby mountain. I checked my phone, found nothing from Juliette. Whatever she decided to tell her son, I knew it wouldn't be the truth, and I knew he already hated me. It happens that way. I promised myself to try to reach out to the kid and set the record straight when I returned. I'd take him to a Knicks game and we'd talk it through, man to man. Just because things didn't work out between your mom and me doesn't mean we can't hang. I was still in touch with one of my mother's old lovers, an alcoholic pathologist named Dr. David Burke. I sought his counsel on certain cases. I envisioned Stevie and me like that, once he was grown and jaded too. *Yeah, right. Whatever you need to tell yourself.* I knew I'd just become another failed father figure in the poor kid's life. *Poor . . . Please, the boy had a trust fund in the hundreds.* He'd be fine. Better off without the series of damaged males that would pass through his privileged life.

I left an hour early for the bus, leaving some bonus time for a few belts at a remembered bar nearby.

The West 40s have always been my least favorite part of the city. It's the filthy armpit of this yawning island mass. Years ago the *New York Times* erected its new headquarters across the street from the bus station in a move that declared the true status of the newspaper business in the twenty-first century. The building looked like a grown-up jungle gym; indeed overgrown man-children have been arrested for trying to scale its ceramic rod façade. To the north were the tourist horrors of Times Square and its eternal fluorescent lightness. One avenue west, over on Ninth, the neighborhood known as Hell's Kitchen continued to live down to its name. There were ugly erections of glass-and-steel condos where razed tenements used to be, and the rents were soaring like everywhere else, but the developers weren't fooling anyone. It was still aptly named: Hell's Kitchen. It just had more character when it was an infested mess of porn shops and prostitutes and transient commuter pubs. The one I remembered was called Rudy's, between West 44th and 45th. Drinkers were offered free hot dogs from behind the bar. It was still standing.

Out front there was a large waving plastic pig dressed in a red jacket and black bowtie. Inside it felt like a good place for a slow, pleasant death. There were cracked red leather banquettes along the wall, facing a worn bar populated by a few day-drinking regulars. Above the cash register was a sign that advertised RUDY'S STIMULUS PACKAGE—a shot of Bushmills and a pint of Rudy's own blonde draft for five bucks. I ordered it along with a hot dog. The Irish whiskey was just right; the beer and the dog were not. Three sips and two bites and I headed for the restroom in the back. Not the way to prepare for a three-hour bus ride. On the way out I was grateful for the jukebox come to life. Some warm soul had put on Sam Cooke's "Cupid." I defy anyone to name a finer voice in human history than the beautiful Mr. Cooke. He lightened my spirits and settled my belly, and I moved down the bar, humming along with an easy smile.

"Hey, sugar," said a syrupy voice to my left. I turned to

find a large black prostitute in a tight red dress that matched
the garish banquette. She mimed a bow and arrow as Sam
sang about letting it go, gave me a wink. "Care to join me?"
she asked. I shrugged, slid in next to her. She placed a
hand over her ample chest and started to sing: " 'Straight
to my lover's heart for me . . .' "

"Buy me a drink?" she asked after the chorus. "What
are you drinking, honey?"

"The Stimulus Package," I said.

She wrinkled her nose. "No wonder you went rushing
to the bathroom." She laughed a thick, throaty laugh. "I'll
take a Bushmills, skip the rotgut on tap."

I agreed, went back to the bar, returned with two more
of the Irish blend.

"Cheers," we said, and downed them.

"What's your name, baby?" she asked.

"Duck," I said. "You?"

She pretended to waddle in her seat. "I'm Melody." She
leaned in, touched my hand. "So, Mr. Duck, you meetin'
anybody or you here all by your lonesome today?"

"Sadly solo," I told her. "Just killing some time before
my bus."

"How much time you got?" Her thick finger circled the
rim of the shot glass. She licked at painted purple lips.

"Not enough time to satisfy the likes of you," I said.

She gave me a Cheshire smile, reached out and squeezed
my hand. "Sugar, it ain't about me. I wanna sa-tis-fy you."

"Sorry, I, um . . ."

"I got a place right down the way," she said. "I get you
to your bus on time, don't you worry."

The jukebox DJ was sticking with Sam. "Everybody
Loves to Cha Cha Cha" came next. I looked into my empty
glass, then up into her glassy eyes. The pupils were dilated.
The whiskey wasn't the only thing coursing through her
system. She kept on smiling through glistening lips. The tip

of her tongue danced against her upper teeth. I felt a hand sliding up my inner thigh. Nothing stirred in me and I felt embarrassed by what she wouldn't find. Then her face was flooded in a flash of daylight. Melody raised her other arm and blocked her eyes, waited for the bar door to shut and darkness to return. I glanced back at the new patron.

He was a well-built, good-looking guy, around thirty. Shaved head, broad shoulders, tattoo sleeves snaked up both arms. His jeans and blank white t-shirt looked fresh off the shelf. So did his smile. It was a cocky smirk that announced physical confidence, a guy who hoped to brush shoulders on the way past. He moved with a slight shuffle, like an athlete trying to walk off an injury.

When he reached our table, he stopped and looked down at us. The smile widened.

"Duck?" he asked.

Melody removed her hand from my thigh, inched away from me, no stranger to bad vibes.

"Wrong guy," I said.

We looked at each other until he blinked. His eyes were lit for action. Up close he had the handsome vacancy of an actor. His face was well proportioned, masculine; he'd get through a few rounds of casting. Beneath the chin, before the tattoos began, there was a thin scar along his neck. The kind left by a blade, I had a few of my own. I didn't want to know where he got his.

"Yeah, it's you, Duck Darley, what's going on, man?"

His accent was distinct, German or Austrian, something central European. He pushed himself into the booth, pinning me in the middle. He stared across at Melody.

"Beat it," he said.

I grabbed her wide thigh and squeezed. "She's with me," I said. "And I don't know you."

Melody started to squirm from my grip, then looked

from the bald stranger back to me. Made her choice. "The fuck are you?" she asked him. "What's good, rude boy?"

"Told you to beat it, slut," he said, leaning in for the challenge. He said it low, but the whole bar seemed to hear. The room quieted and grew tense like someone had just shouted the N-word and now held its breath for retribution.

For the first time in too long, I moved through some aikido progressions in my mind. I was out of practice and out of shape, softened by rich living, unlike this specimen, who looked wired and primed for these encounters. The scar said enough. I placed both elbows on the small table between us, pressed my hands together beneath my chin, breathed through my nose. Slowed my heart rate and tried to focus on the calm before the coming chaos.

"You think you know me?" I asked.

"Sure do," he said. "Lawrence 'Duck' Darley, everybody knows you. You're famous. I'm a fan of your work."

Among the mess of dragons and skulls tattooed up his arms, I noticed an iron cross and the letters *NSM*—the initials of the National Socialist Movement. Neo-Nazis. On the knuckles of his right hand, the numbers *1488* were inked in Gothic type. I remembered the hate numerology from my days inside. The number 14 alluded to the fourteen-word philosophy of white-supremacist groups, something about securing a future for white children. . . . The number 88 was a stand-in for HH, with *H* being the eighth letter of the alphabet. Thus, 88 was the equivalent of the "Heil, Hitler" salute. A real subtle prince, this one.

"Like my ink?" he asked with a grin.

"At least you're up front about it," I said. "Inside, did you only take white cock?"

He stiffened. Blood rushed to his clean-shaven face. The neck scar seemed to thicken.

"You want to make your move and get messy?" I asked. "Or do you want to make your point first? You're obviously an errand boy."

He set both palms flat on the table. A vein pulsed at his temple. Our glasses shook as his knee jackhammered beneath us. Somehow he restrained himself.

"There's no need to be rude," he said. "I just wanted to introduce myself." He stuck out a bony hand. I let it hang. "I'm Oliver. I've read all about you."

"You can read? Good for you."

"I read about your friend too," he said. "The one who likes the whips and chains, yeah? What's her name, Cassandra?"

My heart rate spiked at the sound of her name. I felt every fiber tense.

"You going to see her?" he asked. "Up in the mountains? You don't want to miss your bus." He looked at a tatted wrist with no watch. Then he slid from the booth and peered down at me. "Tell her to be careful," he said. "Both of you be careful. As you might have learned—some things, they're not worth it, yeah?"

I watched his wide back as he walked down the bar without another look. I climbed out and followed. As the door opened and daylight flooded in, I caught sight of an older man waiting for him outside. Tall and trim, he was dressed in a slim-fitting gray suit. Aviator shades covered most of his face. He nodded to Oliver and looked over his shoulder at me. I caught the door as it tried to swing shut.

"Hey, tough guy," I called. "Where you think you're going?"

Oliver turned with a grin, like I was giving him just what he'd hoped for. The man put a hand on his shoulder; he shook it off, stepped toward me.

"You want to tell me how you know Cass and me?" I asked.

"I told you, you're famous."

As he moved closer, he seemed to inflate. It's like that with practiced fighters. The most undersized scrapper can seem like a UFC heavyweight champ when he's coming in with blood on his breath. Oliver had that scent. Fear was a foreign concept. But aikido is made for dealing with men like him. It's all about turning aggression on its head, using force against itself. As he charged, I received him, already anticipating his reaction to mine, a chess match moving at high speed, with higher stakes. There are over ten thousand named techniques in this art; I remember maybe a couple dozen. Inside a cage or alone at night, I would have been doomed. But out on a Manhattan daytime sidewalk, with cops lurking at every corner, I needed one good move to protect myself and make my point. Like a matador, I sidestepped him, stole his energy, and delivered a wheel throw that sent him crashing into the barfront pig. Before he could scamper up and charge again, I went to the older man, grabbed his wrist, and twisted it behind his back. He didn't resist, and though the pressure point exerts extreme pain, he never flinched.

"Who the fuck are you?" I asked in his ear.

"You shouldn't have done that," he said. "My associate is not well."

"If I have to ask again, this arm is broken."

A siren interrupted our street-fighting drama. "Put your hands up," said a voice from inside the car. "Release him."

I did as instructed. A pair of uniforms scurried out with guns drawn. We were forced to our knees, with hands behind our heads. A pedestrian approached, told the officers that I was acting in self-defense. He was a scrawny college-aged kid who said he watched the whole thing go down.

He said he was taking tae kwon do, and that he recognized my moves. The cops asked us to explain. Neither side had much to say. Before the boys could get irritated and take us in for disturbing the peace, another call came in. Shots fired in Times Square. They told us to go our separate ways, waited to see me cross the street, then sped off.

When I doubled back, they were gone.

Chapter 3

When I was twenty years old, I spent thirteen months behind bars for dealing weed. I was hustling all over Manhattan, making some decent money, when I got stopped coming off the 4 train at 59th Street. Over a year in Rikers for a drug that's now been decriminalized in most states, a drug that's about as harmful as a cheeseburger. It should have been probation, maybe some community service, but I was a kid with a sullied last name and a shit attitude.

My second week inside Rikers I was approached by some white supremacists who implied protection. I don't know if they could have protected me or not, but I told them to piss off. Then I tried to befriend a fat black kid named Darreus, who was doing time for crimes similar to my own, and seemed even more afraid than I was. When I sat down across from him in the cafeteria his eyes went wide, like he knew exactly what I'd set in motion. I remember him glancing over his shoulder at the white table in the corner and refusing to meet my eyes. Darreus stared down into his food and grunted one-word answers to my clueless questions. Later that evening Darreus was raped and I was beaten unconscious by those racist fucks.

After being treated for concussion, internal bleeding, broken ribs, jaw, nose, and collarbone, I was returned to the general population. At my first meal back I emptied my food into the lap of my main stomper and swiped the metal tray across his face. The memory of the blood that splashed from his nose still thrills me. It was the dumbest and bravest act of my life. I blacked out from another beating soon after. Deemed a "death-wish dunce" by the guards, I spent the rest of my stay either in the prison hospital or in isolation, which I suppose was my subconscious plan all along. You hear how the deprivation of solitary drives men to madness, but I found it rather peaceful. Better than the anxieties of being around fellow inmates, and the constant fear of rape and assault. I heard Darreus hung himself in his cell some months later. There are only so many nights a man can be sodomized against his will. At the time I couldn't figure why he didn't fight back. Resist, kick, bite, anything but compliant, even if it means a near-death beating—at some point the guards have to protect you, if not from your assailants, at least from yourself. The box is brutal, it saps the sanity, but it's safe. In any case I was released with the resolve never to return, and determined to teach myself skills that would help me defend myself against future attacks.

Enter aikido. I earned my black belt with daily trips to the dojo. For five years I never missed a day. Even out of practice it still filled me with confidence in the face of most any threat.

The threat I learned to loath and fear more than any other during those months inside? White supremacists. They're worse than any Blood or Crip or Latin King. They're the lowest form of humanity, the very worst of America. You see them on the news and all you can think is: *Who raised you? What pathetic in-bred disgrace of genetics produced such idiots?*

I like to think I have a high tolerance for all manner of sin and bad behavior, but nothing fills me with more revulsion than racist white trash. There's nothing supreme about the white race—I had my family as proof.

I was roiling over these memories, allowing the old rage to return. Who was this Oliver? Who was his anonymous keeper? His warning that Cass and I should be careful, that some things aren't worth it? Consider the challenge accepted. I stared out the window of the bus and watched the wasteland of Jersey sweep by.

The landscape turned green and hilly and newly lush as we connected to the New York Thruway and made our way past the suburbs and into the Hudson River Valley. My contact with Cass over the last twenty months had been sporadic, before ceasing entirely after Elvis died. I didn't appreciate being abandoned in a time of need. She loved that hound as much as I did. At the time I considered it unforgivable when she refused to make the trip back to the city to help me bury him in the garden. I told her as much; it had been our last contact until her ill-timed text the night before.

Juliette had every right to her fury. I'd told her about Cass. Tried to put a detached spin on our relationship, but women see through that nonsense. She knew what we shared. She refused to believe we never slept together; it was impossible for a woman of Juliette's appetites to fathom why not. She knew my partner meant more to me than she ever could, and that was not easy for her to accept, no matter how fat the envelopes she left. I considered the cash I'd accumulated over the proceeding months. It was nothing to her, but it would set me up for a while. I'd spent little while holed up at chez Cohen. I was a kept boy, a literal pool boy for her kid. I worked for that cash. There were plenty of nights I could have done without her carnal demands, but I'd been up to the challenge every damn time. It only cost some dignity.

Well, good-bye to all that. It was already a dream fading

from memory, a peaceful interlude between the natural states of chaos that defined my life. I'd miss Stevie though. The little fucker was a funny kid. A sharp, sly sense of humor for an eight-year-old, and smart too. *If I ever had a son of my own . . . Jesus, Duck, really? Deluded bastard you are.*

I untangled my headphones from my jacket pocket and connected to my phone and spun through my library of artists. I needed something with a loveless edge. Found some Libertines. Turned up "Can't Stand Me Now" and listened to Pete Doherty wail about how "the world kicked back a lot fuckin' harder now."

It sure kicked Victor Wingate in the ass—until he went right over the edge of a waterfall and died on impact. Dead or not, the guy had something I envied. He'd won the affections of Cass. I didn't think it was possible. Or in my arrogant haze I considered it only possible with myself. I always thought she'd come around someday. I understood her, like no one else. At some point Cass would grow jaded of the kinky freaks that lined up to pay for her beatings at the dungeon. She'd need an honest relationship, one built on friendship and mutual unbreakable bonds. Like, in our case, a pair of bullets we'd taken for each other, at different moments in our damaged lives. Even as she never allowed a single kiss, never even that extra bit of eye contact that said she was considering it, I never doubted that I was the one for her. The alcoholic's ego, it's unsurpassed.

Instead my partner abandoned me and fled to the country and found someone else. A has-been writer, nothing special to look at, based on his book jacket photo. So he'd won the writer's lottery when his one book was turned into a movie, a good one no less. Probably set up the lucky prick with a nice spot in the woods, all paid off, with the leisure to write as little as he pleased.

The bus stopped in Kingston and the driver informed us that we had ten minutes before continuing on upstate. There was a diner across the lot from the bus station. I walked over in hopes of a liquor license. Alas it was only beer and bad wine available at the Dietz Stadium Diner. There was a loose collection of fat locals spread in the booths, a few travelers grabbing a quick bite at the countertop. I leaned between two of them and ordered three bottles of Beck's. Downed one in a couple gulps, burped it out in silence, sucked at the second. With three minutes to spare I slipped the third green bottle in my bag. I left a twenty on the counter, and limped back to the bus.

At the nadir of the McKay case, my left Achilles was severed with bolt cutters, at the hands of an evil old friend. I could no longer point my toes or rotate my ankle, which made swimming especially difficult. My kick was ruined. I kept vowing to get back into the water on a regular basis. The doctors informed me that would be the best rehab of all, but I'd lost the feel and that's an elusive thing to get back. Besides, I'd been getting my chlorine fix through my lessons with Stevie. I wasn't doing much more than standing in waist-deep water offering some pointers, but it was better than being dry.

That same case also left me with a number of scars down my face, courtesy of an X-Acto knife and the bite of a raving Ukrainian lover. I grew out a beard and tried to forget about them. Clean-shaven it looked like streaks of tears burned down my cheeks, but the scruff covered the worst of it. Juliette offered her plastic surgeon, if I ever wanted to try to laser them away. I told her I liked the reminders.

I cracked my third Beck's as the bus rolled out, picking up the Thruway again, pulling me to Cass and all the intense baggage that came with her. We exited at the town of Saugerties, took a wide left and a quick right, and the countryside opened itself. The Catskill Mountains rolled along the western horizon. The magic-hour light touched them just so, giving the hills a blue glow that could stir even a banker's black-and-white soul. I understood in a guilty instant why Cass had decided to stay. It was everything the city was not, green and open and quiet, with the money—what there was of it—well hidden behind gravel drives. The coach drifted to a stop in front of an inn called Kindred Spirits. I remembered a painting of the same name, in the New York Public Library, and had an unpleasant flash of memory from richer boyhood days when my mother would walk me through the grand spaces of the city, pointing to masterpieces of art and architecture. I banished it, took a last sip of the Beck's, and staggered to the front, thanked our driver and stepped off into the spring evening. She was waiting alongside an old white Land Cruiser.

I cursed the lump in my throat, the familiar ache in my jeans, the Pavlov's response. I moved toward her. She was wearing a long-sleeved black dress, black boots. Straight dark hair framed her porcelain face. All that was missing was the long black veil. Her painted red lips tried to turn up into a smile. They only got halfway there.

"You made it," she said.

"You knew I would."

"It's good to see you, Duck."

She came in for a hug. Our first contact in twenty months and I felt nothing but a cold weariness from her. Our cheeks touched; we kissed at the air. She released me, took my inventory.

"I like the beard," she said. "It suits you."

"Covers some scars."

She nodded, lips pressed at the memory. I looked over her shoulder at her new ride.

"What happened to the Benz?" I asked.

"Had to trade it in," she said. "Couldn't handle the mountain roads in winter."

"You loved that thing." So did I. An '81 silver sedan, 300SD turbo diesel, burgundy interior. A classic. She ran it on vegetable oil, cared for it like a pet. Traded it in? It seemed criminal.

She shrugged. "Straight trade with a local collector. He'll take good care of the old girl." We walked over to the Land Cruiser. I had to admit it had a certain rugged appeal. "Besides," she said, "I've fallen for this beast just as hard. An '85, two hundred thousand miles, and never had a single issue. These things are legend."

That was as deep as we could go, car talk for the reunion. She pulled out of the lot ahead of the bus, turned right, and headed up the mountain. The beauty of it kept me silent. She wove up through the pass, past the towering green and flowing streams and waterfalls falling heavy with the winter melt. Spring came late to these parts. Patches of fading snow were still visible. I rolled down the window and let the cool wind rush over my face. A pack of hikers huffed up the side of the road to their car. Above, ribbons of white clouds decorated the darkening sky. The whole scene had an air of unreality, like a stage set, waiting for an unseen director to shout "Action!" and send a pair of sleek sports cars barreling down the mountain in a high-speed chase.

"I met Victor down in Woodstock," Cass was saying. "Getting coffee at Bread Alone. I was holding a book and he complimented me on it. It was by Jim Harrison, he was a fan. It turned out we both have family in the U-P."

"I thought you were from . . ." I stopped, and realized that I didn't know. Cass had never been one to share personal history.

"Baltimore," she said. "That's where I grew up. But I

had an aunt and uncle with a place way up north on Michigan's Upper Peninsula. Spent some summers there. So did Victor. His grandparents had a cabin in the U-P, not far from my cousins'. He was older than me, so we couldn't have overlapped, but I don't know, that's how we got to talking."

Waiting in line at a Woodstock coffee shop, holding a paperback, and already the bastard knew more about her than her partner of how many years? Partners that had seen the worst together, come close to dying more than once.

"What was it called?" I asked.

"What's that?"

"The Harrison, what book were you reading when Wingate picked you up?"

She gave me a sideways glance; let it pass. "It was called *The River Swimmer*," she said. "I'll lend you my copy up at the house if you want. It made me think of you."

"Shocking."

Cass made a face as she accelerated past a struggling pickup in the right lane. "You do realize I'm the bereaved here? Stop acting so hurt. It's weak."

"Know how you feel about weakness in men."

"Yeah, they deserve a beating."

"He like that?"

She ignored my baiting. Took the hairpin turns with practiced grace, slowed at a passing waterfall as we crossed a narrow bridge. "Up there is Kaaterskill Falls," she told me. "It's beautiful, but hikers have become a nuisance. A few fall and die every summer."

I stared out the window and missed the city. I wasn't interested in sweating and trudging through dirt and rocks to gawk at vistas. Give me a dim-lit bar, good music, amber swirling in my glass. I was a city kid, nature meant darkness and discomfort, and I'd had my share of both. I thought of

Stevie, glazed on video games in his grand apartment, old Duck not even a memory. Thought of Juliette down the hall, splayed across the bed, toying herself to orgasm in my absence. Or maybe she'd already found my replacement. I resolved to call and apologize.

As the mountain crested, Cass slowed and signaled left and we turned into a wooded enclave. On a low pillar there was a sign that read ASHER GREEN, PRIVATE. We crossed a stone bridge over a rolling falls and a view full of déjà vu. A pair of lush green mountains divided by a narrow slice into a deep valley; out beyond, a view to forever.

"This is where Asher Durand painted his masterpiece," Cass said.

"*Kindred Spirits*," I remembered aloud, like the inn down mountain.

"Impressive, Darley. How'd you know that?"

"My mother was big on culturing her kid."

Cass nodded, filed it away. She stopped before a gate, rolled down her window, and punched a code into a keypad that raised a restricting arm. We drove past small shuttered cottages. Some seemed to hang precariously from the edge of the mountain. There were no cars parked before them, no signs of light or life within.

"This place was built as a summer community," she said. "Back in the 1880s. Most of the homes have been passed down through generations, and no one's ever bothered to winterize them. Seems like such a waste. But we loved it empty. It was like the park was just for us most of the year, like our own private ghost town. Victor liked to leave in July, the one month when all these places come to life."

"I'm sorry," I said. Too late I realized I'd never bothered to offer my sympathies. "Sounds like you were happy."

"I was," she said, emphasis on the past tense.

She drove us up two more winding hills past more empty

homes until the woods thickened and all that was left was a two-track road shaded by heavy limbs and new spring growth. A pair of wild turkeys came rooting out of a fern patch and then disappeared at the sound of the car. Inevitable free association: whiskey. Wondered if she had any.

"We're the last house on the left," she said. "Nothing past us but a couple thousand acres of state park. Right up here."

She slowed, turned into a drive, and stopped in front of a gabled Victorian home. The bottom half was covered by a wraparound porch and tree bark siding; the second floor in cedar shake with dark green trim beneath a roof of sharp angles. The entryway was framed by a spiderweb's pattern of twisted mountain laurel. A dim antique light hung overhead. The prevailing aesthetic seemed to be gothic children's tale. Behind the home, lights glittered far off in the valley.

"C'mon in," said Cass. "I'm sure you could use a drink."

I got out, followed, didn't disagree. The house seemed to look down at me with an unwelcome energy.

Chapter 4

Aram's head was mounted on the wall by the door, as if to discourage visitors. Opaque dead eyes, coarse brown fur with a fringed mane under the throat, a stern mouth faded white with age. The horns, thick and weathered from battle, curved down around his face like a well-earned crown. A gold medallion with an insignia of New York hung from his thick neck.

"That's Eddie," said Cass. "He keeps watch over the place."

I was examining the dead beast and didn't notice the live one coming at my crotch. A big, wet nose nuzzled into me. I looked down at a panting chocolate Lab eager to welcome.

"And that's Filly," said Cass. "She's a poor excuse for a guard dog, but she's the sweetest gal in the world." She knelt down and rubbed behind her ears. Straightening up, she said, "Filly's the only thing that's been keeping me together these days. We rescued her last fall."

"Right around the time Elvis died," I said, unable to help myself.

Cass looked away, focused on petting her pup. "I'm sorry, Duck. And I'm sorry I wasn't there too."

I leaned down next to her, gave Filly a scratch, didn't

reply. After a good guilty silence I said, "So you gonna give me the tour?"

We stood and Filly bounded off and Cass began turning on lamps. Each gave off little, the wattage barely enough to read under. She lit half a dozen and the space still seemed to exist in eerie half-light. I looked around a cluttered living room that felt transported from the nineteenth century. Dark stained wainscoting covered the walls and ceiling. Further taxidermy (deer, boar, owl) shared pride of place with landscape paintings in old ornate frames. The furniture looked made more for admiring than sitting, and was arranged around a large stone fireplace. Taking it in, I felt a cool chill to the air. Shivered, my body seizing in on itself. It had been a warm spring day in the city, might have even cracked eighty; but up here in this strange mountain lair of a dead stranger, it felt like winter hadn't released its grip. Cass felt it too. She knelt by the hearth and removed the screen and began crumbling newspaper and tossing it onto a bed of ash.

"It's always freezing in here," she said over her shoulder. "Victor liked it that way. Have you ever heard the term 'hygge'?" she asked.

I shrugged, felt like I should be helping. Took a seat in an uncomfortable cracked leather chair.

"It's Danish, pronounced hooga," she said. "Means something like coziness, but more so. Soft light, sitting by a fire, sipping wine in winter—that's *hygge*." She glanced around the room. "Guess you could say it was one of Victor's philosophies. One of many."

What I thought: *How the fuck did this pretentious clown seduce Cass?* What I said: "Sounds like an interesting dude."

She nodded, kept her back to me, built the fire with expertise. When the logs were positioned to her satisfaction, she lit a long match and began touching the flame to each corner of newspaper. The fire leapt at once. She replaced the screen and admired her work.

"That'll warm things up," she said. "Can I get you a drink? No whiskey, I'm afraid, but we have plenty of wine. Red okay?"

"Guess so."

She left me alone in the shadowed living room and went to fetch the glasses and the bottle. I sat back and gazed into the flames. A memory of Cass bleeding on the floor of my apartment, shot through the stomach. Beside her, two dead Ukrainians, one killed by each of us. Pools of blood intermingled; sirens came closer. Bad times, and it got worse from there. And now here was Cass, cured by *hygge*, before her lover plunged to his death. I wondered when I should mention the warning I received from Oliver and his mysterious boss before I boarded the bus.

She returned with a bottle of Pinot, uncorked it, and poured us two full glasses. We toasted, our eyes met. She looked away.

"Good to see you again," I said.

She settled into a tattered love seat across from me and curled her legs beneath her. We turned our attention to the fire. Didn't speak until we each needed a refill. I topped our glasses, wondered how to begin.

"He didn't kill himself," she said, finally.

I didn't reply. Took a gulp, eyed the almost-empty bottle.

"They've already decided he did. He tried it once before, years ago, so they think that's all there is to it. One attempt and you're forever a suicide waiting for success."

"What happened before?" I asked.

"It was before I knew him, like six years ago. His marriage was a mess, his career too. He said he was depressed and swallowed down a dozen Ambien one night. Chased them with a bottle of gin and went outside to die in the snow. His ex, the bitch, heard him stumble outside and didn't even get out of bed. She said she thought he was just drunk again, going out to get more wood. Victor said he wanted to go die alone like a resigned dog in the woods. But he didn't make it that far. He collapsed in the road, and got lucky. A neighbor, one of the few who keeps his house open through winter, had a lost beagle and was out looking. He found Victor and called 911 and they managed to revive him in time."

"Did he ever find his hound?" I asked.

"I don't know, Duck."

She reached for the bottle, drained the rest in her glass. Didn't make a move to open another.

"So," I said. I set down my glass on the coffee table with a hard hint. "Why are you sure he didn't try it again? Was he saved by the tender whippings of Cassandra Kimball?"

My cruelty hit harder than expected. She recoiled into the cushions, clutched her glass tight in her hand. For a moment I thought she would douse my face with wine. The weary sadness in her eyes was replaced in a rush by rage. I remembered the way she once made her living.

"I'm sorry I called you," she said, her voice all cold control.

She stood, threatening above me. She turned toward the fire and flung her glass into the flames. It exploded against the stone, the red splashed down over the logs like a burst of blood. Glass fragments showered the hearth. Her arm was shaking, her face flushed and mottled.

"Get out," she said. "Get the fuck out, Duck."

I considered my options. I could go off, sulking, say farewell forever to my wounded former partner. Or I could weather her storm, apologize, and take whatever she needed to deliver. No choice at all.

"I'm not going anywhere, Cass. I'm sorry. That was a shitty thing to say."

" *'Shitty'?* " she asked. "You have no idea. You're a stunted drunk, how would you know? You never loved anyone but yourself."

Keep quiet, I told myself, just take it.

"What the hell was I thinking, calling you of all people, thinking you could help me? What a joke. You'll just bring more pain and violence. More death and darkness, your fucking specialties."

All hurricanes pass. Don't fight it.

"Duck, get out. I'm serious."

"So am I, Cass. I'm not leaving. I'm sorry, can we please start over?"

Her fists pulsed by her sides like a fighter before the bell. She extended her fingers, the ends sharp and red. Another memory: Cass slashing a drug dealer across the face with those nails, lacerating his face with five streaks of blood. I met her eyes, braced for the attack. Wanted it.

She turned to Filly. The dog was cowering by the door with concern. Cass went to her, grabbed a leash from a coatrack. "C'mon, girl," she said, hooking it to collar. "Let's get some air."

The door slammed shut behind lab and mistress. I looked back at the fire, and the empty bottle of wine. I seemed to be making a habit of bringing out the fury in women I cared for. Must be me. The thoughtless comments, the snide smirks, they seemed so innocuous at the time. A bit disrespectful perhaps, but nothing to explode over. One more lesson I'd never learn. Maybe something I should work on, or maybe I needed to stop wasting my energy on damaged, attractive women.

Christ, I was an asshole. A friend in need gets back in touch, and what did I do? Callous taunting and selfish sulking—nice strategy. That would get me back into her graces. How many times had she been there for me, sitting and smoking and listening to my shit? Never judging while

I spilled my demons and worked through my scarred past. For ages I'd wished for Cass to return that vulnerability. To confess something, any form of weakness. Let me be there for her. Now she had, and what had I done? *"The tender whippings of Cassandra Kimball . . ."* I didn't deserve her friendship.

I went in search of another bottle. Found a rack of reds next to an old saloon piano in the dining room. A ghostly black-and-white portrait was propped on the thin ledge above the keys where the sheet music should go. A woman in 1920s flapper garb sat at a piano in the background of a bar. Two well-dressed gentlemen in black suits and bowler hats sat at a table in the foreground, whiskeys at their elbows. All three looked out at the camera with unsmiling expressions. I pulled a bottle from the rack, found an opener on top of the piano. Took in the rest of the artifacts around the room as I peeled and uncorked it. There were framed boxing prints from a century past; dull rusted knives hung on a hook by French doors. An old musket was mounted above. Victor Wingate appeared to be a man determined to live in a bygone era. I remembered his single book, the story of that 1920s boxer, Eddie Finn. I glanced over at the eponymous ram's head.

This, it seemed, was where Cass had found some peace, where she healed herself from the horrors I put her through. I could see it. There was comfort in the fantasy of living a century ago. Nothing could be as complicated as the present.

I returned with the bottle to my seat by the fire. Filled up, sat back, looked into the flames. The wine was a Malbec and not too bad. As someone often more interested in alcohol content than taste, I was less than discerning, but after a few months with Juliette Cohen, my palate had grown accustomed to quality. I wondered if there was some weed around to complement it, or better, some nice fat white Vicodin. I considered a recon sweep for substances, but the fire and the wine were making me drowsy. I placed the bottle between my legs, drank deeply, and stared half-lidded at the burning logs.

The flames swallowed up the wood and turned all to ash. When the bottle was gone and the fire was no more than a bed of coals, I got up and tossed on a few more logs and sat back and watched it leap again. I moved rather unsteadily back to the piano and the wine, uncorked another and took a slug from the bottle, then topped off my stained glass. Didn't check what kind, didn't care. I was feeling surly and slurry and knew things would get ugly if Cass decided to return before I had the decency to pass out. Elvis died by my side in bed while she was off rescuing that bounding Lab with her lover, leaving me to grieve in isolation. And I was the bad guy? I was cataloging her wrongs against me when the door opened with a gust and she and Filly were back.

"Should have known," she said, nodding to the empty bottles before me.

"You can take me to the bus in the morning," I said. "I'll crash right here, if that's okay with Her Highness."

"Whatever, Duck." As she poked at the fire, she added, "By the way, Victor was working on something that was going to upset some people. Not that you give a shit."

It was enough to fire up a blast of curious clarity, but I pretended not to feel it. I grunted and took a gulp at an empty glass. Then I closed my eyes and did not dream.

Chapter 5

I was being led through the woods in a hungover guilty haze. Every drinker is accustomed to morning-after shame. Usually I brushed it off after my first coffee, but my behavior last night was weighing heavy. I'd been waiting for her call, rushed off to answer it, torpedoing a relationship in the process, and then I'd reverted to my jaded, cynical settings. Reached for the bottle and spoken words of hurt. It didn't help that she seemed so able to forgive and move past it when we woke.

Cass was sharing more about Victor's project and the powerful folks it may implicate. The rulers of the world of sports, it seemed. Cass was incurious when it came to the games boys played on TV, but even she knew the boldfaces being named.

A cathedral of high trees offered a green canopy above us. Late-morning light filtered through in rays like signs to believers. A couple hundred yards later we emerged from the woods onto rocks and a steep death drop over the face of the mountain. The view unfurled under a hard blue sky, with farms and specks of towns and winding country roads spread across the valley. The Hudson River cut a slate-gray swath through the sightline. Beyond it a faint outline of another mountain range against the horizon.

I gulped at bottled water, leaned over, tried to slow my breathing with hands on my knees. Sweat dripped from my face onto smooth rocks. I tasted last night's stale red on my tongue. "Nice view," I said. "How much farther?" "Few minutes," said Cass. "Think you can manage?" "Doubtful."

She grabbed my water, took a swig, and bent backward, hands on her slim hips. Gave a glimpse of midriff, belly button pierced with a silver hoop. She wore black jeans and a black scoop-necked t-shirt and a loose black hoodie, unzipped. Cass caught me staring and pulled at her shirt. Then she strode off down the trail with Filly at her heels and picked up her story.

I straightened up, cursed them both, and tried to keep the pace.

Upon waking in that cracked leather chair, I was informed that I'd be granted a second chance. A lot of unprocessed emotion flowing between us last night, perhaps she'd been too quick to anger. I offered apologies of my own. She brewed us coffee, brought me Advil. Showed she was the bigger person. She told me she'd explain on our walk.

Victor Wingate had been hard at work on his overdue follow-up to *Walk Through Fire*. A decade removed from publication, it seemed the muse was smiling on him once more. Or to be less poetic and more accurate, he was freed from a bad marriage and was now with a better woman than he had any right to. It was enough to inspire a man. I guessed the movie and the mailbox money from book sales was also running dry. Time to get back to work, and Victor was convinced he had a winner.

He was calling it *The Athlete*, another sports-based book of narrative nonfiction. He told Cass it would elevate him to the ranks of Laura Hillenbrand and Buzz Bissinger, his self-proclaimed competitors, writers who took their time between blockbusters and wrote stories that were translated into A-list films. *Walk Through Fire* had been a classic of the form, so said the critics, and so Victor agreed. Ask me, it was the superior adaptation that extended its relevance and made it a bit more than another dusted-off story of back-in-the-day triumph. Bale was great in the film, or maybe it was Gyllenhaal, or Wahlberg? I couldn't remember, one of those guys.

The comeback book would be the story of Carl Kruger, formerly Hilde Kruger, Olympic javelin thrower—a doped victim of the East German experiment, when a generation of female athletes was treated as guinea pigs in a program that sacrificed thousands of German girls for the greater glory of Olympic success. According to Victor's research the focus was on the young women, not their male counterparts. These were the early days of doping, a frontier far removed from the perfected science of modern-day cheating. Doctors and coaches went in search of big, strong, developing girls, and with their forced drug regime, they transformed them into sci-fi re-creations, performance-enhanced machines of preposterous size and strength. The long-term effects were never contemplated. For Hilde, who already dealt with gender dysphoria before the drugs, it hastened a transition that would have been forbidden in that time and place. When Hilde's body broke down from extensive injections and was forced into retirement, he was one of the lucky ones. He managed to defect, made it to New York City with a fellow East German, a female swimmer named Uli Max. Hilde chose gender-reassignment surgery and emerged a trans man named Carl. The couple wed and settled in lower Manhattan, where they opened a bar called Kruger's.

When Cass shared all this with me, my first thought had been: *How had I never heard of that place?* I fancied myself a connoisseur of Downtown bars; could there be a spot where I'd never lifted a glass, never even walked by and registered? She said Kruger's was way down, off East Broadway, between the Williamsburg and Manhattan Bridges, in a rare pocket of city still resisting gentrification. I looked forward to stopping by upon my return to town.

Cass told me that Victor learned of Carl's story through a childhood friend, now a hotshot restaurateur named Mickey Knight. Wingate and Knight were buddies from the old neighborhood; in their case Soho in the seventies, when the place was still a dangerous cobblestoned community of artists and junkies and cavernous lofts rented for cheap. The writer's interest was piqued. He made a rare visit back to the city and introduced himself to the Krugers. Turned out there was more to the story, with scandal not long buried but still infecting the highest echelons of world sport. Icons implicated, quarterbacks and basketball stars and Wheaties-box champions, wholesome household names beyond suspicion. Victor started to dig, and to write. Cass said she had never seen a man more inspired. It was an attractive quality.

However, in the weeks before his death, Victor began to behave strangely. He insisted he could no longer work from home; instead he drove off in the morning and set up his laptop in local coffee shops or libraries in nearby mountain towns. He blamed it on difficulty focusing among the familiar, in a place so long an idle of little work. He said he needed fresh settings to get the words flowing. But when he came home, there were signs of paranoia. Now the door was being locked at night, the car keys removed from the ignition. This was a part of the country so safe that neighbors seldom did either. He'd been on antidepressants since his attempt six years ago and Cass asked if he was still taking them. He showed her a recently refilled bottle and insisted he was. She figured this was what it was like to live with a writer consumed. She had to admit, she rather liked the eccentricities. But then Victor never returned from that walk and he was found splattered and lifeless at the bottom of those falls. Despite his recent behavior Cass never considered suicide for a moment. There had to be another explanation for the locked doors and new patterns. Someone must have learned of his reporting, someone with a world to lose. Someone must have hunted him down and pushed him.

She said she hadn't mentioned any of this to the authorities. Why should she trust them? They were probably fans of those famous jocks; they wouldn't want to believe what Victor was uncovering. Easier to go with the obvious: a once-depressed man who couldn't shake off the demons and jumped. If Cass wouldn't mention his work and his recent behavior, I could understand why they weren't taking her claims seriously. It sounded like an erratic writer took the final plunge and his special lady friend could not accept the awful truth of it. If not for the encounter with Oliver in the city, I'm not sure I would have believed her either. I still hadn't mentioned that.

I heard the sound of rushing water up ahead. Filly bounded back toward us. We came to a clearing at the top of a high gushing waterfall. Cass frowned, walked to the edge and peered over. When she looked up, her eyes were wet and troubled. Her body, forever a hard instrument of lust and power, looked shrunken in on itself. She wiped at her eyes and looked back over the falls.

"This is where he went over," she said.

I moved toward the edge, stopped a few feet away in a rush of vertigo. I backed off and set my hand on a wet rock. I took in the view. The falls, the rock formations, the birds of prey that circled above, the entire setting felt almost holy, like a place where promises and confessions were made, and sins forgiven.

"Victor used to hike here almost every day," she said.

"He'd bring his bourbon and sit on the rocks and sip it after he finished his writing." She turned to me. "They call this spot All Creation Point."

I swept my arm across the view. " 'All creation, lad.' "

Cass gave me a quizzical look.

"Natty Bumppo," I said. "James Fenimore Cooper's character? That's his line. *Deerslayer, The Last of the Mohicans,* I used to love those books as a kid. They were set up in these parts."

She frowned; her eyes gave a sad smile. "You and Victor would have really liked each other," she said.

We let that settle. It was difficult to believe that I'd have anything but bitterness toward any man sleeping with my Cass. *"My"? Poor deluded fool, just because you both almost died for each other? Had there ever been so much as a kiss, even lingering eye contact and a pause that said she might be considering something more than friendship? "Well, no, Your Honor, but I always thought . . ." Is there anything more pathetic than the platonic sap that holds out endless hope?*

"So, what do you think happened?" I asked.

"Someone pushed him over," she said, a matter of fact.

"He couldn't have fallen?"

She exhaled with impatience. "Duck, I told you, he hiked here all the time. He knew every stone out here. There's no way he just fell."

"Maybe something spooked him, like a bear or something? Are there bears in these parts?"

"There are, and no, nothing surprised him."

"And he couldn't have jumped?" I took a step closer to the edge, tried to peer down and gauge the height. My head spun with another rush of vertigo. It was a long way down, enough to put anyone out of the game. Hell of a dramatic place to check out.

"I told you, I've never seen anyone as inspired as Victor.

The story, Carl Kruger, it was consuming him. He was anything but suicidal. There was something closing in on him, something that had him terrified. And we were . . ." Her voice caught. "We were happy, Duck. He could not have jumped."

"But he tried before," I said.

"He tried before because he was depressed, in a shit marriage with an awful woman, and hadn't written a word in years," she said. "If you have any doubt about what I'm telling you, then let's go back now. No one else will believe me either."

She turned and headed back toward the trailhead. "C'mon, Filly," she called.

"Cass, hang on, I believe you," I said. "And there's something I haven't told you."

She stopped. "Tell me," she said, her back to me.

"I don't think he killed himself either," I said. "I think you're right—someone probably pushed him."

She turned, a threatening energy pulsing off her. "Why?" she asked.

"Before I left," I said. "I received a warning from a guy in a Hell's Kitchen bar. We had an, um, altercation. He knew I was coming to see you. He told me that we should be careful, that some things aren't worth it."

Cass inhaled through her nose. She placed a hand on a tree trunk to steady herself. She looked at me with those black eyes, processing my withheld information like a cop who's finally getting his confession.

"You're telling me this now?" she asked.

"Cass, last night it got ugly fast," I reminded her. "This morning I was surprised you were willing to forgive me, that you still wanted me around. Then we were off hiking and you were doing all the talking. . . ." I glanced back toward the view, unable to face her. A hawk plunged down past the waterfall, on the hunt, ending the life of some small woodland animal. "I'm telling you now," I said.

"Who was he?"

"Some punk. His boss was waiting outside, I didn't get his name."

"Describe them," she said.

"The guy I talked to called himself Oliver. Some kind of accent, German, I think. Shaved head, fit, about thirty, he had tat sleeves down both arms. I noticed some racist ink, an iron cross and the numbers 1488 across his knuckles. That's prison symbolism, white-supremacist jargon. He must have done some time."

"And the guy outside?"

She was entering into that eerie calm zone of contained rage. I remembered it well. It must have thrilled and terrified many a slave in her dungeon. Her stillness, the slowing of her breath, the way her chest seemed to rise and fall with each imperceptible inhale and exhale, it chilled me and made me move farther from the edge.

"He was tall and trim," I said. "Older, maybe fifty, wearing a suit and aviators."

"Tell me about your entire exchange."

"The younger guy, Oliver, walked in and came down the bar. He stopped by my booth and called me by name," I said. "He slid in next to us, started acting ugly. Then he gave his warning and left." I regretted the first-person plural as soon as I said it.

" 'Us'?"

"Just some prostitute I was sitting with."

"Nice, Duck. You have time to pay for some head after that?"

"We were just talking. I'm sorry I didn't tell you right away."

"That's it?"

"That's it," I lied. "Look, I haven't heard from you in ages. Then you get in touch late night and ask for my help. Now I'm up here in the woods talking about your fallen lover. C'mon, Cass, I know you're hurting, but can you stop giving me a hard time?"

Her look stung more than any whip could. She turned and walked back through the woods toward the house. Filly tossed her head in her master's direction and gave a quick bark. I followed her command.

Walking back, I tried to picture Victor Wingate and his daily routine, before something spooked him out of the house and caused him to start locking doors. Waking next to Cass, was there sex first thing each morning? The normal kind, or the kind Cass liked? Their obvious connection came together and I felt a kind of prudish relief. It wasn't about physical attraction, at least not for her. It was about finding a partner who shared her specific, kinky tastes. Maybe Victor was an eager slave that she would whip for free, or at least for free lodging. Then what? After a morning session, would they slip into a domestic routine? The writer at his desk, tapping away at the keys, sipping his coffee, while his lady puttered about the house, took out the dog, planned their lunch. Then shared a midday feast, followed by the ritual whiskey and his walk in the woods. A chance to turn over that morning's sentences in his mind; do some mental editing, work out what came next. And when he returned, would Cass be waiting in leather, ready to tie him up and administer the pain that filled them both with pleasure?

I watched her hiking up ahead, the way her legs and ass flexed in her jeans with each stride. Wished my tastes weren't so vanilla.

When we emerged from the woods and saw the house up ahead, I noticed another car in the driveway. Cass tensed at the sight of it. It was a yellow Volvo sedan, a few decades old, with weather rust along the wheel arcs. Next to it stood a weathered woman in a long tan coat and a wide-brimmed hat. Her body was full and curved, country bred, and fit into the environment as if she'd been painted there. Tangled brown hair spilled from under the hat and down her coat. She saw Cass and me and moved toward us with huffed shoulders.

"Fuck," said Cass. Then to me: "Don't say anything, okay?"

When we were within ten yards of each other, the woman raised an arm and pointed. "Bitch," she shouted. "You don't waste any time, do you?"

"Hello, Susie," said Cass. "This is my friend Duck." Then to me, "Duck, this is Victor's sister."

I hung behind a few paces, the bad energy coursing between the two women.

"How was she?" asked the woman named Susie. "How was this slut?" I realized she was talking at me, looked to Cass for some guidance.

"Duck and I are old friends and business partners, Susie," she said. "He's visiting from the city."

"Hey, I asked you a question, Dick or Duck or whatever your name is. How was this whore? How much you pay her?"

"Susie, what are you doing here?"

She eyed Cass with an aggression I thought would turn physical. "I'm here, whore, because this is my property. Victor left this place to me, which means you're trespassing, which means it's time for you and your friend to get the fuck out of here."

"Hold up, Susie," she said. "I haven't heard anything about this. If that's the case, could you give me some time to pack my things?"

"I don't have to give you anything," she said. "I want you off my property. I'll throw your shit in the street when I feel like it."

"Susie, I know we're both grieving. Please, if you'd just—"

"Mickey Knight told me this place is mine, along with everything in it," she said. "He was the executor of my brother's will. If you have a problem with it, call him."

"She's just asking to gather her belongings," I said. "I'm sorry for your loss, but let's be decent here."

The sister eyed me with contempt. "Old partner, huh?" she asked. "What, were you her pimp at that kinky house of whores?"

"I'm gonna suggest you stop calling my friend names," I said.

"Oh yeah? Or what?"

"Duck," said Cass. "Please."

"Or I'll come up with some names of my own, like white-trash bitch," I said.

The words found their mark and Susie seemed to go rabid upon hearing them. She let out a grunting growl. Her eyes glazed with rage. "Motherfucker," she snarled. She lunged at me.

Cass stepped into her path and sent her tumbling onto the grass. Susie scrambled to her knees. She eyed us like a kicked dog, her coat whipping back behind her.

"I'm calling the cops," she said. "Assault and trespassing, I'll have you in jail."

Cass grabbed my shirt and pulled me toward her car. "Let's go," she said. "I'll deal with her later."

Chapter 6

When I returned to the city, an evening storm was blowing through the streets. A hard rain fell through the lights, streaked across windshields, and splashed against the asphalt. Traffic lights of glittering green and red struggled to retain order. Umbrellas were up and shoulders were hunched and the collective mood was foul as I moved east from the Port Authority, not a lit cab in sight. There were dry bars of refuge every half block or so, but I kept moving. My thoughts were a scrambled skillet of violent memories and regret.

How many nights had I spent missing Cass, indulging frantic fantasies that would never come true? Toasting oblivion in post-traumatic stress and tragic longing. Rescued by a rich divorcée and her son. I thought about stopping by unannounced to see Juliette and Stevie. Soaked and smiling, I'd offer bended-knee apology. It wasn't too late. She'd take me back, if only for the improbable positive influence I'd had on her son. I removed my phone from a damp pocket and found no messages. Scrolled to Juliette's number and typed: **Can we talk?** Erased it and wrote: **I'm sorry, can we talk?** Erased again, and wrote: **How's Stevie?** Hit SEND, slid it back in my pocket.

Cass said there was little cell service up on the mountaintop. She told me she'd call from a landline after she gathered her things and checked into a hotel. Through the window of a crowded bar on West 26th Street, I noted an attractive bartender pouring drinks. The call from Cass was the only thing keeping me outside. I wanted a dry, quiet place to chat, the comfort of my couch, where I could hear whatever happened next between her and Susie Wingate. In the car on the way to the bus, she shared a bit about the Wingate family. Victor and Susie moved upstate when they were kids, after their artist parents could no longer afford the city. They'd finished raising son and daughter in a farmhouse outside of Bearsville; their mom made ends meet by teaching at Woodstock Day, while the dad supplemented his failing artistic ambitions with pot sales on the side.

It was a sideline I could relate to. I thought of my own father and namesake, serving 150 years in federal prison down in Butner, North Carolina. His crimes were a little more severe than a bit of soft-drug peddling. When I was twelve, we learned that he'd been defrauding his investors for decades. The scheme cost his clients a few billion dollars. The Darley name was rather sullied. My driver's license says *Lawrence Darley, Jr.,* which makes the occasional cop raise an eyebrow, but I've been Duck since before dad's fall. I've never made the trip to visit him, and I don't intend to.

Anyway, Victor Wingate made good after his family's city-to-country move. He studied hard, went to nearby Bard College on scholarship, and served his required years of journalistic servitude at various magazines before breaking through with a number of award-winning features. When he hit his profession's version of the Powerball lottery with *Walk Through Fire,* he bought the place in the Catskills, a half hour's drive from his parents' homestead. Sister Susie didn't come out quite as adjusted. Diagnosed schizophrenic as a teen, she'd been an unstable mess forever. Medication and men came and went, usually in a flurry of fury and bad scenes. When their parents died, she moved into the old farmhouse, where she lived like *Grey Gardens* and got by through direct deposits each month from the good brother—deposits that had shrunk in recent times as Victor's income dwindled. When Victor met Cass, the sister assumed that she was the reason for her reduced donations. She did some Googling on her brother's new woman and did not like what she discovered. The horrors of our last case with the McKay family produced plenty of headlines, many of which mentioned Cass's other profession as a dominatrix. As "Page Six" once alliterated, Cassandra Kimball, aka Mistress Justine, was the "private eye of perverted pleasures." Not something that will endear a woman to a half-crazy potential sister-in-law.

If we were working on the assumption that someone helped launch Victor Wingate over that waterfall, sister Susie had to be a logical suspect. Unstable, capable of violent outbursts, and in difficult financial straits: a classic combination for murderous action. But why go after her own brother, why not the harpy she hated, the one playing house with her benefactor and last-remaining blood? Then again we were talking about family—and family real estate. Things were never rational. Perhaps Susie became consumed with loathing for the big brother made good, the one who'd always gotten the grades, the opportunities, and the professional success. She must have resented his financial care while she languished in the borderlands of madness at their parents' crumbling farmhouse.

It must have fascinated her to watch him finally struggle a few years back, to fall apart and attempt the worst, the way she'd considered—and maybe attempted—so many times before. And then to watch him emerge from that darkness, the one time she felt he might be able to understand her, to emerge happy and inspired, in love with *that* woman, that kinky, damaged slut from New York?

Presuming to grasp the motivations of this woman was a dangerous business, but it made a certain degree of sense. Though it did not explain the visit from Oliver and his boss. Susie may have been a nutter ready to lash out, but it was hard to imagine her capable of enlisting guys like that to do her dirty work.

I was mulling these things in the rain when I turned onto my street and sensed something off. Two teenaged boys were stopped on the sidewalk in front of my stoop, looking at my front door. One black, one white, dressed in hoodies and holding oversized umbrellas. When I reached them and stepped past, down my steps, they shook their heads.

"That's messed up, man," said the white one, pointing to my door.

The black one said, "We know what that means."

I looked from them to my door. Spray-painted in red across the front were the numbers *1488*. I pictured Oliver's tattoo across his knuckles, his ugly smirk as he leered at the prostie next to me. Blood at a boil, I turned to the boys.

"Me too," I said. "And when I find the fucker who did this, I'm gonna tear his head off."

"Let us know if you want some help," said the white one.

They walked away, huffed and puffed with teenaged outrage. I remembered the private school around the cor-

ner, where they were probably students, where Stevie
Cohen was in third grade. For fifty grand a year fortunate
sons and daughters learned more than just math and science; they were also enlightened in social justice, and
taught the signs of intolerance all around them.

I found some cardboard boxes beneath the trash canisters,
tore off a piece, and went inside to grab a roll of duct tape. I
taped over the offending numbers, went back in, and
bolted the door. Checked the rooms for signs of B and E,
found none. After I boarded the bus, Oliver and his boss
must have headed over to my place. They seemed to know
plenty about me, and I didn't like it. It appeared Wingate
had pissed off some folks with his latest project. Maybe
they thought I could be spooked away with a bit of intim-
idation. Maybe my altercation with Oliver would help
them reconsider.

I turned on some Pogues and settled down with my laptop to do some homework. "If I Should Fall From Grace
With God" came out of the wireless speaker as Shane
MacGowan growled about going "where no murdered
ghost can haunt me." Hearing the drunken bard made me
long for whiskey, but there was not a drop in the apartment. I resisted a run to the liquor store. I typed in some
searches for Susie Wingate. Nothing much, a Google
nonentity, a Facebook page with few friends and infrequent updates. I typed in *Carl Kruger* and got a bit more.
Cass's report on our walk was all verified: the forced doping of Hilde Kruger, from the town of Merseburg on the
wrong side of the Wall. Plucked from his family at the age
of eight, sent to the sporting institute and probed like a
high-performance lab rat. His Olympic title, followed by
the defection and gender reassignment, reduced to a suc-
cinct Wikipedia entry; all facts, no story.

East Germany had been a doomed state from the beginning. Under the yoke of the Soviet regime, they were denied the basic freedoms and pleasures of the West. Merseburg was just an hour drive from the border, yet it existed in a different gray universe. It was a land of deep insecurity and deprivation. Sport, they realized, was a way to gain recognition and respect on the international stage. Long before the drugs produced superhuman Olympians, these were a hearty, hardworking stock. The genetics and the work ethic were there first. Add in heavy doses of Oral Turinabol to still-forming female bodies, and you've got an unnatural army of world-beating athletic machines. Historians noted the echoes of the Third Reich. The Germans were still obsessed with perfecting humanity in the most inhumane ways. Now they'd lowered their ambitions from the battlefields to the fields of play. It was the world Kruger was born into. Country-strong parents who were proud members of the Party produced strapping offspring: Hilde, the youngest. Now they had three sons.

World champion, and then an Olympic champion, in the javelin before twenty, the pictures of Kruger throwing that spear in full doped-to-the gills glory were disconcerting. Soon after, the drugs began to exhibit their side effects: joints could not support the artificial muscle and started to snap. Knees and back and shoulder problems halted any future success. It was rumored that excessive injections kept Kruger out of the next world championships. There were worries about a failed test. Kruger was sent instead to a detox clinic outside of Leipzig, and by twenty-two, was a broken-down, used-up piece of athletic meat. He'd served his country's purpose, brought them glory at the Games, and now was expected to live out his days on a paltry stipend, with ironic work as a physical-education teacher at a Merseburg grammar school. The story should have ended there, as it ended for so many others, except Kruger possessed the courage of self-awareness. He escaped, along with his lover, the swimmer Uli Max. Their defection to New York, Kruger's transition, and his subsequent marriage to Uli were matters of record. There had been some press on it at the time, but there had been nothing reported since. I longed to know more. I understood how Victor Wingate had become hooked on the tale.

Emerging from the K-hole of searches and clicks, I realized I still hadn't heard from Cass. I tried her cell—straight to voice mail. Texted her and stared at the screen, but those ellipses promising a reply never appeared. I told myself she must have forgotten, staying somewhere out of service in the sticks.

She mentioned that Victor had discovered a link in Kruger's story to present crimes and some very famous athletes. It wasn't just a history lesson, another twisted chapter of warped goals and expendable bodies. He uncovered something current, implicating icons that would not appreciate the attention. My mind began tripping through the connections, from the echoes of the Third Reich to the East German doping experiment to the present-day sports landscape of performance enhancement and big money. I thought of fit, aggressive Oliver and his waiting master outside the bar. Wondered what else Kruger had told Wingate.

I opened a new tab on my browser and typed in *Kruger's bar NYC*. Google spit back the result in 0.57 seconds. It was located at 168 East Broadway, a few blocks from the Manhattan Bridge. A century and a half ago much of the Lower East Side of Manhattan was known as Little Germany, boasting the third-largest German-speaking population in the world, behind only Berlin and Vienna. Waves of new mass immigrations diluted the Deutsche presence over the decades, but German inscriptions could still be spotted on the facades of plenty of landmarked buildings. And now here was Carl and Uli, part of the old lineage, just another proud couple dreaming the American Dream, shedding past identities and slipping into new ones in the city that let you be whatever you damn well pleased.

I grabbed an umbrella and headed back out into the rain.

Chapter 7

The bar was full and relaxed, with the air of regulars disinterested in a scene. The Stones' "Torn and Frayed" was playing, but not loud enough to disrupt conversation. The demographic was all over the map. A Chinese couple, a table of Rasta black guys, some fading beauties on the wrong side of forty, and the usual collection of bloated dudes with hunched shoulders curled over their pints at the bar. I joined them on a stool in the corner. Felt more comfortable than my own living room.

The décor was dive basic: neon beer signs as the only art, worn bar, low ceiling, and a few Formica tables with mismatched chairs behind the stools. There was a drum set and two guitars standing unused on a tattered green rug in the corner. Above the cash register behind the bar, I noticed the only personal touches: a cheaply framed black-and-white photo of a large woman heaving a javelin. Above that, mounted on hooks over the mirror, the spear itself.

The bartender took her time making her way over. I didn't wave or force eye contact. I wanted to establish myself as a patient sort, in for the long haul. When she reached my corner, she jutted her chin, waited for my order. A Hofbräu and a Maker's, little ice. She turned without reply and began to pour. She was a wide, tall woman dressed in a loose black frock. Hands like a man's, her left swallowed up the pint glass as she pressed the tap with her right. "Handsome" was the proper word for her type of female face: strong jaw, strong Germanic nose, hard blue eyes. Her hair was auburn and pulled back in a careless ponytail.

"Sixteen," she said.

"Start a tab?" I asked, offering a card.

She shrugged, took it, left me with my drinks.

I forced myself to sip them slow. I had no plan beyond remaining until the bar started to empty. Then I'd venture some chat with the bartender, whose identity was confirmed soon after my first Maker's, when a regular two stools down called over for "Uli."

Uli Kruger, née Max, Carl's beloved. Once upon a time behind the Wall, they were doomed and doped lesbians, world-class athletes cut adrift after their playing days. Now, all grown-up, they were husband and wife, proprietors of a low-key, Downtown bar, where all felt welcome. The romance of it, the long odds of triumph to normalcy, was touching. I remembered one of my mother's old boyfriends, in her dissipated drinking days after the fall. He was a cokehead Turk with wild moods and a warm heart. He owned a bar, off the Bowery. I couldn't remember his name or the bar's, but I always remembered a piece of wisdom he once shared, while serving me underage after he packed mom off in a cab to pass out.

"Duck," he preached, "owning a bar is one of man's most noble endeavors. Because no matter how bad things get in the world, if you have one, you'll have a place where people can come to raise a glass and forget their lives, and at least laugh for a little while."

I raised mine at the memory. Then raised my hand and

ordered another. Uli returned with wordless refills. Her manner behind the bar was unsmiling, but not unhappy. On her side of the taps, this was work, not playtime, and she did it with unhurried efficiency. She sipped water from a pint glass, and granted an occasional crack of a smile for a witty regular or two. She began to grow more attractive as I watched her work. Part of it was the inevitable softening of standards from the booze, but more than that, there was something about her, a dignity in her movements. Though anything but lithe, she moved through her space in a smooth, almost sensual way. I remembered her past as an elite swimmer, one of her country's high-performance guinea pigs. For some athletes, no matter the ravages of time, the body never lost its grace of movement. The back stayed straight; the shoulders rolled back; the body was forever aware of energy expended.

We were part of the same tribe. In my own damaged youth, I was once a swimmer of promise too. It would be my "in" when the time was right. If she read the tabloids, she'd probably heard of me, or at least remembered the case of Charlie McKay, the devil in a Speedo, so said the *Post*.

Midnight slid to two a.m. over the course of silently sipped whiskeys and beers. I was feeling rather fine. A nice buzz, Cass was back in my life, and I was back on a trail, albeit on a pro bono basis. As the bar began to clear, Uli's musical tastes became more eccentric. I recognized Klaus Nomi's cover of "You Don't Own Me." An otherworldly scenester who arrived in the East Village from Bavaria in the seventies, Klaus sang backup for Bowie and slept with every boy in town, before falling to AIDS in the eighties. Now he was a cult figure for cool kids who missed the edgy arty days of a Downtown they never knew. I used to deal to an aging drag queen that claimed he knew him.

I was smiling at the memory, nodding along to Nomi, when Uli approached, granting her first acknowledgment. "You know Klaus Nomi, yeah?" she asked.

"Brings me back," I said.

"To what?"

"Life."

She reached behind her and grabbed the neck of the Maker's and refilled my glass. "On house," she said. "For Klaus."

I raised it in thanks, took a sip. She lingered. I was about to play my fellow swimmer card, blurt out an intro, when the bar door opened and in stumbled a drunken beast. He staggered through the entry with a leering recklessness that shattered the room's kind vibe. I felt Uli tense at his presence. She stepped away from me and braced herself.

The beast scanned the room with bleary eyes. All that was left was the table of Rastas and myself. The black guys gazed back under heavy lids, then tipped back the remains of their beers in unison and moved to leave. They seemed to recognize him and didn't need the drama.

"Who needs a drink?" shouted the beast.

But they were already moving toward the door. Uli had her arms crossed behind the bar. He didn't seem to notice me raise my empty glass an inch to accept the offer. I sized him at about six-three, 250 pounds or so, but he identified bigger, like a retired linebacker now lost in a fog of pills and concussed memories. He was dressed in wide jeans, work boots, and a worn black sweater that would have fit across the chest of a bull. His head was shaped like a Halloween pumpkin, lumpy and carved into something both frightening and ridiculous. The features were all oversized and misshapen. Face and scalp were covered with the same length of patchy stubble. His movements made you think of falling china.

"Carl," said Uli. "Go home."

Carl Kruger snorted and weaved down and around the bar and helped himself to a pint glass and a bottle of Jameson. He poured it half full, gulped at the amber, and wiped his mouth with a meaty forearm. Uli pushed past him. She started gathering her things by the register. The electricity between husband and wife crackled, on the verge of igniting. Neither looked in the other's direction. Uli tossed a purse over a wide shoulder, circled the bar to leave.

"You close up," she said. *"Betrunken schwein."*

"Fotze," said Carl.

Then the door opened and shut, and it was just the two of us. Carl seemed to deflate in her absence. His shoulders sagged with a heavy exhale. He shook his big pumpkin head and tried to rub some clarity into his watery eyes. He grabbed another pint glass from the shelf and poured himself a Bud from the tap. He was slurping it down when he seemed to notice me for the first time.

"What can I get you?" he asked.

"Another Hof and a Maker's would be great," I said.

"Geil," he grunted.

I watched him pour. He sagged and swayed against the taps as Klaus Nomi continued to serenade us like a soprano alien. He pushed the drinks before me, held up his glass, and said *"Prost."* Drained it down and poured himself a refill.

"Sorry about all that," he said, waving toward the door. "The wife, you know . . ."

"Rough night?" I asked.

"Genau," he said. "Rough night, rough week, rough life."

"I can relate."

He turned and sized me up, took the measure of just how much I could. My look back seemed to satisfy him.

"Scheisse happens, eh?"

Raised my whiskey. "This helps," I said.

"*Ja, ja,* so it does."

He came over and poured me another, helping himself to the same. Carl saw me looking over his shoulder at the javelin mounted above the bar, the framed picture beneath it.

"Another life," he said.

"Who is that?" I asked.

Something passed across that ruined face. It was covered by a glass as more beer slushed down his throat. When he set it down, he sighed and said, "She is no longer with us."

"I'm sorry."

Carl pushed away my condolences like a bad meal. "No 'sorry.' It was a long time ago." He went back for the Jameson, stopped midpour, and tilted his head at the music. "What is this shit she's playing?"

"Klaus Nomi," I offered.

"I know who it is," he said. "I'm German, *ja?* Our music is shit."

He knocked back the Jamey, found the iPod by the register, and scrolled for something more suitable. Motörhead's "Ace of Spades" began to rip through the bar. Carl turned it up. Venturing conversation over Lemmy was pointless, so I just watched as he placed both hands over the taps and began to rock his head and sing along to the metal. "The Chase Is Better Than the Catch" came next and Carl cranked it even louder. I'd never been much for the harder stuff, but like many I harbored a fascination for Lemmy Kilmister, the ultimate speed-fueled, bottle-a-day rock star. Somehow, despite his best efforts, the hard-living bastard had made it just past his seventieth birthday. He was an example to the rest of us who insisted on challenging our vices to take us down.

Carl emerged from his metal trance after the second track ended and lowered the volume back to a level that wouldn't violate noise ordinances and send neighbors dialing 311 to complain. Despite his rapid refills of Jameson

and Bud, he seemed more sober now than when he arrived. And his headbanging had mellowed him. He came
back over.

"So, what do you do?" he asked.

"I find things," I said. Then realized it had been a long
time since I found anything I could be proud of.

"What sort of things?"

"People, mostly. Whatever folks pay me to look for."

"Like a private eye, *ja?*"

"I guess," I said. "I'm not though, not officially. I don't
have a gun or fancy spy toys or anything like that."

"So, who hires you then?"

"Rich women," I said.

Carl liked that. He raised his glass, waited for me to do
the same. We clinked. "To rich women," he said. *"Prost."*

We drank. I thought of Juliette Cohen and that big,
beautiful apartment. It was beginning to feel something
like home. And her kid, Stevie . . . I missed those two. I'd
miss that life. What was I thinking, turning my back on
that peace? It had everything a man could want: sex, security, fulfillment as a father figure, even health. In my time
with Juliette I hadn't touched the amber, didn't drink anything harder than good red wine; hadn't done a drug
harder than weed since I started teaching Stevie. The life
had, well, maybe not everything. It lacked a certain dignity, perhaps. I'd spent years trying to renounce ambition
as the deadliest of sins. I took pride in never seeking work.
I let the cases—those rich women—find me. But that was
just passive-aggressive ego and whiskey-soaked laziness. I
longed to be pointed in a direction, like a hound on a
hunt, and told to sniff and howl until I found it.

"So, what are you looking for now?" asked Carl.

I waited until he made eye contact. Then I said, "I'm
looking for you."

Too forward, perhaps; too cute a move to pull on a

drunken beast behind a bar. I was out of practice and maybe the booze altered my judgment. We had been getting along so well. But Carl didn't hesitate. He flung his pint glass at my head like a fastball aimed at brain damage. It grazed my ear as I dodged and it shattered against the door behind us. The stinging contact sparked instant sobriety. I was up off my stool and braced for Carl's onslaught before he could reach for another glass. He let another fly and this one I stepped past easily. It exploded behind me next to the first one.

"Wait!" I shouted. "Wait! I'm here about Victor Wingate."

Hearing the name, Carl flung one more glass, then turned and reached behind the register. He came out with an old German Luger and pointed it at me. The gun looked like an antique relic that hadn't been fired in ages, but it did not shake in Carl's hands.

"Victor is dead," he said. "And you will be too if you fuck with me."

I raised my hands, moved back toward my barstool. "Can I sit?" I asked. "I'm not here to fuck with you, Carl. I'm investigating his death. I'm sorry for setting you off. That was the wrong way to begin."

I pulled out the stool and sat down, put my hands back in the air. The nine-millimeter hole at the end of the pistol stared straight into my eyes. A short black tunnel, with death coiled at the bottom, waiting for a touch of the trigger. He held it like a man familiar with firearms. I looked back like a man familiar with guns being pointed at him. We had our standoff, and then Carl lowered the Luger and said, "Talk before I shoot you."

"My partner thinks he was murdered," I said. "She was his girlfriend. Her name is Cassandra. Do you know her?"

He shrugged. "Maybe."

"Has she been here before, with him? She told me—"

Carl swept the gun up and pushed the barrel of the

Luger against my forehead. A twitch of that drunken finger and I'd have a bullet lodged in my brainpan.

"Carl, please, if you'd let me—"

"Call her," he said. "Let me hear it from her."

I glanced down at my phone on the bar. "Okay," I said.
"No problem. Could you please lower the gun while I
dial?"

He removed it from my forehead, but kept pointing it at
me. I showed him the screen as I opened my CONTACTS and
scrolled to her name. "See," I said. " 'Cass,' she's my
friend. I can show you our texts too."

Carl snatched the phone away with his free hand and
put it to his ear. He frowned as he listened. "Straight to
voice mail," he said. "Too bad for you."

"She's upstate," I said. "There's no service up there. I've
been trying to reach her all night."

He considered that, tossed my phone back on the bar,
and lowered the gun. "She at Victor's?" he asked.

"No," I told him. "It sounds like Victor's sister, Susie,
inherited the house. She threw us off the property earlier
today."

"You met Susie, eh?"

"Batshit crazy, that one."

"*Genau,* both of them. He's the one who jumped off
that waterfall."

"Cass thinks he was pushed."

Carl shook his head. "Pushed himself maybe," he said.

"Why would he do that?" I asked. "He was writing
about you, isn't that right?"

"*Genau.*"

"What about?"

Carl nodded toward the picture behind the bar, the
javelin above it. "My old life," he said. "When I was her."

"What else?"

"What else, he asks. All of it. Those who fed me pills,

stuck needles into me when I was young. Made me a big, strong champion."

"It's a horrible story, Carl, but Cass said—"

" 'Horrible'? No, it's a sad story with a happy end. Uli and I, we made it out. We built a life. We love each other." He paused, remembering the scene I'd witnessed earlier. "Despite our little arguments, *ja?* I have not been so good since Victor died."

"Cass mentioned there was something more. That the people who abused you are still out there. She thinks maybe you told Victor something that got him killed."

"They are still out there, *ja,* of course," he said. "No one was punished, not really, a few small fines, slaps on the wrist. When the Wall came down and it all came out, the doctors, the coaches, they left and found new jobs in new countries. They were very smart. There are many opportunities for smart guys in sport, lots of money in improving performance." He reached for a clean pint glass on a shelf that had been cleared considerably since his arrival. Poured another Bud, swallowed half in a gulp. "As for Victor, I guess it became too much. He fought the depression."

"You really think he jumped?"

"Of course—they say it was suicide." Another gulp finished off the beer. He turned for another refill. "If they think it was anything else, why would they not look into it?"

"Because Cass hasn't told them everything," I said. "It sounds like Victor was being threatened. It sounds like the two of you were talking about exposing some very powerful people."

He smirked down at me, said, "Your partner, Cassandra, she is very beautiful, very sexy, *ja?* You have a thing for her, don't you? You'll do whatever she asks. She says someone killed her boyfriend. She called you, fed you the scent, and sent you out hunting. You are her bird dog."

The truth of his assessment, perhaps meant critically, fired me with pride. Who else could she call? Only her faithful Duck . . . I looked down into my empty glass. Carl didn't need to be asked. He refilled it while I relished his words. I tapped the bar, asked if I could use the men's room.

"Why do you need my permission to piss?" he asked.

I looked toward the Luger, still hanging forgotten in his hand.

"*Bitte,*" he said. "I'll put it away. Do what you must."

I climbed off the stool and moved toward the back. After the jolt of adrenalized sobriety, the accumulated booze reasserted itself. My head was a fog of amber and hops and troubled visions. The imprisoned landscape of Kruger's youth, a well-trained captive stuffed with pills and pricked with needles until he could throw a spear farther than anyone. The thought of Victor Wingate's final moments in flight over those falls, pushed or not, the terror would be the same. For a few accelerating seconds the fact of death would have rushed through him before impact on the rocks below.

I locked the door and unzipped and heard Lemmy return at high volume outside. Couldn't make out the song. Chainsaw guitars and the growling roar of hard-lived lyrics. Cass had spent time here, Carl knew her, a fact she failed to mention. I pictured her seated regal in black at the bar, chatting with Uli, while Carl poured out his life story to her boyfriend. Perhaps they double-dated on trips to the city. The dominatrix and the damaged writer, the strapping German couple of unlikely origin: a fine foursome fit for a Downtown of lost days. Cass had been back and hadn't even bothered to tell me.

A bird dog, I thought. *Called when needed, when a scent needed sniffing and tracking. Poor dead Elvis and I, two of a kind.* I missed the hound. But I felt no submissive shame at that truth. It was the only time life felt worth living: when there was something to chase, secrets to uncover. I washed my hands, accepted my face in the mirror, and unlocked the door. When I stepped out, Carl was no longer behind the bar. I called his name over the metal.

Then there was a sharp crack of pain at the back of my head. My legs crumpled beneath me. I heard breathing behind me, the clang of a weapon hitting the floor.

And then it was black.

Chapter 8

It was an unpleasant way to wake. Shaken on a dirty bar-room floor, blinking at lights and hard voices through the searing pain of concussion. Events flooded back in flashes. Every thought and image brought blasts of nausea and confusion. I was slapped in the face by a large palm and pulled to a seat. Around me a collection of cops came into focus. Another pack was grouped behind the bar, fixated by something on the ground.

"Wake up," said one, with another slap to my cheek. "Time to wake up."

I was yanked to my feet. My knees buckled. A pair of officers caught me on my way back down. Steadied, found my sea legs, pulled myself from their grasp. "I got it," I said. "I got it. What the fuck?"

"Bring him over," said an un-uniformed one behind the bar.

He was dressed in a baggy blue suit. Tie loose under a fleshy throat. His haircut was high and tight, military grade all the way, but now his saluting days were behind him. Twenty years and fifty pounds later, with jowls hanging and eyes drooping, he was the detective in charge.

The two uniforms grabbed my arms and pushed me over. I stumbled behind the bar and looked down. Carl's bulk was splayed across the narrow back-bar floor around broken glass and pools of blood. His javelin was standing upright, embedded deep in his neck. His mouth hung open; his eyes were wide in final breathless thought. His arms were rigid, his fingers splayed out as if he had beseeched his executioner. The Luger lay by his thigh near a tide of blood. I looked back at Carl's body, at the spear now driven through his throat. His large pumpkin head was shrunken, drained of blood and life. I looked to the detective, opened my mouth; I failed to find words.

"Sit him down," he said to his uniforms.

They led me around the bar and pushed me down into a chair at the table where the Rastas had enjoyed their peaceful night, before Carl burst in and they'd been wise enough to head out. I remembered being glad to see them go, feeling that smug sense of a night going to plan. It was just as I'd hoped; I had a solo audience with the man I wanted to see. Now that man was dead behind his bar, while I was in for some questions that I would not be able to answer.

The detective came over. He pulled out the chair across from me, sat, and adjusted his too-big blazer. His eyes were bloodshot. His mouth drooped down with his jowls. He crossed his arms. I looked over his shoulder at the first morning light out the window, guessed it to be about six a.m.

"Hell of a fight you two had," he said.

"I didn't do that."

He shrugged as if I was talking about a spilled drink.

"What'd you say to set him off?" he asked.

"I . . . We were talking," I said. "I got up to use the bathroom. When I came out, I got hit. Someone must have hit me on the back of the head." I raised a hand, felt the swollen lump behind my right ear. Remembered the sound of the weapon clanging away as I crumpled to the ground. "I was knocked out."

He nodded in that understanding, keep-going way that signaled it was time to shut my mouth.

I crossed my arms, waited for his questions.

He didn't react, just stood, then nodded to his uniforms. I was pulled up and led out of the bar into a cool Downtown morning. Above the stench of Chinatown you could smell the inventions of spring. The air had the hint of damp promise, the chill no longer to the bone. A few early risers with dogs on leashes were loitering around the pack of police cars. It was too early for a scene, and no one seemed too interested. Nothing to see here, just a former world-class athlete turned bar owner, executed with a javelin shoved through his throat. Just a cursed pseudo private eye caught in the midst of more mayhem. The *Post* would be thrilled by my return. "Death Darley," as they dubbed me, back in action, back under the black cloud of tragedy he could never escape. Twenty months prior, in my search for Madeline McKay, I'd given them a nice run of headlines, cover stories that had culminated in the worst of human suffering.

As I was shoved into the back of a cruiser, I recalled my old friend Roy Perry, "Page Six" reporter and blow-fueled bon vivant. He had witnessed a similar moment of me sliding into the back of a police car, leaving another scene of death and coming scandal. I pictured his wide, wild eyes that filled a bloated face, aged too fast from hard living. I searched the sparse crowd for any signs of press. Roy wasn't among this dog-walking group of morning gawkers, but I knew I'd be hearing from him soon.

I was taken to the 5th Precinct on Elizabeth Street in Chinatown. We parked across from a fish delivery truck. When the back door opened, bile bubbled up the back of my throat at the stench. I climbed out, leaned forward, prepared to heave on the sidewalk. The guiding officer took a step away. The nausea passed and then I was being led up the steps to the 5th. The building was a nineteenth-century relic, white stone with long windows and a pair of cast-iron gas lamps on either side of the entrance, lit in green glass. The numbers *1881* were carved above the arched front door, marking the year of construction, back when this neighborhood was filled with Chinese immigrants being denied basic human rights. They were the Muslims of today. The feds did their best to block new arrivals, while denying the rights of those already here. The natural response was a new, underground order: Chinese gangs known as Tongs. They established the opium dens, the gambling parlors, the houses of prostitution, and they kept their own protected when no one else would. The free associations kept tumbling as I was guided inside the station house.

I was led past a carved oak staircase, under original molding, and pushed into less attractive décor, into a holding cell. I had two roommates at this hour on a quiet weekday morning: one young, one old, both Asian. The kid looked like a low-level dealer, the kind I used to be, crisscrossing the city with a backpack full of weed, maybe some gram bags of blow or molly. The older one looked like a wizened drunk, the kind I might someday be, brain fried with no flame left in his eyes. He sat on a steel bench in careless clothes, his head lolled back against the cement wall, knees splayed out, arms limp at his sides, in a posture that invited any intrusion. He was past the point of caring. Beat him, bend him over, take what you will, there was no more dignity left to steal. He looked at me through dark slits, his expression as impassive as the guest of honor at a wake. At the other end of the cell, the kid was a contrast in life force. He stood as I entered; his body tensed in defense, a fist curled. He had self-conscious style—clean kicks, bright blue jeans, and a black Brooklyn Nets jacket. Long black hair fell around a high-cheekboned face. His look was hard, but his face was smooth, free of scars and the violent lessons that would come if he stayed in his line of presumed work.

I nodded to the pair, found a separate corner, and sat against the cold wall, trying to piece together what had brought me here. I returned from the mountains to find my front door tagged with hate, so they knew where I lived. I headed down to Kruger's bar on East Broadway and settled in. Had I been followed? Carl burst in drunk after midnight; fought with wife, Uli; the bar cleared. Carl and I engaged in friendly banter, listened to some Motör-head, and then I set him off.

There was the volley of violence, thrown glasses, and a pointed pistol, before the moment deescalated and I managed to regain his trust. I learned that Carl knew Cass. She and Victor had visited him at the bar. I learned more about his childhood as an abused, oversized athlete–guinea pig behind the Wall. And then what? That I was Cass's bird dog, sent out on another scent in the darkness?

Despite his protestations I didn't believe that Carl thought Victor jumped off that waterfall any more than Cass did. They were still out there, Carl admitted, the needle-wielding doctors who doped children for the greater good of Olympic glory. They just moved on to new countries. The secrets to enhanced performance were a valuable commodity, worth billions.

My head ached; my vision kept filling with black discs. It wasn't my first concussion, nor would it be the first to go untreated. Between the head trauma and the wet brain of whiskey, doctors would predict dire consequence in my later years. Not that I expected to make it that far. I shut my eyes, pressed my hands over my face, willed the echoes to pass.

It wasn't long until my name was called and I was summoned out of the cell into an interrogation room. I sat on a folding chair behind a steel desk and was left alone inside the cement room, facing a one-way mirror of smoked glass. It all felt preordained. My choices were irrelevant. What I said, where I went next, none of it came from anything as deluded as free will. The flashes that some called déjà vu, those were just peaks behind a curtain, fleeting reminders that your course was long set before you. And some courses were cursed from the first.

The detective from the bar came in a few minutes later. Despite the jowls and the bad suit, he was a proud man passing into middle age with life in his eyes. He moved with the air of a man devoted to a calling, a true-blue believer in justice. He approached the desk and extended a hand.

"I'm Detective Fitzpatrick," he said as he took the seat across from me. "Your reputation precedes you, Mr. Darley. You must have the worst damn luck of any guy in this city."

"You make your own luck," I said.

"If that's true, I'd consider some life changes if I were you."

"Thanks for the advice."

"My pleasure." He smiled at me like he was an old pal with his shit together, just trying to help a wayward buddy. "You ever consider AA?"

"Fuck off."

He held up his hands in mock apology. "Hey, I don't buy it either. Swearing off everything forever? Sounds like a time bomb to me. I'm just saying, some folks, when they hit it hard all the time, they find a way of landing in troubling spots. As you said, you make your own luck."

"Is this an intervention or an interrogation, Detective?"

"I'm sorry, not my place, you're right. I'm just trying to figure out how you've managed to find yourself, yet again, at the scene of a murder."

"I didn't kill him."

"No one said you did." He looked over his shoulder, left to right, feigning confusion at my statement. "I'm just curious about your presence there."

"Then why was I tossed in a cell? Being treated like a criminal usually means you're a suspect."

Fitzpatrick gave a thin smile, gentle, almost. He leaned forward and set his forearms on the table. "Like I said, your reputation precedes you, Darley. You're a convicted felon, with documented substance abuse issues. You've been a party to—and a victim of—extreme violence in the past. You've been diagnosed with PTSD. Hell, I had it too, after I served in the Gulf. It's no joke. I get it. Sometimes you feel like you're going to snap, like you want to mow down every smiling face you see. And some guys do. Not everyone makes it out the other side."

"So, did I snap last night?" I asked. "Before I hit myself across the back of the head and knocked myself unconscious?"

"Let's back up," said Fitzpatrick, drawing back and crossing his legs. "Why don't you tell me about your night. You go to that bar often? Know the bartenders?"

"First time there."

"What brought you down there? It's not too close to home, is it?"

"I like to discover new places to drink."

"Not me," he said. "I like my locals. Creature of habit, I guess. I've got one or two spots out in Bay Ridge near home. Can't remember the last time I had a beer anywhere else. But, hey, I suppose that's my loss. I wish I was more curious, like you."

A silence settled between us. I tried to maintain eye contact, but a new wave of concussive symptoms swept through and the black discs returned to my vision. I squeezed my eyes shut, rubbed at my temples.

"You okay there, Darley?"

"Fine."

"Good. Now, can you tell me what brought you to that particular bar last night? Someone tell you about it? You read a review—'Best Downtown Dive Bar' or something?"

"I was in the neighborhood," I said. "And I was thirsty. As you've noted, Detective, I'm frequently thirsty."

"What time did you get there?"

"About nine, I think. You can ask the bartender, she was serving me all night, before her husband came in and took over."

"How'd you know they were married?"

"Because he came in a bit drunk and they fought," I said. "Wives don't like it when their husbands drink too much, or so I've heard. She was upset with him and she left, and then he went behind the bar."

"You guys talk much?"

"A bit."

"Introduce yourselves?"

"He said his name was Carl. We were both a little drunk, and the bar emptied out, so we chatted."

"About what?"

"Lemmy," I said. "He was a big Motörhead fan."

"Is that a band?"

"Was. Lemmy's dead."

Fitzpatrick nodded, uncrossed his legs, leaned forward again on the desk. His brow tightened, his eyes narrowed. "Now so is Carl Kruger," he said. "And you were the last person—or perhaps the second-to-last person—to see him alive. Tell me what happened next."

"Next I got up to use the bathroom. When I opened the door and headed back to the bar, I was hit on the back of the head. Last thing I remember is hearing the weapon, a pipe or something, clang away. I heard it hit the ground, right before I did. Then I was slapped awake by your boys and dragged up and shown what happened to Carl behind the bar. And now here we are."

"Here we are," agreed Fitzpatrick. He pushed himself up and turned his back to me and faced the mirror, shaking his head at whoever watched from the other side. He turned and said, "We believe you. We do. Despite our precautions due to your past, no one thinks you killed that guy. Turns out the back door to the bar was left open, where the killer or killers could have entered and escaped. Maybe they were waiting for the bar to empty and they got tired of waiting on your drunk ass to leave. Knocked you out, then held up Kruger. In any case the cash register was emptied. Also looks like they grabbed a few top-shelf bottles on the way out. Looks like your basic late-night bar robbery."

"Then why am I sitting here?" I asked, knowing full well. I pictured the javelin that had impaled Carl on his bar's floor. So did Fitzpatrick.

"Well, it's about the murder itself," he said. "Or the weapon involved, I should say."

He came and sat back down, crossed his legs with ease. He pursed his lips and gazed into his lap, like the final answer to the Sunday crossword was on the tip of his tongue. Without looking up, he said, "Someone hits you on the back of the head, knocks you out, and you hear the weapon hit the floor?"

I didn't answer.

"Then, he—or they—go to Kruger behind the bar. Maybe a gun is being pointed at him. They demand the money from the register, make big old Carl lie facedown while they take the cash." Fitzpatrick peered up at me with a look of genuine fascination. "But the thing is, Carl had a gun too—a German Luger—that was right by his side. Maybe he reached for it when he saw them and they convinced him to set it down, promised he'd live if he didn't resist."

"Maybe," I said.

"Hard to figure a guy like that would stand down so easily," said Fitzpatrick. "Big guy like that, drunk and cranking heavy metal?" He rubbed at his clean-shaven jowls, turned his head in profile. "Then there was all that broken glass on the floor, like someone had been throwing pints. Except it was in the opposite direction. It seems the intruders entered through the back, past the bathrooms. Hit you first and then approached Carl. But someone made quite a mess tossing glasses at the front door. Hell, I don't know." He sighed with bewilderment, forever perplexed by the reenactment of crimes. "Maybe it was a couple methheads. They charge in there, take you out, start trashing the place, and Carl resists and they decide to get creative. They see that long, sharp spear hanging above the bar. While they've got him on the ground, and one of them is emptying the register, the other one takes it down. Carl rolls over, tries to grab it, and, *bam,* too late, it's driven into his throat. Game over. And off they go."

"Sounds like you've got it figured," I said.

"We might, we might." He offered that gentle smile again. "The simplest solutions are usually the correct ones, aren't they?"

We regarded each other across the desk. The black discs returned, another wave of stabbing pain through the backs of my eyes. He saw me wincing, said, "When you get out of here, you really ought to have that bump on your head checked out."

"Does that mean I can go?" I asked.

"Soon enough," he said. "It's just . . . the thing that bothers me is that spear, that javelin or whatever. There was a picture above the register, of a woman throwing one at some kind of competition."

"He said it was another lifetime."

"Ah, so you two talked about more than just music, huh?"

"I asked him about it," I said. "I'm guessing many people do. It stands out in a place like that."

"And what did he mean by 'another lifetime'? Was that his sister or something?"

"Got me. It didn't sound like he wanted to elaborate, so he changed the subject."

"To rock 'n' roll."

"Yes."

A buzzer sounded in the room and Fitzpatrick frowned with irritation. "Hang on," he said, and went to the door.

I was left alone looking into the black mirror, too tired and pained to care about the details I was omitting. Fitzpatrick didn't seem like a bad guy, as cops go, but I'd been hardwired for most of my life not to give them a bit more than necessary. All I wanted was a cool, dark room and a pillow and about fifteen hours of silence and sleep.

A minute later the door opened again and Fitzpatrick reentered without his gentle smile. He was followed by a familiar figure.

"Seems you've got a friend on the force," he said. "Wouldn't have guessed it."

He moved aside and Detective Lea Miller stepped forward.

"Hello, Duck," she said.

Chapter 9

It was late morning by the time I was released in her care. She agreed to give me a lift home in her unmarked Prius. The day was bright and blue, and there was a lightness to the city. Spring had settled in to stay. We didn't speak as we inched through Chinatown and Little Italy, over on Grand, and up the Bowery. Despite the relentless development of the former flophouse stretch, the undercurrent of seediness remained. I hoped it always would.

When I was a kid in the city, the Bowery was the land of bums and junkies and rock 'n' roll. CBGB was long gone now; a John Varvatos boutique took its place, desecrating the holy spot with hipster threads that the Ramones would have spit on. Yet the homeless were still scattered in pockets along the sidewalk. They knew this land was theirs first. There were encampments flourishing along the east side of the avenue, never mind the outrageous rents behind the doors and up the elevators.

I appreciated Lea's quiet, her willingness to let a silence run its course. There had been a time, in the wake of my troubles with the McKay family, when she and I had something together. It was a matter of comfort. She had become immersed in the madness of that case too. Miller was the first cop to question me, after the first murder. She was a small, compact woman with a mousy beauty that she made little effort to enhance. Everything about her was sensible—from her shoes to her corduroys, to her diligence as a detective. A few months after the case I started to meet her at the Union Square dog run with Elvis and her mastiff, Freddy. Our pups would ignore each other and sniff around the perimeter of the pen as we sat together with few words exchanged. One afternoon I invited her back to my apartment, where she initiated the next step in our bleak, mute courtship. She was kind and warm-blooded in bed, with a hunger that surprised me. It might have led to something more if I had been less of a mess. As my drinking unraveled again, Lea stopped texting about doggie dates and I made no effort to follow up. Nothing felt worth it, least of all a relationship with a well-meaning cop.

"How's the hound?" she asked as we waited at a light.

"Dead," I said.

"Oh, Duck." She reached across and squeezed my hand. "I'm sorry. When?"

"Last fall." I stared straight ahead. Watched a pack of giggling stoners stagger across the street to St. Marks. The world went right on, no matter the horrors. "How's Freddy?" I asked.

"He's good. Getting up there, but still going strong."

We drifted the rest of the way up Third Avenue in silence. Elvis used to get jealous and howl anytime Freddy would jump up and collapse in my lap. I wondered when it would be time to go back to the shelter and rescue a new one. Not yet, maybe not ever. I wasn't even sure I'd be able to pass a shelter's loose standards of adoption anymore.

There was a hydrant in front of my building and Lea pulled in next to it and put an NYPD placard beneath the windshield. She looked at the cardboard taped over my front door.

"What happened there?"

"Just some kids," I said. "Tagged it with graffiti. I haven't bothered to fix it."

Lea nodded, didn't push it. "How have you been, Duck? I mean, since we last saw each other? I worried about you."

"All's well," I said. "Or it was until last night. I was actually doing better. Even cut back on the drinking."

"I can tell. You look healthier."

I gave her a side-eye, put my hand on the door.

"So, are you going to tell me what happened last night?" she asked.

"I already told your colleague down there."

"Yeah, you were always so forthcoming with law enforcement."

"I don't know what else you want me to say."

"I want to know why you were there, and how you knew that guy?" She placed both hands on the steering wheel at ten and two. Gripped it until her knuckles whitened. "When I get back to my desk," she said without turning. "And I start digging into this Carl Kruger's life, I'm not going to find any connection to you? You're telling me I won't find any weirdness to this guy's life, anything that might have interested you?"

I pulled the handle and stepped out into the street. "It was good to see you, Lea," I said. "Give Freddy a rub for me." I closed the door. Heard the electric Prius click into gear. She pulled out and was already at the light by the time my key reached the lock.

Inside, I tapped out two Xanax, four Advil. Tossed all six pills into my mouth at once, leaned under the faucet, and gulped them down. Wished I had something stronger. My painkiller connection had OD'd. He lived, but was scared straight and got out of the life. A fistful of fat white Vicodin would put me right in no time, or even better, some of those power-packed Oxies that he started getting

toward the end. I knew I could have found that stuff elsewhere with minimal effort, but it had been a part of my
chez Cohen rehabilitation. Now it would take a number of
calls and conversations with past associates I didn't care to
contact. Lea said I looked healthier. It gave an odd dose of
pride, before I remembered how I'd been with her: a
bloated, catatonic corpse lucky to get it up.

I needed to see Juliette Cohen and Stevie again. Those
two were responsible for whatever health I could muster. I
needed that stability. There's only so much you can unravel in the presence of a kid in grade school. I knew another bender was inevitable living alone, with not even an
animal to keep me accountable. If I had any sense, I'd go
over there and grovel for forgiveness, beg to be permitted
back into their gilded fold. I'd been so quick to flee the
moment I was summoned by Cass. I didn't hesitate. Hell,
Juliette caught me smiling when I read Cass's text. *Good
little bird dog, run back to your master, or mistress, as the
case may be.* I resolved to get some sleep after the Xanies
kicked in. Then I'd reach out to Juliette. Convince her to
take me back. I'd promise to cut Cass out of my life. Her
lover's fall over that waterfall was not my problem. Forget
I ever spoke to Carl Kruger, banish the image of that
javelin impaled through his throat.

I felt the pills making me woozy with little else in my
belly. I staggered to my bedroom with a book, some devilish
Nick Tosches, and tried to read a page. I made it through a
paragraph where the narrator bit through the femoral
artery of a gorgeous young coed. He sucked the blood from
her thigh, and then rushed her to the hospital. It was the
last image I had before the black discs returned and the
book fell from my hands and I was out.

It was dead of night when I woke. I reached for my
phone by the bed. A few past three a.m. The soul's mid-

night, I'd read, the hour of darkest depths. My headache was gone. I felt the egg on the back of my head and found it shrunken. My body felt rested and strangely right. I considered my options. There would be no more sleep tonight; my eyes had opened without the urge to snooze. If I hustled, there was time for a few rounds at a nearby pub before the four a.m. call. I resisted that option. *See, Lea, I wasn't lying, I'm improving. . . .* Instead, the prosperous path: a morning swim with my old Masters group. It had been too long. The swim lessons with Stevie provided the chlorine fix, but it wasn't the same as those sensory-deprived laps, slogging up and back under fluorescent light, vision a dreamscape of moving water and body parts. Finding the breath again, feeling the body stretch and ache and pull over the black line on the bottom, flipping at the cross, pushing off in a streamline. A few languid dolphin kicks. I knew it was what I needed. Knew it would always be my tether to sanity.

But first there were two hours to kill. The Masters group did not meet until five thirty a.m. The darkest hours still needed to be filled. A few episodes on Netflix perhaps, some porn on the laptop, or back to the Tosches novel and more of his bloodsucking, all options that held a certain appeal, but not as much as my curiosity about Carl Kruger. I would return to Juliette and Stevie soon, but first a bit more research was required. Victor Wingate was a best-selling author, albeit years ago. He must have an agent, an editor. Would he have told them about his new book? Cass said he was thrilled, filled with inspiration, and immersed in the tale of Carl Kruger, investigating the villainy that consumed his childhood. The villains were still out there, infecting the highest levels of sport. Mad scientists with potions of performance enhancement, it was the dark art of athletes, whose multimillion-dollar contracts depended on it, whose multibillion-dollar teams and federations looked the other way.

It wasn't difficult to find Victor's past representation. *Walk Through Fire* had been a hit, earning enough for all parties involved to ensure the author a follow-up whenever he was ready. I found Wingate attached to an agent named Alex at Writers Room, and an editor named Colin at Anchor Press. Both were thanked prominently in the Acknowledgments. But there was nothing recent in the search results, nothing within the last six years. No indication that his comeback book on Kruger had been sold, or was even making the rounds. Maybe Wingate was still in the early stages and was keeping a wrap on his research. Or maybe agent and editor had given up on the one-hit chump, left him to his has-been career in the country. I emailed both from an incognito AOL account. It was easily tracked, but who cared? A short note with the subject heading **Inquiry About Victor Wingate.** I introduced myself as a source for his most recent project, and asked if they knew what would come of it now, after his untimely demise. I didn't elaborate, hoped it was enough to elicit a reply. Hit SEND.

Besides Cass, and the Krugers, who else would have known he was writing this story? If he was immersed in it, that meant he must have been speaking to plenty of folks. Word would spread, perhaps among those with a vested interest in silencing it. Where was his computer? Was there a working manuscript, transcripts of interviews, research compiled?

I considered Victor's loony sister, Susie, intent on ejecting Cass from her brother's home, now hers. I remembered Cass mentioning Victor's paranoia in the days before his death. Locking doors, rushing off in the mornings to write elsewhere. Someone had been circling. They were taking measures to shut things down, until the most extreme measure was taken.

I felt myself caught in the rip current of curiosity, felt the pull of the tide sucking me out to sea. What was it that lifeguards said about riptides? Don't fight it. If you try to swim against it, you'll lose. All you can do is let it take you, and when the current is through with you, swim around it and back to shore.

My phone buzzed. A 518 number, upstate, it must be her.

"That you?" I asked by way of greeting.

"It's me," said Cass. "I'm sorry we didn't connect earlier." No explanation offered.

"Carl Kruger is dead," I said.

"I know." Her voice was clear and hard, with midday clarity.

"How? Did Uli call you? You didn't tell me you knew them."

"Duck, it's in the news," she said. "You're in the news. I just saw it. Where are you?"

"Home, it's the middle of the night, Cass. I was in custody for most of yesterday. I think I have another concussion. Somebody hit me, before killing Carl."

"I know," she said again. "It's online, in the *Post*. Your old buddy Roy Perry wrote the story."

"Lovely." I hoped to make it to the pool before the paper made it to the newsstands. At least give me that final underwater respite before the insanity began.

I was surprised I hadn't heard from Roy. We'd been close once, or as close as a friendship can be that revolves around drugs and heavy boozing. Last I saw him, it looked like the blow had taken over his face. He was unimpressed by my houseboy cleanup, courtesy of Juliette Cohen. I told him I wasn't using anymore, which meant there was little reason for us to hang out.

"You sound wide-awake," I said.

"I've barely slept since Victor. I'm sorry to call at this hour, I didn't even realize it was so late."

"Where were you the other night? You never called."

"There was a storm up here," she said. "Blew the power out for a couple hours. I checked into an inn nearby, but it didn't have a generator." I heard her exhale into the phone, pictured the angry shake of that beautiful head. "Poor Carl," she said. "He was a good man. And Uli, I need to reach her."

"Did you manage to get back into the house to get your things?"

"For a supervised few minutes," she said. "When I got back Susie had called the cops. There were a couple uniforms waiting with her. One of them finally convinced her to let me in so I could pack a bag."

"Any chance you can get back in there when she's gone?"

"That would be breaking and entering."

"That's not what I asked."

"I'm sure she'll be changing the locks, but I could probably find a way back inside. Why?"

"It would be helpful to take a look at Wingate's laptop."

"We might not need the computer itself," she said. "I'm sure Victor had everything saved in his email, or in the Cloud. He was fastidious about backing up his work. I might have another way in."

"Which is? You know his passwords?"

"No. I'll tell you later. But you're right. A sweep of the house might turn something up. Until you got there, I could barely bring myself to set foot inside. I just sat on the porch staring into the trees."

"It's worth a try," I said.

"She wouldn't even let me take Filly. That dog was mine as much as Victor's, and Susie refused, said her brother had left her *everything*. The poor pup was crying by the door when I left."

"Listen, why don't you come back down to the city?" I asked. "Just for the time being. Staying alone up there in some inn can't be healthy. You can stay with me. There's plenty for us to look into here. We can head back up together and get into the house in a few days. And we'll bring Filly with us, I promise."

I listened to her breathe in my ear. Then she whispered, as if someone was listening in the next room, "First they killed Victor. And now they killed Carl."

Chapter 10

I arrived at the pool an hour later, strapped on the cap and goggles for the first time in too long. Old lane-mates welcomed me back warily. I wondered if any had seen the news today, or if it was just the old stuff—the torture and the multiple murder scenes I'd been a part of—that spooked them. I offered empty smiles, kept the smoked goggles over my eyes. At least I didn't smell like booze. The sense memory swallowed me back in. It was ingrained down to the soul, the smell and taste and texture of an indoor pool, something I could never shed. I kept my head down and tried to make the intervals. It was what I needed: to be released into the swirl of a morning workout, lost in the present tense as the seconds swept away on the clock.

Before she hung up, Cass agreed to return to the city. I told her to wait until dawn, try to get a few hours of sleep. She said that wasn't happening, she might as well leave now. The thought of her driving sleepless down the blurred line of the Thruway worried me.

Maybe killing the writer and the source was enough. Others would hear about it, but, with those two freshly dead, would anyone have the courage to come forward? They had been playing a dangerous game. For every high-profile scandal and public shaming of an athlete who crossed the line and cheated in pursuit of success, there were scores of others who did it without detection. Hall of Fame careers, public hero worship, stadiums built on the backs of brands they helped create. It was in the best interest of many powerful folks to keep these things quiet. Lawsuits were a given. That was the easiest weapon, and often the most effective. When someone with less financial might wrote something you didn't like, use libel law as a weapon. Sue their ass. Even if you were guaranteed to lose, that wasn't the point. You'll injure the erstwhile whistle-blower financially, and you can crow about defending your proclaimed innocence. I wondered if Wingate had already been threatened with that prospect. Maybe he was so blinded by his righteous reporting that he declared it wouldn't stop him. Maybe he already had proof.

Accusations of doping went on daily, in every sport, across every country. It was a parlor game by this point. Rivals point fingers back and forth, certain countries are more suspicious than others, but it was mostly impotent outrage. It usually amounted to nothing. There was too much at stake for it ever to stop. Those enhanced athletes were part of an economy and a culture that would not be permitted to fail. As long as fans delighted in seeing out-sized achievements, there would be those committed to de-livering them—through any means necessary. Notions of cleanliness and fair play were quaint in the end. Lock the doors to a Hall, threaten lifetime bans, it would never be enough. Not with all the money up for grabs, not when the world would forever hunger to witness eye-popping performance. Money, I knew, was only part of it. It moti-vated, of course, but as much as standing up and doing something with your body that had *never* been done be-fore, by any human in history? No, the ego that drove ath-letes could never be measured by any dollar amount. The same went for the coaches and the doctors and the team owners that all prospered from that performance.

I remembered a story about the soaring value of sports franchises not long ago. It seemed there was no better investment on earth, for those with a couple hundred million to spend prior to the year 2000. By the early years of the twenty-first century, the value of those teams—even loser franchises that rarely made the play-offs—was rising well over a billion dollars. It came down to eyeballs and the ultimate value of seeing something live. The only time the suckers on the couch were willing to watch a commercial was during a live competition. The rest of the world's small-screen entertainments were scheduled at whim, but not sports. Watching athletes play their games, live, that was the highest currency there was on television. Combine that with the almighty athlete ego. There was only one sin left: getting caught.

An hour later I touched the wall for the last time and removed my goggles and listened to my heart hammering through my chest. I took my pulse, found it soaring over 180, worried about cardiac arrest. I climbed from the pool and staggered to a bench and sat slumped over with my elbows on my knees. Water dripped from my face and pooled at my feet. The other swimmers shuffled past to the locker rooms, giving me a wide berth. I sat there air-drying, listening to my heart settle, until I heard them clearing out, headed for offices or airports or God knows where. Then I limped to my clothes, stripped and changed, and wondered if I felt better or worse than before.

Outside, the blossoms were bursting. The leaves were speckled with night rain, the sky a soft blue streaked with pink. It was the time of year when the city was forgiven again. After the months of freeze and hunched punishment, pressing against winter winds and bad spirits, when everyone contemplated flight to warmer, saner ways of life, finally there was reprieve. We all fell for it, every time. Spring in New York—it's an illusion of a season, one that may last no more than a week, before the oppressions of summer take over. I even caught smiles on the sidewalk. Amnesiac fools slipping into light coats with a lighter step as they skipped down to the subway and off to the same cubicles.

I told myself to savor the brief bliss. Circling Gramercy Park, I stopped and admired the blooming patches of yellow tulips erupting from tree stands in formations. Dogs pulled at leashes and sprayed them before being yanked away by owners. Behind the iron gates of the park, gardens flowered while the old and the rich lingered on benches with the *Times* spread before them. Strollers rolled past carrying children no longer zipped in coats and sealed like contraband. It was a time of fresh starts, of forgetting, but only for the foolish. As I turned on Third Avenue, I confronted a newspaper stand outside a green grocer. My spring reverie slipped away on a breeze. There was the headline horror:

STAFF OF DEATH, read the *Post*.

IMPALED, said the less-clever *Daily News*.

I kept walking. I'd learned to ignore the tabloids whenever I was a recurring character. A year and a half ago I made a series of covers, had my fifteen minutes in the darkest of ways. The McKay case was now a part of the New York roll call of scandal known by shorthand: the "Preppy Murder," the "Central Park Jogger," the "Mob Cops," the "Millionaire Madam." They were the stories that revealed the sinful undercurrents of the city, and just as much, the unique hunger of New Yorkers for a certain kind of high-profile cruelty. Money and power and privilege, rough sex and lurid violence, madness that cracked open into the light with that special resonant something. The McKay case joined the pantheon recognized as the "Sicko Swim-

mer." *Dateline* and *20/20* did segments on it. *Law &
Order: SVU* did the requisite ripped-from-the-headlines
episode based upon it. And then it drifted away, leaving
the characters destroyed in its wake, remembered by the
rest at dinner parties, preserved for posterity on Wikipedia
and true-crime compilations.

Maybe this would be another. Or maybe it would lack
that sticky ingredient that those master story chefs at the
Post were so brilliant at sniffing out. Aside from the murder weapon—and my presence on the scene—it looked on
the surface like another bar robbery gone wrong. Carl
Kruger's backstory would raise the dial, but he wasn't the
only trans bar owner in town, and I wondered if his background would even come out. Who was I kidding? The
broad strokes of his past were a Google away. This one
could unravel all over again. I wanted no part of it.

A block from home I spotted Cass's Land Cruiser parked
on the corner. I was still incredulous that she traded in the
old Benz, winter roads or not. It was more proof of the way
she shed her city life, her life with me. No longer the Downtown dominatrix and detective sidekick, Cass had settled
into her quiet country idyll, in love, a hundred miles and a
universe away. But then her lover went over those falls,
and now she was back. I smiled to myself. The great mag-
net of Manhattan will always pull you back.

I saw her waiting in front of my place. She leaned
against the gate along my stoop and placed her Parliament
between her lips. She blew smoke at the sidewalk and did
not look up. She was dressed in jeans, black hoodie, her
style careless, a long way from her curated city look. Her
straight black hair was tied back in a ponytail, setting off
her sharp profile. She was a woman rarely without makeup.
I noted her exposed beauty without it. She looked less severe, more vulnerable. Cass took a final drag, lifted her
chin as she flicked it into the street, and turned to me.

" 'Bout time," she said.

"Went for a swim."

"Good for you."

"You eaten?" I asked.

"Not hungry."

I remembered her diet of energy bars, coffee, and wine. I'd never seen her ingest anything else, aside from the endless string of cigarettes. I stepped past and opened the gate, unlocked the door, and welcomed her in. She stopped in the doorway, scanned the sparse room. On her last visit she lay dying on the floor, a bullet in her stomach, two dead Ukrainians around us. The ghosts still lingered.

"Place feels different without Elvis," she said.

"I know, I'm thinking of moving."

"Where?" she asked.

I shrugged. Went to the kitchen and filled a kettle with tap water and turned on a burner. I opened the fridge and took out the coffee, poured a half-dozen scoops into the French press. She joined me in the kitchen, peeked over my shoulder, and scanned the countertops.

"No bourbon in sight," she said. "What's gotten into you?"

"Been cutting back."

"Good for you."

She turned and paced the apartment. I could sense her reenacting the past violence. Cass had flatlined in the ambulance that day. They managed to restart her heart, but that had marked the end of our partnership. Now we were even, or so I thought. Years before I'd taken a bullet for her too.

We didn't speak as I let her absorb the remembered horror. When you've lain in a pool of your own blood and felt life seeping away, you know there is little to say. It's a memory that will forever feel disembodied, as if it happened to someone else. You can look down at the spot where it happened and sense that other self there on the ground dying, and you'll realize that past, present, and future are all delusions, and self, the grandest illusion of all. Cass stood over that spot by the door and looked at it for a long while, until the kettle whistled and she shuddered out of herself.

"Milk, please," she said. "No sugar."

I poured our coffees and settled onto the couch and waited until she was ready. Set out an ashtray for her. She came over and lowered herself into the leather chair that was always hers; I hadn't sat in it since. Cass raised the mug and took a sip, set it down, and sparked a cigarette.

"How does it feel to have me back?" she asked through a plume of smoke.

"Feels good."

"Wish I could say the same."

"At least you're honest."

"It's a curse," she said. She looked back over at that spot. "It's good to see you, Duck, it is, just not here. I agree . . . I think you should move. I don't know how you've been able to stay."

"I haven't really been spending much time here," I told her. "Not since Elvis died."

"And where have you been staying?" She ground out her cigarette with an arched eyebrow.

"I was seeing someone." I pictured Juliette and Stevie, the three of us seated around their dining table like an actual family. "I was staying at her place."

She smiled with her eyes over her raised mug. "I'm glad. You needed someone to bring you out of all that." She gave another glance over at the spot by the door. "We both did."

"Yeah, well, now that's over and I'm back to this humble, haunted abode."

"How long ago did you break up?"

"When you called," I said.

"Oh, Duck, really? That is ridiculous."

I pushed myself up, went back to the fridge. I stared at the empty shelves and longed for a nice long row of green Beck's bottles. I closed it and poured myself water from the tap.

"She saw your text before I did," I said. "She took it the wrong way and threw me out."

Cass shook her head, lit another cigarette. "You need to fix that shit," she said. "Want me to talk to her?"

"No thanks."

She stood and went back to the spot by the door, transfixed by the memory of her near death. I pictured her there, bleeding, with eyes resigned, the gunshots echoing through the small room.

"It wasn't easy to get all your blood out of the floorboards," I said.

"Is that why you stayed?" she asked. "To keep the trace of me left behind?"

Chapter 11

We were sitting at the counter of Coffee Shop on Union Square, waiting on my California wrap, and Cass was talking about what happens to email when you die. It used to be old letters in a trunk that gave voice to the dead as survivors picked through past correspondence. Now it was the mountain of data left behind, and it wasn't as easy as opening a trunk to find it. If you were without the passwords of the dead, Google and the other guardians of the gates required a long, legal process of discovery.

"I need to get into his Gmail," said Cass. "His iCloud too. There might be some drafts or transcripts saved to his desktop, but Victor was diligent about sending his work to himself. He said it was the best way not to lose anything."

"You never asked to see some of what he was working on?"

She gave me a look. "No, Duck, I didn't."

Secrets, I remembered, were her lifeblood. The Cass I remembered demanded souls lay bare, be it kinky desires or daily communications. I couldn't imagine her alone in that house and not indulging her curiosity. I also couldn't conceive of any man hiding things from her. Not when she set those dark eyes upon him and asked . . . for anything.

The waitress brought my food, grapefruit juice, and more

coffee. She refilled Cass's water glass, asked again if there was anything she could get her. Cass ignored her. She was a tall redhead with translucent, lightly freckled skin and high, sharp hips that jutted over a pair of low-cut jeans. An expanse of pale bone and belly was offered at the midriff. A small chest without a bra pressed beneath a white t-shirt. Her green eyes sparkled with an innocence that wouldn't last long. Coffee Shop was a long way from the lower-case version of your classic greasy spoon. Situated on the western border of Union Square, it was more Brazilian bistro, staffed by aspiring models and actresses forever on audition. The décor was Art Deco, dominated by a curving bar through the center, where assorted cute young things lingered in every eye line. It was open seventeen hours a day, and full for most of them.

The waitress retreated, but not before an appraising glance in my direction. Interested by association, I'd forgotten how much attention was refracted my way anytime I sat with my partner. Cass pretended not to notice.

"Did Susie know what her brother was working on?" I asked.

"All Susie knows is that big brother wasn't floating her the way he used to. She blamed me for it. The fact is Victor was almost broke. He worried all the time about what was going to happen to his sister when he couldn't support her anymore. Not that she showed any gratitude."

"Is there any chance she could have been involved?"

She shook her head. "I thought so at first. The woman's a full-on nutter. You should see how she lives down at the place in Bearsville. She needs to be committed, but Victor would never consider it. He paid for her doctors and all her meds and basic living expenses, but insisted that she was better off in the family home. Susie Wingate might be capable of plenty of fucked-up shit, but she didn't kill her brother. I checked—she was drinking at Landau's in Woodstock all day on the afternoon Victor died. I was told she got there at noon. A bartender drove her home when they closed at ten. She was passed out in her living room when the cops went by the next morning to break the news."

"She seemed to be taking it well."

Cass gave me a glare. "You shouldn't have provoked her like that," she said. "I told you not to say anything. We're lucky she wasn't armed. She often is."

I shrugged, dug into the avocado, egg, and cheese. "I didn't like the way she was speaking to you."

"Yeah, well, you could have gotten us both shot."

"Wouldn't be the first time."

"Next time will probably be the last time," she said. "I hate that tough-guy routine."

"Apologies, now back to the emails," I said. "How do you propose we open them? You have any idea what his passwords could be? Any chance he might have written them down somewhere?"

"Doubtful," she said. "Victor prided himself on his memory. I can't see him writing down passwords. That would defeat the purpose. I could make some educated guesses, but we don't want the account disabled after too many wrong tries. That would just make things more difficult when we ask for help."

"Who do you suggest we ask? Any old hacker friends?"

"Like I was saying, every company has its own procedure for recovering the data of the dead. Google, Microsoft, Yahoo, Apple, they all have slightly different policies. Victor used Gmail and iCloud for everything, so I looked into those two. Apple's policy is just one paragraph, claiming that all content on a person's iCloud account is terminated and deleted upon death. Pretty harsh if you think about it, all those endless family photos that so many folks have stored there. They have a support section that says it can help, so maybe they're not wiping everything out the second they see a death certificate, but going through Apple seems like a long shot."

"But Google seems easier?"

"For an authorized representative, yes," she said. Cass reached over and helped herself to my grapefruit juice. She drained half of it and set it down without apology. "They have a two-part process where representatives of the deceased can submit a bunch of info and then wait for a case review to see if you can proceed to step two, where I guess they take a closer look into the person requesting the emails and determine whether or not to release everything. The whole process can take a few months."

"You're willing to wait a few months for that?" I asked. "And how are you an authorized representative? Unless you were married without mentioning it."

"We weren't, and no, I'm not. We'd need Susie to help us. Which is unlikely, but we may not have to go through the front door."

Cass's dark eyes lit. She helped herself to the rest of my juice. The corners of her mouth turned up as she drank. Setting it down, she licked her top lip and said, "I think I know someone who can help us."

"Old client of yours?" I asked.

"Old colleague," she said. "At the Chamber. Girl named Natalie Shaw. Went by Mistress Nikita. She was a really talented domme, a natural. She whipped her way through NYU, majoring in computer science. I was sort of her mentor at the dungeon. We used to session together sometimes, when slaves wanted two at once. Anyway, when she graduated, she got a job at Google and moved out west. She works in their security department. Nat was always obsessed with cybersecurity and privacy. She would always say we had no clue how vulnerable we were, how easy it was to find anyone's so-called 'private' data. We haven't stayed in touch, but I think she might be willing to help."

"What would you tell her?" I asked. "You think this girl would risk her career at Google just to help a former fellow dominatrix?"

"I would tell her the truth, Duck," she said. "And yes, I do. You don't understand the bonds that can form in a dungeon."

"And what would that truth be?"

She paused. Her nostrils flared as she inhaled and exhaled.

"That I was in love," she said. "The truth is that I was in love with someone and he died, and I don't think it was an accident or a suicide. And now I want to find out what happened to him. Natalie will understand that. Mistresses know how hard it is. After you've spent enough time in a dungeon, the thought of a real relationship, even the concept of love, can seem impossible."

I gulped at my coffee to wash away the sting of her statement. Cass, in love . . . Now heartbroken, she'd whistled for her loyal bird dog to help her investigate. I set down my cup and stared at the second half of my wrap. I wanted a drink, and another after that. I wanted to launch myself on a three-day bender and come out of it to find myself abandoned, alone with only myself to blame for the pain. Cass excused herself and slid from her seat. As she walked to the ladies' room in the back, I watched the eyes of other diners follow her. I slipped my phone from my pocket and regarded the backlog of messages awaiting my attention. I ignored the voice mails. I'm unable to understand why anyone leaves them anymore. Listening to them has become a tedious anachronism. I looked at my texts. The number *13* was lit in the red bubble at the upper right of the green icon. A handful were from past clients, curious about my reappearance in the *Post*; there was some badgering from Roy Perry, looking for a comment; one from detective Lea Miller, telling me to take care of myself; and to my surprise, one from Juliette Cohen.

Are you ok? Saw the news.

I wrote her back at once: **Can I come see you?**

I saw the ellipses appear in her reply box. I saw Cass returning, and tried to shield the screen. She sat back down and glanced at my phone just as Juliette's reply came through:

I don't know if that's a good idea. . . .

"That your lady friend?" she asked.

I didn't look up. Typed: **Please. I'd really like to see you and Stevie. Been a crazy few days.** Then, after hitting SEND, I added: **I'm sorry.**

I set the phone facedown next to my plate and motioned to the redhead for the check. I felt Cass watching me.

"So, what's your plan for today?" she asked. "Gonna go grovel for your lady's forgiveness?"

The irritation in her voice gave me a dose of satisfaction. I didn't think she was capable of jealousy, but she wouldn't like someone else holding my leash.

"Maybe. I'd like to see her," I said. "And her son. They're worried about me, after seeing the news."

"You should."

"What's your plan?"

"I'm gonna see if I can reach Natalie, see what we can do about these emails. Then I thought I'd stop by the Chamber. It's been a while. I feel like I should say hello to Rebecca."

Rebecca was the head domina and owner of the Chamber. Cass's ostensible boss, though I knew all mistresses worked on a freelance basis, giving a cut to the house for use of the various dungeon rooms. I also knew Cass had been the most popular mistress Rebecca ever had. She would be welcomed back with open leather-clad arms.

"Maybe you can book a few sessions while you're at it," I said.

"Maybe I will."

"Easy money."

"There's nothing easy about it," she said. "But I know a few gentlemen who might be glad to see me."

"I'm sure the line is long."

Cass shook her head, stood, and left me with the check as the redhead cleared my plate. She offered a sympathetic smile, asked if I'd like anything else.

"Do you have any serenity?" I asked.

"Is that a drink?"

"I wish," I said. "How about the wisdom to know the difference?"

But she didn't get it. I watched her smile fade.

"Never mind. Could I have a mojito?"

The redhead nodded and retreated while I watched Cass walk out the door without looking back.

I looked at my phone to find a reply from Juliette: **Okay. Come over around 2. We should talk before Stevie gets home from school.**

I said I'd see her then. I salivated at the thought of my coming cocktail, considered the odds of staying sober until then. If only for Stevie's sake, I told myself this would be my only beverage of the day, at least until night fell. But my hands would be idle for another few hours and the devil was already dancing in my head.

Chapter 12

The day was brisk and blue, with wisps of clouds in Rorschach patterns above the buildings. Pollen burst from tree buds and tortured the allergic. I stood at the corner of Fifth Avenue and 16th Street behind two young women moaning about the season. One sneezed in rapid succession, covering her face with a black-sleeved blouse, while the other, dressed dimly for the weather, hugged her bare arms and stared at the blue sky and sighed how she couldn't wait until summer.

I crossed over to the west side with no destination in mind. There was a massage parlor halfway down the block that advertised table showers and body scrubs on a sidewalk placard. Euphemisms for "hand jobs," not that anyone cared. Houses of various forms of prostitution existed on every block in this city. "New York values," said a failed Republican presidential candidate as he knelt before Goldman partners for interest-free loans to fund his hate-filled campaign. The city had a generous heart, too generous for some. It was a place where everyone could be honest about desire. It required only the will to knock on the right doors. Transactions were a given, some more up front than others. As long as the parties were consenting and of age, I didn't have a problem with any of it. I'd never understand the men who longed to be whipped and wounded and pissed on by Cass and her fellow dommes, but I had my own issues with masochism to deal with. They just didn't happen to be quite so literal or fetishized.

The memory of Carl Kruger's impaled body came back to me as I passed through the Village. The javelin forced through his trachea as he lay on the sticky barroom floor. After I was knocked out, how had it gone down? Carl would have put up a fight. He was not a man to stand down and accept his fate. Was he forced to the ground at gunpoint? Did the murderer have an accomplice? Why was I spared?

Despite our brief volley of pint-throwing violence, I liked the man. Under different circumstances there could have been a hazy raised-glass friendship, nights drank away at Kruger's with wife Uli pouring and Carl laughing along to his loud music behind the bar. There was a bravery to him, an honesty, that shone through. Here was someone with demons to match my own, and he was fighting the good fight. He rose from the abyss, found someone to love, found a measure of peace and prosperity. Until a nosy, has-been journalist turned up with his striking lady friend and started asking questions about his past. Victor Wingate had muddied the long-still waters of his memory, got him talking about criminals—child abusers—that never paid for their crimes.

I turned south and walked down Seventh Avenue with One World Trade filling the sky at the bottom of the island. The replacement to the Twin Towers offended me at first, with its lost potential for greatness and its heavy-handed symbolism, peaking at 1,776 feet. The city could have delivered something iconic, worthy of sharing world's greatest skyline with the Empire State and the Chrysler, the Woolworth and the Flatiron. Instead it sent up another bland monolith of glass and steel. But there was something about its simplicity, the long triangular symmetries, and the way the sun lit the glass and blended it into blue spring days. I kept moving toward it without realizing where I was headed. It wasn't until my legs turned right on West 4th and took a left on Cornelia Street that I became conscious of my destination.

Charlie McKay's former home was a block farther, on Leroy Street. I hadn't gone near it in the twenty months since I was tortured there. I'd been a part of horrors inside that house that would never heal. Two of us emerged alive, and two more were left dead I seldom thought of Madeline McKay any longer. I tried not to envision her post-traumatic sufferings since she escaped her brother. When I thought of her, I pictured an illusion that I knew would never materialize: Madeline healed and happy on a beach somewhere, smiling in the sun, as the warmth soothed her scars. I didn't care to conjure the more likely reality, of a young woman forever shattered, who would turn back to drugs and reckless sex to numb a past she could never get over.

I stood across the street, facing the house, not daring to step closer. The façade had been altered since I last saw it. The ivy that covered the front was gone now. The front door, garage, and windows were now period appropriate, the modern design stripped away. I approved of the changes. I hoped the inside had been gutted as well. Charlie's taste, minor among his many evils, was horrendous. The soulless white décor spoke to the vacancy inside him. I remembered the floating stairs, the modern art, the blade slicing down my face, the teeth of the bolt cutters wrapped around my Achilles, and the sound of Charlie's grunt as he pressed them together and snapped my tendon apart.

The panic of PTSD rose inside me. I felt the anxiety bubbling, wished I had some Xanies to swallow. My eyes scanned for an open bar down the block. The need to pour whiskey on the circuits was consuming me. I searched the faces of passersby; the paranoia was returning. There was someone following me. I was sure of it. There was someone tracking me and waiting for the right moment to strike. *There's no such thing as paranoia,* I reminded myself. *The voices are real and so is the presence behind you. It's all true.* I explained this once to my therapist. She replied that I'd reached the height of the disorder.

I saw movement behind the second-floor windows of the house. An older woman peered out of the diamond panes. For a moment I mistook her for Margaret McKay, the mother who set it all in motion by hiring me to find her daughter. Could she have moved into her dead son's home, where such sibling horrors unfolded? No, impossible, the woman looking down at me was not her. Just another well-dressed wealthy lady with a face-lift and a fine-looking ivory dress, there was hardly any resemblance beyond the checkmarks of class. A look of concern crossed her face as she gazed down at me. Concern shifted to fear as I held her eye contact. A phone appeared in her hand and she tapped at the screen and held it to her ear. She turned her back and moved from the window. I blinked, tried to bring myself back. My pulse was pumping, sweat leapt from my forehead. The block spun. I thought for a moment I might faint. I sat down on the nearest stoop, put my head between my knees, and closed my eyes. *Just breathe. Go home, lie down, take three Xanies, this will pass. You should never have come here.* I realized that a cop would soon be rolling down the block in response to her call. I forced myself to stand, staggered south. I needed to lose the hellhounds on my trail.

I wove through the maze of the West Village, where the numbers disappear and the city grid shifts off center. I've never lived anywhere but Manhattan in my life and I can still get lost in this pocket of streets. It was still before

noon and all the bars I passed were closed. A blessing, I
knew, but I could always find somewhere that was serving,
or wave down a cab and head home and drink myself into
a soothing stupor. Something stopped me. It was Stevie, I
supposed, and Juliette. My only tether to sanity—an eight-
year-old kid who probably didn't want to see me, and his
mother, whose affection had now turned to pity. I would
stay sober for them today, even if it meant risking a break-
down on the sidewalk. Every half block or so I glanced
back and searched the faces of pedestrians, the make of
the cars, certain that I would recognize something. Paranoia was a protective instinct, a survival mechanism. It
was only a disorder if there was no one coming for you.
And there always was.

I must have walked for an hour or so before I found myself turned around and back on Sixth Avenue, facing Uptown. The IFC movie theater was on the west side of the
street across from the West 4th subway stop. The façade
advertised a retrospective of contemporary Japanese cinema. I chose a documentary about a famed sushi restaurant in a Tokyo subway station. I remembered reading a
review, three or four stars, but I didn't care about its content. It started in ten minutes and its running time was an
hour and twenty-three. Enough to kill the remainder of
the afternoon, keep me away from bottles, and get me to
the Cohen apartment, sober, by two p.m.

The film sucked me in. The master sushi chef toiled in
his ten-seat subterranean temple of fish, spurning bigger,
more profitable opportunities, and instead devoted his life
to excellence and simplicity. He was described as a
shokunin—someone who has embraced the persistent pursuit of perfection in his art. His apprenticeships for aspiring sushi chefs took a decade.

I envied that purity of purpose, remembered it from another time, my interrupted childhood as a swimmer. I was

good too, fast enough for whispers of Olympic potential. I cared about little else, nothing beyond faster times and moving up the rankings, and pleasing my own master—my coach, Teddy Marks. But then came the fall: my father's disgrace and imprisonment, the overnight identity shift from rich to poor, moving with my mother from the Upper East Side brownstone to that Lower East Side tenement.

Mom tried to drink away the disorientation. She succeeded. She drowned in the bathtub during my last year of high school, an empty bottle of Popov vodka by the tub. I found myself annoyed by the chef's sons in the film, conflicted by the pressure to succeed the patriarch. Poor boys, heirs to a master, their worries revolved around the temperature of rice, or how long to massage an octopus.

But at least the anxiety settled. The fear subsided, the paranoia wasn't quite so consuming. I felt a certain pride in handling the symptoms without self-destruction for once. I could have reached for the booze and the pills and erased the panic in a fog of oblivion. Instead I had taken a long walk and watched a fine film. Now I could see Juliette and her son with a clear head, without shame.

The denouement was wrapping up. The master chef summed it up for his oldest son, groomed to take over for his father: "He just needs to do it for the rest of his life," he said. I straightened in my seat. I remember exhaling, with something like peace of mind. Then my theory about paranoia and its nonexistence was proven true.

I sensed movement in the seat behind me. Before I could turn, a strong arm wrapped around my eyes and yanked my head back. I felt the edge of a knife press into my neck. I resisted and felt the blade break skin.

"Miss me?" he asked.

His voice was hot and close in my ear. I didn't dare kick the seats or shout for help. I'd have a severed carotid artery and three or four minutes before I bled out on the theater floor. My assailant would race for a side exit and may or may not escape, but it wouldn't matter. One deep cut and I'd be done. So I listened.

"I could kill you now," he said. The blade pressed deeper. "But that would be no fun." I felt blood trickling down my neck and under my shirt. "First there must be fear. And suffering. Do you like to suffer, Duck? Do you like to hurt those you love?"

I shook my head, felt the knife move with my skin.

"I do," he whispered, the voice, that same German accent—Oliver.

He released his hold and pushed me forward. My forehead hit the seat in front of me. I reached for my throat, unsure if the wound was real. For a moment I doubted whether the episode occurred at all. I heard footsteps behind me, and the theater door swung open and there was a flood of light, but even that seemed like an illusion. My therapist told me in severe cases there could be physical manifestations of my disorder. The paranoia could intensify into full delusional psychosis. That must be what happened. When I looked up, the other moviegoers were staring at the credits, shifting in their seats, untroubled by any disturbance.

It wasn't until I touched my neck and felt the sticky warmth. I put my fingers to my lips, tasted my blood. It made me feel better. It proved I wasn't crazy.

Chapter 13

On my way to Juliette's I stopped in a Duane Reade and bought gauze and Neosporin and some Band-Aids. I'd managed to stop the bleeding with a batch of napkins from the theater, but now they were soaked red and the girl at the counter was careful not to make contact. I thanked her, apologized for the mess. She told me there was an Urgent Care two blocks south. I turned north and went into a Starbucks on the corner. There was a long line and every eye was fixated on phones. No one noticed as I dripped blood on the way to the bathroom. A fat white boy opened the door as I reached for the handle. He pushed past, left a stinking bomb behind in the small dirty room.

I bolted myself in, regarded the cut in the mirror. It wasn't so bad. About three inches, very thin, the blade had been sharp. I rinsed it and applied a layer of ointment, ripped and folded the gauze and placed it on, then covered the wound with two Band-Aids. I'd tell Juliette that I cut myself shaving. That's right, I was shaving in the dark with a knife as I watched a movie. She'd believe that.

Next stop: the nearest venue that served strong drink. All discipline was canceled after that blade to the throat. Some things can only be treated with the proper medicine.

I wouldn't overdue it, at least not until after I left Juliette and Stevie. I'd buy some breath mints on the way over, but resisting drink was no longer an option.

I remembered the Marlton Hotel a block away, over on West 8th Street. There was a stylish bar off the lobby that would be open for lunch. It was the former home of Jack Kerouac and Lenny Bruce and plenty of other back-in-the-day coolsters. I heard it was where Valerie Solanas lived when she shot Andy Warhol. Now, of course, the Beats and the artists and the would-be artist killers had been replaced by Gold Coasters content to pay ten bucks a beer. But this was no time for judgment or nostalgia. I needed a goddamn whiskey down my throat.

It was 1:45p.m. when I walked through the oak-paneled lobby. A fire was lit and an attractive pair of professional women lounged on plush love seats before it. I noted the light fixtures and the crown moldings. It was a fine spot. Overpriced or not, the original character was still in place; the dead voices of the past would approve. I gave myself eight minutes. Enough time for two or three belts, then a stop at a bodega for mints, then a speed walk five blocks up to the Cohens'.

The bartender examined my face and neck with blithe curiosity. He was bearded, with slicked-back hair, dressed in a tweed suit, in character behind the meticulous bar. The bottles were lined on glass shelves before a mirror trimmed with carved-oak inlay. He tossed a cocktail napkin on the marble bar top in front of me. Didn't ask about my bandages.

"Double Bulleit," I said. "One cube."

He nodded, turned, and poured. Placed it on the napkin and watched as I lifted it and drained the bourbon down in one swallow.

"One more, please," I told him. "And a Stella."

Another unquestioning nod and he delivered the rest of my order. When he set the green bottle and amber glass before me, I had my card waiting.

"I'll settle up. Don't have much time, unfortunately."

He shrugged, went to swipe it. I sipped the second whiskey a little slower. Savored the warmth it brought to my belly, the calm it delivered to my mind. I rinsed each sip with a pull of Stella. I checked my phone. It had been six minutes since I walked in. I was no longer feeling so out of control. I gave myself two more minutes to finish, signed the tab with a five-dollar tip, slid from my stool, smiled at the ladies by the fire as I passed, and returned to the streets with a comforting haze.

The sun was shining and the day had warmed. Spring was springing. Well-dressed women walked expensive dogs down Fifth Avenue. Couples walked, hand in hand, oblivious to all but their happiness. A pair of European men in tailored suits laughed and smoked in front of the Salmagundi Art Club. They all felt like extras in a movie version of my reality.

I bought the breath mints at a deli and added a Gatorade for hydration. Wondered if Juliette might smell it on me despite the mints. Showing up with whiskey breath and a sliced neck, eager to reunite with my lady and her son—*Real nice, Duck.*

The Cohens lived in one of the few new apartment buildings with a degree of taste. At least the windows weren't that same infuriating geometric pattern—one large rectangle, one narrow rectangle, one square in the lower corner—that appeared to be de rigueur for every steel-and-glass disgrace being slapped up these days. Their building at 12 East 13th Street offered some red brick between the oversized square-paned windows. It was still too contemporary, with pretensions of artistic vision, but it was hard to argue with the interiors—or the private parking places that came with every residence.

The doorman's look was not happiness to see me. Ernie was his name—a short, courtly fellow with a bright smile of crooked teeth, which he flashed for every tenant. I was always friendly to him, but he seemed to see through me. The boyfriend interloper of the attractive divorcée Ms. Cohen, I was tolerated with fake cheer in her presence. Alone I was welcomed with the indifference shown to a Seamless deliveryman. I also made the mistake of calling him Bert once on our way in, after a few bottles of wine, and I don't think he ever forgave me.

"Ernie, my man," I said. "Long time, how you been?"

He ignored my outstretched hand, ignored my neck wound. "She's expecting you," he said, without looking up.

"Thanks, good seeing you too, buddy." I slapped the desk on my way past just to make him stiffen.

Each apartment was its own floor, with the elevator opening onto a glassed foyer. Juliette was not waiting by the entrance. I called out for her and got no reply. Peeked my head into the long living room, found it empty. I kept calling her name until I found her seated at the kitchen island, staring down in silence.

"Juls? It's me, everything okay?"

She looked up. Her face was tear-streaked with terror and blame. Her body shuddered as she pushed a piece of paper toward me.

"I just got back," she said. "This was waiting downstairs with Ernie. It was sealed and addressed to both of us."

"To you and me?"

If she noticed the bandages on my neck, she didn't mention it. She showed me the torn envelope it came in. On a typed label, it read: *To Ms. Juliette Cohen (and Mr. Duck Darley), Residence 4*

I picked up the letter. It was typed and printed on thin white paper:

> Dear Ms. Cohen,
> Please share this note with your friend, Mr. Darley.
> Your son, Stevie, is a good boy, isn't he? So smart, so full of promise, I'm sure he's an excellent student at his school on East 16th Street, where he arrives each morning by 8:25am, and where he leaves each afternoon at 3:10pm, picked up by his nanny. On Tuesdays I hope he enjoys his afterschool piano lesson. On Wednesdays I understand his swimming is coming along nicely, with the help of your friend, Duck. (I do hope he's reading this, as well!) It would be a shame if Stevie did not come home one day, wouldn't it? I know how busy you are, Ms. Cohen, with your lunches and your photography course, and the good work you do with the Whitney Museum. You and your son seem like lovely people, leading lovely lives.
> Do be careful, won't you?

It was unsigned. I set the letter down on the counter. "*Do you like to suffer, Duck? Do you like to hurt those you love?*" Adrenaline fired through me, the effect of the drinks vanished.

"Who left this?" I asked.

"Ernie said it was some kid, looked like a student from across the street at the New School."

"Probably paid a few bucks to drop it off," I said.

Juliette looked up, confused. "What? What are you talking about, Duck? Paid by whom? Who would do this?"

"Juls, it's okay, it will be okay. I'll find him. Nothing will happen to you or Stevie, I promise."

My words shook her from her stupor. She stood and her face split into hysteria. "Nothing will happen?" she shouted. "Someone is threatening my son! Because of you . . . because of something you're involved in! And you tell me it will be *okay*, you'll find him? Who, Duck? Who the fuck would send something like this?"

She flung herself at me, her fists lashing at my chest. I caught her by her wrists and did my best to restrain her. "Please," I heard myself saying over and over. "Please, Juls, let me explain. Let me talk, okay?"

"No," she said as her attack waned. "I don't want you to talk. I want you to leave. I'm calling the police."

She reached for her phone on the counter. I put my hand over hers. "Juls, wait."

"Don't you touch me," she hissed. "Explain it to the police."

"Let me call," I said. "There's someone in the department, a detective I know. She'll be able to help us—faster than anyone else."

I removed my hand. She looked into my eyes with revulsion. "Then call," she said. "Call your detective. Get her over here. Now." Then the panic returned. "My God, I have to call the school. Why haven't I called the school? I have to get Stevie, what if . . ."

While Juliette dialed, I tried Detective Lea Miller on my cell. When it went to voice mail, I sent a text: **Lea, it's an emergency. Call me asap. Kid I know is being threatened. Must be connected to Kruger murder. Need to reach you. Please.**

I set down my phone and listened to the temporary relief in Juliette's voice as she was assured that Stevie was safe in class. She told the school that she would be over to pick him up early.

When she ended the call, she looked back at me. "What did your detective say?" she asked.

"Left a message, I'm sure she'll call back any second."

She reached for her purse on the counter, stuffed her phone in, and moved for the elevator. "I'm going to get my son," she said. "That detective better be here when we get back. If not, I'm calling 911."

Left alone in the apartment, I read the letter again. Its precise, mocking tone, the pride it took in its intel, seemed aimed at me. I remembered the first warning I received at the bar before our sidewalk altercation. That white-supremacist punk with the 1488 tattoo on his knuckles, what had he said? That some things weren't worth it . . . before spray-painting those same hate-filled numbers across my front door while I was away. There was Carl Kruger's death by javelin, while I lay unconscious on his barroom floor, then the knife to my throat in the theater, and now this threat to Stevie. They were taking sadistic pleasure at my expense. I felt like a voodoo doll, with pins being inserted at various points of pressure. Why was I being tortured while others were being killed?

I went to the living-room windows and looked down at the street as Juliette rushed from the lobby doors and turned east toward her son's school. For a moment I felt a need to go after her, to follow behind and make sure nothing happened to either of them on their way back. But I stayed put. I needed to get Lea here in a hurry.

At least I knew I wasn't paranoid. There really was no such thing. Someone had been following me. They were watching Stevie and Juliette. They wanted me to feel the pain and the panic of their looming presence. If I continued to approach, so would they. Ever since Cass reached out, the night I read her text in Juliette's bedroom, when she shattered my delicate domestic bliss, there had been someone watching. It started with Cass. I needed to reach her. If they were preying on the people I cared most about, she would be the first target. As I reached for my phone, it lit up—Detective Miller responding to my text.

"Start talking," she said.

"Lea, thanks for getting back. I need your help."

"I said start talking, Duck. I asked you to be honest with me, after this mess with the Kruger murder, and you weren't. And now you need my help, so start talking."

"I wasn't lying," I said. "I don't know how any of this is connected, but I'm being threatened, and now so is an eight-year-old kid. He's the son of a woman I was seeing."

I heard a sharp exhale through her nose. Either expelling a flash of jealousy, or more likely a snort of disgust. "How was he threatened?" she asked.

"We got a letter, left with their doorman," I said. "It detailed his school schedule, said it would be a shame if he didn't come home one day. It was addressed to both of us—to his mom and to me."

"Where is the kid now?"

"At school on East Sixteenth. The mom, her name is Juliette Cohen, she just went to pick him up. The school said he was fine."

"And where are you?"

"At their apartment, 12 East 13th Street. Can you come by?"

"I'll see if I can send someone over."

"Please, Lea, can *you* please come by? I was told that if you weren't here by the time they got back that she would call 911."

"Jesus Christ, Duck. I'm investigating a murder."

"Right, a murder that might be connected to threats

being made to an eight-year-old boy—whose mother has enough money to launch a full-on manhunt."

"Un-fucking-real," she muttered. "Where are you again?"

"12 East 13th. Thank you, Lea."

"You call me by my first name in front of that woman and I'm turning around, that clear?"

"Thank you, Detective Miller."

Chapter 14

The kid did not run into my arms, or offer a high five, or even a smile in my direction. Seeing me there, back in his kitchen, sipping his sparkling water, Stevie gave me a hard look—a rich eight-year-old's version of *hard*—and put his head down and went straight for his bedroom. Down the hall his door slammed shut. I looked at the two women arriving in his wake.

Ernie had refused to allow Detective Miller upstairs until the lady of the house returned. They entered together, an unpleasant energy between them, collectively directed toward me. Neither spoke. Juliette walked past and indicated the letter on the island.

"This is it," she said. "It was left at the front desk around one thirty this afternoon. I received it when I arrived home, about fifteen minutes later."

Detective Miller glanced around the moneyed space, offered me a professional nod, and joined Juliette in the kitchen. She examined the letter without touching it.

"Your doorman said it was left by what looked like a college kid?" she asked.

"Probably paid a few bucks to drop it off," I said.

Lea looked at me like a disruptive student. "What happened to your neck?" she asked.

I shrugged.

"Ernie said he looked about nineteen or twenty years old, white with longish blond hair," said Juliette. "He was wearing jeans and a hoodie, a backpack over his shoulder. He told Ernie that he was asked to drop it off. Left the letter on the front desk and turned and walked out before Ernie could ask him anything. All deliveries usually must be signed for," she added.

"We'll try to help your doorman ID him. Mr. Darley is probably right. Whoever wrote this likely slipped the kid a few bucks and asked for a favor. Maybe we'll get lucky and he'll recognize the face coming out of class."

"And then?"

"Has anyone else touched this letter?" asked Miller. "Besides you and Mr. Darley?"

"No. Just Ernie, and the kid who delivered it, but I guess that was only the envelope."

"We'll have both dusted for prints. But seeing the printed label and the fact that it was typed, it seems probable that precautions were taken."

"Which means you have little to go on. Which means my son is being threatened and the police won't be able to do a goddamn thing."

Miller indicated toward the family room. "Could we sit?" she asked. "I'm going to need you both to walk me through everything."

"Duck can walk you through it," said Juliette. "I want to hear it myself. I have no idea what's going on here and I expect some answers. I expect both of you to fix it very fucking quickly." She was finger-pointing now, the octaves rising with every syllable. "I want to know who wrote this. Whoever it is will live to regret it, I can promise you that."

In the face of danger, some will wilt and seek protection. Some will weep and want to hide. Others will respond with fury and indignation. Juliette Cohen was not a wilter. She was a woman confident in her place in the world. The divorce settlement might have made her financially invincible, but Juliette had been a fearsome lady long before her marriage. Born in Greenwich and forever gorgeous, the woman knew the score. She also knew how to settle one. But everyone has her soft spots, and when kids come into the picture, no one is as invulnerable as she projects. I knew the cursing fury would give way soon enough to helpless fear. So did Lea. She didn't react to Juliette's demands. She just turned and walked toward the family room.

The ladies settled at opposite ends of a sectional leather sofa. I took the club chair next to it. I sat forward and faced them, afraid to speak.

"So, Duc—Mr. Darley, I'm going to need you to walk us through your connection to this," said Miller. She averted her eyes, inwardly scolded herself for her stumble over my name.

"Is this why you were begging to see me?" asked Juliette. "To warn me?"

The women glanced at each other, engaged in a silent power play. Miller leaned in and placed her elbows on her knees. She was a small, compact woman without wasted space. In contrast, Juliette was long and curved and full. Her indulgent, high-priced beauty was a threat to every woman competing in the infinite ways of city women. She leaned back and crossed her legs and draped an arm over the back of the couch. "Well?" she said.

My instinct—with both cops and with women—was to lie, or at least to omit. Shape the story to fit your needs. Add little else. The whole truth was almost never advisable. It only caused more trouble, more questions, more mistrust. But I thought of Stevie down the hall, and the threats made against him. Omitting details now could place him in further danger. I couldn't have that on my conscience.

"This started with a text I received from my partner, my former partner, Cassandra Kimball," I said.

Juliette stiffened at the sound of her name. I avoided her eyes.

"Her lover died recently," I told them. "He fell over a waterfall, upstate in the Catskills. A writer named Victor Wingate. His death was ruled a suicide. Cass thinks he was pushed. She asked me to help her look into it. I agreed and went to see her. She told me Wingate was writing a book about Carl Kruger. Kruger was a doped Olympic champion from East Germany. My understanding is that Kruger was helping Wingate to expose a current doping ring that was connected to back then, behind the Wall. My first stop when I returned to the city was to see him at his bar down on East Broadway." I looked at Juliette. "And you know what happened next."

Lea was glaring at me.

"What?" asked Juliette.

"Your boyfriend here insisted that he had no connection to Kruger," said Miller.

"He's a liar. And to be clear—he is *not* my boyfriend."

"In any case, after Kruger was found dead, your boy . . . Sorry, Mr. Darley here was taken in for questioning. He failed to mention any connection to the deceased."

"Why did you lie?" asked Juliette. "You went there to see him the night he was killed." She turned to Miller. "Is he a suspect?"

Miller pursed her lips, gave a slight shake of her head.

"I went there to talk to him. Cass thought Wingate's death might have something to do with what Kruger told him."

"What does she think he said?" asked Miller.

"You'll have to ask her. Like I said, it had something to

do with a current doping operation, connected to some very powerful players. The doctors that doped Carl and thousands of others got away without any punishment. They scattered across the world to ply their trade elsewhere. Performance enhancers for hire, it's big business these days. Appears Wingate may have been looking to expose some folks. Which might have something to do with the threats."

" '*Threats*'?" asked Miller.

"The letter, about Stevie."

"No, you said 'threats,' plural. Have there been others? What happened to your neck, Duck?"

Juliette glanced over at the detective's use of my first name. It confirmed her initial instinct. I marveled at their gender's intuition. Miller ignored it. She was too pissed now to care what this rich, foul-mouthed woman thought of her.

"I cut myself shav . . . ," I began. Then I thought of Stevie back in his room. "Someone put a knife to my throat," I said. "In a movie theater."

"Where?"

"IFC cinema, down on Sixth Avenue in the West Village. It was about twenty minutes before I came over here. Someone came up behind me at the end and pressed a blade against my neck."

"What did he say?"

"He asked if I liked to suffer," I said. "He asked if I liked to hurt those I love."

"And then you came *here*?" asked Juliette. She stood and pointed down at me. "You motherfucker! You came here and put my son in danger? You son of a bitch."

My phone buzzed in my pocket. To incredulous stares I took it out and checked my message. Text from Cass: **My friend Nat hooked us up. Have access to Victor's email. Come home soon, ton to discuss . . .**

I stood and told the women that I needed to leave. Miller told me to sit my ass back down. I sat.

"We're going to need to speak with your partner," she said.

"Of course."

"Is she still upstate?"

"No, she's living, um, staying with me."

"Is she there now?"

"No," I lied. "I'm not sure when she'll be home."

"We're going to need you both to come in to answer some more questions," she said.

"What about my son?" asked Juliette. "I don't care what happens to this prick and that slut partner of his. Protecting my child is the priority here."

"It will be, Ms. Cohen," said Miller. "I'm going to have someone keep an eye on your building, and on your son's school. We'll keep him safe, you have my word on that."

"My son isn't going back to school, not until we find the bastard who sent that letter." She stood and strode to the kitchen. She opened her wine fridge and withdrew a bottle, started slamming drawers, looking for an opener. I watched as she plunged screw into cork and glared back at us. "We're not going anywhere until you people do your jobs."

"I understand if you'd like to remain at home for a little while," said Miller. "This letter is extremely unsettling. But I can assure you that the great majority of threats are just that, and nothing more."

Juliette removed a glass from a cabinet, poured, and turned toward Miller. " 'Nothing more'? How reassuring, Detective, now I feel so much better. The person who wrote this letter might be connected to two murders. He's probably the same person that held a knife to Duck's neck earlier today. But I'm sure you're right – it's just empty words. We should go about our lives without taking it seriously. *Jesus fucking Christ.*"

She gulped at her wine, wiped at her upper lip.

"We take every threat seriously, Ms. Cohen. The safety of your child is paramount. We'll have an officer stationed outside your building. We'll see if your doorman can identify the kid who dropped off the letter. I'm going to have it dusted for prints, though as discussed—"

"Precautions were probably taken, I know. Which means you're not going to find shit."

"Ms. Cohen, before I leave, would it be all right if I spoke to your son?"

"No, it's not all right."

"He might have seen something, or someone, that didn't seem quite right. I don't want to alarm him, but—"

"I did see somebody," said a young voice behind us.

We turned to find Stevie watching us from the front of the hall. God, I hoped he hadn't been there long. He stood with a bravely puffed-out chest. Both fists were clenched and his eyes were narrowed at his mother. He wasn't a wilter either. He'd inherited her fierce confidence. But his jaw gave him away. It trembled as he spoke. "I saw somebody weird yesterday," he said. "He stopped and talked to Aidan and me on our way home."

"What did he look like, honey?" asked his mother. "What did he say?"

"He was bald and had a lot of tattoos. And his voice was funny, like he wasn't from here."

Oliver, I thought. The same racist fuck from Rudy's, the same one who must have tagged my front door, and held a knife to my throat in that theater.

"What did he say to you and Aidan, sweetie?"

"He asked if we'd like some ice cream. Before we could answer, he said, 'Didn't your moms tell you not to talk to strangers?' Then he started laughing. He slapped Aidan pretty hard on the back and ran away."

"Where did he run to, honey?"

"I don't know. He just took off running down the block, like fast. He was weird."

"Where did this happen?"

"I told you, on our way back from school yesterday."

"Where was Gloria when this happened?"

"She was talking to other nannies, farther back. We went back to her right away. She said he was probably just some crazy guy. She said we shouldn't have been talking to him, but we didn't, Mom. He just came up to us. We didn't do anything."

His mother went to him now and wrapped her son in a hug. She bent down and kissed the top of his head and squeezed him to her. When she released him, I could tell the helpless fear had arrived.

"Was that man bad?" asked Stevie.

She nodded and promised her son that he would never see him again.

Chapter 15

On my way out Juliette told me not to come back. Stevie wouldn't look at me. Detective Miller made clear that Cass and I were expected to report for questioning first thing in the morning. If we were not there by nine a.m., she would have us arrested for obstruction. She stayed behind as both women watched me walk to the elevator. I felt their stares on my back. Didn't turn. On my way down I touched my bandages. I recalled the words whispered in my ear as the knife pressed to my neck. Someone must have seen him entering or leaving. I turned west and returned to the theater.

The kid issuing tickets said he had no clue what I was talking about. He'd never seen a guy who looked like that, but then he said he'd never seen me before either, and I'd bought a ticket from him a few hours before. His eyes were stoned to slits. He had to tilt his chin up to look at me, his eyeballs invisible behind a curtain of lashes.

"I told you, man, I've never seen that dude before, and I've never seen you either," he said. "Now do you want a ticket or not?"

"Do you mind if I go back in and ask your colleagues behind the snack bar?"

"My 'colleagues'?" He yawned and laughed at once. "That's pretty funny, man. But yeah, I do mind. You gotta buy a ticket to get in."

I pushed a twenty under the glass and asked him to pick whatever he recommended.

"You like Japanese horror?" he asked.

"Perfect."

"Seriously?"

I waited until the hamsters in his head could inch the wheel forward. He blinked and smiled. "Oh, right, you're just, like, buying a ticket so you can go talk to my *colleagues* inside. You're sly, man."

"Like a fox," I told him.

He pushed the ticket and my change under the glass and tried to wink. His head lolled to the side like he was having a stroke. "Enjoy your show," he said.

The kids working behind the snack bar were about as helpful. Maybe not quite as stoned, but glazed with indifference. No, they'd never seen the man I described; and yes, they would remember someone who looked like that. They thought. At least they were pretty sure they'd remember. But no, man, they hadn't seen a bald, tattooed dude in the last few hours. I thanked them for their uselessness and left with even less hope for humanity.

On the way home I returned to the Marlton for another pop. Double Bulleit, bottle of Stella—the previous rounds were burned away too soon by the scene at the Cohens'. I felt the pull of a bender coming on. I'd kept it in check long enough. In times of extreme stress it was a necessary medicine.

Taking in the surroundings, I realized I couldn't get used to this. I'd grown accustomed to good living with Juliette, where drink prices were not looked at and dives were be-

neath consideration. But I'd been expelled again from the
gilded ranks, and the money I'd saved would not last long
if I persisted in drinking in places like this. Better enjoy it
while it lasted.

"You got some more time now?" asked the bearded bartender. "Or is this another hit-and-run?"

"On the run, as always," I said. "But I think I can manage one more round."

He nodded toward my neck. "What happened there?"
he asked. "I noticed it before."

"Rough play," I said. "She ignored my safe word."

He didn't have much for that. Gave a faint smile, turned,
and went to the other end of the bar, where a middle-aged
tourist couple was getting toasted on Manhattans. The
paunchy husband raised his glass and asked too loud for
two more "Manahattas." His wife cackled and slurped off
the dregs of her current one.

I looked at myself in the mirror above the bottles. It
hadn't taken long for the whiskey bloat to return to my
cheeks. I wondered if my latest cut would leave a scar. *One
more for the memoir,* Duck Down in Darkness, I thought.
I'd come up with that clever title one afternoon during my
convalescence after the McKay case. In my self-absorption
I resolved to write it all out someday—the betrayals and
the madness and the violence of one wasted city boy's life.
But all I'd managed to write so far was that title, which
probably wasn't as clever as I thought.

Cass would be waiting at home, eager to share the latest. I had plenty to tell her too. Returning with a hazy
head of booze wouldn't be appreciated. I waved down the
bartender and asked for one more and the check. But this
time, no need to make it a double. A single shot would be
fine. It was the little shows of temperance that mattered.

I walked home in a mostly straight line, enjoying the
magic-hour light. This was when the city liked to reveal its

full charm. In the spring twilight hour was when the sun bowed and granted that special glow against the buildings, when everyone stopped and gazed, if only for a moment, at the city posing for its portrait. At Broadway and 10th I paused to admire the steeple of Grace Church. Turning north toward Union Square, I felt transported to another, more tasteful era. The old loft buildings with their high windows and decorative facades still lined the boulevard. The Strand was still there, unchanged as ever, with its miles of books beckoning. The Empire State and the Con Ed stood tall and proud, standards of a city built right. But then my eyes drifted to the new soaring glass disgraces that continued to insult the skyline, and my reverie was broken.

I returned to the apartment in odd spirits. Given the events of the day, I should have been distressed. I should have been rattled by my assault in the theater, enraged by the threat to Stevie, panicked by all the violence that was back in my life. Instead I was rather calm, peaceful even, like I'd rediscovered a chaotic equilibrium that was my natural setting. I strolled in with a beatific smile and went to the fridge and poured myself some ice water. Took a gulp and leaned against the kitchen counter and said, "What a day."

Cass was watching me from the couch with distrust. "Are you drunk?" she asked.

"Nah, just feeling a little surreal, I guess. A lot's happened today."

"Then why do you look so happy?"

"I've got nothing to be happy about, trust me." I felt myself smiling as I took another sip. "Maybe I'm in shock."

"What happened to your neck?"

I touched the bandage, pressed the cold glass against it. "I suppose that would be a good place to start."

"Duck, you're acting seriously strange," said Cass. "Talk to me."

"Shall we begin with the knife to the neck in a darkened theater?" I asked. "Or perhaps the anonymous threat made to an eight-year-old boy? Oh, and we're both expected at the Ninth Precinct tomorrow morning. We have to share all we know about the deaths of Victor Wingate and Carl Kruger."

"Christ, Duck . . ."

"Had no choice, darlin'. The mother of said eight-year-old was less than pleased by the letter she received. I was just lucky she allowed me to call Detective Miller, instead of dialing 911."

"Come, sit," she said. "Talk to me."

She sparked a Parliament, exhaled, and kept her eyes on me through the plume of smoke as I refilled my water and joined her in the living room.

"Here we are again," I said.

She scanned the small room like it was a foreign space. "It feels different now."

"It's Elvis. The hound's left the building."

Her eyes fell shut as she nodded. "Poor boy," she said. She leaned forward and stubbed out the burning filter and rested her forearms on her knees. She was wearing a scoop-necked black t-shirt that revealed a black lace bra beneath. She caught me staring, sat up and pulled at the neck. She crossed her leather-clad legs and sighed. "Tell me about your day," she said. "From the time we left the restaurant."

"Don't you want to tell me about the emails?" I asked. "That your ex-dominatrix friend managed to hack into?"

"After," she said. "Now talk."

I did. I held nothing back. Lying to Cass had always been impossible. She possessed the power of a priest in a confessional. The compulsion to spill and ask for penance was the same. Whispering secrets, sharing battled desires, asking to atone and be forgiven for sins—and the church wondered why it had issues with sex and abuse. It was all the same dance. I'd rather kneel before a gorgeous lady in leather.

I told her of my walk through the Village, returning to Charlie McKay's home and trying to resist the urge to drink, determined to stay sober for Juliette and Stevie. I told her about the film I watched, the sushi chef's monk-like devotion to the perfect bites of fish. I described the tattooed arm around my eyes and the knife pressed to my throat, and repeated the words breathed in my ear. I confessed going to the Marlton and told her what I tossed back before going to the Cohens' and finding Juliette there, shaken and staring at that letter. Then there was the arrival of Detective Miller, and finally Stevie coming out and telling us about his run-in with the guy who must have been Oliver.

When I finished, Cass's expression was unchanged. She absorbed it through perpetual drags, lighting one stick after the next, exhaling upward through the side of her mouth.

"Fuck," she said.

"Fucking hell, right?"

"We gotta figure out how much to tell your detective friend tomorrow."

"You tell me," I said. "Your turn. What did you find out today?"

Cass stubbed out her latest cig, pushed herself up, and stretched her arms over her head. Her shirt inched up to reveal an expanse of pale stomach, the piercing in her belly button. She pulled it down before my eyes could linger long. "You got any wine here?" she asked.

"Apartment's dry, if you can believe it," I said. "You want me to order a bottle?"

" 'Order'?" She smiled at that. "I forgot everything is deliverable here. In the country you actually have to get in the car and drive to get things you need."

As opposed to Manhattan, that offered five-star-hotel room-service options from any room in the city. It was better than any hotel. From the comfort of my couch I could have any service imaginable delivered to my front door within the hour. There was Seamless for any cuisine, numbers and websites for endless, more unsavory options. In less than sixty minutes, without stepping outside, you could have a feast of lobster and champagne spread before you on the coffee table, followed by a dessert of the highest-quality cocaine and a two-thousand-dollar-an-hour escort who would treat you to the full Girlfriend Experience. Money was the only requirement. Oh, Gotham, you abusive lover.

"Duck? Earth to Duck?" Cass was snapping her fingers in front of my face.

"Huh? Sorry, spaced out."

"I said a couple bottles of Pinot Noir would be nice. Want me to call?"

"No, no, I got it, they know me. Hang on."

I called Beta at Gramercy Wines, didn't have to give my name or address. He recognized my voice. My orders had become more restrained, less frequent than the past, but he knew not to question a top customer. When you start buying a few less pills from the dealer, he doesn't question it either. Sometimes scaling back is good for business. When your product is an addictive substance that provides pleasure, a good seller knows that long-term addicts are the best kind. The hell-bound, death-wish types, they never work out in the end. Plus, dealers don't like the guilt. Folks assume they have no conscience, but that's not true. They want their customers functioning for as long as possible.

I ordered a couple Pinots for Cass. Then, before hanging up, I added a bottle of Bulleit. I could sense Beta smiling on the line. "You got it, buddy," he said. "Julio will be over in five minutes."

"I'm quite the enabler, aren't I?" asked Cass.

"We make our own beds," I said. "Now tell me about these emails."

Chapter 16

Over the previous year Victor Wingate and Carl Kruger exchanged over a thousand emails. It was the first draft of a story that seemed bound for best-seller lists. The inspiration and flushed excitement that Cass witnessed in her lover had been warranted. In Carl Kruger he discovered a character and a source that writers dream of. Abused and talented girl transformed into a doped champion, and then transitioned into a determined, proud man. Somehow he found the improbable happy ending in the city—married and in love with a partner that respected his past, had lived it too, and together they operated a business where they welcomed other souls to sip away their demons.

But this was no biography that Victor was writing. Perhaps it should have been. If he'd stopped there, if he kept quiet about the rest of it, both of them might still be alive. It was what Carl told him next that must have set off these storms of violence. Inevitable lawsuits should have been minor among their worries. These guys were plotting to out some of the standard-bearers of sport itself. If exposed, it threatened to topple the entire edifice. Teams and leagues worth billions could not let that happen.

My bones were weary after the spikes of adrenaline

through the day's events. I brewed a French press of strong coffee and resisted peeling open the new bottle of bourbon. There was something calling me back from my usual annihilation, my factory setting for dealing in times like this. I kept recalling the words in that letter.

"Your son, Stevie, is a good boy, isn't he? So smart, so full of promise . . ."

The mocking tone addressed me personally: *"I do hope he's reading this . . . !"*

Followed by the almost-playful, rhetorical warning: *"It would be a shame if Stevie did not come home one day, wouldn't it?"*

I bummed a rare smoke from Cass and told her I was taking a walk. Since Elvis died, I hadn't been able to shake our evening ritual. As night fell, I was compelled to walk around a few blocks, stopping by the same trees. Maybe it was a form of mourning, or maybe a sign of denial, probably both. Either way it provided a measure of comfort that I did not feel any need to end. Cass glanced up as she handed one over with her lighter and went back to the trove of emails. I lit it, said I'd be back in a few.

It was a gorgeous spring evening, the sky a cobalt blue lit by an almost full moon. Wisps of clouds were visible in the night sky, but never any stars. The city lights below would forever drown the universe above us. I crossed the street and strolled tree to tree around the perimeter of Stuyvesant Square. There were thin maples standing in fresh mulch, which was always a roadside attraction for dogs on the leash. Many street trees were now protected by low iron fences and admonishing signs, asking dog owners to please take their business elsewhere. They were trees, for Christ's sake, isn't that where dogs were meant to go? I always took a perverse pleasure when Elvis decided to spray right on one of those signs. At the gates on Second Avenue I turned and entered the park. Inside, it was all darkness and shadow under a canopy of thick oaks and elms. They were among the oldest living things in this city. Allowed to grow free for centuries, they were the true natives of New York. How many dogs had pissed on them through the ages? How many bewildered men and women had sought brief shade and refuge beneath their limbs? The city was still beneath them, in these carved-out parks, and quieter, though we remained just steps away from the traffic moving down the avenue. There was a whispered danger in these parks at night that I relished. It wasn't the bums or the junkies littered on nearby benches, or the antiquated threat of petty crime. It was something more elemental than that. In certain parts of New York, in aged darkened rooms and under ancient trees, you could almost feel the ghosts reaching out and touching your shoulder. They were malevolent spirits, there to remind you of all the suffering and evil that had come before in this fallen city.

I considered Carl Kruger, impaled through the throat with his javelin, on the floor of his bar. I remembered the blood around his neck like a bright red scarf. I remembered the vibrations of death that hovered over the barroom. It was a black energy I knew well; I'd become acquainted with it on multiple occasions. I wondered about the dead in each of those cases. The spirit of each of them was out there somewhere. I had no faith to speak of, but I was sure that death in this life was not final. The soul moved on. Sometimes it didn't move far, and seldom did it go happily, without a fight.

I stopped walking and found myself standing before the statue of Peter Stuyvesant, the peg-legged OG leader of this island. Back in the mid-1600s, when the settlement was still owned by the Dutch, Peter was the director-general of New Netherland. This was his land I was standing on now. At least land he'd stolen from the Lenape natives and claimed as his own. His presence was still pronounced over these parts. His grave was just a few blocks south.

My mother, when she was sober, loved to regale me with city history. In college she'd written her thesis on the "inevitability of Manhattan" as the world's center. It had everything a settlement could wish for: a port, fertile soil, and that spirit of place that vibrated beneath the feet of anyone paying attention.

My thoughts were scattered as I stared up at peg-legged Pete. I read that he lost his right leg during an expedition in the Caribbean, while working for the Dutch West India Company. A cannonball hit him during a battle with a rival Spanish fleet, and medicine being what it was back then, the lower leg was amputated with a lack of surgical precision. They say you can still hear that wooden stump tapping against his coffin in the cemetery next to St. Marks Church on certain nights. Soon enough I figured I'd be joining him, along with my mother and countless other spirits still tossing and turning in the soil and the winds around the city. I never expected a long life and a peaceful old age. I couldn't imagine it. I knew my end loomed sooner than later.

The breeze stirred and rustled the leaves overhead. I nodded to Peter and walked under the moon and the trees along the path and exited beneath the high black iron gates. I checked my cell for messages, found none, and returned to the apartment.

Cass was yawning in front of the computer as I walked in.

"Death," I said. "It takes a lot out of you."

"I can't believe this stuff I've been reading," she said. "It's so fucking disturbing."

"Enough to kill for?"

She nodded, closed the laptop.

"Look forward to catching up on it."

"Think I'm gonna turn in," she said.

She squeezed my shoulder as she shuffled past. I tried not to look at the full sealed bottle of bourbon on the counter. I needed clarity now, and memory. If I was going to continue pursuing this, and I knew I had no choice, then I was putting Stevie in danger. The least I could do was make an honest, sober effort of it. Well, sober-ish. I settled on the couch and reopened Cass's computer, read an exchange between Carl Kruger and Victor Wingate. It was dated February 16, time-stamped at 3:13 a.m. It read:

Herr Viktor,

You sure you want to keep going with this? It will get unpleasant, ja? Too much money and power is at stake. Too much fame too. When they learn what you are doing they will try to stop us. They will sue, as you said, but maybe worse. Uli is worried. She tells me I should keep my mouth shut. She reminds me of the people we once knew who did not keep quiet. Another time and place, I tell her. No, she says, it is no different, only now is more dangerous. There is even more to lose. Perhaps she is right. I am torn.

CK

Victor's reply was full of righteousness. He was blinded by the story. He refused to acknowledge the dangers that so worried Carl's wife. In response, he wrote:

Carl,

I hear you, but we need to forge ahead. Remember what wise Edmund Burke said – "The only thing necessary for the triumph of evil is for good men to do nothing." You are a good man, Carl. I'd like to believe the same of myself. And this is evil. Neither of us can deny that. We need to expose it. We're talking about some of the most famous men on earth, treated as far back as their teens, their achievements built on endless layers of lies and drugs. The guilty have not only escaped punishment for too long, they've continued to practice their dark art. They feel no shame or remorse for those they've hurt, and they will continue to enrich themselves

with their sinful science until the day they die. You were brave to tell me about it. We cannot stop now.

Vic

Carl did not reply for a few days. When he did, it appeared he'd chosen to side with the writer over the wife. He asked Victor to meet him at Kruger's that Friday. Uli would be away for the weekend. There would be time to talk. The next email came from Victor the following Monday. He was thrilled and outraged.

C,

I am still buzzing from all we discussed. I need to get down to that clinic in Coral Gables as soon as possible. This Dr. Lipke is shameless. Did you know his bio on the BioVida website boasts of having over 50 years of experience in the field? Unreal! Does he tell these clueless parents what his early years involved? Does he tell them he was convicted in German court of child abuse, for his role in all that doping?! How is this allowed to go on? They operate in plain sight and no one seems to care. All these parents care about is their kids' sports, how they can boost performance by any means possible. Who cares about the damage or dishonor if it might mean millions later! It used to be state-sanctioned, by an unconscionable few. Now it's open season. This country is worse than any communist regime. And Lipke's partner, this Dr. Crowley, what do we make of him? BioVida claims to be "an anti-aging and hormonal health clinic." What does that even mean, that they treat old folks, desperate to find the medical fountain of youth? It's a convenient front, especially down there with all the retirees refusing to admit their mortality. Do you realize that the names you mentioned, many are icons across the globe? This isn't Lance or A-Rod or Barry Bonds. Everyone always knew they were bullshit. We're talking the most beloved, beyond suspicion, the most powerful of all. Do you realize how much they have to lose by being tied to something like this? And yet, they continue to go to BioVida. They can't help themselves. As soon as their skills begin to fade, they get desperate. They'll do anything to extend their time in the sporting sun. But fuck them. They're not the ones who trouble me. They're soulless self-obsessed stars who need to feel worshipped. I'll be happy to bring them down, but they're not the real problem. No, my friend, our target is those parents who sacrifice their children at the altar of performance, and those doctors who'll inject anything into these kids, never mind the side effects, just to make them faster, or stronger, or physically superior in any way. We are going to stop this, you and I. You are a brave man, Bruder.

Vic

I read late into the night. I Googled every unfamiliar name and company mentioned in the correspondence. A picture began to form of the world we were entering. It was an underworld of shameless cheating and warped ideals, of parents determined to juice their children to college scholarships, at the least. If all went according to plan, their enhanced offspring would perform all the way to the pros, where they'd sign eight- and nine-figure contracts that would set up generations of family. The stakes were high, the risks deemed worth it, or not contemplated.

Dr. Eberhard Lipke knew all about those side effects. In the 1970s in East Germany he had been one of the regime's top sporting scientists: Director of High Performance was his title. From his lab in Leipzig, Dr. Lipke oversaw the doping programs of all East German athletes in track & field and swimming. He was among the first to pioneer the use of a little blue pill called Oral Turinabol, an anabolic steroid that bolstered athletes' hormones—and helped transform their bodies into unnatural gold-medal-winning machines. Tinkering with the chemistry of young bodies, as if they were his personal property, Lipke fed them a rainbow of drugs. With the blue pills came yellow ones and gray tablets and green powder, and then came the syringes, needles to hard-muscled asses. *Do not ask what's inside. Ignore the troubling changes to your body—the morphing facial structure, the back acne, the deepened voice, the sudden sexual urges. Pay no mind to such things, just enjoy the added strength and speed. Enjoy standing atop the podium.*

Yet the real problems came later. The drugs bulked bodies to such artificial size that the bones and joints could not accommodate the muscle. Soon these doped bodies began to break down like brittle thoroughbred horses. But that did not concern the doctors and the coaches; the athletes were easily replaced. As they aged, the ones cast aside would often suffer brutal long-term effects: children born with birth defects, heart problems, infertility, not to mention the psychological damage inflicted on a generation of athletes abused with needles and pills without their consent.

When the Wall came down and the records poured out, Dr. Lipke was among those arrested and tried in a unified-Germany court. The evidence against him was overwhelming. He was convicted on eighty-five counts of causing bodily harm to minors. His punishment? A fine of 7,500 German marks, less than four grand, and a fifteen-month suspended jail sentence. Lipke got off with a shrug of a check and served no time. He left Germany and offered his in-demand expertise elsewhere. First, in Austria, for their vaulted ski program; then in Norway, leading a performance center for Winter Olympians, until it appeared he tired of cold, dark European winters.

He moved to South Florida and founded BioVida. His partner was a clean-cut American doctor named James Crowley. A university diploma and medical degree from Stanford, an athlete himself, Crowley's bio boasted of his dozen Ironmans and All-American past as a cross-country runner as a Cardinal undergrad. While other anti-aging clinics had come under fire for having doping ties to professional athletes over the years, BioVida had escaped scrutiny. It appeared to be a cottage industry in South Florida, a land of body-beautiful worship, masses of aging folks determined not to die, and a fertile sun-drenched ground for developing young athletes. Miami was also a place where a dubious past in another country had never been a problem. Lipke was just another drug dealer, allowed to set up shop and blend into the sunny, shady landscape.

As I finished the emails and my Googling, I was left with two nagging questions: How much of this did Cass already know? And how did Carl Kruger come by his information? Cass must have heard something from her dead lover. She had accompanied him to the city, to Kruger's, where she must have listened to at least some of Victor's conversations. And Carl, how would he have known about those superstars allegedly lining up at Lipke's clinic, or about the parents of young athletes, eager to dope their children to success? There was so much I longed to ask them.

But dead men keep quiet.

Chapter 17

The next morning I woke on the couch to the smell of coffee brewing and bacon sizzling. I heard Cass cracking eggs over the stove. I heard Dylan's "Romance in Durango" playing from her phone on the counter. I stretched my arms overhead and yawned loud enough for her to hear.

"He's risen," she said.

I rose. Ambled around the corner to the kitchen. "Smells damn good in here," I said.

"I picked up some basics from Raffi's deli. Got you a fresh six-pack of Beck's too."

"To what do I owe this generous display?"

She glanced over her shoulder, a smile in her eyes. She wore black leather pants and a Clash t-shirt with Simonon smashing his guitar. Dark eyeliner circled her wide eyes. Crimson lipstick was painted across her mouth. It hadn't taken her long to assimilate back to her city look. I watched her scramble the eggs and turn the bacon, resisted the urge to grab a slice from the skillet. I poured some coffee, then reached into the fridge and grabbed a Beck's. It would have felt rude not to.

"I was thinking, last night in bed," she said. "You don't have to keep doing this, for me, I mean. It's not like you're getting paid. And now I've put that boy in danger too."

"No, you didn't," I said. "I did. I was warned and I ignored it. That's why Stevie was threatened."

"But I set it in motion. I asked for your help, and now Carl is dead and someone put a knife to your throat, and they're threatening to hurt a young boy."

"Who are 'they,' Cass? Who's this Oliver working for? He can't be acting on his own. Who was that older man with him?"

"I don't know. Someone associated with Dr. Lipke and his clinic? Victor mentioned that he needed to go down there and investigate. We were going to go together, make it a little getaway from the upstate winter. But we never made it. . . ."

"So, you knew about BioVida?" I asked. "Before your friend helped you hack into those emails?"

She paused as she turned the bacon, seeming to consider the question. "No," she said. "I told you, I didn't ask Victor about his work. He made it clear that he didn't want to discuss it while he was immersed. I respected that. He told me a little, just what I've told you, and said that the story was taking him down to Miami. He asked me to come. I was going to lay by the pool."

Cass turned off the burners and scooped the eggs and the bacon on a spatula and served them on a plate. She handed it to me. *"Bon appétit."*

"What are you having?"

"Already ate," she said.

In all our time together I'd still never seen her take a bite off a fork. She poured herself a fresh cup of coffee and followed me to the living room. While I devoured her breakfast, she lit a Parliament and watched me.

"So, when are we headed down there?" I asked between bites.

"Where, to Miami?"

"Of course. We need to pick up where Victor left off."

"Duck, are you sure you want to do this? I think maybe you should stop. Why put that boy at further risk? It's clear that you care about him. Both the boy and his mother, what's her name again?"

"Juliette."

"Juliette." She let the name linger between us. I remembered Cass's late-night text, the way it had shattered our domestic play, the way Juliette saw it in my face. A woman recognized where there was competition, despite any man's best efforts.

"You know I have no choice," I said. "What am I supposed to do, pretend like nothing's happened and stop searching? Just because someone puts a knife to my throat and sends a threatening letter?"

She laughed. "Actually, yes. That's what a normal person would do. Someone with any sense of mortality."

"Yeah, well." I took a swig of the Beck's, rinsed it with a gulp of coffee. The pairing had always been my favorite way to wake.

"All right, listen," she said. "Before we go down there, I need to talk to Carl's wife, Uli. She's a sweetheart. I know she was worried about what our men were working on. For good reason it turns out. She and Carl, they were the sweetest couple you've ever seen. They'd been through hell together, and they made it out."

"He should have kept quiet," I said.

"Some people can't help themselves."

The bar was no longer a crime scene. The yellow tape was balled in a trash can in the corner. Uli was sweeping when we entered a little before noon. She glanced up, and seeing Cass, stopped and leaned against the broom for support. Her eyes began to well, but she blinked away the tears with a shake of the head. A silence stretched between the two women.

"Our stupid men," said Uli.

"Dumb bastards," said Cass.

They went to each other and embraced in the center of the room. They held the hug while I lingered in the doorway. Uli whispered something in Cass's ear and she nodded, then released her and stepped back and looked over her shoulder at me.

"Uli Kruger, Duck Darley," said Cass.

"We've met," said Uli.

"We have. It's nice to see you again."

"Not nice at all," she said. Then, to Cass, she asked, "Would you like a drink?"

We took the stools next to the taps while Uli went around the bar. I watched her wide, elegant frame move with that same unhurried grace. Uli wore a long peasant's dress washed almost colorless, with a brown leather string wrapped around her ample waist. The neck was open and untied and her full chest breathed braless. She placed both hands on the bar top before us. "What can I get you?" she asked.

"Just an orange juice," said Cass. "Thank you, Uli."

"A Hofbräu for me, please," I said.

She poured our drinks and pushed them in front of us and then crossed her arms and looked at Cass. "So, how do you know this one?" she asked.

"He's my partner. I asked him for help. I hope that's okay, Uli."

"You should have told me first."

"I know, I'm sorry," said Cass. "After Victor died, I was so messed up. I knew he didn't jump. I called Duck the next night and he came upstate and I told him what happened. I mentioned Victor's project with Carl, and—"

"So that's why you were here," said Uli.

"That's why," I said.

"I should have told you," said Cass. "I think he can help us."

"How?" asked Uli. "They're both dead. What is there to do now?"

"Don't you want to know what happened? Don't you want to catch whoever did this?"

Uli shrugged. "Why?" she asked. "It will not bring them back."

"No, it won't," said Cass. "But I need to know. I need to find out who killed them."

"Suit yourself," said Uli.

"You really don't want to know?"

Uli turned her back to us and began straightening rows of glasses that did not need straightening. Looking at us through the bar mirror, she said, "If you grew up the way we did, the way Carl and I did, you would have learned that asking too many questions never helps. It only brings more trouble. I reminded Carl of this. I told him to keep quiet, but he wouldn't listen. Victor got him too excited. He convinced him they were crusaders. It was so stupid."

"It's an important story," said Cass. "It should be exposed."

" 'Exposed'?" Uli snorted. "Who cares? The doping, it is everywhere, why does it matter anymore? Why do you care?"

"I care about finding out who killed the man I loved," said Cass. "You should too."

The women made eye contact through the mirror. Uli gave a pained smile and nodded and turned around. "So, what do you want to know?" she asked. "How do you expect me to help you?"

"How did Carl know these things?" asked Cass. "How did he hear about Dr. Lipke's clinic in Miami? How did he know about the athletes he's treated?"

Uli removed a wineglass from the shelf. She opened a fridge beneath the liquor and brought out a bottle of cold white wine. She uncorked it and filled her glass, then topped it off with a splash of soda. She took a sip and gave me a withering once-over.

"That night, did you talk to my husband?"

"A bit," I said. "Not about any of this though. We mostly talked about music."

"Oh?"

"Carl was cranking the Motörhead," I said. "We bonded over Lemmy."

"God, he had such shit taste in music."

"Uli," said Cass. "How did Carl know about the things he told Victor?"

She ignored her friend. "And then you got up to go to the bathroom, and when you came out . . ."

"Someone hit me on the back of the head. I was out cold."

"And then he went to Carl," she said.

"Who do you think it could have been?" I asked.

Now she turned back to Cass. "My husband was rather famous in certain circles," she said. "In anti-doping circles he was a case study. You can Google him and see. I told Carl that, but he would not see it that way. I think he liked the attention."

"Do you think he was exploited?" asked Cass.

"Of course he was. I told him that. But he did not care. My husband was easily seduced by the media. Many are, I suppose."

"So, because of his stature, in those circles . . ."

"People told him things, yeah? He became someone others would reach out to. He was like the face of a movement. People sent him things—information, gossip. He never did anything about it, until Victor came."

"How did they meet?" I asked.

"I told you," said Cass. "Through his friend, that restaurateur, Mickey Knight. He introduced him."

"Oh, yes, Cokey Mick," said Uli. "I remember. He used
to come late, after his restaurants closed, and do cocaine
in the bathroom. Then he would come out and hit on
everything that moved."

"Sounds about right," said Cass. "He came to visit us
once on the mountaintop. He never stopped sniffing and
wiping his nose. He made a pass at me when Victor left the
room. Some friend."

"A prince," said Uli. "But he spent a lot of money here,
and he was very generous, so we tolerated him. Sometimes
Carl would share his drugs, which I hated."

"So, one night on coke Carl must have started talking,"
I said. For some, I knew, blow could be a sloppy truth
serum. An evening of key bumps in the bathroom and the
late-night secrets and buried desires would start spilling
forth.

"I suppose," said Uli. "I would leave whenever I noticed
Carl doing that. I didn't want to be around it. It led to
many fights."

"Did Victor ever join them?"

Cass shook her head. "No, he wasn't into that. But
when Mickey came to visit, he told Victor about his new
friend Carl. He told him about his past, the abuse, how
those responsible were never punished. He even suggested
that Victor write about it."

"We might want to talk to Mickey," I said to Cass.
"How close was he to Victor?"

"They grew up together," said Cass. "Victor said he was
like a brother when they were city kids in the seventies, before his family moved upstate. Victor's parents were typical unreliable artists, high half the time, and Mickey's
father was a cop. I think they wanted each other's lives.
Mickey was a wild kid who wished he had the freedom

that Victor had, while Victor longed for more structure and the comfort of rules. They were two sides of the same coin."

"A fine analysis, Ms. Freud," said Uli.

Cass raised her glass of juice, gave her friend a nod. "My area of expertise," she said. "Analyzing the needs of men."

Both women looked to me. I drank, avoiding their eyes. They let me squirm a moment, before Uli said, "The police, they think it was a robbery gone wrong."

"Did the killer take anything?" asked Cass.

"Yeah, smashed open the register and took all the cash. A few hundred dollars."

"Anything else?"

"Also a bottle of vodka," she said. "Grey Goose. That is all."

"But the way your husband was killed," I said. "There's no way a panicking junkie does that."

Uli took a drink of her wine. I watched her chest rise and fall as it rinsed through her body. She sighed. "It could be. You don't know. It could have been a meth-head, out of control. Maybe he saw the javelin and wanted to play with it. Carl was very protective of it. No one was allowed to touch it."

"But there was no sign of a struggle, right?" I asked. "Your husband was a big man. I saw him upset. If he wanted to stop the killer from touching that thing, the place would have been a wreck."

"Not if there was a gun pointed at him," said Cass.

Uli refilled her wine and set it on the shelf next to the register. She leaned back against it and crossed her arms. "Why was he upset?" she asked.

"That night? You saw him when he came in, he was a mess."

"Yeah, and then I left, and you stayed, just you and my husband. Why was he upset . . . with you?"

"He wasn't, I mean not really, or not for long. I said something that set him off. I brought up Victor's death in a clumsy way."

"The police said there was broken glass at the front of the bar," said Uli. "A few glasses were gone from the shelf."

"Thrown in my direction," I said. "But he calmed down."

"Jesus, Duck," muttered Cass.

"Listen," I said. "I only spent a short time with your husband, but I liked him. He seemed like an honorable, good man. I never met Victor, but I'm sure I would have liked him too. If he liked my partner here, he must have been okay. I want to help. I want to find whoever killed them. I know the cops are looking too, but with access to their emails, we have a head start. Let me help, okay?"

Neither woman spoke. They looked at each other in silence, until Uli shook her head and smiled. "Where did you find this one?" she asked. "So earnest, like an eager hunting dog."

Chapter 18

Mickey Knight, aka the Neighborhood Maker, owned a half-dozen restaurants in Manhattan. For three decades his model had been both simple and self-fulfilling: Enter a questionable area where leases were still cheap, where crime still lingered, where the gay settlers were beginning to tidy up. Open one of his see-and-be-seen bistros and watch them flock. It had worked every time, in TriBeCa, the Meatpacking District, the Lower East Side, Alphabet City, all areas where it was once inadvisable to walk alone at night. But now, thanks in part to the Knight touch, they were bright bazaars full of bright young things, blithely ignorant to the dangers of the past. In a *New York* magazine profile, I remembered Knight declaring that every neighborhood in Manhattan was now done. There was nowhere else to go. He spoke of taking his model on the road, to the inner cities of Baltimore or Detroit, perhaps, anywhere but Brooklyn, where his model had been plagiarized to the point of cliché.

We spoke to three of his managers—at Musette, Allard, and Jadis—where we received various degrees of unhelpful snootery. No, they didn't know where Mickey was; and no, we could not have his number. Maybe he would be stopping by later tonight, sometime between eight p.m.

and midnight. We were welcome to come back then and wait to see if we could catch him. On our way out of Jadis, on Avenue C, a handsome young waiter came running out after Cass.

"Excuse me!" he called. "You're Cassandra, right?"

Cass turned and eyed him, shoes to hair. He was tall and thin, with a face made for commercials. A shaggy mop of styled blond hair fell across his eyes. He pushed it aside and smiled at my partner. "Do I know you?" she asked.

"No, I'm Tad, we haven't met." He stuck out a hand, which Cass did not take. "Mickey's mentioned you. You were with that guy, his friend, who died?"

Cass stiffened, said nothing.

"He kept talking about you," said Tad. "He said you two had some crazy connection. After his friend died, he was saying how he needed to see you again, but he didn't know how to reach you."

"Victor," said Cass. "His friend—my boyfriend—his name was Victor Wingate."

"Oh yeah, he was like a writer, right? Anyway, I thought I recognized you, based on how he described you, and I know Mickey would really like to hear from you."

"I'm sure he would," said Cass.

"So, listen, I don't, like, have his number, but I know he's going to be at Musette this afternoon, probably around four. He has this rotation, where he goes, and, well, I don't really know what he does, but he stops by his places at different times based on his rotation. It's supposed to seem like it's random, so he surprises us, but we all know his pattern."

"Thanks, Tad," I said. "Musette, that's on Suffolk, right?"

Tad turned to me for the first time. "Yeah, on the corner of Suffolk and Rivington. Why are you guys looking for him?"

"We'll check it out," said Cass, already walking.

"Cassandra, one more thing!" he called. "When you see

Mickey, would you mind mentioning that I put you in touch? It's Tad."

Cass didn't answer. I felt bad for the pretty boy, so I said, "Sure, buddy. Tad, from Jadis, got it."

"Th-thanks, dude," he stammered. "I really appreciate it."

It was a clear, bright day on the Lower East Side and the hipsters were out in force. This was no longer the neighborhood where I spent my unhappy teenaged years—the one where I got into sidewalk fights and tried not to get jumped by local kids who smelled my rich-boy scent still lingering. Back then, it was a tough, untouched pocket of the city. We lived on Pitt Street—so far in spirit and style from the Upper East Side that it felt like we'd traveled back in time, to a town closer to Scorsese's *Gangs of New York* than the gilded safe place I knew as a boy. But all that was gone now. At the bottom of every tenement there were bars and restaurants, galleries and coffee shops, all catering to the young and the clueless. Like the Meatpacking District before it, the Lower East Side came and went in a blur—it was rough and ugly one minute; hip and exciting the next; then over, having been invaded and ruined by douche bags and bag-ettes. I hated the threatening streets of my high school years, but this pillaged place was even worse.

Mickey Knight, as much as anyone else, was responsible for it. When he arrived with one of his bistros, it was like waving a wand over a neighborhood. He brought the models and the musicians, and everyone else followed. Then the cool kids would leave as soon as others discovered it, but Mickey's brand would remain, cashing in for years to come with the bankers and the wankers and the tourists in search of the "real" New York.

When Cass and I entered Musette, the staff family meal was just finishing. A bartender looked up from polishing glasses and called, "Sorry, guys, not open yet, about ten minutes, okay?"

While we waited on the corner, I remembered our missed appointment with Detective Miller that morning. We'd been so consumed with the emails, the Miami connection, then visiting Uli . . . Lea would be pissed. I hoped she wouldn't make good on that threat of obstruction. I mentioned it to Cass. She shrugged, lit a Parliament.

"I figured you were blowing it off," she said.

"So you remembered and neglected to mention it?"

"I've got nothing to say to them. If they need a statement, let them come get us."

It wasn't the time to argue. We probably had a pair of uniforms at my front door, awaiting our return. May as well meet with this Mickey character first. I regarded his restaurant, had to acknowledge his taste. Musette was spelled out in unlit neon script over the entrance. I remembered the cover of a famous novel, of a lone figure standing beneath it. I couldn't remember the author or the name of the book, just that enduring image. It was on the cusp of memory when a waiter came out and set a placard before us. The neon flickered above our heads and the sconces glowed in the daylight around the perimeter. As Cass took a final drag, a black Suburban came to a stop on the corner in front of us. A heavy man in a sharp black suit emerged from the back. On the other side the back door opened and shut.

"Be still my heart," he said. "It's you."

"Hi, Mickey," said Cass.

"How did you—" He went to her with open arms, but before he could reach her, his passenger came into view.

"The fuck are they doing here?" asked Susie Wingate.

"I don't . . . I'm as surprised as you are," said Mickey.

They turned and regarded us, eyes settling without welcome on me.

"Uli Kruger suggested we speak to you," I lied. "We're investigating a pair of murders, and the significant others want to find out who did it."

"'Murders'?" asked Susie. "My brother jumped to his death. This bitch must have driven him to it. What's he talking about, Mickey?"

"I don't know, honey, but I'm sure Cassandra here has a good reason for her visit." He looked from Cass to me, stuck out a meaty hand. "And I'm sorry, I don't know you."

"Duck Darley," I said, taking it.

"How do you know this lovely lady?"

"We're partners, Mickey," said Cass. "We're here—"

"Oh, wait," he said. "I remember you. 'Death Darley,' isn't that what the *Post* called you? After that mess a while back? And then you were with Kruger the other night, during that robbery, the poor bastard. You've got some shit luck."

"I'm glad I'm not me," I said.

"Ha, clever." His phony smile faded. He looked to Victor's sister for some direction.

"I want them out of here, Mickey," said Susie. "She's probably here trying to get something from my brother's house. She knows you're the executor of his will. I told her he left me everything, but she wouldn't believe it." She glowered at Cass. "She'll probably fuck you for it."

Before I could provoke her to violence with more name-calling, Mickey put his hand on Susie's shoulder and tried to soothe her. "There's no need for that," he said. "This is a difficult time for all of us. We all loved your brother, Susie. Why don't the four of us go inside and see what they have to say?"

He led her past with a firm grip and pushed open the door to his restaurant. The staff froze at our entry, waited for their boss to explain. He ignored them and moved straight for the bar. Cass and I followed a few paces back without glancing at each other. I admired the room. The walls were done in the same white tiles that covered the exterior. The floors were a checkered black-and-white tile, the ceiling a salvaged pressed tin. The tables were small two-tops with four chairs crowded around them. Black-and-white prints of old bicycle races, the only art. We followed Mickey to a curved bar that filled the back of the space.

"A couple quality ones," he said to the mustached bartender. "A white and a red." He turned to us. "I detest wine lists," he said. "No one understands them, except the real tools, and everyone else just pretends. At my places I make it easy. I give you three choices—Table, Good, and Quality. People love it, it cuts out the bullshit."

The bartender set out two carafes of wine and four small glasses. Cass nodded to the red, and Mickey joined her. Susie reached for the white. I waited until she filled herself to the rim, and then poured myself. I didn't want either. I wanted a double Bulleit with a Stella back, but it didn't seem Mickey was taking orders.

He raised his glass. None of us moved in to clink.

"To Vic," said Mickey. "May he rest in peace."

"To Victor," said Cass. "And to Carl."

"And to Carl. Good men, the best." Setting down his glass, Mickey looked for Cass's eyes and said, "You really don't think their deaths could be connected, do you?"

He had a wide, puffy face, the bulbous nose of a drinker, and a head of tight black curls. His body had the kind of bulk made to absorb hard living. Not handsome by any standard, but he carried himself with an animal confidence. He was a man who knew what he wanted, and knew how to get it. It took two swallows for him to finish his wine. I was already ahead of him. We reached for the carafes, poured ourselves refills, looked to the women before us. Susie was sulking with her shoulders curled in. She refused to look up at any of us. Just standing in our presence seemed to bring her physical pain. But Mickey held some kind of sway over her.

"We're sure their murders are connected," said Cass.

"Murders? Victor jumped. He killed himself," said Mickey. "And poor Carl, they said it was a robbery gone wrong."

"We don't think so," I said.

He ignored me, kept his eyes on my partner.

"Victor didn't jump, Mickey," she said. "He was pushed."

"Why? Who would . . ." He looked away and stared at himself in the distressed mirror behind the bottles. He gulped from his glass and wiped at his stained lips.

"You knew them both," I said. "You knew what they were working on. I'm told it was you that introduced them, that you suggested Victor write about Carl."

Mickey kept regarding his reflection. Without turning his head, he said, "I'm sorry, why are you here again?"

"I told you," said Cass.

"No, I meant your friend. Why is he here? To come into my place and drink my wine and insinuate . . . What is it you're trying to say? Two of my friends die, within a few days of each other, and you think I had something to do with it?"

"Throw him out," said Susie, perking up at his flash of anger. "Throw them both out. She's a whore and he's a rude prick."

"Remember what I told you about name-calling?" I asked. "I know you're a crazy bitch, but are you stupid too?"

Mickey squared his shoulders toward me. He drank his wine, raised the glass, and flung it down on the marble floor. The sound of it shattering silenced the room. "This woman is a sister to me," he said. "You mouth off like that and we're going to have a serious problem, my friend."

I stared back at him. Took a sip of my wine and mimicked his raised-glass display. Then I threw it down and took a step forward.

Mickey let out a low growl and lunged forward and tried to grab me by the shirt. I caught him by both wrists, stepped back, and used his own momentum to pull him forward and flip him over. It was a simple aikido progression, subduing a large, impulsive attacker. I stood over him and turned his wrists, made him feel how easily I could snap the tendons. Before I released him, Susie was on my back, clawing and hissing like an alley cat. I let go of Mickey and staggered forward against the bar. I felt Cass trying to peel her off, but Susie clung to me with vicious, feral intent.

"That's enough!" shouted a voice through the madness.

I looked up to find the mustached bartender holding a .38 Special in shaky hands. His thumb was on the hammer, his finger tight around the trigger. The damn thing was liable to fire at any moment in that amateur grasp.

"Get the fuck out of my place," wheezed Mickey from the floor.

"You want me to call the cops, boss?" asked the bartender.

"No need," I said. "I'm leaving as soon as this bitch gets off my back. And your boss here is fine. I didn't hurt him."

Susie released me and stepped away, no stranger to firearms. She was probably thinking the same thing as me: that finger needed to get off the trigger, fast. She raised her hands. Cass did the same. The room waited until the bartender figured out the threat was subdued. We let out a collective breath as he lowered the gun and set it behind the bar.

"We're going," I said.

I stepped over Mickey Knight's heaving mass and walked out without meeting the eyes that followed me. My pulse was pumping from the unexpected altercation. I could have prevented it. I didn't need to provoke them by name-calling, by tossing down my glass the same way. But folks like that need a gentle reminder at times. Their success, the arrogance it brings, does not grant them the right to bully everyone.

Though I suppose I wasn't much different. I was a bully without money, abusing a martial art to humiliate a guy who'd achieved more than I ever would. Still, I had a feeling I'd done his staff a favor, and not just those on hand to witness it. Word would spread among his restaurants. Waiters and chefs and managers would talk at family meals and over late-night drinks and blow, and they'd toast to that little episode. *You're welcome.* It always felt good to use the aikido again too. I didn't practice enough anymore. My trips to the dojo were infrequent. I needed to get back there, before my own arrogance in my black-belted abilities failed me.

I waited outside for Cass. When she emerged, she was not pleased to find me waiting. A disgusted shake of the head, a lit Parliament, and she walked off. I tried to catch up, called, "I'm sorry! Wait up." She didn't stop until she reached Houston Street. She turned at the light and laid into me.

"Asshole!" she shouted. "Did that make you feel good? Mister tough guy, breaking glasses, throwing him around like that, did that make you feel like more of a man?"

"Cass, listen, he stepped into it first."

"Oh, so he started it? What are you, twelve?"

"He's a fucking bully," I said. "He was trying to impress you. I didn't like it."

"So you showed him? What, that you can beat up a fat fifty-year-old? Wow, Duck, you're so badass."

"C'mon, Cass, it's not like that. I didn't even hurt him."

"It's exactly like that," she said. "And whatever we might have learned from him, we're never gonna hear now."

"What did he say after I left?"

"He said he was going to press charges, you dick. I stayed in there trying to convince him not to. Susie was begging him to call the cops."

"*Please.* I can't be charged with anything," I said. "I doubt there's a scratch on him, and he made the first move."

"Well, he has a dozen people on his payroll who witnessed it. They might say otherwise. Susie certainly will."

"That chick is strong. She's a lot more dangerous than he is."

"I'd like to know what she was doing there with him."

"Want me to go back in and ask?"

"Fuck you, Duck."

"I jest," I said. "Just trying to lighten the moment, partner."

The light changed and the WALK sign lit and Cass gave me a final disgusted look. Then she turned and crossed Houston, offering a raised middle finger in her wake.

Chapter 19

I stood on the corner like a scolded spouse. The sun was low in the sky and bright in my eyes. Traffic honked and sat and swore alongside construction in the middle of the street. A jackhammer pounded at the moods of pedestrians. I remembered an old alkie bar a few blocks down. A real shithole, the kind that opened at eight a.m. each morning and welcomed the same doomed crew. Milano's—that was it. You could smell the decay of livers and dreams the moment you walked in. It was a place that made me feel better about myself. Drinking there would cause any man to reconsider his definition of "rock bottom." It was a suitable venue for the moment.

But before I could go abuse myself with my people, I felt my phone vibrate in my pocket. I took it out and was surprised again to find a message from Juliette Cohen: **My son would like to see you. Could you please come over?**

I considered a few pops before going, decided against it. There would be time for that after I saw the kid. I hailed a cab and told him to take Lafayette up. I offered a bow of the head as we passed David Bowie's old place. When he died, after his silent, dignified battle with cancer a few years back, the city had embraced him as one of its own. He stood for the best of this town: eternal cool, sexy to all, private and proud, but, above all, stunningly creative and successful. It was that last word that most endeared him to New Yorkers. It was the prerequisite to the pantheon. You could be all the other adjectives you liked, but this city spit out failures. It priced them out and locked the doors with ruthless disregard. Sent them packing to cheaper towns, where maybe they could find their level. Bowie might have been British by birth, but he was a New Yorker by choice. He spent his final decades here and served as an ambassador in ways mayors or masters of the universe never could.

I patted my pockets for headphones with a sudden urge to hear "The Jean Genie." Finding none, I sat back and conjured the chorus in my head as we drove past Astor Place, went up Fourth Avenue, and turned a block before Union Square.

The cab let me off behind a cop car in front of Juliette's building. There was a doorman waiting outside, and another behind the lobby desk. I recognized neither. When I told them whom I was there to see, they stiffened. The muscles in their back and neck didn't relax until they called upstairs and listened to Ms. Cohen approve my arrival. I was escorted past the overpriced abstract art to the elevator in the back. One of the new doormen joined me on my ride up. I asked him his name. He ignored me.

The doors opened onto a pair of heavies standing in the entry foyer. They looked like retired linebackers still obsessed with weight rooms and a low-fun diet. Arms like thighs, barreled chests. Necks nonexistent. One was white, early thirties; one black, around forty. The older one had gold hoops in both ears and a scar that stretched like a headband over his scalp. The younger one came over and patted me down without introducing himself. Finding nothing, he stepped back and nodded to his boss.

"She's in the back," he said. "In her room."

I moved past them and walked down the hall toward the bedrooms. Passed the housekeeper, Lucia, in the kitchen. She frowned when I pointed back at the company. Stevie's room was on the other side of the apartment. I considered tiptoeing past Juliette and going to see him. But figured that would be frowned upon by the lady of the house. I knocked once and cracked her door.

She was halfway dressed, in a pleated green skirt and black lace bra. Calves and stomach and shoulders bare, every surface smooth and toned. Her blond hair was swept up, drawing attention to her neck, where I'd spent stretches licking and nibbling the warm flesh. It would become mottled the more she became turned on, until she would grab me by the ears and force me down.

Juliette seemed to read my thoughts. She rolled back her shoulders and thrust out her chest, and with a wicked look she said, "Don't go getting any ideas, hotshot."

"I'm just here to see Stevie," I said. "As you asked." I tried to ignore the ache and the involuntary thickening in my jeans.

"I know that glazed look you get. Like what you see, do you? Well, too bad for you."

"Where'd you find those two out there?" I asked.

She picked up a black silk blouse from the bed and slipped her arms in and began to button it, a little slower than I thought necessary. She seemed to revel in the silence between us, pleased by the fact that she still held carnal power over me. The moods of any woman are a dark mystery, but Juliette's mercurial states were on another spectrum. She claimed it wasn't her fault, that it was genetics. She was a mix of Colombian and Italian. Her maiden name had been Fuoco. And, boy, could she burn. She could swing between seething hatred and the warmest embrace in seconds.

"They're ex SEALs," she said. "Real beef hearts, aren't they? Part of a company called Warrior Security, out of

D.C. The older black one out there, Terrance, he runs it. He recruited a bunch of guys under his old command when they got out. I'm told they're the best."

"By who?"

"By people who know these things," she said. "I have no faith in public servants, and I thought current circumstances were a little beyond your grade."

"No offense taken."

She finished buttoning her blouse and raised a hand to her neck. She traced manicured nails along the skin without taking her eyes from me. "You missed me, didn't you?" she asked.

"I'm worried about you," I said. "About you and Stevie. I'm sorry for all of this."

She took a step closer, smiled. "You certainly owe us some apologies," she said. Another step. Her hand rose to her mouth. She tapped her lips with an index finger. "How's your partner?" she asked.

"In mourning," I said. "We just had a difficult meeting with Mickey Knight."

"The restaurateur? God, what a revolting man. I heard he raped one of his waitresses and paid her off. It's a wonder he hasn't been Me-Too'd yet."

"Wouldn't surprise me."

"Why were you meeting with him?"

"He was friends with her dead ex," I said. "Now he's the executor of his estate. We were trying to ask him some questions. The dead guy's sister was there too. We had an altercation. It was nothing, but he's threatening to press charges."

"Naughty boy." She finished closing the distance between us, her body an inch from mine. Our pheromones collided. She peered up at me, placed a hand against my chest. "Always causing trouble, you."

"Juls, the last time I was here, you told me you never wanted to see me again."

Her hand dropped. "Please, my son had just been threatened. I wasn't in a clear frame of mind."

"But now you are?"

"Now I am taking the proper precautions," she said. "We'll be well-looked-after until we figure out whoever sent that note." She put both hands on her hips and inhaled through her nose, held it, and exhaled. "And if you must know, I haven't been laid since the last time you were in my bed. Before you left to see your slut."

I looked down at her. The skin around her face was tight and moisturized. Despite the soft makeup around her eyes, her sleeplessness was visible. Her pupils were shrunken to pinpricks, constricted in response to whatever pills she'd been prescribed. She squirmed beneath my gaze.

"Me neither," I said.

Her eyes fell shut, her chin tilted up, her lips parted. I kissed her hard and deep. One hand wrapped around the back of her neck, the other grabbed the small of her back. I pressed her to me. She panted into my mouth, moaned against my teeth. Her hands were under my shirt and she was pulling me toward the bed, when we heard a knock at her bedroom door.

"Mom?" asked Stevie. "Duck?"

We leapt away from each other, wiped at our mouths. I tried to turn my hips to shield the bulge. "Hey, buddy," I said.

"Sweetie, I'm sorry, Mommy was just very happy to see Duck," she said. "Aren't you happy to see him? He came over just like you asked."

Stevie looked from his mother to me and I saw his eyes well up. Then he turned and raced back down the hall. We heard the door to his room slam shut.

"Shit," said Juliette.

"I'll go talk to him."

He was sitting on his bed, playing a game on his phone, when I peeked in. I knocked once and took a step across the threshold. He didn't look up.

"Hey, mind if I come in?"

He shrugged, tapped harder at the screen. He lct out a huff, tossed the phone aside, and crossed his arms. "What?" he asked.

"Sorry about that, back there," I said. "I was glad to see your mom."

"She said she hated you, you know."

"I made her upset."

"She's psycho," he said. "How can you say you hate someone one minute and then want to make out with them the next?"

"Grown-ups are complicated that way," I said.

A smile escaped from his face, before he caught it and turned away. I walked farther into the room and turned his desk chair and sat down to face him. The room was uncluttered, decorated with prints by Picasso, alongside framed school art by Stevie. His queen-sized mattress was nestled in a heavy sleigh bed of dark mahogany, covered by a plush comforter and no stuffed animals. Stevie was tall for his age, but he looked small and helpless on the edge of the wide bed. He wiped a brown curl from his forehead.

"Your mom said you wanted to see me," I said.

"What did you do?" he asked.

"How do you mean?"

"I mean, why do we have two soldiers out there pro-tecting us? My mom said it was because of something you did—that could put us in danger."

"What else did she say?"

"That's it. When I kept asking her, she told me I should talk to you myself."

"And here I am."

"So, what did you do, Duck? Does someone want to hurt us because of you?"

"Of course not, buddy," I lied. "I'm just helping out a friend, that's all."

He gave me a look that demanded I stop insulting his youthful intelligence.

"Remember what I told you I used to do?" I asked.

"You were like a private investigator, right? You said you used to help find missing people, for their families. Stuff like that."

"That's right."

"You told my mom you weren't gonna do that stuff anymore."

"And I don't, but do you remember my partner I told you about? My friend Cassandra? Well, something bad has happened to her. She asked me to help her."

"What happened, did somebody hurt her?"

"No, something happened to a man she was seeing, a man she loved. He died."

"How?"

He straightened up now, engaged, blue eyes unblinking. There's nothing kids disdain more than a demeaning adult who doesn't tell it straight.

"He fell off a waterfall," I said. "We think someone pushed him. But the police think he jumped. Either way we want to find out what happened."

"Why would someone push him?" he asked, inching forward with interest.

"He was working on something that might have upset some people. They wanted him to stop."

"What was he working on?"

"A book."

"About what?"

"I don't really know, buddy. You know how pro athletes sometimes get in trouble for cheating, for taking drugs?"

"Yeah, like Lance Armstrong and those guys?"

"Yeah, like Lance, and lots of others. I think it has something to do with that."

"Cool."

"No, it's not cool, my man, it's really not cool."

"No, I didn't mean like that, I just mean, like, it's interesting. Your partner's boyfriend was writing about that stuff? But, Duck?" he asked.

"Yeah, buddy, what is it?"

"Why would that have anything to do with us, with my mom and me? Is it because you're looking into it and you know us?"

The smart little fucker, there was no sense lying. "Here's the thing," I said. "There are some really bad guys out there, and usually they just do their thing and we do ours, and we pretend like they're not there. But sometimes our lives overlap, and the bad guys, they don't like that. They want everyone to be quiet and not ask questions, act like we don't know anything."

"So, why don't you? I mean, just, like, be quiet and not get in their way?"

"Most people do," I said. "Most do. But sometimes we can't."

"Why not?"

"Let me tell you a quote that you'll learn in school at some point," I said. "A guy named Edmund Burke said it. He said, 'The only thing necessary for evil to spread in the world is for good men to do nothing.' Maybe that's not his exact quote, but you understand what he meant?"

I watched the wisdom get absorbed in that bright head of his. After a moment he nodded and said, "I get it. If everybody did nothing and let the bad guys do whatever they wanted, eventually they'd take over. The Dark Side would win."

"Yes, the Dark Side would win," I said. "And when those Sith Lord fuckers mess with people we love, we can't back down and keep quiet, can we?"

"Fuck no," he said, then blushed at our shared profanity.

"So you'll take care of your mom for me? I don't want her to be worried."

"I think she's got it covered, Duck. You see those guys out there? Who's gonna mess with them?"

"I know, buddy, you'll be safe as can be. But you still gotta take care of your mom, okay? When she gets scared or upset or anything, you're the man who's gotta cheer her up, deal?"

"Deal," he said.

I offered a fist bump, which he returned. I told him I'd see him soon. Left him there on the edge of his bed and went back to see Juliette. Her room was empty. I heard laughter down the hall and found her with her hired warriors. They were lapping up the charm—and the legs—of their new boss. She turned when she heard my footsteps, placed a hand on Terrance's biceps as she made eye contact with me.

"How is he?" she asked.

"He's all set," I said. "Want to walk me out?"

"Hold up," said Terrance. "We need to talk."

He stepped away from Juliette, walked toward the kitchen, motioned for me to follow.

"Sorry, boys," I said. "Gotta run."

Terrance's younger partner moved in front of the elevator. He crossed his arms over that bull's chest, tried not to smirk. I thought about putting my aikido to another test, but decided I'd already subjected Stevie to enough drama for the day.

"All right," I said. "I suppose I can spare a few minutes."

Chapter 20

The spring pollen was blowing in gusts through Union Square. Skaters rattled and stumbled through their tricks on the pavement. The usual scattering of the homeless and the mad were slumped on park benches beneath the trees. A huge, heavily 'roided man in a torn pink tank top walked mumbling next to a small disheveled woman. She held him by the forearm like her son. The man was known in the neighborhood as Hercules, a city creature of morbid renown. The *Post* once did a piece on him. He lived somewhere around the Square in a space inherited from an OD'd junkie lover. Hercules was a needle freak. He shot whatever he could into his body, anything from smack to speed to the steroids that ballooned him to those grotesque proportions. He could be seen most days wandering either Union or Madison Square like a walking-dead Schwarzenegger, always with an aged addict attached to his arm. I nodded to him like a good neighbor. He looked back with vacant, unrecognizing eyes.

I'd talked until Terrance was convinced I wasn't holding anything else back. His interrogation technique was more persuasive than any cop's. I sensed he had practice, given free rein to go as far as necessary to get the answers he needed in plenty of far-off hellholes. There was no need for further measures with me. There was a time I would have talked back, taken the beating just to feel it, but not with Stevie down the hall.

I felt a kinship with the kid, even before that note. It was the easiest way to rattle me. The kid might be rich, but what did he have, really? A father worth a fortune who had no interest in seeing him, a mother whose erratic moods and revolving door of lovers would not set a healthy example for future relationships with the opposite sex. He had few friends, no siblings, not even a pet. Yeah, I could relate. A little damaged Duck, Jr.

Jesus, whatever you do, Stevie, don't follow this path. An ex-con alcoholic with a death wish—ready to mentor your fortunate sons!

When I returned home, there was no sign of NYPD waiting. I reminded myself to call Miller and apologize. I found Cass seated with her legs crossed, surrounded by a stale cloud of smoke. She hadn't bothered to open a window. The ashtray runneth over. She didn't look up as I entered, fixated on her laptop. I walked past and went to the fridge and took out a Beck's. I cracked it, took a swallow, said, "I'm sorry about earlier."

She ignored me. The artificial glow from the screen and the hanging smoke gave her face a ghostly pallor. I finished my beer in silence, waited for her to speak, then took out another. She glanced up at the sound of it opening, snorted, and shut the computer. On her way past to the bedroom, she said, "Our flight to Miami leaves at ten tomorrow morning. Don't get too wasted tonight, the car's picking us up at eight."

The door slammed behind her. I resisted the urge to charge after her, point out that she was a guest here, sleeping in my goddamn bed, and who did she think she was? Certainly not my spouse, she'd made that clear. She was here like a haughty mother superior expecting me to drop everything, put myself—and a kid I cared about—in danger, just so I could help her find who killed the man she loved? The man I could never be. Fuck that. I reached for the bourbon, unsealed it, and took the bottle and a glass with me to the living room. No ice needed, thanks very much.

I poured a tall one. Savored the amber cure. Kept drinking until the world stopped mattering and I fell sideways on the couch.

She kicked me awake, disgusted, in the morning.

"I'm leaving," she said. "You don't have to go. I'll call the airline on the way there and cancel your ticket."

"I'm coming," I said, sitting up with a thundering head and a desert-dry mouth. "Just give me a minute. What time is it?"

"It's seven forty-five, Duck," she said. "I'm not asking, I'm telling you—I really don't want you to come with me. I'm sorry I ever called you about any of this."

"Yeah, well, too late for that. You did call, and I answered, and now I'm involved. Which means I'm coming, no matter what you're *telling* me to do."

Cass stood over me with hands on her hips, looking down at the almost-empty bottle of bourbon.

"Why do you do this to yourself?" she asked.

"Because I like the taste," I said.

"I'm serious. Why, Duck?"

I looked up into her eyes and locked them there until she knew I was serious too. "Because," I said, "sometimes it's either a drink or a rope around my neck."

"I feel sorry for you," she said.

"Your pity has been duly noted," I said. "Now give me five minutes to get ready, okay?"

She didn't step aside as I raised myself from the couch, steadied the spins, and staggered to my room to pack a bag. I swallowed down four Advil, gulped for hydration beneath the faucet, brushed, deodorized, splashed water across my face and through the hair, and straightened up, already feeling almost human again. I threw a few t-shirts into a bag, remembered my suit and goggles for the possible hotel pool, and didn't bother with much else.

When I emerged, Cass was waiting outside on the stoop, sucking down her Parliaments. We didn't speak as the car pulled up and we slid in the back. Falling blossoms flashed in the morning light. The day smelled fresh and unspoiled as the city can be. Down the avenue an ambulance wailed.

She scooted all the way over against the door, rolled down her window, and stared out. I spent a few lights looking at the back of her head, willing her to turn, and if not forgive, at least berate me further. But she insisted on her silent treatment, so I turned and looked out my window at the tired masses trudging off to work. So was I, in a matter of speaking. I might be forever unfit for an office, but that didn't mean I lacked their work ethic. I'd shaken off hangovers harsher than those lemmings could ever handle. Burned the candle down at both ends, and did what needed to be done to find whatever it was I'd been hired to find. Except this time no one had hired me. There was no money, no job, only the presumption of my former partner. She asked for my help and never considered that I might turn her down.

Now this bird dog was feeling beaten and weary. The snakes and the midnight demons were taking over my mind. I pictured them up there in my brainpan, swimming through rivers of whiskey and filth, clouding any hope of clarity, ready to lunge and strike at the slightest disturbance. I was afraid to shake my head for fear of rattling their nests.

We were emerging from the Midtown Tunnel, slowing for the toll, when I noticed them out the back window.

They weren't trying to hide. Behind the wheel of a white
Ford Explorer sat Oliver, grinning back at me. I don't
know what made me look back. Maybe I sensed his smug
gaze. By his side was the older man, unsmiling with eyes
covered by aviators. Oliver nudged his companion, nodded toward me, and laughed. The man did not react. His
face was so still he could have been sleeping behind those
sunglasses. He had the air of a scaly predator, laying in
wait before rising up with fast, brutal violence.

We passed through the toll, accelerated onto the Long
Island Expressway. Oliver caught up and began to tailgate
too close. Our driver noticed, cursed him in Arabic.

"Bastard," he said in his rearview. "What do you want,
you bastard? Get off my ass."

"He's following us," I told him. Then, to Cass, I said,
"We've got company."

She turned and looked. Oliver waved. His boss didn't
move.

"Fuck," she said.

"You recognize them?" I asked. "Because I do."

She turned back to our driver, leaned between the seats.
"Could you pick it up, please?"

"I want no trouble," he said. "Why are you trouble?"

"Just keep going," I said. "Let us off at LaGuardia.
Everything is cool."

"No," he said, "I don't want your trouble, I let you off."

I read the name on the back of his headrest and leaned
in. "Sardar, listen," I said. "We don't want trouble either,
but if you let us off anywhere but the airport, that's what
we're going to have. Just drive. A New York airport is the
last place anyone's going to make trouble, you know that,
right? There's security everywhere."

He shook his head at the rearview, gave the mirror his
middle finger. Oliver waved again. But our tail would be
short-lived. As Sardar exited on I-278 toward LaGuardia,

they did not join us. Oliver drove past and continued east on the LIE. He bid us farewell with a raised salute of his left arm out the driver's-side window. I saw Cass jotting down their plates on her hand.

"Same guys from the bar, weren't they?" she asked.

"The very ones. Looked like you recognized them too."

"What? No. How would I . . ."

I shrugged. "You tell me."

She shook her head, crossed her arms, and stared, troubled, out the window. She'd seen them before. I knew it from the way she froze at first turn. Decided to wait and probe further on the plane.

A few minutes later Sardar pulled to the curb in front of the American terminal. He muttered about hating trouble while he waited for payment. I handed over eighty bucks, told him to keep the change, apologized for the drama back there. He took the cash and did not offer to help with our bags. Cass lit a Parliament next to the curbside baggage checkers. She pretended not to notice their lingering looks while I called Juliette. It took two missed calls and a few texts to get her to pick up.

"Listen, I just saw them," I said.

"Where?" she asked.

I watched as Cass flicked away the filter and then stalked inside the terminal without a glance in my direction.

"On the LIE. Could I talk to Terrance?"

"Not until you tell me what's happening."

It was pointless to argue with her. All communication between employees would be vetted first by the lady of the house.

"They were tailing us on the Long Island Expressway, on our way to LaGuardia."

"Where are you going?"

"Miami," I said. Then wished I hadn't. "We need to investigate something down there."

I listened to her breath as she digested that, deciding whether to push for details or plate it until later. "They followed you to the airport?" she asked.

"No, when we got off on the Grand Central, they kept going, heading east on 495. Gave us a Nazi salute out the window. That's it. Now can I talk to your bodyguard?"

I heard her steps across the cavernous apartment, finding Terrance, then his hard voice on the line.

"You have something to report to us, Mr. Darley?" he asked.

"Listen, you guys need to run some plates," I said. "A white Ford Explorer, recent model. New York plates, DKY 2117, you writing this down?"

"Yes," he said. "Who was behind the wheel?"

"Same guy who's been fucking with me, probably the same one behind the note about the kid. Said his name was Oliver, no last name. He was following us on the LIE. When we got off, he kept heading east on 495."

"You're sure it was the same guy?" he asked.

"Positive."

"Was he alone?"

"No, there was the other guy, his boss, sitting shotgun. Same one I mentioned, older, early fifties, serious. Thin blond hair, hollow cheeks, he was wearing aviators."

"Thank you, Mr. Darley," he said. "We'll look into it."

"You do that."

"Check in when you land," he said.

I heard the dial tone in my ear. *Typical SEAL,* I thought, *the heavyweight champs of military arrogance. Everything is a yawn compared to the incomparable hardships they endured.*

I'd known one well, my coach Teddy Marks. A man I once admired more than any figure of authority in my life. And what became of him? He paid for his arrogance in the end.

Inside the terminal I checked in at a kiosk and searched

for Cass. Spotted her toward the front of the security line. I handed my ID and boarding pass to a bored TSA agent, waited for her to glance up and confirm my identity. Joined the queue. The snakes had stopped rattling upstairs. I knew the hangover would descend again at thirty thousand feet. A Beam or two and a nap would help. I wondered what awaited us in Miami, wondered what Cass had in mind. Did she intend to storm into the BioVida offices and confront Dr. Lipke? Was she envisioning some sort of stakeout?

My knowledge of South Florida was limited, but the town left an impression. I once tracked a cheating art dealer down to Art Basel. I'd been impressed with the guy. He was pushing sixty and I watched him blow lines and down magnums of champagne, before taking a pair of models back to his suite at the Raleigh. He must have been chopping blue lines of Viagra to go with the coke, because when those models emerged at six a.m., they had that unmistakable freshly fucked look. One even walked with a slight limp. I snuck my pictures from a lobby club chair by the elevators and returned to the city and presented the tawdry evidence to his second wife. She made off with more than the first.

I remembered the BioVida offices were in Coral Gables, a neighborhood whose name rang a bell, but I'd never been. I pictured strip malls of boutiques and avenues lined with palm trees and hair-gelled machismos climbing out of red sports cars. I wondered how Dr. Lipke ended up there, from the drab landscape of Eastern Europe. Wondered what else Victor Wingate had learned about him, and how he could be connected to the murders and our current troubles. I was turning over these things in my muddled mind when I saw an officer approach Cass and ask her to step out of line. She complied, handed over her ID. The officer examined it, seemed to tense with confirmation, and placed a hand on her upper arm. He took a firm hold and guided her off, past the metal detectors, into a security room.

The interaction happened so quickly it took a moment to process. I kept expecting Cass to emerge with carry-on in hand and an annoyed look on her face. Just another excuse for the TSA to feel up an attractive traveler in the name of terrorism prevention . . . but Cass did not emerge. *Detective Miller, making good on her threat,* I thought. We were both being charged with obstruction, warrants out. I waited for my turn, but no one approached. I was permitted to pass through security without question.

I walked to our gate in a confused trance. I tried calling and texting Cass. Got no reply. Wondered if I should leave without her. I lowered myself into a chair by the gate and sat paralyzed by indecision. Boarding began. The first-class passengers moved past with entitlement, followed by harried parents traveling with young children, before the grouped pens in coach waited their turn and trudged toward the Jetway. I waited until the entire flight was full. Finally, at last call I pushed myself up and boarded without her.

Chapter 21

The flight attendant, familiar with the desperate red-eyed look of certain travelers, handled me with care. When her cart stopped alongside my row, she was reaching for the mini-bottles before she took my order. When I asked for Beam, she gave me two, said she'd be back around. She was a petite brunette with a pixie cut and a second-look beauty. Thought I caught an Irish lilt to her voice. Her nametag read *Clara*. Her look reminded me of Detective Lea Miller. I resolved to call her when we landed. Apologies were in order, not that that would be enough. Cass was about to face an unpleasant grilling.

I couldn't figure why I hadn't been pulled out of line with her. I had three hours in the sky to contemplate. I tried reading my book—an underlined collection of short stories by Mary Gaitskill called *Bad Behavior*. I'd been through them many times before and the nihilism in her writing always brought comfort. Now I found myself re-reading the opening paragraph of the first story, "Daisy's Valentine." A character contemplated how it was fun to think that his life was in danger of further ruin.

Fun indeed. Why was it always the times when the earth seemed to open and swallow people up that sparked these giddy blasts of endorphins? I couldn't explain, but it couldn't be denied. It took the scent of death and ruin for me to sit up and smell. I might have looked the part of resigned alcoholic, but I felt myself awakening inside, renewed to the presence of all the evil that lurked across life.

Someone had pushed Victor Wingate over a high waterfall. Someone, perhaps the same one, had driven a javelin through the throat of Carl Kruger. A blade had been pressed to my neck in a darkened movie theater. Someone threatened to hurt an eight-year-old boy because he was close to me. These events had all been accumulating abstractions. I hadn't been conscious of their weight. Like those cocky SEALs, I'd faced my share of horrors. It was hard to get too worked up about anything. I needed a strong hit. But now Cass had been taken. The arm of the law, and whatever it was attached to, had reached out and plucked her from a security line at the airport. Just like that.

I gave up on reading, tucked the Gaitskill in the seat pocket in front of me, and plugged in my headphones. Turned on some Emmylou Harris, *Quarter Moon in a Ten Cent Town*, and listened to her sing about things being all right: "'cause it's midnight and I got two more bottles of wine . . ."

Clara returned with two more little bottles of Beam and set them down on my tray with a fresh cup of ice. She gave me a sympathetic wink, and moved on down the aisle with a devilish spring to her step. I wondered how long she'd be staying over in Miami. I could use the company and she seemed to have me pegged from first glance. When she brought a third round, those little potions started to work their magic. I gazed out the window. Outside the skies were bright and blue and cloudless. I sat back and tried to form a plan.

* * *

It was ninety degrees on the ground at Miami International. As we shuffled down the aisle into a blast of humidity, I saw Clara offering her smiling farewells to each passenger. I palmed one of my cards and slipped it to her on the way off. "Not sure how long you're staying," I said. "But I'd love to hear from you."

Her smile dropped before she caught it and tried to recover, without success. I'd misjudged pity for affection. "Thank you," she said with an even mouth. Then she looked over my shoulder at the next passenger and replastered that fake smile.

I knew I'd never see her again. I felt the eyes of my seatmate on my back, laughing at my bold failed pickup attempt. The cheap thrills of a flight attendant's attention, the wisdoms of Gaitskill and Emmylou—ladies out of reach who kept reality at bay. And now, here I was alone and sweating in South Florida, with nowhere to go. I took out my phone to search for a place to stay. Found it dead. What did we do before we became slaves to these damn devices? Approached strangers with questions, I guess, used pay phones, lived in the world, as opposed to our modern cloistered existence.

Outside the terminal I joined the cab line and felt sweat leap from every pore. I wasn't wired for warmer climates. My body cannot process the upper extremes. Northern European blood, perhaps. Fierce humidity feels like an assault on civility. It sours the mood, soaks the skin. Makes me want to plunge underwater and come up only for meals and strong drink.

I climbed in the back of a cab with sputtering air-conditioning. A young Cuban with glistening mocha skin turned and asked where I was headed.

"Coral Gables," I said.

"Where in the Gables?" he asked.

"Got me. Know any cheap hotels with a pool?"

He drove off. My face was bursting with booze sweat. I stuck my head out the window; the breeze didn't help. Out the window the air smelled of salt and fetid decay. A white Range Rover pulled next to us at a light. Behind the wheel a lurid Latina woman dressed in green silk and heavy jewels. She glanced over. Her windows were down and she had not a drop of sweat on her.

"Beautiful day," said my driver. "So nice this time of year, you know? Not too hot yet, just right."

"Says you."

"Where you from, my man?" he asked. "First time in Miami?"

"Manhattan," I said. "And no, just don't get down here often."

"New York City, got some family up there. It gets plenty hot there too, don't it? And no beach to cool off."

I fiddled with the air vents between the seats. "You mind turning up the AC? I'm dying back here."

"Going full blast, man. Sorry, not reaching back there?"

I wiped a few ounces of sweat from my forehead, looked out at the hazy landscape. The heat rose from every surface. It gave a shimmering unreality to the streets passing by.

"Got a good place for you," said my driver. "The Chateau-Bleau Hotel."

"Don't want anywhere too pricey, okay?"

"Don't you worry, it's cheap, but nice. And a pool too, like you asked."

I leaned forward. "What's your name, buddy?"

"Miguel," he said. "You?"

"Duck."

"Like *quack, quack*?"

"That's right."

"So, what brings you to Miami with no place to stay, Mr. Duck?"

"Last-minute business trip," I said.

"What do you do?"

"I look for people. What do you do, Miguel? I mean, besides drive this cab?"

"You needing some help around town?" he asked. "Like you need some hookups?"

"I might. Think you can help me?"

"I think you got into the back of the right cab—yes, I do. I hook you up. What you need?"

"Not sure yet. When we arrive, can you leave me your contact?"

"I can do that," he said.

He was right about the ChateauBleau. It was cheap. And it had a pool—a kidney-shaped tub of glistening blue alongside the parking lot. Palm trees and cheap white lounge chairs interspersed along the concrete deck. The hotel itself was a three-story, taste-free affair that looked like it was untouched since the seventies. Outside the smoked lobby doors a man and a woman argued. Neither looked like they had slept in a few days. The guy was wearing jean shorts and a loose Miami Dolphins jersey, with a matching Dolphins hat turned backward. He was jabbing at her with a lit cigarette. His body seemed to twitch involuntarily. The woman stood wobbling on unstrapped heels in an orange tube dress that started just above her nipples and ended with the curve of her ass. She pressed a cigarette to painted lips, exhaled, and shook her head angrily. They turned at the sound of the taxi door, stopped talking, and eyed me. Miguel rolled down his window and stuck out a card.

"My cell's on the back," he said. "Call me. I hook you up, anything you need."

I thanked him, said I'd be in touch, then stepped past the bickering tweakers and pushed into a stark lobby with a blast of AC and the heavy scent of bleach. A young gay desk clerk, too chipper for his surroundings, told me rooms were a hundred bucks a night. There were plenty of vacancies. He informed me there was a Greek restaurant called Mylos, off the lobby, that was open for lunch, if I was hungry, or after he looked into my watery eyes, just needed a drink.

"Let me know if I can get you anything else," he said with a wink. "Anything at all."

Nice town. My first two encounters with natives and it seemed I had two leads to the illicit.

Upstairs, the bleach smell of the lobby was replaced by a thick, musty odor in the room. The space was large by city standards, and barren of warmth. White walls devoid of art, low white ceiling, stained white carpet. The only splash of color was the bloodstains I found at the foot of the bed. I went to open the door to the balcony and found the lock tampered with. A crime scene at one point in its past . . . but the pool below was empty and beckoning. I tossed my bag on the bed, plugged in my phone. Stripped and stepped into my suit, and headed back downstairs.

I had the pool to myself. Whatever lowlifes and low-rent business travelers used this place, it wasn't folks inclined to take advantage of the water-filled asphalt hole. The sun was hot on my pale shoulders. I noted the absence of sunscreen, reminded myself not to stay out in it too long. I strapped on my goggles and plunged in.

The water was a tonic, the only safe place I knew in the world. I stayed under in the silence, exhaled and watched the burst of bubbles float to the surface. I crossed my legs and settled on the bottom of the deep end. I stayed in that position until my lungs ached and my throat constricted, then surfaced with a gasp and looked out through my goggles with renewed perspective. I repeated the process a half-dozen times. Forced myself to stay under a bit longer with each round. Then I floated on my back for a while with eyes shut, soaking in the hard sun.

For all the suffocating humidity and poor taste, there were certain attractions to life in a tropical city—first among them, the opportunity to swim outdoors daily. It was a different sensation than the indoor pools of the north. No matter how cavernous and clean and fast, a pool indoors is an impostor. It misses the essential point. The experience of swimming should be one of immersion under the sky, below the surface, enveloped by layers of blue. Floating there with my ears submerged in silence, my face up to the sun, I convinced myself that New York had lost its appeal. All I needed for a new, sane life was a daily dip in a pool outside.

An hour later I returned to my room feeling cleansed and rebooted. I knew I'd stayed out in the sun for too long, but welcomed the coming burn. I needed some color. It was worth a night or two of discomfort. I unplugged my phone, found no messages, tried calling Cass. It went straight to voice mail. Considered calling Juliette, but didn't have anything to say. Then I remembered Detective Miller.

"Where are you?" she asked by way of greeting.

"Listen, I'm sorry."

"I asked where you were."

"Miami."

I listened to her ragged breath, too exasperated to form words.

"At LaGuardia," I said, "why did they take Cass and not me?"

"It wasn't for obstruction, Duck. You failed to come in as instructed, but that's not why she's in custody."

"Then why?"

"Your partner's been arrested," she said. "For murder."

Chapter 22

The fix was in. I knew that much. They always suspect it's the spouse first, and usually it is. But hadn't Wingate's death been ruled a suicide? What caused them to reconsider? What had Victor's crazy sister, Susie, been telling those Keystone Cops on the mountaintop?

"You need to get back to the city," said Miller. "I don't know what you're doing down there, but I've about had it with you."

"Murder?" I asked. "Why would Cass call me and ask for my help finding out who killed him? What, the murderer enlists her old partner to investigate a crime that she committed?"

"A guilty conscience can be an unpredictable thing."

"*Please.* You know damn well this is bullshit. What do they have on her?"

"Enough to issue a warrant for her arrest."

"And I suppose she killed Carl Kruger too?"

"Where was she when that happened?" she asked.

"Jesus Christ, Lea. Are you serious?"

"I am, Duck. Where was she?"

"Upstate," I said.

"Where upstate? We know she was no longer in Victor Wingate's home."

"She said she was staying at an inn nearby. Then she came down to stay with me the next day."

"So you don't know her exact whereabouts at the time of Kruger's murder, when you were also assaulted, but not seriously hurt. And then Ms. Kimball showed up at your apartment the next morning?"

"I'm done with this," I said. "I thought you were smarter than that, Lea."

I hung up. Threw my phone against the pillows, shouted, "Fuck!" Then went out to the balcony. I rested my forearms against the hot metal railing and stared down at the pool. The arguing couple from the lobby walked, hand in hand, onto the deck. It appeared they'd made up. The guy pulled his Dolphins jersey over his head to reveal a lean torso covered with tattoos. The woman peeled off her orange tube dress. I couldn't tell whether it was a black bikini or lingerie beneath. They stepped out of their clothes and joined skin and made out at the edge of the water. The guy took her hand and placed it on the bulge in his jean shorts. She broke the kiss and slapped his ass, pulled away and leapt into the pool. He let out a loud laugh and joined her with a rowdy splash.

I went back inside, got in the shower. Turned on a blast of cold for a shot of clarity. Opened the curtain and regarded my wet, naked body in the mirror. Somehow my genetics had helped it beat back time and sustained abuse. But I knew it wouldn't be long before the entire structure started to crumble. I needed to get back in the pool on a regular basis, needed to return to the dojo and stay on top of the aikido. I made the usual promises to my reflection, then dried off, dressed, and forgot about them.

I looked up BioVida on my phone. Its offices were less than a mile away, according to Google Maps, at the corner of Ponce De Leon and Alcazar. Without any sort of plan I left the hotel and followed the blue dot on the app in that direction.

The heat hovered over the sidewalk like a curse. Sweat seeped from my forehead. The sky was baby blue with wisps of clouds and no wind. There were few pedestrians, and those I saw moved slow and deliberate, reconciled to the sun's rule. The boulevard was a faceless stretch of low-slung office buildings and bland condo developments. BioVida was located a few blocks before the Miracle Mile. I'd do some exploring later. Find a bite and a bar, and watch the natives.

Past an elementary school on the corner of Alcazar, I found the address. The building was a black, mirrored cube about ten stories tall. The directory in the lobby listed BioVida on the fourth floor. The security guard at the front desk didn't look up as I walked past. I rode the elevator up and was deposited into a lobby full of bright pastels, fit middle-aged men, and a few strapping teens accompanied by fathers. I lingered in the doorway.

"Can I help you?" asked a blond receptionist.

She looked like she'd been created in a beachside lab. Her lips and chest were enhanced to an unnatural degree. Her tan, the product of years of worship; her hair was the color of salt and sunshine. I looked above her at the company logo on the wall and pretended to squint at it.

"I'm sorry, is this Sun Lasik?" I asked.

"Sixth floor." She smiled. "Two more up."

"Whoops, my bad," I said.

I turned toward the elevator, but paused as I heard a door open behind me. I looked back to an attractive black nurse scanning the waiting room. She was tall and curvy and her dark skin seemed to glow against her white nurse's uniform. She called for an "Alex Nestor." One of the teens stood up and looked down at his father. The older man winked at his son and gave a knowing smile. The nurse regarded me with a hand on a hip; the kid, Alex, turned with her. The rest of the room followed their gaze and stared at me.

"Have a good one," I said, holding eye contact with the nurse.

I rode the elevator down and returned to the blinding sunlight. In two blocks I found a bar called The Bar. Its white exterior was as plain as its name. But inside it was dark and cool and Loretta Lynn played on the jukebox. I found a stool at the round bar and ordered a Beck's and a burger. It was a little after three p.m. I'd go back to the BioVida building at five, around the time the doctor's staff should be getting off. If I wanted to follow anyone, I'd need to rent a car, but with any luck one of them would leave on foot, perhaps for a nearby happy hour. That was the half-ass plan anyway. I ordered another Beck's when the food arrived and inhaled both. I thought about Stevie and Juliette. I pictured Terrance and his partner from Warrior Security lingering around the apartment, stealing peeks at Juliette's ass while she flirted and soaked up the attention.

I told myself I should forget this nonsense and return to the city. Lay low for a week or two, to prove I wasn't interested in pursuing this further. Whatever happened to Wingate or to Carl Kruger wasn't my business. I should be grateful I'd gotten off with warnings. I needed to get back and do what I could for Cass and those bullshit charges. What was I supposed to accomplish, playing snoop down in South Florida, a thousand miles from the folks that needed my help? Had this really been set in motion over a couple doctors distributing performance-enhancing drugs? Was that enough to kill for?

My gaze fell across the bar to a poster of a Miami Marlins slugger. He posed with hard eyes, bat propped on his shoulder like a weapon. His forearms were each the size of toddlers. He'd recently signed a contract for 250 million dollars. I didn't know if his prodigious power was natural or came from some "supporting means," as the East German party liked to refer to cheating, but I knew what a quarter of a billion dollars meant to people. And I also knew only a fraction of that fortune would end up in the slugger's pocket. The rest would be distributed to extended family and friends, hangers-on, to agents and the small army that helped him put up the numbers necessary to earn that salary. The slugger was just one of an innumerable lot. World-class athletic performance was worth billions. Doctors that helped ensure that performance—it was hard to overstate their value as central figures in a dark market that operated under bright stadium lights.

When I asked for the check, the bartender told me it was Whiskey Wednesdays that night. Starting at six, and going till two a.m., every bottle of amber behind the bar would be half off. He said I should come back. I couldn't disagree. He poured two shots of Jameson as a teaser, offered me one, and we tapped glasses and knocked them back. The Irish swill fired my insides, burned away the rest of the hangover. I was ready to go now. Ten more and I'd be howling on the beach under the moonlight. I looked forward to it. But first, a bit more work to do. I told the bartender I'd be seeing him later, dropped thirty bucks on the bar, then slid from my stool and braced myself for another assault of sun.

Back on the corner of Alcazar and Ponce de Leon, I lingered under a palm tree in the shade and eyed the entrance to the building. The exterior reminded me of Darth Vader's eyes. The blond receptionist exited at 5:05 p.m. She moved with a jaunty walk on heels, wearing a red miniskirt and a tight low-necked white tee that demanded appraisal of her hard-earned body. The outline of nipples could be seen across the street. She stopped in front of a black BMW coupe and reached in her purse. The car blinked and un-locked and the blonde slid into her ride. As she drove off, I jotted down her plates.

Another ten minutes passed before the nurse came out. She had changed out of her white uniform and was wear-ing a green sundress covered in palm fronds that clung to her curves. Her dark hair was tied back tight against her scalp in a ponytail. Her cheekbones were high and sharp beneath a set of watchful eyes. For a moment I thought she spotted me across the street as I moved behind a car. When I peered over the trunk, I saw her opening the door of a silver Camry. So much for following on foot . . . no one walked anywhere outside New York. I didn't bother to write down the plates as I watched her pull out on the boulevard. Oh, well, at least I had Whiskey Wednesdays to look forward to. But then I saw the Camry break and signal at a parking garage a few blocks down. I walked toward her fast, feel-ing the booze sweat leap forth. At the intersection I spot-ted her exiting the garage and approaching a business under Spanish arches and a terra-cotta roof. Over a row of brown awnings, it read BOOKS & BOOKS.

It was a brilliant bookstore, the kind that should exist in every town. Under the arches there was a newsstand full of magazines, mass and niche, along with a dozen different newspapers. In front of an interior courtyard there was a small bar run by an old-timer in a Hawaiian shirt unbut-toned to his navel. He gave me a nod as I entered, went back to sipping his rosé. The store itself existed in the rooms surrounding the courtyard. Some reserved for fic-tion, nonfiction; another for children's books; another for art; a small coffee shop in the back, facing a section for local history. I almost forgot about the nurse. Wandering a well-done bookstore with a slight buzz, one of life's great pleasures.

Then I saw her. She was standing over a table of staff

recommendations. I couldn't see the title she was holding, but she looked down at the pages with an immersion I appreciated. She flipped the book over and read the back, gave private approval and pressed it to her chest. Sold. I turned and examined the nearest row. It was the YA section; a few teenaged girls eyed me with suspicion. She passed behind me toward the register. I watched her pay, chatting with the clerk like a regular. She had a bright, easy smile, a kind air about her. With new book in hand she went to the bar in the courtyard and opened it and ordered a drink.

I waited a few minutes, wandered the stacks, scanning for a suitable title, one that might spark some conversation. I settled on a Charles Willeford called *Miami Blues*. The back cover said that if I was looking for "a master's insight into the humid decadence of South Florida," then no one did it better than Willeford. That worked. I paid and strolled out to the magazine racks, examined the covers, before I moved to the bar and took a seat one down from the nurse. She was sipping a white, gazing down at the opening pages. Manicured orange nails grazed her cheek. I ordered a beer, received it in a frosted glass. I glanced around the bar and the courtyard. Every patron had a nose in a book and a drink at the elbow. I'd stumbled into a lotusland of readers and drinkers. Outdoor pools and a spot like this—the town was growing on me.

I kept an eye on the nurse's glass. I couldn't wait until she asked for the check, and therefore missed my window, but I also couldn't move in too quick. I polished off the Peroni after a page or two. The old-timer behind the bar placed a new one in front of me before I asked. He knew how to spot the thirsty ones.

"Old Hoke Moseley," he said. "That your first Willeford?"

"It is," I said. "You a fan?"

"Guy's a legend. You're in for a treat. No one better to give you a sense of this town. You're not from here, are you?"

"How could you tell?"

He laughed. "You're either a Yankee or a shut-in," he said. "No one around here's pale as you."

I noticed the nurse smile at his comment without taking her eyes from the pages. I turned to her. "That obvious?"

She looked up and appraised me. Her eyes glimmered with recognition. "It's you," she said.

"You work at that place, what's it called, where I stumbled in earlier?"

"BioVida," she said. "You find the Lasik office upstairs?"

"How'd you . . ."

"My girl at the desk told me."

"Ah. Yeah, I did, thanks."

She considered my reply. Let her eyes linger on my face, then down below my neck. Whatever she saw, her smile faded. She closed her book. The cover read *Talent Is Overrated*. She placed a hand on it, turned her shoulders toward me.

"Why you pulling a shuck?" she asked.

"A what?"

"A shuck. Why you messin' with me?"

"I'm not," I said.

"That why you hit the 'down' button on your way out?" she asked. "I asked my girl Tiff what you were doing there and she said you were looking for Sun Lasik. 'Cept that's on the sixth floor, and you went back down."

"I know. I forgot what she said and went down to look at the directory."

"Right."

"Why do you think I'm lying?" I asked.

"Show me your contacts," she said.

"Why should I?"

" 'Cuz you ain't wearing any, and I don't see any glasses. Which tells me that you're full of shit. So, like I was saying, why you pulling a shuck?"

I nodded to her glass. "If I tell you, can I buy you another drink?"

"From a lying stranger? Thanks, I'm good."

"What if it's a really good story from a guy who's not so bad?"

"Tell it to the bartender. He's paid to hear it." She reopened her book. Eyes returned to the page, body language shut me down.

I pointed to the cover. "You're gonna like that," I said. "I read it a while back."

Without looking up, she said, "Thanks, now if you'll excuse me . . ."

"Sorry to bother you. I just . . ."

I waited, hoped she'd pick up my ellipses.

With an exhale she said, "You just what?"

"It's funny, that's all. Your book sort of relates to what I'm doing down here."

"Which is what? Wandering into offices and lying about your presence?"

"I'm sorry about that. I had my reasons. Can I tell you about it?"

"Why?"

"Because I believe in kismet, and because I think anyone who buys that particular book would be interested in what I'm up to."

She looked from me to her glass, then raised it and swallowed down the rest. "Okay, fine," she said. "Let's hear it, big boy."

Chapter 23

I really had read the book: *Talent Is Overrated* by Geoff Colvin, a Malcolm Gladwell-esque examination of "What Really Separates World-Class Performers from Everyone Else." Alas, it was not about performance-enhancing drugs. It was one of those feel-good, pop-psychology narratives that tried to make mortals feel a bit closer in potential to their sporting heroes. A nice idea, with a nonsense thesis.

I really did believe in the kismet of a shared book too. Is there a better way to spark conversation, discover some common bond with someone new?

But after that bit of sincerity, I told her a tall one. That I'd been hired by a divorcée troubled by what her ex husband was doing with their teenaged son, a budding baseball prospect. I'd stopped by the clinic in hopes of catching father and son in the waiting room. That kid she called, Alex Nestor, had he been going there for long? She shrugged, a few months maybe? She asked if I was sure I wasn't a reporter. They had some problems in the past, journalists poking around trying to catch athletes procuring drugs. I promised her I wasn't. Showed her my card, shared a bit about my pseudo private-eye business. Always lie with a side of truth. She started to open up a bit.

Her name was Tasha. A New Orleans native, she had

settled in South Florida after college. She'd been with
BioVida for a few years now, and she knew damn well
what they were up to. Not that it bothered her much. The
way she saw it, sports were a dirty business all around.
But the science of aging fascinated her. Her grandma used
to moan that she was sick and tired of being sick and tired.
After racing her way through a nursing degree at LSU on a
track scholarship, Tasha learned about the boom in inte-
grative medicine practices down here. She headed over the
Gulf and found work with Dr. Lipke's clinic.

"How you like him?" I asked.

"Herr doctor? He's all right, he looks like a little German Santa Claus," she said.

"Sounds like he's got plenty of goodies in his work-
shop."

"Ha. They all keep coming back for more, that's for
sure."

"And you don't have a problem with it?" I asked.

"What, his patients? He's making 'em happy. Bunch of
old dudes, can't get it up no more. He's helping 'em out. I
don't judge."

"I'm talking about the younger ones. The ones going to
your clinic to cheat."

"I know who you're talking about, but for the record,
I've never seen or heard anything myself. Still, if you ain't
cheatin', you ain't tryin'. Isn't that the American way?
Every white boy getting rich up on Wall Street knows that.
If some jocks wanna pop some pills, get some shots that
make 'em run faster or whatever, I mean, I get it. It's gonna
upset some people, but there's a lot worse stuff to worry
about in this country, you ask me."

"I've got a problem with it," I said. "Things are unfair
enough without folks cheating to get ahead."

"Says the privileged white boy." Her eyes teased over
the rim of her glass.

" 'Privileged'? Not me."

"Hey, I didn't say you got money. Maybe you do, maybe you don't. You're still a straight white male."

No denying that. I waved down the bartender, asked for a Bulleit. I was informed that it was wine and beer only. He added that there was a pub nearby, Whiskey Wednesdays if he wasn't mistaken.

"Already got it penciled in," I told him. Then to Tasha, "How'd you like to join me?"

"A date at a dive with a lyin' Yank?" she asked. "Be still, my heart."

"Who's calling it a 'date'?"

"You sure you're not press?"

"I'd rather be a cop than a journalist," I told her. "And it doesn't get much lower than the boys in blue."

"Ah, I see," she said. "What we got here is a bona fide hater. You go poking around, asking questions, judging like you do, but you say you don't like the folks who do the same thing. Just different masters, is all."

"Gotta serve somebody," I said.

"Too true, honey, too damn true."

We clinked glasses and drained our remains. Held eye contact for a promising beat. Her eyes were wide set and deep brown with lashes so long they couldn't have been real. She fluttered them.

"So you'll join me?" I asked.

"I didn't say that, no." A fingernail traced around the rim of her glass. "So you're not a cop or a reporter, just a pasty snoop with a thing for black girls?"

"Just a book lover that likes a lively conversation," I said.

"What happened to your neck?" she asked.

"Fight with a vampire."

She laughed at that, so loud and throaty that the rest of the courtyard turned and regarded us.

"Tell you what," she said. "I'm not interested in slamming whiskey in dive bars. I gotta work tomorrow. But there's a Spanish place I like down the way. If you want, you can join me for some tapas and sangria."

"It's a date."

"No," she said, winking. "It's just a nice fellow book lover who wouldn't mind some company."

The restaurant was a few blocks down on Ponce De Leon, off the Miracle Mile. There was a Lamborghini, a Ferrari, a Bentley, and a Porsche Carrera valet-parked curbside in front. Each was polished in a primary color. The Italians call the drivers of these things "tomatoes." Apt. I wanted to key all four right in front of their overcompensating owners. Tasha saw me looking without approval.

"You get used to it," she said. "Miami's so damn flashy. It used to drive me crazy, now I just laugh."

The place was called Bulla, and despite the douche mobiles out front, it was a fine-looking space of blond wood and high leather seats. We found two chairs at the mostly full bar. The bartender was a Ronaldo look-alike with comparable vanity. He was long accustomed to charming every lady and less-than-straight man that he served. He greeted Tasha like he knew her, with a hug over the bar, and turned to me with a frown.

"Carlos, this is my friend," she said. "He calls himself Duck."

"*Quack, quack,*" he said. Then to her, "Pitcher of white sangria?"

"Sounds delicious, thanks, hon." She turned to me. "You'll love the sangria here. It's dangerous, sneaks up on you."

"Thought you had to work tomorrow?"

"It's early yet. Don't be getting any ideas, Mr. Duck."

"I'm full of bad ideas, darling."

And I almost forgot all the troubles that brought me down here after that. The sun sank in the sky, the day's swelter becoming bearable. A breeze passed through the restaurant's open doors. The light had that special golden hue seen only in towns surrounded by water. Much is made of the magic-hour twilight and the palate of soft colors it brings, but it's the glow that precedes it that is the true seducer. It's the last, best promise of day, before the darkness announces itself. It's a time to exhale and to raise a glass and look into the faces of beautiful strangers.

I was feeling downright poetic and my hand found its way onto Tasha's thigh. My fingertips rested there, not daring to advance farther. She allowed it. She offered a playful smile while we sampled the *croquetas* and *pintxo*.

"So, what do you have planned for tomorrow?" she asked.

"We'll see," I said. "Probably sit outside the kid's house, wait till he gets out of school. Follow him and his dad. See where they go."

"How glamorous."

"Hurry up and wait, that's the job."

"For a boy who hates cops, you sure sound a lot like one."

"Known some cops, have you?"

"Maybe a few." She pushed my hand away. "I think somebody's getting some bad ideas."

"I told you I was full of them."

"That you did. Now if you'll excuse me for a minute."

Tasha dabbed at her lips with a napkin, placed it on the bar, and pushed her chair out. She turned her back to me and I watched her weave through the crowd toward the ladies' room. It was up the stairs. With each step men stole glances at her ascending figure in that green sundress. I liked her, in more than that giddy I-might-get-laid sort of way. She had a clear-eyed bluntness mixed with manners that could be so charming in many Southern women. I sipped at my sangria. Wondered what Tasha would think of the ChateauBleau Hotel, and if I had any chance to lure her back there. But when she returned, it was with a serious expression. The mood had changed.

"Listen," she said, climbing back next to me. "I was thinking about what you're up to, for the mother of that kid. I don't want to get the boy in trouble. It's not my place. It could mess with my job."

"Not to worry, I didn't hear anything from you."

"Yeah, sure you didn't. You been pumping a source all night, haven't you?"

"That comes later," I said.

She slapped my arm. "Keep dreaming, big boy," she said.

"Can you tell me more about Dr. Lipke?" I asked.

"What you wanna know?"

"What's he like, where's he from? I'm curious how a doctor crosses to the dark side. Seems to me he doesn't think much of the Hippocratic oath."

"You make it seem so sinister. It's not. I told you, he's good to me. His patients all like him. He just seems like a friendly old German grandpa. Harmless, you know? He's a whole lot better than his partner, I'll tell you that."

"Who's that?"

"Dr. James Crowley, a real cracker, from up in Jacksonville."

"So, Lipke partnered with an American."

"I don't know if they're fifty-fifty or what, but it's both of them who run BioVida. I'm from down south, I can smell a racist a mile away, even if he smiles and says all the right things and pretends to respect you. Dude's bad news. I try to keep my distance. It's been nice lately, he's been gone for a while."

"What does he look like?" I asked.

She raised her eyebrows. "What's that got to do with this job of yours?"

"I'm just trying to imagine this lovely fucker."

"Oh, he thinks he's lovely, all right," she said. "Probably treating himself to his own medicine. Always running, crazy fit, tall, too damn skinny if you ask me, but he likes the mirror, that's for sure. Oh, and we started to notice—Crowley only likes treating the white boys. Dr. Lipke, he doesn't care, he treats anyone, but his partner? His client list looks like a Trump rally. You believe that?"

The thin man by Oliver's side . . . his henchman's racist numerology tattooed on his knuckles. . . . Yeah, I could believe it.

"What you thinking about?" she asked. "You got a funny look."

I tried to slow my thoughts as they flooded forth. Vic Wingate gets on the story of Carl Kruger, the abuse he and so many others endured back in East Germany, at the hands of men like Dr. Lipke. He follows the story down to Miami, to the BioVida clinic. He thinks Lipke is the story; he's not expecting to find a neo-Nazi American business partner. Both doctors shun attention. They're concerned about Wingate's intrusion, the threat he brings. Their client list, if they hear about it, will be even more concerned. Crowley, the more aggressive and younger of the two, demands they do something about it. Lipke, an old Communist, knows a few things about staying under the radar. Then the writer turns up dead at the bottom of a waterfall. His subject impaled with his own javelin on the floor of his bar. I'm warned, a boy is threatened, and Cass is framed. And then I walked right into their office and chatted up the nurse. I'd probably put her in danger too.

"Damn, boy's gone quiet on me," she said.

"I'm sorry," I said. "A long time ago I did some time, for dealing weed. Inside, I had some problems with some white supremacists. Hearing about a racist fuck like Crowley, it brings back bad memories."

My presence beside her might have been based upon a lie, but that part was too true. My face grew hot. I gulped at the sangria and sucked on a piece of ice. I felt her hand touch my thigh, felt her watching me. I turned, cupped her warm cheek in my hand, and kissed her lightly. Waited, brushed against her lips, to see if she'd return it. She did. Tasha wrapped an arm around my waist and pulled me closer. She opened her mouth and breathed me in. I felt her tongue on mine. A shudder went down my spine. When we broke the kiss, we turned together to the bar with fingers raised for the check. It was already placed before us.

Chapter 24

The glow of streetlight slipped through the crack in the curtains. The quiet in the dark felt alive, suspended. I watched her walk naked to the bathroom. Her ass was athlete firm and high, and she moved with a spine-straight pride. Her smell lingered on my skin, in the sheets, on my lips. It was a rich, musky scent that could not be mistaken for anything else. Like a primitive mating call, it announced hunger. I breathed it in, exhaled, and stared, smiling, at the ceiling. I tried to remember the last time I felt so sated.

When Tasha emerged from the bathroom, she began to gather her clothes at the foot of the bed.

"No," I said. "Come back."

"Told you, I gotta work tomorrow." She moved to the side of the mattress and leaned over me. Her tangle of hair fell around my face. Her lips met mine, tasting herself. I felt a small wiry hair in the back of my mouth. She straightened up, touched my cheek. "I'm gonna be cross-eyed at work tomorrow," she said. "Thanks to you."

"Not yet."

I sat up and reached for her, tried to pull her back. She

resisted, but not entirely. I began to kiss her stomach. My eyes peered up and connected with hers. She smiled me down to my knees.

"What are you doin', mister?" she asked.

I kissed lower. My hands cupped her ass. I pulled her to me. She gasped and relented and down I went.

Round two exceeded the first. The raw thrill of the first time was heightened by a proven quantity. We knew what we could bring out of each other. With Juliette everything had felt like theater. She took great pride in her bedroom abilities, but it was always once removed, as if she were watching herself from across the room, taking measure of the action. Mental notes on volume, creativity, duration . . . With Tasha everything was present tense. I savored her and lost all memory of past, all worry of future.

Finally she was dressing at the foot of the bed and we were both laughing in disbelief. The room reeked of sex. The comforter and sheets had all been pushed off the side; the pillows were flattened. There was a wide wet stain in the center of the mattress. She fastened her bra. Picked up her sundress and slipped it over her head. It fell across her body and stuck to her sticky skin.

"How long did you say you'd be in town?" she asked.

"I didn't."

"Stick around," she said. "I think I'm gonna need that again."

"You and me both."

"Well, you know where to find me."

"Here," I said, reaching for my phone on the night-stand. "Enter your number for me."

She took it and looked at the screen. I saw her face drop.

"What?" I asked.

She handed it back. "You better take a look," she said.

There was a text from Detective Miller. It read: **Your partner is now being charged with double murder. There's evidence. Call me.**

"The fuck you doing down here?" she asked.

"I told you, a mother hired me—"

"Oh, bullshit. I shoulda known you were full of shit. When I go in tomorrow and ask about the Nestor family, what's the doctor gonna tell me? I bet he says the boy's mother and father are still married, that's what I bet. How about it, Duck?"

I stared up at the ceiling, without the sated smile of before. "I have no idea what you'll find," I said. "Until you called that kid's name in the waiting room, I'd never heard of him before. Maybe his parents are still married. Maybe that wasn't even his father with him. I have no clue."

"Mother. Fucker," she said.

I sat up. She stood before me with crossed arms, her feet set wide, like a pissed-off bouncer. The doors had been shut, the latches pulled tight. I wouldn't be entering again anytime soon.

"Can I explain?" I asked.

"You damn well better."

And I tried. I started with Cass, my now-incarcerated partner, facing a double-murder charge. I told her about the death of Victor Wingate, and my presence at the scene of Carl Kruger's execution. I told her about Oliver and the thin man, the guy I thought I could now identify as Dr. James Crowley. The only thing I neglected to mention was the threat to Stevie Cohen. There were enough layers for her to digest. I didn't need to add that last one, and try to explain my relationship with the kid and his mother. When I finished, she was seated on a chair by the window. Her arms were crossed as she looked out the crack in the curtains.

"You think Dr. Crowley is behind all this?" she asked.

"It seems likely," I said. "What about the other guy, this neo-Nazi errand boy, Oliver? He sound familiar?"

She shook her head. "I'd remember a man like that," she said. "I'm pretty sure he's never been to the clinic. At least while I've been there."

"I'm sorry," I said. "I'm really sorry for lying. . . ."

"I don't want to hear it." Tasha stood and peered out the curtains to the pool below. "You have any cigarettes?"

"I don't," I said.

She looked toward the door. Bit her lower lip, refused to face me. We'd had such a time. It was no mere hookup and we both knew it. Moments earlier I'd been contemplating how long I could stay down here, or if she had any vacation time coming to her, wondering if I could convince her to visit me in the city. Now I was just scrambling to say something that would make her *not* hate me.

"Tasha, I'm sorry," I said. "I never expected—"

"You 'never expected' what?" she asked. "To fuck me after you pumped me for information?"

"It's not like that."

"Yeah," she said. "It's *exactly* like that."

I watched her gather her purse on the dresser. Her body was stiff with her back to me. She was a proud woman who didn't allow her heart to be opened often. I sensed I'd inflicted a deep hurt, one that she would try hard to banish from her mind. Just a one-night stand with a lying white boy, she'd tell herself. Connection or not, she'd be right.

"Bye, Duck," she said.

I listened to the door open and shut.

Once again a text concerning Cass had wrecked the

postcoital moment and enraged a woman I'd just pleased. And once again I didn't hesitate in reaching for the phone.

Miller picked up on the third ring.

"You got my text," she said. It was after midnight, but there was no yawn to her voice.

"I think I know who's setting her up," I said.

She sighed like I was a cuckolded spouse, always the last to know.

"Duck, her prints were all over Kruger's javelin," she said.

"So what? She'd been there before, she probably asked him to see it."

"The widow, Uli Kruger, insists that her husband never let anyone handle it."

"And Victor Wingate?" I asked. "I suppose her prints were all over her boyfriend's clothes too? And that must mean she's the killer."

I listened to Lea breathing on the line. "The autopsy on Wingate's body revealed marks consistent with torture," she said. "It was badly damaged by the fall, but his sister, Susie Wingate, insisted on further examination."

" 'Torture,' " I said. "Lea, you do know what Cass did for a living, when she wasn't working with me?"

"I'm aware that she was involved in S and M, yes. You told me as much."

"So, doesn't it stand to reason that any man she was with would also share those certain tastes?"

"That is for her attorney to parse out," she said. "I'm only telling you what we've found."

"You want to tell me what Cass's motive was? You're telling me she went on a murderous rampage and then called me for help in finding out who did it?"

"Duck, how well do you know your partner?" she asked.

"As well as anyone," I said. "We worked together for years. We've taken bullets for each other. You know this."

"I also remember you telling me how private she was, how little she let you know of her personal life."

"So much for trusting a cop in bed," I said.

That jab hit the mark and left her quiet for a moment. I was beating up the messenger. Detective Miller had never been anything but decent to me. I'd seldom returned that decency.

"We'd like you to come in for questioning," she said.

"I'm still in Miami," I told her.

"I realize that, and I'm going to suggest—as your friend—that you wrap up whatever it is you're doing down there and come back to the city."

"What if I'm investigating something that could clear Cass?"

"Then we'll look forward to hearing about it, and picking up where you left off."

"Stay tuned," I said.

"Duck . . ."

"What, Lea?"

"Take care of yourself, okay?"

"Not my style," I said.

She ended the call with a sigh and no good-bye. I looked at the screen, hated it for being the source of such trouble. I missed a world of no text messaging, of pay phones and privacy, a time when we weren't perpetually reachable, always on hand to receive the bad news day and night. Without that goddamn device this night would have ended with blissful sleep after rounds of stunning sex. Instead I was up. Sleep wouldn't be possible. Tasha hated me. So did Lea. Juliette was probably being serviced by one of her Warrior Security studs. And Cass was imprisoned, suspected of multiple homicides.

In the dark hours that followed, I played pillow karate for a while. At three a.m., I got out of bed and pulled on jeans and went out in search of booze. The streets were warm and damp in the night, with a film of condensation over every surface. I walked back to The Bar to find it closed. I remembered that few cities outside New York kept bars open until four. I went in search of a bodega or an all-night supermarket for beer, but struck out there too. I'd have to go without, as much as the prospect of a sober head sounded like torture.

When I returned to the hotel, I stopped by the pool. I hopped the locked gate and went to the edge of the water. The underwater lights gave off an unsettling glow, like a Hockney painting come to life. I contemplated a clothed plunge, but resisted. Instead I rolled up my jeans to the knees and sat on the lip and dangled my legs in. I watched the surface ripple and spread as I moved my feet in slow circles. Contemplated the way the slightest disturbance can awaken still waters and send aftershocks in all directions. Then I thought about all the half-bright metaphors and quotable wisdoms subscribed to the ways of water. Bruce Lee said, "Be water, my friend." Leonardo da Vinci described putting a hand in a flowing stream, how you touched the last that's gone before and the first of what's still to come. Fitzgerald claimed that all good writing was swimming underwater and holding your breath. So said the man who drank himself to an early grave. Step into liquid, said a surf movie I'd seen years ago. Yet again I felt the pull. Those dark whispers that pushed for the final solution. It would be so easy. Just step in and exhale. Let yourself sink. And stay there. Sleep would come then, the big one.

I shook off that siren song and padded back to my room. The first light of morning was beginning to creep through the curtains when I finally managed to doze off.

Chapter 25

It was after eleven when I woke. The room remained shrouded in false dark, except for that uncloseable crack where the light got in. A bright, thin line crossed the floor and ended at the foot of the bed. I rolled away from it. The events of the previous night flooded back. I closed my eyes again, but it was no good. Despite my longing for apathy I couldn't just lie there. Cass was being accused of two murders she couldn't have committed. I climbed from bed and moved toward the bathroom. I smelled Tasha's scent still clinging to my skin. Decided to skip the shower. I wanted to keep the sense memory close, for as long as it wanted to linger.

The first matter of business was transportation. I had a vague plan in mind, and cabs or Uber wouldn't work. The desk clerk was the same well-dressed gent from the day before. He offered a cheery smile and asked if I'd slept well.

"Nope," I said. "But it's not the bed's fault."

"And what can I do for you this afternoon?"

"Where's the closest place I can rent a car?"

He thought about it for a moment in a theatrical pose with thumb and index finger pressed to his chin. He gazed off, pressed his thin lips together, and narrowed his eyes in actorly thought.

"There's an Enterprise," he said at length. "About two miles away, on Ponce De Leon, this street right out here? Would you like me to call you a car?"

"That's okay, I think I'll walk."

He gave me a twisted look.

"I'm from New York," I told him. "I know it's an unfamiliar concept elsewhere."

His eyes lit. The bright lights of Broadway were a long way from the lobby of the ChateauBleau. "God, I adore Manhattan," he said.

"Try living there."

I turned to the exit and paused as the doors swung open. Two miles in which direction, that would be helpful.

"Turn left!" he called. "You can't miss it."

The heat outside hit me like a wet fish to the face. The sky was dull, the humidity absurd. I almost turned back and asked for that cab after all. But I'd made a prideful point about walking. Dumb ego prevented retreat. I was drenched within a block. At the intersection of Alcazar I lingered in front of the BioVida building. I spotted Tasha's silver Camry parked curbside; I ignored the impulse to leave a note. I'd be back this way in a few hours. Much as I stirred at her scent and the memory of her contorted face below me, I needed to let her be. I spotted a Starbucks around the corner and sought air-conditioned refuge, along with a supersized iced coffee. Fortified and temporarily cooled, I made it the rest of the way without heatstroke.

The Enterprise lot was tucked behind a bland beige stretch of businesses. It was empty midday on a Thursday and I had my choice of rides. I chose a black Crown Vic for its cop sensibility. And then I was pulling out into the jungle climate of Miami with windows up and AC blasting.

I drove north on U.S. 1 through Coconut Grove, past the AmericanAirlines Arena, home of the Heat, and followed the signs for the MacArthur Causeway toward Miami

Beach. On one side of the bridge there was a long, ugly stretch of industrial need—stacked rows of shipping containers and cranes and utilitarian tankers being loaded in the trench. On the other side there were the glittering gated islands of the loaded. First Palm and Hibiscus, then a little farther down, Star Island, home to a certain type of celebrity and the stupid rich. They said Shaq lived there, along with Sylvester Stallone and Gloria Estefan and P. Diddy. Those sorts, you get the idea. Their neighbors were families of dubious fortunes, often drug related, pharmaceutical and otherwise. I remembered that Al Capone used to live on one of those island enclaves. I couldn't remember which one. This was a town so shameless that it didn't matter where your money came from, as long as you had it—and just as important, as long as you flaunted it. Not unlike Manhattan, but at least there the big wealth would always be hidden behind doormen and wrought-iron gates, with the six-figure cars parked underground, and no nine-figure yachts parked out front like neon advertisements for the self.

I had no plan in Miami Beach other than to walk on the sand, people watch, and clear my head in the salt water. I found a spot near Joe's Stone Crab and crossed through a cluster of new condos to the water.

The ocean was more Caribbean here than the clouded coastal waters along the eastern seaboard. There was no surf and the turquoise sea lapped placid on the white sand. Under a palm tree at the edge of the beach, I took off my shirt and wrapped it around my waist in a modified deck change. I slid off my jeans and pulled on my suit. Yesterday's blast of sun had left a light red burn across my layer of pale skin. I ignored the need for sunscreen. I walked straight to the water like I was being summoned by some unseen power, strode in without hesitation, until it was up to my waist. Then I dove forward and under. Bliss, instant brain-clearing bliss . . . Why did I live in a place where I didn't have this tonic on offer at all times? An indoor pool was such an inferior substitute. So were any pools for that matter. Nothing could compare with the cleansing shock of diving beneath salt water. I told myself I'd have fewer problems if I could be near this more often. Maybe I could patch things up with Tasha; I could convince her to quit BioVida and find work elsewhere; we could make a life down here. Fool, what a fool I was, always musing on the impossible, that it might be possible for me to leave New York. I was a prisoner there, like everyone else. I remembered a line from wise old Jim Harrison. Written soon before he died at his desk, with pen in hand, an unfinished poem before him. *"We are all on death row living in cells of our own devising."* As I swam underwater, with open eyes in the blurry brightness, I resolved to toast that line with a whiskey when I got out and found a place to eat.

I considered Dr. Eberhard Lipke and his partner, Dr. James Crowley. I needed to learn more about them, needed to chat with Dr. Lipke, whether he liked it or not. Tasha had painted him as a kindly aged doc, beloved by his patients and staff. *Bring me your old and your impotent, your young and strong. Are you desperate to enhance performance without detection? Come on in.* Her moral blindness was difficult to reconcile with the sharp woman I'd spent the evening with. I doubted she was aware of his past activities behind the Wall. This was no order-following innocent. This was a man who injected poison into developing bodies, someone who fucked with body chemistries in the name of sport. He helped lead a mass sacrifice for the greater good of the state.

Lipke drugged thousands, with substances that gave no high, no pleasure, beyond the false pride of winning by cheating. He got away with it all. Maybe he wasn't a card-carrying member of the Aryan Brotherhood like his partner, but he had plenty to answer for.

I swam around for a half hour like an agitated manatee. Then I walked across the sand, gathered my jeans, and let myself drip-dry under the hard midday sun. I strolled along the low tide, taking in the bodies around me. Everyone was fit and bronzed and proudly exposed. I saw men in their sixties that could have passed for *Men's Health* models. I saw women in G-strings that I could have sworn I'd seen on YouPorn. It was a raw parade of the body beautiful. I found myself walking with a straighter back, a sucked-in gut, but it was no use. I was a pasty Yankee visitor, made all the more obvious by my increasing burn. When I touched my finger to my shoulder, I saw the telltale blotch.

Driving back over the Causeway, I was feeling almost sane. It would all work out. Cass's prints were on the javelin: There was sure to be a good reason for that. Even if Kruger forbid others from touching it, it was difficult to deny Cassandra Kimball any request. There were marks of "torture" on Victor Wingate's body. He had to be into some kinky shit if he was with Cass. That didn't mean she followed him out into the woods and pushed him over a waterfall at his favorite spot, where she knew he hiked every day. What was her motive? Did she think she would inherit that house of his? Had I been called to help establish her distress and innocence, as the grieving ersatz "widow"?

I remembered telling Lea about her. It always bothered me, the unequal footing of our relationship. Cass knew it all, from my father's fall to my mother's death, the details of my time in jail to my rehabilitated badass years on parole, when I learned aikido and established my reputation as an investigator, albeit unlicensed. She was there for my descent with the pain pills and the bottle after taking a bullet in the gut trying to protect her from a stalker. She'd been with me ever since. And in those years, I'd learned little about her. I'd never been to her apartment in the city, knew only that it was in Chinatown, or at least that's what she said. I knew about her dungeon work at the Chamber, where she whipped and berated conflicted men desperate to submit. But what else did I know? Our relationship was about the cases we worked together. Despite my affection for her and our rather unconventional working arrangement, she was always careful to keep it professional. Lea was right, I didn't really know her, especially since she reciprocated with a bullet of her own, taken for me during our last case together. She disappeared after that. I'd seen her once in the hospital while we both recovered, and then she fled the city. Joined a Zen retreat upstate near Woodstock, and met Victor Wingate. Fallen in love . . .

Is it a sign of clarity or madness when you begin to doubt those closest to you? Is it paranoia closing in, or an overdue recognition of the truth behind the layers? I tried to banish this tumbling line of thought. If I couldn't trust Cass, then all my instincts as an investigator were a joke. It would bring down the whole delicate construct. The swim gave me illusions of lucidity, but as I recrossed the Causeway, my mind was muddied with doubt and confusion.

It was a little before four p.m. when I returned to Coral Gables. I found a spot across the street from the BioVida offices and settled in for a late-afternoon stakeout. I searched Miami's FM radio options. The majority of stations were either Spanish or hip-hop. I settled on 105.9, a classic-rock station that had decided the nineties were old enough to be classic. I could abide the Nirvana, but when Pearl Jam came on, I turned off the radio and chose silence over Eddie Vedder.

The building began to empty a few minutes after five. I noticed the platinum-haired, fake-titted Tiffany talking to a toned Latino stud in a shirt that was two sizes too small. I'd spent untold hours watching workers leave their offices back home, while I was spying on something or other. They all looked the same in the city, moneyed and exhausted, too past it to look back at anyone. Down here folks moved with a peacocking that was disconcerting. Instead of eyes cast down and inward, everyone seemed to search out, scoping for connection. When I spotted Tasha, I sank low in my seat and looked away. She had no reason to recognize the Crown Vic, but I was a little disappointed when she climbed into her Camry and drove off without a glance in my direction.

I was beginning to think I had missed Lipke's exit when a black S-class Mercedes sedan pulled from the lot beneath the building. My only image of the doctor was a decades-old photo posted online during his German court trial. But Tasha's description was apt. Behind the wheel he looked like a kindly Kraut Santa. His cheeks were ruddy, his hair and beard white and neatly trimmed. The vanity plates on the Benz read: AGE DOC. He turned right and I pulled out and followed a few cars back. Lipke turned onto U.S. 1 and we headed north. Just before we reached the downtown, he signaled and turned onto the Rickenbacker Causeway bound for Key Biscayne.

The bridge was longer and prettier than the MacArthur artery to Miami Beach, with clear expanses of Biscayne Bay in that soft shade of blue unique to South Florida. As we reconnected with land, we passed through a stretch of protected mangroves before reaching the settled patch of the Key. It was a short drive from the mainland, an island hop from showy South Beach, but Key Biscayne felt like a separate civilized universe.

There was the sense that mothers and children seldom left. There were schools and playgrounds and all the water sport you could wish for. The breadwinners would be forced to leave each day to Miami proper, but there was a peace and calmness here not present in the rest of the city. Still, that didn't mean the wealth was any less conspicuous. As I followed Lipke down Harbor Drive, the homes behind the gates announced themselves like loud art spread beneath the palms. There were no cars between us now. If he'd been paying attention, he would have made me. When Lipke slowed and signaled in front of a high white gate, I passed without glancing over. In my rearview I watched as the Benz went through and the gates closed behind him. I turned around and double-parked on the corner. There were cameras visible in the treetops, no pedestrians, and a Neighborhood Watch sign in front of me. I wouldn't be able to loiter for long.

Five minutes later the gates reopened and the man himself appeared between them. He was short and paunchy, with a proud manner. He moved lightly in his loafers. Lipke was dressed in blue linen pants and an orange silk shirt, which covered a deep tan. He looked at my car and lifted an arm and waved like he was greeting an old friend recognized across a room. I almost waved back. I watched him approach, rolled down the window. If he wanted to talk, wonderful, so did I.

"*Guten tag,*" he said, leaning in.

I looked down at his fingers resting on the window frame. They were small and stubby and expertly manicured. Trumpian. He waited until I met his gaze and gave me a relaxed smile. He was a man in confident control of his environment. I didn't know when he picked up my tail, but I'd done a shit job.

"Why don't you join me inside?" he asked. "It's much

more comfortable in there." He glanced up at the dull, heavy sky. "It is too warm out here. Come, I'll get you a drink."

He nodded and walked back toward his property, never doubting that I would follow. I turned off the car and opened the door and tripped after him like a kid late for school. He pressed an opener in his pocket and the gates swung wide. He didn't wait for me to catch up. As we approached the house, I noticed her car. Tasha's silver Camry, parked by the front door. Lipke glanced over his shoulder.

"Yes, she is here too," he said. "We'll all talk, the three of us, *ja?*"

I sensed him smiling with his back to me. I looked up at the house. It was a white beast of right angles and dark glass, an emblem of the eighties, when the city preened in its *Miami Vice* heyday. It looked like a film set, a home fit for a fictional drug dealer with a cache of automatic weapons in the closet and bodyguards lurking in the shadows. At the door he turned and said, "I'm so glad you followed. We have much to discuss."

Chapter 26

The open interior was an expanse of marble, in white and black, with matching black or white furniture and lighting. The walls were covered with a thorough looting of Art Basel. Some savvy art advisor had whispered in his ear and helped Lipke pick out an array of inexplicable work. His Italian loafers tapped over the marble, leading the way without a word. We found her seated at a white kitchen island with a tall glass of white wine before her.

"There you are," he said.

He went to her and kissed her on the forehead, wrapped an arm around her shoulders, and turned to me. "I understand you met Natasha yesterday?"

"Nice to see you again," I said.

Tasha didn't raise her gaze. She took a sip of wine, crossed her legs. Yesterday's green sundress was replaced by a cream skirt and fitted black tank top. Her feet were bare. Despite the evident betrayal the sight of her flesh stirred an instant longing.

"You bought her a drink, *ja?*" asked Lipke. "At Books and Books? I do love that store."

"I did."

Lipke looked at his nurse. I wasn't sure how much she'd

told him about our encounter, but I wanted to believe it ended there.

"It seems you had a nice chat," he said. "Natasha, would you mind repeating what you told me earlier about your conversation with this gentleman?"

For the first time I sensed the menace beneath his jovial veneer. His request carried the undertone of demand and threat of punishment. I remembered my coach Teddy Marks, and other coaches I'd encountered as a kid. They often had that same note of smiling cruelty. Within many adults who've worked with young athletes, there exists a seed of sadism. It was easy to spot in Lipke.

"I told you, Eberhard," she said. "He was asking about you and Dr. Crowley."

He positioned himself behind her and rested his small hands on her shoulders, close to her neck. Tasha tensed as he squeezed; Lipke smiled. "What else, dear?" he asked.

"He said some divorced mother of one of our clients hired him," she said. "Apparently, the woman doesn't like us treating her son, and wants to get back at her ex-husband. Something like that."

" 'Something like that,' " he repeated. "It was the Nestors he mentioned specifically, is that right?"

Tasha nodded, took another nervous sip.

"Was that all?" he asked.

"It was a short conversation. I first saw him in our waiting room, pretending he was lost, then I spotted him following me at the bookstore, and he sat down next to me and started a conversation. It creeped me out."

"Interesting," said Lipke. "How interesting." He massaged Tasha's shoulders. It was all she could do not to hunch them up and swat away his little hands. Then he asked me, "What would you like to know about Alex Nestor and his treatment at BioVida?"

I decided to join the game. Maybe the kid's parents really were divorced. Maybe that's all she told him. "You're helping him cheat, aren't you?" I asked. "Along with plenty of other athletes. Just like you used to do back home in East Germany."

"Ah, now I see," he said, pleased with the engagement. "Our friend here has done his homework, Natasha. What did you say your name was again?"

"I didn't."

"What did you say it was, love?" he asked his nurse. "Dick, was it?"

"He calls himself Duck," she said.

"How original. And does this Duck have a last name?"

"Darley," I said. "I'm curious to learn more about your background, behind the Wall. I'm curious to hear how a convicted felon is able to continue practicing medicine."

"Another time and place," he said. "The West always liked to be outraged, when, in fact, our means of assisting performance was no different than yours."

"So you were stealing from thieves?" I asked. "The classic rationale."

"Poetically put," he said. "In my decades as a sports physician, I never had an athlete test positive for any banned substance. Not once. I paid a fine for that ridiculous political persecution. In any case my business now is treating older clients, men like myself, who do not wish to grow old quite as quickly as nature intended."

"That must explain the teenagers in your waiting room yesterday."

"Many young men experience testosterone deficiencies. I'd be happy to explain these conditions further if you have the time."

"Tell me about your partner," I said. "This Dr. Crowley."

He glanced at Tasha, said, "Dear, would you mind if Mr. Darley and I spoke a bit in private?"

"Of course not," she said.

As she slid from her stool and Lipke's grasp, she flashed me a look beneath her lashes. There was complicity in her eyes. It wasn't betrayal that brought me inside this house but collusion. Tasha was making it easier for me. Whatever her previous relationship with her boss, she'd served him up for me now. At least that's what I wanted to see.

We watched her walk to the back of the house, open a sliding door and step out onto a shaded patio. She took a seat in white wicker with her back to us. Drank from her glass, tapped at her phone.

"Loyalty is the most valuable of commodities," said Lipke, still staring after her. "She is a special one."

"She seemed very nice."

The doctor looked back at me with dark eyes. The false cheer and easy jousting was over. "Enough," he said. "Alex Nestor's parents are married. The mother did not hire you. Enough of your charade, tell me why you're here."

"Tell me about Crowley," I said.

"Who are you working for?"

"Myself."

He snorted. "So this is just professional curiosity?"

"Amateur," I said. "Strictly amateur." When he smirked, I added, "You can also tell me about Carl Kruger. I understand he could really toss the javelin. While you're at it, tell me about Victor Wingate."

Lipke grinned. "Which one would you like to know about first?" he asked.

"Crowley," I said. "Tell me about your partner, and then tell me about the racist skinhead he likes to keep company with. He told me his name was Oliver."

"Very well," he said, "but first let's pour us a drink. You strike me as a whiskey man, is that correct?"

"It is."

"Good, as am I, but not the crude American kind, I cannot

abide bourbon. Only single malts for myself, will that be okay?"

"You pour it, I'll drink it."

Lipke opened a cabinet in the kitchen and produced a bottle of Macallan, a stainless-steel measuring shot, a pair of Waterford tumblers, and a couple coasters. "Eighteen year," he said. "I do hope you enjoy it."

He filled each serving in the shot, then poured the precise amount and handed it over neat. It was not even a finger in the heavy glass.

"*Prost,*" he said.

I raised the amber, met his eyes. It tasted fine, in that fussy way of old scotches. My tastes were cruder.

Lipke walked past with his glass and the coasters and said, "Come, we'll talk in the dining room."

I joined him in a soulless space dominated by a long, glass table, a crystal chandelier, and an abstract canvas of slashing black paint framed on one wall. He took a seat at the head of the table and motioned to the chair next to him. He slid a coaster, with the initials *EL* etched in glass, beneath my drink before I could set it down. We had a sip in unison, and sat back and regarded each other.

"So, what would you like to know about my associate, Dr. Crowley?"

"I understand he has a rather select clientele," I said.

"Did Natasha tell you that?" he asked.

I waited for him to reply further. He crossed his short legs, glanced over at his ridiculous art.

"Dr. Crowley was once a champion runner himself," he began. "A world-class miler. He broke four minutes, when it still meant something. He came from the northern part of Florida, in Jacksonville. When I arrived in the U.S. in the mid-nineties, I did not know this country well. I didn't grasp the ways of your South, in particular. In Germany we have our sins, our dark history, *ja?* But here, you must believe me, it is much worse in certain parts. Maybe not in Miami or New York, in your liberal coastal areas, but where Dr. Crowley comes from the tension between the races is more open. And he was a runner, *ja?* A sport once dominated by white gentlemen, ages ago, but no longer. Dr. Crowley has an interest in correcting certain perceived genetic disadvantages."

"Sounds like an alt-right man of medicine. That must explain his henchman, Oliver. Your partner must approve of his tattoos."

"We all have our little obsessions," said Lipke. "I don't consider my partner to be racist. The concept is fundamentally foolish. He is fascinated with the human body, by its potential. Each of us has certain advantages and disadvantages according to our genes, our environments, or any number of factors. The field of play is never equal, is it? One could argue that so-called performance enhancement is a way of striving for more fairness, not less."

"One could also argue that racist crackers like your partner are actually the inferior ones," I said. "What about Oliver, Doctor? I've had the displeasure of meeting him a few times now."

Lipke sipped his scotch, his Santa's eyes twinkling over his glass. "I never will get used to that aggressive American way of speech. Where does your confidence come from? You all have it, even those who seem to have no right to their convictions."

"As opposed to hiding behind walls and lies and fake manners?"

"No, as opposed to understanding there is more than one obtuse side to every story."

"Then tell me your side, Doc."

"You don't see yourself as you are, do you? So righteous, so convinced that you've zeroed in on the enemy, in your narrow way of perceiving things."

"From what I understand—from your own employee out there—your business partner is a bigot, and from my own experience and observations, the man I've seen him with is a blatant neo-Nazi. I know what his tattoos mean, I've seen them before."

Lipke shook his head, tried out a frown. "The gentleman you're referring to is very close to me. It pains me to hear you refer to him that way. He is not what you say, not anymore. We have discussed having those tattoos removed, due to the fact that some folks, felons like you, will recognize its unfortunate meaning."

He pushed a hand in his pocket and brought out his phone and began to thumb through it. Finding what he was looking for, he handed it over for me to see. "I'm showing you this so you know that I have nothing to hide," he said.

It was a picture of Lipke and Oliver standing on a beach, arms around one another, smiling for the camera. "My son," he said. "My adoptive son, Oliver Lipke. He took my name, bless him."

"All undue respect, Doctor, but your son is still an ignorant racist punk. We had an altercation when he and your partner came to see me. They wanted to send some sort of message. I don't think I got it. Maybe you could share it in person?"

Lipke glanced away toward his art. He crossed and uncrossed his legs, fidgeted in his seat. "You should not have provoked him," he said. "It will not help matters."

"Wasn't that the point? You sent those two to the city to warn me off, to shut me up. They haven't succeeded."

"Oliver is quite intelligent," he said. "Despite your assumptions. And he is also dangerous, someone you do not want to provoke. He is a well-trained man of action. You'd be wise to remember that."

"And you'd be wise to remember the blood on your

hands. Two people are dead—and your boy has provoked *me*. I wonder how he'd react if I put his daddy in the hospital right now?"

Lipke rolled his eyes. "I abhor threats. I told you, I have nothing to hide. I understand you attacked my son, in the presence of my partner. If you'd like to assault me too, go ahead." He swept a little hand around his airy home. "I could always use more money."

"Where are Dr. Crowley and Oliver now?" I asked.

"I'm afraid I don't know."

"You sure about that? It would be a bad idea to lie to me. Your boy, Oliver, might have done his homework, but have you? Do you know my history of violence? PTSD, the works, you're dealing with an unstable man, Doc."

He took a sip of his scotch, set it down on his monogrammed coaster, and folded his arms across his chest. "Perhaps you didn't hear me," he said. "I abhor threats. Now, if you'll excuse me . . ."

"Carl Kruger," I said. "You ordered his execution, didn't you?"

"I did no such thing. I've had no contact with Kruger in many years."

"When was the last time?"

"Never, not with *him*," he said. "I only knew Hilde Kruger, one of the most brilliant athletes I ever treated."

" 'Treated'—as in, *abused as a minor*. One of thousands you forced to dope, as has been proven in a court of law."

"A political circus, a sham of justice," he said. He swallowed his scotch. Blood rushed up his ruddy face.

"Correct me if I'm wrong," I said. "They were just guinea pigs, weren't they? These days it's been more perfected. You can produce supermen that make hundreds of millions of dollars. Must make you feel like a kind of god, doesn't it?"

He scoffed. "Another Internet expert. What, did you spend a few minutes Googling, read some Wikipedia, and

now you think you know about me? I don't have time for
this." He pushed out his chair, stood, and waited for me to
do the same.

"I was with him when he died," I said. "Carl was murdered with his own javelin. Impaled through the throat."

I watched his flushed face go as white as his beard. "I
have nothing to hide," he said again. "And I can assure
you, neither my son nor my associate had anything to do
with that."

"What about Victor Wingate?" I asked. "You sure no
one you know might have followed him into the woods,
gave him a push over those falls?"

"We are done here, Mr. Darley. I've had about all of the
disrespect and accusations that I can stomach. If you wish
to assault me, go ahead. I invite your attack, and the retribution it will bring."

And I almost did. It would have been so easy to mop
those marble floors with the supercilious Kraut. Rub his
face in his own blood. Let him feel some real pain. But it
would have been like attacking a child. A craven act of
temper, it would result only in my arrest—and would put
Stevie in further danger. Instead I reached out and grabbed
his cheeks in my hand and squeezed. Leaned in close until
our noses almost touched and looked into his eyes.

"I do hope you'll remember this meeting," I said. "Do
be careful, won't you?"

Chapter 27

I waited for Tasha to follow me out. When she didn't, I sat in the Crown Vic across the street, expecting her to appear between the white gates. After an hour of sitting and seething, I gave up on her and drove back to the mainland. I could have sworn that glance said she was on my side, not the doctor's. Or maybe I was an arrogant fool, convinced that a hot romp in a hotel room was enough to shift her allegiances.

It was Lipke who wrote that note about Stevie. That child-abusing disgrace of a doctor who abhorred threats, who claimed he had nothing to hide, he was behind it all. He had to be. *"I do hope . . ."* I knew the moment he handed me that scotch and said those words. And Oliver was his adopted son? Had he raised that neo-Nazi? Did he really believe his kid had changed? No, true character can always be measured by who it is that you surround yourself with most. In Lipke's case it was an alt-right Southern supremacist and a kid covered in racist hate ink. The man had plenty to hide.

When I returned to the ChateauBleau, I gathered my bag and checked out and headed for Miami International. The skies went from dull to dark and then opened with the region's patented late-afternoon monsoon. The rain in South Florida is like nowhere else. It is a reminder that the land is a temporary condition, a low-lying peninsula that will someday be swallowed from above and below. The water rules these parts. Street flooding is as natural an occurrence as Midtown traffic in Manhattan. You learn to live with it.

When visibility became zero, I had to pull over and wait it out. Traffic continued to move past at the speed limit, unfazed by driving blind or hydroplaning through busy intersections. I turned off the wipers and let the storm envelop the car. It felt biblical. Yet ten minutes later it was gone. *Just passing through, thanks, see you tomorrow at the same time.* I pulled back onto the avenue, feeling cleansed. Maybe that was the secret to South Florida sin— it was always rinsed away by those fierce daily storms.

I returned the Crown Vic as the floodwaters began to recede in the Enterprise lot. Took the shuttle to the terminal, shrugged when the driver asked what airline. I had no return ticket, but it didn't take long to find a cheap one with Frontier Air. Two hundred bucks one-way, departed in two hours. Perfect, enough time for a few drinks.

Perhaps my retreat home was too hasty, but after my conversation with Dr. Lipke, I knew it was time to get back and find his associates. Lipke was a self-righteous bastard who would never own up to his crimes. He told himself he had nothing to hide, while living for decades inside a moral vacuum. Sure, he doped thousands against their will back behind the Wall. Sure, it was cheating, but he was following orders. Now he continued his dark art at BioVida, using vain old men as his cover patients. He refused to acknowledge his hand in the health problems that came later: the ruined bodies and souls of a generation sacrificed on the altar of sport. But I knew he and Crowley were guilty of much more than that. They may not have pushed Wingate or driven the javelin through Kruger's throat; they had probably ordered Oliver to do it.

I remembered Crowley outside that Hell's Kitchen bar, not flinching as I twisted his arm behind his back and prepared to take on his henchman. I pictured Lipke composing that letter to Juliette Cohen, threatening her son. Taking private pleasure in the fear and panic it would provoke in the mother, the rage it would fuel in me. I remembered his partner seated alongside Oliver as they followed us to LaGuardia, thin-lipped and hard-faced behind dark glasses.

I realized I hadn't heard from Juliette since I arrived in Miami. I took out my phone, shot her a text: **Hey, just checking in, all okay?** Looked at the screen and waited for the teasing ellipses that indicate a reply is forthcoming. None appeared. I put it away, found a gate-side bar and ordered a pint. Knocked it back and added a Maker's alongside the next one.

An hour and a half later I was good and sauced as I weaved down the Jetway to my flight. I didn't bother to check my phone before slumping into my window seat and passing out. I dreamed of knives and torture and suffocation, all standard fare since my last case. I woke to the sound of the landing gear lowering over the Manhattan skyline. Drenched in sweat, dry-mouthed, desperate for a flight attendant to bring water. But it was too late. Time to stay strapped in and compliant as cattle.

My passage from plane to terminal to cab to apartment was made in unconscious transition. One moment I was blinking away nightmares above the city lights, the next I was seated on my couch, reaching to pet a dog that wasn't there. I'd received no word back from Juliette, nothing from Detective Miller since our conversation the night before, no call from Cass either. I remembered she had a lawyer, a for-

mer slave at the dungeon. He helped us through the legal
morass last time. Anytime you're involved in death, the
law likes to have its say. We each killed someone, very bad
someones. It was justified, the definition of self-defense,
but still. It was never as easy as explaining the circumstances to a cop and then heading home, free and cleared.
I'd find the lawyer's number, reach out to him tomorrow.

Sleep came late and troubled. The nightmares on the
plane picked up where they left off. I was back in a darkened room bound to a chair with all manner of horror
around me. Chained bodies were strewn about with needles hanging from arms. Heads lolled sideways, the floor
filled with vomit. Pets were being killed and cooked and
fed as last meals to the captives. I learned that I had committed some unnamable crime, something deserving of
great punishment. It became clear that my sentence would
involve the loss of something vital, a hand perhaps. But no
one would tell me what I did. The terror was real, the
threat imminent. I dreamed that I would negotiate with
my captor. How about a foot instead? That was less essential than one of my hands. How would I type?

It was nine a.m. when I woke on the couch, uncertain of
my surroundings. Home stopped feeling like home, ever
since Elvis died. I needed to find a new apartment, a clean
new space that had never experienced death. But I couldn't
imagine living in one of those modern glass towers that
scarred the skyline. I used to tell myself that I welcomed
the ghosts in these haunted rooms. As far as I was concerned, admirable architecture ceased to exist following
the Second World War. When materials grew cheap and
labor expensive, taste was the sacrifice. Out with the ornate exterior flourishes, the crown and base moldings in
high rooms full of wide hardwood floors and marble fire-
places. In with the white boxes and flat lines and bad windows.

Cass told me I had the taste and the judgment of old money, but without the pedigree. My brief gilded days as a boy were just a blip. My father's fortune had been nouveau and false, built on a pyramid of lies with a crooked foundation. Ever since, my relationship with money had been, well, complicated. I managed to earn a living, though my fees amounted to little more than scraps from the trough of real wealth held by my clients.

I sat up and rubbed at my puffy face. Scanned the sparse room, never refurnished since it was torn apart a year and a half ago. I loved the place, with all its original accents untouched, but I really did need to move. Thanks to Juliette's envelopes of cash, I had a bit saved now. I could afford something with fewer demons. Nothing fancy, just a decent studio or a one bedroom without memories. I got up and made coffee in the French press. Heard the usual phantom patter of Elvis's footsteps coming down the hall.

I tried to burn off the hangover under a scalding shower. Considered going for a swim, but it sounded like too much work. Caffeine and Advil would have to do. I found the name of Cass's lawyer searching through old emails. It was Edward Lutelman, Attorney at Law, with an office on East 44th Street, near Grand Central. I'd met him once, in a painkiller haze soon after getting out of the hospital. I couldn't pick him out of a lineup, just another interchangeable Midtown suit. I remembered him being in thrall of his mistress. Whatever Cass did for him behind those padded dungeon walls, he was forever grateful. There was no hourly rate mentioned, no invoice sent. I opened our last email exchange from two years ago. Hit REPLY and changed the subject line. I typed **Cass arrested, have you heard from her?** I reintroduced myself in the body of the email, explained the present situation, and asked when he was free to talk. Hit SEND. He replied in less than ninety seconds: **Yes, in**

touch with her, call you shortly. The phone rang five minutes later.

"Duck, it's Eddie," he said. "How you doing?"

His voice was hushed, loaded with concern.

"Thanks for getting back to me so fast," I said. "How's Cass?"

"Not well, I'm afraid." He was silent for a breath, before he added, "Things aren't looking good."

"What's not looking good? She's being framed."

"I believe you, but they're doing a hell of a job of it," he said. "Her prints are all over the murder weapon, that javelin from the bar, the one that killed this Kruger fella? As for the boyfriend upstate, he was in pretty bad shape, I mean before that fall killed him. Marks all over his body, load of drugs in his system."

"Eddie, you of all people ought to know what their relationship was like. Of course there were marks on the guy's body. I'm sure he asked for them."

If he was embarrassed by my knowledge of his kinky pleasures, he didn't let on. "I know, I know," he said. "We'll be pointing that out. This is all bullshit. Not to worry, I'll get her out. I'm just telling you, it's not going to be easy. Someone is working her over good."

"Who's behind it?"

"I was hoping you could help me with that," he said. "I've been waiting to hear from you. I'd like to discuss the rest in person."

"Tell me when and where."

He suggested an Irish pub called the Wheeltapper downstairs from his office on East 44th, between Third and Lexington. We agreed to meet there at one. I hung up and tried Detective Miller next. Straight to voice mail, told her to call me, that I was back in town. I texted Juliette. Nothing. At least the slave lawyer was taking my calls.

I arrived early at the pub, found a seat in a narrow banquette surrounded by stained wainscoting and crimson walls. There were framed prints of old Guinness ads and distressed antique signs giving the space a curated clutter. The bar was about a century too young to be authentic, but it got points for effort. I ordered a Harp and a Jameson in deference. My waitress was cute, ginger, with a striking pair of blues and a winking Irish lilt. I listened to Shane MacGowan growl out "The Sick Bed of Cuchulainn." Even cranking the Pogues—yeah, this place was really trying. I ordered another round soon after the first, scrolled through my phone, and started to wonder about Lutelman. No messages, twenty minutes late, the guy worked right upstairs. I tried his office line. A secretary told me he'd left for lunch. I set down my phone, faceup next to my drinks. Lifted my pint and gazed out the windows at a crowd gathering by the entrance. The lights of an ambulance pulled up in front of the pub, siren wailing. I placed cocktail napkins over the mouths of my glasses and got up to investigate.

There was a group on the sidewalk looking down at a body in distress. A Good Samaritan was performing CPR. He got up and let the paramedics take over. They knelt around him and tore open his shirt and stuck the electrodes on his chest. Gave him a zap, then another. Their body language did not look encouraged. I elbowed my way to the front of the crowd to get a better look. I didn't think I'd recognize Lutelman, but there he was: bloated and blue-faced and unmistakable. They strapped him to a stretcher and loaded him into the ambulance. The paramedics closed the doors and moved slow to their seats. The siren wailed as they pulled into the gridlock of Midtown. I pictured the lawyer in the back, wondered if he was having any final thoughts or was seeing any lights at the end of tunnels.

The crowd began to disperse. Just another poor fallen suit in this fallen city . . . maybe they'd raise a glass to him at lunch. Maybe they'd wait till happy hour. Many would forget about it by the time they got back to their desks. I lingered by the entrance of the pub, remembered my unfinished beverages and unpaid tab. I felt a hand on my elbow.

"You look like you could use a drink," said a voice in my ear.

I turned to find Dr. James Crowley standing by my side.

Chapter 28

We went back inside, sat down at my banquette. Crowley was grim-faced and smartly dressed in a slim-fitting blue suit and high white collar. What was left of his hair was blond and combed down flat. His eyes were a dark watery blue that seemed unaccustomed to light without sunglasses. Veins were visible in his neck and throbbed at his temples. His entire countenance was one of perpetual intensity.

There are usually two extremes when it comes to the second lives of athletes. Some have had enough of all that exercise. They let themselves go, find new, less healthy excesses to indulge in. Others take private oaths never to lose that hard-won six-pack. They're the ones who take up marathons and triathlons and treat their bodies like temples. They worship clarity and energy and performance. They will do anything to keep looking back at a sculpted form in the mirror. They are the ones I fear.

He crossed a leg and looked in judgment at the pair of drinks aligned before me. I removed the cocktail napkins from the mouths of each. I raised the Jameson and held his eyes as I knocked it back. I slammed the glass down on the table. He did not jump. Those blue eyes stared back over sharp cheekbones.

"What happened out there?" I asked.

He ignored the question and extended a bony hand. "We haven't had a proper introduction," he said. "I'm James Crowley."

I let the hand hang over the space between us. "I know who you are," I told him.

He lifted his offered hand higher and motioned for our waitress. She turned wary at the sight of him. "What an awful scene," she said. "I hope the gent's okay."

"Awful, indeed," said Crowley. He turned to me and asked, "Would you like anything else?"

"Another round of each."

"And I would like a nice big glass of ice water, if you'd be so kind," he said.

We watched her retreat to the bar. She was the shapely sort I would have spent all night and a dozen pints pining for, until I was too drunk to make a move. I made a mental note to return under more relaxed circumstances. Crowley eyed my empty glasses.

"I'm told you like to indulge," he said.

"And who told you that?"

"Your partner, Cassandra. She didn't mention that we knew each other? We became acquainted while Mr. Wingate worked on that book of his. Tragic what happened to him, isn't it? She didn't strike me as the type, but I suppose you never know what past traumas can bring out of a person."

I reached across the table and grabbed Crowley's wrist and gave it a quick turn, just enough for him to feel the pressure point. "I'll snap this arm in two if you don't cut the shit," I said.

I knew once again that the pain had to be intense, but Crowley was not a flincher. He looked back and waited until I released him as the waitress returned with our drinks. She'd seen enough to know not to interfere. She set our glasses before us with averted eyes. Crowley set both hands in his lap. His pint of ice water sweated before him.

"I'm aware that you are angry and confused, Mr. Darley," he said. "But I'm afraid I could use your help." He glanced outside to where Cass's lawyer had collapsed. His thin lips pressed together; his jaw clenched. "That was not supposed to happen out there. Many things were not supposed to happen. We are dealing with someone very dangerous, and very unwell."

"And what exactly happened?"

He sipped at his water, set it down precisely on the wet ring of the coaster, and re-crossed his legs. "You remember my associate, the young man you upset outside that bar?"

"Oliver, your partner's son. I understand you share the same racist tendencies."

"His *son*," he said, putting the second word in air quotes. "I'm surprised he told you that."

"Lipke insists he has nothing to hide. He showed me a photo of him and his boy on the beach. He appeared quite proud that Oliver took his last name."

"His 'boy,'" said Crowley. "There might be a better word for it."

"What are you trying to stay?"

Crowley sighed, seemed to consider how to begin, how much to share. "Oliver Lipke, previously Oliver Zesner, has not been a part of Eberhard's life for long, perhaps a year, less than two. Their relationship is rather unique, not what you would call 'parental.' They are uncommonly close. For reasons I have not been able to clarify. He feels a responsibility to the boy."

"And you? What's your relationship to this prince? Common interests of hate?"

He ignored my taunt. "He is a troubled young man, Mr. Darley. We've tried to help him, but the drugs appear to have taken over. Oliver is addicted to methamphetamine.

He has also been diagnosed as a paranoid schizophrenic. I fear he is off his medication. He's out of control. And he is particularly interested in hurting you. Your altercation humiliated him."

"What did he do to my lawyer out there?"

"One of his fighting tricks, it happened so quickly I can't be sure. He ran off. It seemed more prudent to remain at the scene and wait for you than to chase him and draw further attention." He shook his head, exhaled. "This was all meant to be a simple matter. As I'm sure you've noticed, we've been monitoring your whereabouts. But no one was supposed to be harmed. This was about Cassandra—I knew she would contact you after what happened to Mr. Wingate."

"So you sent in a hopped-up neo-Nazi to warn me?"

"Eberhard insisted that he accompany me. I did not think it was necessary. You could say our roles have switched since we arrived in the city. Oliver has done some work for us in the past, he had his value, but I've been trying to rein him in since we got here. Most of the time I don't know where he's been."

"Carl Kruger?" I asked. "Was that his handiwork?"

"May I attempt to clarify things?" he asked.

I took a gulp of the Harp, a nip of the Jamie. Sat back in the banquette, stretched an arm over the back. This I wanted to hear. "Go ahead. Is there anyone else from your Aryan Brotherhood that you've enlisted?"

"I understand you've spent some time in prison," he said. "That must be how you identified the numerology behind Oliver's tattoo."

"You have until I finish this drink to start explaining yourself." I took a swallow, set it back down. "As you know, I drink fast."

"Very well," he said. He shifted in his seat. "Your partner, Cassandra, came unhinged. She killed her lover, Victor

Wingate, and enlisted you to help her pin it on someone else, namely me. She knew that the suicide explanation would not hold up if they had a look at the body. It was clever that she refused to believe it. The grieving spouse in denial—she is clever, isn't she? Then she followed it with the execution of Carl Kruger, after she knocked you out. Again, with the intention to frame me, with your help."

"Why?" I asked.

"Indeed, why? That's always the most interesting question, isn't it?"

"This drink is getting pretty low, Doctor."

"He asks 'why,' the great question of the universe. Unanswerable, really, but there are a number of explanations. First, her relationship with Victor Wingate was coming to an end. It was not sustainable, the games they played. Poor Victor thought he'd discovered a kinky soul mate, when, in fact, he'd been lured by a black widow. I'm sure she enjoyed herself at first, strapping him to crosses and administering all manner of punishment under those high, beamed ceilings. But these things don't last, do they? One grows weary as a master, as I well know. That is how I met her."

"You spin a hell of a story, Doc."

"You don't wish to believe me, that's understandable," he said. "But I must ask, how well do you know your partner, really?"

"Better than you."

"No, Duck, you don't. Of that, I can assure you. Now, may I continue? Would you like to order another drink?"

"Talk."

"Very well. As I said, that's how I met your partner, in a role as a master. Cassandra liked to come back to the city on occasion, when she tired of playing house in the country, to attend a certain kind of gathering. Very discreet,

very well done, at a private home on the Upper East Side.
I'm sure you can infer the details."

"No," I said. "I can't. Tell me."

"Very well, they were S and M parties. An exclusive
scene, the owner of the home was very discriminating.
When we learned of her boyfriend's book in progress, and
how our clinic might be implicated, we had her followed.
Then I flew up to learn more. I assured Eberhard that I
might have an efficient means of getting to her. He was becoming panicked over this book. I was concerned as well,
for obvious reasons. And so I managed to secure an invita-
tion to attend one of these gatherings. It was an effective
place to make her acquaintance."

"Bullshit," I said. "You said these things were exclusive,
and oh-so-discriminating. Why would they let your out-
of-town ass in?"

"Because I could afford it." He shrugged. "And it also
happens that I have some experience in such worlds. It's a
rather small community, particularly at the higher end. I
was able to offer a suitable referral."

"So you were another slave looking for her attention.
Nice way to mix business and pleasure, or should I say
pain?"

"Quite contrary. I prefer the other side of the whip, as it
were. Your partner was tiring of Mr. Wingate. As you may
or may not know, many women who work professionally
on the dominant side of our lifestyle will often prefer the
submissive role in their private lives. So it was with Cassandra. Her relationship with Wingate had become an ex-
tension of her past work. Her visits to these parties were a
chance for your friend to indulge in the other side of her
nature. It was not Victor's inclination to play that role, but
I assure you, it is very much mine. We connected at once. I
admit, I went with a motive, on a fact-finding mission, but

her web really is quite sticky. I thoroughly enjoyed playing the master for her. At least for a time."

My mouth was dry and my drinks were gone. I raised my hand for refills, asked for water as well. Crowley spoke with such blunt confidence that I couldn't doubt him. The layers so carefully concealed by Cass were beginning to fall away.

"You're sweating," he said. "Are you okay? Would you like me to continue?"

"Go on." I lifted the empty pint and put it back down.

"Very well. I know this must be difficult to hear. As I mentioned, you don't know your partner as well as you thought. So, yes, I was pleased to play the role of her master at first. I knew it could become a conflict of interest. I was there for information, after all, not a sexual encounter. But we connected that night and I agreed to see her again. She was quite keen. After our sessions, she tended to open up. It's a common side effect. Our lifestyle can bring incredible release. She told me about this book her boyfriend was working on, just as I'd hoped. She was a wonderful source, and an even better lover, if you enjoy what we do."

"I don't know who's more full of it," I said. "You or Lipke. You think I buy this forthcoming, nothing-to-hide bullshit? Why are you feeding me all this crap?"

"Because, sir," he said, "my motivation is in saving myself. My partner's interests, and those of his unstable son, are no longer aligned with my own. Now, may I continue? There is more you should know."

"I'm listening," I said. "Not to say I'm believing, but let's hear the rest of it."

"Thank you. When I've finished, you are free to believe whatever you will. Now, as my affair with your friend continued, I think a part of her wanted to be caught. Despite our rather specialized tastes, it was all quite typical, I suppose. An overlapping romance, a soon-to-be jilted lover, but then Cassandra's cracks began to appear. I'm afraid your last case took its toll. She needs help. I think it broke her in some essential way. Severe trauma will do that to some. She began to exhibit erratic behavior, bursts of rage. She spoke of getting rid of Victor. I became concerned, and truth be told, I was tiring of her drama. I told her we needed to end it. I'd learned all I could from her. She did not take it well. A week later Victor was dead and I knew I was being set up. Her boyfriend had learned certain things about our practice that could be misconstrued in the press."

"You mean, like exposing some of the most famous athletes on earth as cheaters? I can see how that might be bad for business."

"That was Mr. Wingate's wish, but no, he would only be making false accusations, and we were prepared to sue for libel. We indicated as much, but he appeared eager to play the role of crusader. A false role that would have bankrupted him, but some gentlemen cannot be reasoned with."

"Even the whiff of scandal would have been bad for your biz as well, I'm guessing."

"Without question. Eberhard and I just wanted the story, this proposed book, to go away, for the good of all involved. But then things became more complicated. I am partly to blame, of course, due to my relationship with Cassandra. Now there is Oliver's behavior, a much greater problem, and one that Eberhard refuses to acknowledge. His addiction is worse than we thought—the meth, along with opioids, anything other than the antipsychotic drugs that he needs. He's beyond rational thought. He's going to kill you, Mr. Darley. You and maybe others too."

"I don't think you're a bit concerned with my safety or anyone else's. It sounds to me like you're just interested in saving your own ass."

"Interpret it however you like," he said. "But I think you'll see that our interests are now aligned. We both need to find Oliver before he hurts anyone else."

Crowley crossed his arms and let it all sink in. He wasn't lying and he knew that I knew it. At least about his relationship with Cass . . . but that did not make her a murderer. Pushing a lover off a cliff in a deranged rage—okay, I could maybe see that. But executing Carl Kruger like that, in such a personal, vicious way, after knocking me out? It couldn't be. What did Kruger have to do with her love triangle? That one had to be on Oliver—perhaps acting at the behest of his father, or whatever they were to each other.

"I know this is a lot to process," he said. "Kruger had become very close with Victor. He never trusted Cassandra. I think he knew a few things about the edge of madness, and he recognized it in her. He told his friend as much. When Victor died, she knew that Kruger would suspect her first. So she sent you to him. It gave her a lovely alibi."

"You're telling me that Cass sent me to talk to a man she intended to kill, about the guy she'd just killed? That's pretty clever."

"Let me ask, where was Cassandra that night, do you know?"

"Upstate," I said. "She dropped me off at the bus that afternoon and went back to deal with Wingate's crazy sister."

"When did you next speak to her?"

I considered the fallout after Kruger's murder. Waking on the barroom floor at dawn around a crowd of cops; the time spent being questioned at the 5th Precinct; Detective Miller driving me home; drinking until I passed out on the couch; waking late in the night and getting the call from Cass. How long had it been between Kruger's death and her call? Around twenty-four hours, and where was she in that gap of a day? I remembered her lack of surprise when I told her. *"It's all over the news,"* she said. I couldn't remember Cass ever glancing at the news.

I needed to banish this line of thought.

Crowley was examining me like a patient. There appeared to be a glint of sympathy in his eyes as he delivered his unwelcome diagnosis. "We tried to warn you," he said. "Before you left to see her on that bus."

" 'Some things, they're not worth it,' I believe that's what Oliver told me. And then when I returned home, I found that graffiti sprayed on my front door, the same as the tattoo on his knuckles. As you noted, I've done time. I know what that means."

"It was a mistake for him to join me. I blame my partner, who thinks he can control him."

"Were you aware that your partner sent a letter threatening an eight-year-old boy?"

" 'Letter'?" he asked. "I'm afraid I don't know what you're talking about."

I looked at him over a gulp of lager. Wiped my mouth and kept on looking. He never blinked. "You're a hell of a liar, Doc. I'll grant you that."

"I think you know I've been very open with you. I've not heard of any letter."

"A close friend received a note that threatened her son," I said. "Typed, no prints, but no matter, I know it was Lipke, and I'm going to prove it. You get one chance at some mercy on this. Are you telling me this is the first you've heard of that?"

"I have no idea," he said. He spoke the words with conviction. Like the rest of what he'd told me, it was difficult not to believe him.

Crowley sat back and clasped his fingers in his lap, his thin mouth turned down. "When people you love let you down, it can be one of life's most difficult experiences. Though I think you know all about that, don't you?"

I didn't reply. I finished off the beer and stood up. Slid out of my seat, still holding the glass. "Thanks for the drinks," I said over him.

Then I raised the pint and brought it down hard on the back of his blond head.

Chapter 29

I left Crowley sprawled on a table of blood and glass. Left him there with a six-drink tab and a head wound, and maybe something to think about. It was impolite to be quite so honest with one's cruelty.

The daylight was blinding, a slap to the senses. I waved down a passing cab with a shaky forearm. The ginger waitress and her manager came out after me as I climbed into the back and told him to drive. Without considering my destination, I called out East Broadway and Canal, the cross streets of Kruger's bar on the Lower East Side. Before I visited Cass in Rikers, I needed to retrace the scene with new eyes. I needed to talk to Uli. Their affection for one another had been evident. Cass's lawyer might be dead, and if there was truth to Crowley's claims, she could be going away for life.

I thought about trying Juliette again. Decided she wouldn't like what I had to say: My partner, the woman who set all this in motion, was now a presumed killer. The guy who sent that letter was an insidious doping doctor, with a meth-head adopted son on a rampage. I had nothing positive to report, nothing that could set her rich, worried mind at ease. Better to keep Juliette ensconced with that crew of

Warrior Security. Instead I tried Detective Miller. This time she picked up.

"You may want to check out an assault and a suspicious heart attack at a Midtown pub called the Wheeltapper," I told her.

"Where are you?" she asked.

"Did you hear me? I'm reporting a crime, I thought cops were supposed to care about that sort of thing."

"I heard you fine, Duck. Where are you?"

I gazed out the window as the cab turned toward the FDR. We inched past the United Nations complex with its expanse of white marble along the south façade. I thought of all the earnest peacekeepers inside, all the delusions of democracy and cooperation preached in there. So far removed from folks like Carl Kruger, another victim of Cold War nonsense. A soldier in a tracksuit juiced for nationalist glory; defected; changed genders; embraced American dreams; and was killed with the instrument of his success. He was one of the doomed. Marked for strife until his number came up, too soon, and ended a difficult life.

The East River waterfront was an ugly blight of barges and cranes. The speed of the tide flowing north always surprised. Across the gray water was the developing skyline of Long Island City and Greenpoint. The traffic loosened and picked up as we passed the Midtown Tunnel exit and continued south.

"You there?" asked Miller.

"I'm on the FDR," I said. "Back in town and causing trouble."

"I suggest you go back to your apartment and stay there," she said.

"I just had an interesting conversation with a Dr. James Crowley, that name ring any bells?"

She paused, enough to indicate her surprise. "Listen,

Duck, I can't talk right now, but I strongly urge you to stop whatever it is you're doing and go home."

"I can't do that, Lea."

"Duck . . ."

I hung up wondering why I bothered to call in the first place. Did I want Crowley to report my assault so I could join Cass inside? My violence was as illegal, as unprovoked, as the lawyer's curbside attack. I wondered what Oliver had done to him. Maybe pressed a Taser to his chest, maybe a quick strike to the trachea. There was any number of ways to incapacitate an out-of-shape overstressed New Yorker. I knew a few of them. Oliver had been tracking me since Cass first called, even after he shed his boss. I doubted Crowley knew about his knife-to-the-throat warning inside that darkened theater. Much as I hated to acknowledge it, Crowley had shared facts, at least as he believed them. I knew with a certainty that the love triangle he described was accurate. Cass wanted to rid herself of Wingate, and Crowley was sick of the unstable lady that wanted him. He'd already learned enough from her.

Or perhaps another scenario, one with pieces that fit more cleanly into the emerging puzzle: Crowley and Cass were together when Wingate went over that waterfall. They'd been partners in the crime. He wasn't sick of her at all. They were united in their desire to eliminate the unwanted third side of the triangle. He'd turned her, convinced her to help him in the suppression of that book. Crowley had been present when she called me for "help." Indeed he'd been given instructions on where I could be found, when to approach. But then something shifted between them. Another murder had been necessary. I had been spared. And while I lay unconscious, someone had gone to Carl Kruger and executed him, driven his spear through his throat and watched the blood drain from his body and stain his barroom floor.

The cab let me off in front. KRUGER'S glowed in neon over the entrance. Back open for business and scrubbed clean, that was where I found Uli Kruger at work behind the bar, slinging drinks. A widow needed to eat. She glanced sideways as I entered and eyed me as I found a stool in the corner.

The life of the bar hummed on a low, boozy frequency. The only thing different about the space was the missing javelin hanging over the bottles. The room did not hang its head in mourning for its fallen proprietor. The city cannot afford to pause for every death. There is rent to pay.

It was the same eclectic mix of patrons, a diverse crew of Asians, blacks, and whites collected in shared union around their chosen sacrament. They sipped from their pints and their spirits with murmurs of conversation. Early Tom Petty, "Here Comes My Girl," played from unseen speakers.

Rest in peace, Tommy boy, you were one of the kings. Drinking music, if I ever heard any. I lifted a finger toward Uli, waited for her to make her way over. Decided to stick with the day's double: another pint of lager, another hit of the Jamie. As many as it took, until I got some answers or collapsed drunk. Both, I hoped.

Uli took her time about it. When she approached, she offered no acknowledgment, just nodded at my order and turned to pour. When she set them before me, she lingered and asked, "How's your head?"

"Just fine," I said. "How you holding up?"

She gave a shrug.

The space may have looked the same to every regular, but to the widowed owner it had become a tomb. Each day she was forced to walk over the spot where her husband was slaughtered.

"We didn't have much savings," she said. "I have no choice but to stay open."

"They've arrested Cass," I said.

"I know."

"She couldn't have done this. I don't believe it."

"I do."

"Why? You sounded like friends? How could she kill Carl?"

She suppressed a shudder at the *K*-word. Then she looked back at her customers lining the bar. Noticed a few half-empty glasses. "I must get back to work," she said.

So I stayed. Drank slowly through the afternoon, getting more two-word answers to my questions each time she served my refills. I felt myself reaching a zone where drunkenness was impossible. I could mainline the whiskey and my brain would continue to function on its same fuzzy frequency until morning. There are times when successive drinks cease to matter. It's like the accumulation of snow in a blizzard: Does it really make a difference whether it's fifteen inches or twenty in the end? Either way you'll be crippled for most of the next day.

The bar emptied a little before five. She could expect another swell in the happy hours, but for now Uli Kruger had just one customer to serve: a surly pseudo investigator a dozen drinks in.

"Alone at last," I said.

She came and topped off my Jamie without asking. Poured one for her. *"Prost,"* she said.

We knocked them back, set down the glasses, and looked at one other. She was a fine-looking woman whose size disguised her beauty. Her almond-shaped eyes were almost Asian in their lines. Her mouth was wide and full, with plump natural lips, the kind that ridiculous women on the Upper East Side pay for, only to look in perpetual need of Benadryl. Her skin, even in mourning, was flawless. She wore the same loose frock as before. It covered a thick, powerful body. Once a swimmer, always a swimmer, there was no mistaking her.

"I used to swim too, you know?"

It was the first thing I'd said that seemed to interest her.

"Where did you grow up?"

"Right here."

"They have teams here in the city?" she asked. "I would not think—"

"Ever hear of Charlie McKay?"

"Ah, of course, I'm sorry. I know about him, and all that happened. I'm sorry, my mind has not been working so well since Carl . . ."

"What was your stroke?" I asked.

"Butterfly," she said.

"Nice. Same here. Though you were probably faster than I was."

She gave a faint smile without pride. "Well, we had some help in those days. The drugs worked well."

"It's not like you asked for it."

She poured us another shot, raised hers, and knocked it back.

"Not many appreciate that," she said after a wince. "They think we were all evil cheaters."

"Were you given a choice?"

She shook her head. "Of course not. If we refused, terrible things would happen. Not only to us, to our families as well."

"So you have nothing to apologize for."

"We are all atoning for something, I think."

"Guilt doesn't get anyone anywhere," I said.

She poured us another round and this time we sipped it

slow. I kept stealing glances at her blue almond eyes. She didn't look away. When she leaned forward against the bar, I caught a glimpse of the bra beneath her frock. It was a simple number, no lace or leather, but the sight of it stirred my thoughts.

After a stretch of silence Uli met my gaze and said, "You're a good man, aren't you, Duck?"

I had nothing for that. So I excused myself and moved to the bathroom. The floor rose and fell as if I was on a ship in high seas. I steadied myself on passing chairs, lurched the rest of the way, and acknowledged that perhaps the drinks were having their desired effect after all. When I was locked inside the men's room, I took a look in the dirty mirror. Remembered what happened the last time I was in this room. A killer hid in wait outside the door. Waited for me to emerge, hit me over the head, and went to Carl. It happened just like this, alone in the bar with the owner, after too many rounds for clear thought, much less decisive action. When I finished, I looked back in the mirror, splashed water on my face until my eyes came back into focus. I opened the door and jumped at the sight of her.

Uli was leaning against the wall across from me. I thought for a moment that she was waiting to go next, but the ladies' room was open next door. She stepped forward without expression. I moved aside and let her enter the room and watched as she locked the door behind her. Together we filled the small space to capacity. Wordless, she draped her arms around my neck and kissed me. Her strong hands moved down my back as she pressed her body against mine. She moved with a hunger it would have been rude to deny. Then she broke the kiss, let go, and turned her back to me. She hiked up her dress and bent over the sink. Let out a low growl. I did not need to be told twice.

Jeans were dropped, underwear pulled aside, and then I was inside her. I held her hips as she pressed back into me.

Watched as her hands clutched either side of the sink until her knuckles turned white. Dispensed of any building rhythm and took her as hard and as fast as she required. She felt me building and thickening and rocked back in time with my thrusts. We both looked into the mirror at the same moment. Stared into each other's reflected eyes as I let out a cry and came deep inside her.

We panted against each other until I slipped out. She tore a strip of toilet paper from the roll and wiped herself off. Then she hiked up her underwear, smoothed her dress, and offered a parting kiss.

"I'll get us another drink, yes?" she asked.

I nodded and she let herself out.

I looked back in the mirror, sober as can be.

Chapter 30

The bar began to fill soon after we emerged. Uli put on Klaus Nomi again, turning it loud without her fallen husband to object. A song called "Total Eclipse," which fit the mood. I watched her move with a freshly fucked air that I could be proud of. It meant nothing and everything. I told myself I helped ease a widow's pain. I told myself a lot of things.

Uli kept my glasses full and delivered each refill with a wink. If anyone knew of her recent loss, her spirits wouldn't seem right. But I knew better. I'd only offered temporary reprieve. The crash tomorrow would be even darker than before. I wanted her to myself again, couldn't wait for the bar to empty. I kept willing customers to drink up and get lost. Around ten there was another lull. I watched a tattooed couple leave, hand in hand, and then it was just the two of us again. Uli tapped at her phone with a frown, then set it down and approached with a look I couldn't quite read. Another purging romp bent over the bathroom sink perhaps? No, it wasn't that kind of look. She glanced at the remains of my latest lager.

"Finish up," she said. "We're closing early tonight, there's something I want to show you."

I swallowed it down, knew better than to ask. She settled

the register, checked the back, and turned off the lights. The Nomi was the last to go; "Valentine's Day" played in the fluorescent darkness as she gathered her purse and said, "Shall we?"

I was lingering on the sidewalk as she locked the front when a pack of drunken hipsters approached.

"Sorry, boys," she said. "We're closed."

"It's only, like, ten o'clock?" slurred one.

"This is bullshit," said the biggest of the bunch. "I know Carl, lemme talk to him."

I moved between them, a little too eager for confrontation. "He's not here, tough guy. You'll have to find somewhere else to drink."

He stepped into my chest, snorted like a provoked bull. His eyes were high and wide and glassy. One nostril held the remains of telltale whiteness. He sniffed and wiped at his nose. "The fuck are you?" he asked. "Carl owns this place."

I'd had enough booze and sex and violence over the last twelve hours that my impulse control was nonexistent. Another sniffle from this cokehead and I was ready to break both his arms, and then take on his buddies. Uli placed a hand on my shoulder.

"Carl was my husband," she said. "He died. Now please leave us be."

That took the fire out of the moment. They muttered their apologies and moved off down the sidewalk with bowed heads.

"Fucking hell, Duck, really?"

"Sorry," I said like a scolded schoolboy.

She stalked off to Canal Street. I followed. Three blocks west she turned right on Orchard without looking back. It was a warm, moonless night and the Chinatown markets gave off a rank stench. Interspersed with the old tenements and the faded signs of Chinese characters was new construction that announced the future of the neighborhood. It was one of the last frontiers of almost-affordable Manhattan, but it wouldn't be long. Buildings were being bought and gutted, or torn down—and in their place were new, sleek condos with all the conveniences a banker could want. It was a short cab ride over to the Financial District, an easy commute. The bars announced the transformation. Bars designed for white collars, playacting at Downtown cool; for prep school grads pretending they were on the edge of something long blunted to cliché. In time the leases would run out on those Chinese markets and dumpling shops and appliance stores, and the landlords—sons and daughters of families that went back generations in the neighborhood—wouldn't be able to resist any longer. It was time to cash out and welcome the Duane Reade drugstores and the Chase banks like every other pocket of the city.

Uli was waiting halfway down Orchard, under a blue sign that read SUCCESS and beneath it HOSIERY FOR MEN-LADIES-KIDS. Upon closer inspection, I saw it was an antiseptic art gallery, where someone's unsuccessful hosiery business had once been. The sign left up in the name of irony perhaps.

"You can't help yourself, can you?" asked Uli.

"What?"

"Back there," she said. "Was that necessary?"

"Nothing ever is."

Uli made a face. "Who finds that nihilism charming?"

"I don't know how you deal with those people behind the bar," I said. "I'd lose it having to be nice to coked-up dicks all the time."

"They pay my bills," she said. "And thanks to you, I've just lost four regulars."

"I'm sorry. I promise to come back and drink for four."

That got a smile at least. "I don't know how Cassandra put up with you." She approached a red door sprayed with graffiti, wedged between a new coffee shop and a Chinese trading market with a FOR RENT sign in the window.

"Have you ever been here before?" she asked.

"Don't think so."

"I thought not."

She unlocked the front and walked us into a dim, narrow hallway. One light flickered by the stairs, the rest were burned out. "It's at the end of the hall," she said over her shoulder.

The building was still holding on to its slum past. There was little regard for the tenants in the shared interior spaces. The hall smelled of weed and stir-fry and sweat. The floors were faded green linoleum, worn down by decades of shuffling feet. Uli stopped by the last door on the left and found the key. "It's helpful to have a space on the first floor," she said. "Less eyes on the comings and goings."

She turned the key in the lock and we stepped inside. The space was cramped and claustrophobic in the gray darkness. There was a galley kitchen with a bathroom to its left and a tiny living area on the right, furnished with a black futon, walnut coffee table, and no television. Despite its modest size the place was meticulous. Every surface clean, no clutter anywhere. On the only wall space wide enough for art, there was a framed print by Gustav Klimt. *Judith and the Head of Holofernes*—the beautiful femme fatale holding a severed head . . . I knew at once whose apartment it was. I once imagined Hieronymus Bosch or Albrecht Dürer on her walls, but I should have known it would be this Klimt. Uli saw me looking.

"She loved that work, obsessed you could say."

"Not surprised."

"So you know whose place this is, yes?"

"Cass."

"An illegal sublet, technically. Her name is not on the lease, which is why it wasn't searched, but yes, it has been hers for some time. She never brought you here, did she?"

"Never."

"Come," said Uli. "Let me show you the rest."

She produced another key and went to a locked door next to the futon. It opened onto a darkened room, the windows covered with blackout shades. Across the back of the door black foam egg crates were pinned up to absorb the noise. Uli turned on a standing lamp in the corner and let me take in the furnishings without comment.

It was a small, impeccably outfitted dungeon. Along one side was a high massage table in black. Across from it was an assortment of whips and straps and torturous toys hanging from hooks. On the wall next to the door, there was a Saint Andrew's Cross. Restraints hung from each end of the X. In another corner a leather-padded high-backed chair, also outfitted with restraints. The floor was painted crimson, and it looked clean enough to eat off. Every other surface was black.

Uli crossed the room, took a seat in the chair, and crossed her legs. "What do you think?" she asked.

"Did she live here?"

She nodded. "For a time. This was the bedroom at first, before she transformed it. When Cassandra moved upstate, she kept it and rented it out. A sort of Airbnb for the kinky set." Uli sat back and gazed around the room, familiar in the surroundings. "The four of us loved this room."

"You and Carl?"

"And she and Victor. We shared similar tastes."

"Where did she sleep?" It seemed important as I took in this private space of my former partner.

"On the futon, I presume. Cassandra seldom slept. Didn't sleep, didn't eat, she really is a sort of vampire, isn't she?"

"You think she killed them, don't you?"

Uli ignored the question. "Sit," she said. "Let's chat. You look so troubled, poor boy."

I walked to the massage table, though I couldn't imagine much massaging went on atop it. I tried not to consider the acts that had been performed here. No wonder the space was immaculate. As I sat upon it, my legs dangled over, not touching the ground. I felt like a boy indeed. A drunken boy out of my depth and reeling with revisions of the past . . . Across the room on the hooks I noted a selection of strap-ons in various sizes and colors. I squirmed at the thought. In our past conversations about Cass's slaves, it had all existed in absurd abstraction. She hadn't been shy about mentioning the diaper training or the pegging or the whippings administered on the cross. I just chose never to comprehend its reality. I never imagined she had her own personal dungeon at home, in addition to the work she did at the Chamber.

"I never knew her at all," I said.

"Oh, don't be dramatic. She spoke of you. I know she cared for you very much."

"I know nothing about her." It was true. "She knew everything about me, but she never let me see any of this, or anything else."

"That's the way she is," said Uli. "Cassandra is a private person. Particularly when it comes to people who do not share her tastes. But that does not discount what you shared together, or what you both went through."

"How much do you know?"

"Quite a bit, I'm afraid. We became very close, very quickly. She shared your history, your relationship, one late night."

Uli uncrossed her legs, pulled up her dress past her knees.

She lingered with parted thighs before crossing the other leg. I couldn't tell if the gesture was for my benefit. Under the circumstances I couldn't be sure of anything. "Your last case," she said. "It took a difficult toll."

"You could say that."

"I'm sorry. It sounds horrible."

I didn't care to recall the horrors. I'd learn to recognize the simmering spikes of PTSD, the dissociative trauma, the flashbacks lingering at the fringes of my subconscious. I tried to push it away, focused on the subject at hand.

"Victor and Carl, they were your slaves?" I asked.

"No, they were our spouses, our partners. We were all lucky to find mates who shared similar desires. But in here"—she gave a wicked smile—"yes, you could say that Cass and I were in charge."

I remembered Crowley's account, how he'd met Cass in similar environs. "I heard she liked to switch roles on occasion."

"Oh, really? And whom did you hear that from?"

"From her latest master," I said.

"*Her* master? What was his name?"

"James," I said, watching her reaction.

Uli sat up straighter. She recognized it.

"And his last?" she asked.

I shrugged. "You tell me."

She stood and stepped toward me. The room seemed to shrink; she seemed to grow. When she was standing over me, she reached out, held my chin in her hand, and leaned in to make close eye contact. "This is no place to be coy," she said.

"I don't know," I lied. "Honestly."

She held the stern pose until I pulled back, rattled by the shifting dynamic. She gave a strange smile and let go, patted my cheek. "Dear boy," she said. "I see what Cassandra saw in you."

"And what's that?"

"Damaged, untamed, so angry, such a challenge." She turned and went back to her chair.

"You know who I'm talking about, don't you?" I asked. "Your look said so."

"Afraid not, love. You fancy yourself quite the perceptive investigator, don't you?"

"Just an observation. I've been known to be wrong."

Again she uncrossed her legs, paused, and crossed the other. Her eyes never leaving mine.

"What happened between the four of you?" I asked.

She gazed around the room, scanning all the implements of pain and pleasure. Her eyes settled upon a long black flogger. She sighed, said, "We were so close, for a short time, but so close. What happened was our boys' book project, launched the night Mickey Knight made the introduction. The three of them were thick as thieves, so pleased with themselves. After that, Cassandra and Victor would come down from the mountains to see us. We would take turns playing here and then return to the bar, where Carl and Victor would talk and drink and plot their story, while Cassandra and I would chat and indulge our men. Then Victor wrote a proposal and began to search for a publisher. Carl was thrilled. I was surprised he was so eager to share his story with the world. I thought he had more dignity than that, but I was mistaken. At first, Cassandra was happy for them. She loved seeing Victor so inspired. It's an attractive quality, inspiration. I understand he'd written another book once, years ago, but that he had not worked for some time. I think Cassandra liked being his muse. Though that changed."

"Why?"

"Perhaps it has something to do with this other gentleman you've referred to?"

"Dr. James Crowley," I said, done with the games.

Uli gave a sad smile. "Ah, yes."

"You knew him. You knew about their affair."

"I knew," she said. "It is not so unusual in our world. Many times even the most committed mistress will tire of all the control, all the responsibility, and we long to submit. I think Cassandra was also feeling a little bit neglected. Victor was an obsessive person. For a time he was obsessed with Cassandra, and she liked that. But then this story took over, writing the book became his new obsession. Combine that feeling of neglect with a growing desire to let go and submit to someone else's control. Those on the outside may not understand, but it very much made sense to me. I didn't approve, I knew it meant the end of our foursome, but I understood."

"She told you?"

"She did."

"That doesn't mean she'd kill him," I said. "And why would she have any motive to kill your husband?"

Uli waved her hand around the room. "Do you see all this?" she asked. "It is fantasy, yes? A harmless means of release, a form of satisfying therapy for most. We are all attracted to it for different reasons, but there are those drawn to its darker side. Some are true sadists, sociopaths. Others begin innocently, and change. Years of inflicting pain can desensitize some, especially those working through fresh trauma."

"So you think Cass cracked? You think she got rid of her slave boyfriend and then went after Carl? Why?"

"Because he knew," she said. "He knew she was cheating on his friend. When Victor died, Carl instantly suspected her. He never warmed to her, even when the four of us were playing family. But when he learned she was with this Dr. Crowley of all people, then she was dead to him. You understand who Crowley is, don't you?"

"The doping doctor. Dr. Lipke's partner at their clinic in Miami."

"The boy has done his homework," she said. "Yes, Dr. Eberhard Lipke, our former doctor in Leipzig. He treated both Carl and myself, when we were young athletes in the DDR."

"You knew each other back then?"

"Not well, but yes. I was a few years younger. We were both a part of the system, among the guinea pigs. We were in different sports, so there was not much contact, but we all dealt with Dr. Lipke. He was the scientist responsible for all those gold medals."

"And all the side effects that came later."

"Yes, those too."

"So, when Cass took up with Lipke's partner . . ."

"My husband was outraged. It was unforgivable, a betrayal of the worst sort. He was going to tell Victor. I don't know if he ever had the chance. We heard of his death soon after, and then you came to see us at the bar the night that Carl was killed."

"Have you ever crossed paths with Lipke's son?" I asked. "Name's Oliver. I understand he adopted him, somewhat recently. I had the displeasure of meeting him."

Uli gave me a quick look. Then she blinked, looked away for the first time. "No," she said. "I wasn't aware he had a son."

She couldn't look back at me.

"He works for both of them," I said. "A neo-Nazi scumbag who seems to be at the center of all this. I think *he* killed your husband, not Cass."

She shook her head. "I think you drink too much. You have crazy ideas. A neo-Nazi? No, I do not believe that."

"Seems Crowley has some bigoted tendencies himself," I said. "Maybe Lipke too."

"Duck, we are both friends with Cassandra, yeah? Do

you really think she would associate with someone like that?"

"Maybe she didn't know that side of him," I said. "She was skilled at keeping certain sides of herself hidden. Maybe Crowley was the same way."

I couldn't be confident of what fit and what didn't, but I was sure that Cass had lied to me when she first called. Used me to establish her alibi. Played me like a pawn as she pretended to help with my investigation. I wondered what might have happened if she'd made it through security at LaGuardia that day. What if we'd flown to Miami together and gone to see Lipke? Was she setting me up for a fall as well? All betrayals that couldn't yet be processed, but what I couldn't shake was what she failed to do before all this.

She never got in touch, after our last case together, when we barely escaped with our lives and maybe not our sanity. She fled upstate. Claimed she stayed there, in love in the mountains. When, in fact, she had been returning to her dungeon lair, renting it out to others in the scene, enjoying double dates with a like-minded kinky couple at their bar down the street. While I was a five-minute cab away . . . never a word from someone I once considered my closest friend. We took bullets for each other, almost died for one another. I was never anything more than an amusement to her. And when it got too hot and too real, when the pain and the blood was no longer a game, she was gone.

"Dear boy, look at you," said Uli. "You look shattered. Come here."

I slid from the table and crossed the room to her. She opened her arms and I sat on her lap like a troubled child.

"She took my Carl too. I will never forgive her either. But it's over now. She's going to pay for her crimes."

"But there's still this Oliver character," I said. "You're

sure you've never heard of him? Dr. Lipke claimed him, proudly, showed me a picture of them together. Then Crowley put that word 'son' in quotes. He said it wasn't the way it sounded. I just can't believe that Cass would—"

"*Shhh,*" she said. "Enough for now. In the morning, with a clear head, I'm sure it will make more sense."

Uli wrapped her arms around me, pulled me close, and stroked the back of my head. I burrowed my face, breathed her scent. Felt her sigh beneath me. Then my lips found her neck as her hands slipped under my shirt. I raised my face to kiss her, but she stopped me.

"Let Uli take care of you now," she said.

I nodded in submission.

Let her do her worst.

Chapter 31

I escaped with my dignity, barely. I limped home through the Lower East Side and up the Bowery, eschewing lit cabs. I needed to walk it off. The warm spring night brought out the drinkers in happy droves. The bars were full, and in front of each, smokers smoked and spoke too loud next to ignored signs about respecting the neighbors upstairs. I felt no urge to enter any of them.

I thought of dungeons and jails and violations. I remembered my time spent inside Rikers as a young felon, locked away for dealing weed, the horrors I'd endured. I considered Cass there. My former island of incarceration was her new home. I wondered if her lawyer was still alive. Cass, so secretive, so dishonest with one true friend, and now there she was, up on double-murder charges with no lawyer, no one left to help her. It was cruel to feel a streak of schadenfreude, but I believed Uli, and Crowley too, maybe even Lipke. I was a cuckold that never even had the pleasure of consummation.

For so long I'd accepted her secrecy, romanticized it even. Plenty of relationships are one-sided, and those protective of their privacy always maintain an upper hand. I'd submitted to that dynamic from the beginning. My questions were brushed aside until I stopped asking; her questions were answered in waves of words and revelations about my past. I shared it all because I needed someone to talk to about it. She was my therapy. I presumed myself to be a lot more interesting than I was. Everyone has a past. Almost everyone thinks his or hers is more fascinating than the next. I was sure of it. I'd experienced the heights of wealth; parental betrayal and heartbreak; lost it all; done hard time; come out a badass. I had stories to tell. And Cass listened to them. I told myself I was respecting her privacy by not doing the same. Fool, arrogant fool, I had been another of her slaves. I was too blind to see it. It wasn't sexual, not in the way I longed for, but she held a power over me that I could not resist.

She still did. The moment I arrived home I looked up the visitation schedule at Rikers women's prison.

There were no visits permitted on Mondays or Tuesdays. On Wednesdays and Thursdays you could see inmates from one p.m. to nine p.m. On Fridays, Saturdays, and Sundays the visiting hours were from eight a.m. to four p.m. I had vowed never to set foot on that island again. Suicide sounded better. I tried to repress most of it. I couldn't remember if anyone had visited me there. My father was locked away in a prison in North Carolina; my mom drank herself to death a few years earlier. Were there friends from that era who cared enough to come say hello? There must have been, but I couldn't remember a single one.

It was Friday evening, approaching midnight. I could be there in eight hours. But first my body was demanding recovery. I couldn't begin to tally the drinks I consumed. Didn't want to. After this was over maybe I'd go back on the wine-and-weed wagon that worked so well in my time with Juliette Cohen. But not yet, my mind was anything but limber.

I poured myself a nightcap. Savored the sweet bourbon burn. Plugged in my dead phone and took my beverage with me to bed, set it on my nightstand, where a healthy man's water might have gone. I picked up the Nick Tosches again, *Me and the Devil*. More dark visions, more indictments of what this city had become. I set it on my chest after a page or two. Sleep came quick. I was treated to another drowning dream, a recurring favorite. I'm in a swimming pool surrounded by fellow swimmers. Naked, able bodies are nearby. Anyone could reach out to help, but no one does. I try to take a stroke, turn my head for a breath. I can't. I'm paralyzed. I sink under, beneath bodies doing blithe laps above. Strong limbs and ripped torsos, blind to my struggles, the applause of splashing. I panic as I reach the bottom, silent and helpless. If I'm lucky, that's when I wake. If not, the nightmare really begins. I black out and the demons invade, taking me down farther. The pool bottom melts away. I'm pulled into a dark, wet earth, toward something I identify as hell, but can never see. It's only blackness and the shrill screams of demons all around.

A restful sleep it was not. I woke at seven, with the deserved headache and dry mouth, and a subconscious terror that the dream was an all-too-real future. I made it to the bathroom in a sweat, gulped water from the tap, and then stood under the shower until I drained every drop of heat from the pipes. Coffee, Advil, the usual morning Band-Aids, they weren't helpful. So I cracked a Beck's and sucked it down. I started to feel better after the second one.

It's only ten miles to Rikers Island from Union Square, but few New Yorkers could find it on a map. It sits at the mouth of the East River, next door to LaGuardia Airport. Technically a part of Queens, it's separated from the free world by a mile-long bridge. For those dreaming of the shortest escape route, it's less than a hundred-yard swim from the eastern edge of Rikers to LaGuardia's nearest runway. I spent many days in solitary thinking of what I'd do when I made it across that strait. Maybe run unseen across the tarmac and stow away in the luggage belly of a departing plane. . . . Get lucky and find it was a flight to the Caribbean, where I'd manage to sneak off to the nearest beach and run into those turquoise waters and swim away. Then I'd emerge near some fine resort and find work as a bartender, where I'd screw visiting cougars after pouring them rounds of strong mai tais. Such are the thoughts that get young men through time inside.

The fear was coming back stronger than expected as we passed the welcome sign before the bridge. It was burned into memory: RIKERS ISLAND, HOME OF NEW YORK'S BOLDEST. I always wondered about that last adjective. It seemed such an odd, mocking choice: *Bring me your bold convicted masses. We'll beat that boldness right out of them.*

Then we were traveling over the East River to the land of the unwanted. The water below was the color of slate. It hardly rippled in the windless morning haze. A hot day ahead, promises of the suffocations of summer. At the center of the island the prison complex sat like a joyless fortress. My old Haitian cabbie let me off in front of the Benjamin Ward Visit Center. The fare was forty-five dollars; I gave him sixty out of appreciation for not asking about my destination. He took the bills with a nod, drove off as soon as I closed the door. I wondered if Lyft did pickups out here.

Visitation schedules were divided according to inmates' last names, *A–L* one day, *M–Z* the next. Fortunately, today was the *A–L* turn, so Cassandra Kimball could accept visitors. She was being housed in the Rose M. Singer Center. How did one earn the honor of having a jail named after oneself? I pictured Benjamin Ward and Rose Singer as a pair of sadistic wardens that ruled for decades over these doomed masses. And when they died and the city pushed through more funding for upgrades, their names could live on in eternity over new centers that housed new generations of criminals. Or maybe Ben and Rose were lovely people, full of empathy and forgiveness for these lost souls. I doubted that. I'd done my time. The captors were more dangerous than the captives.

While I waited, I remembered the alternate reality of time inside. It didn't just pass slowly; it stagnated. The red arm of the clock seemed to stop flowing at times, or even circled counterclockwise. You soon learned to stop watching it. I slumped in a steel chair and stared at my phone. There was nothing from Detective Miller, nothing from Juliette Cohen. They wanted me out of their lives. I brought little but pain and suffering and danger.

"Lawrence Darley?" called a female guard. "To see Cassandra Kimball?"

I leapt up. The prospect of seeing her stripped away all self-pity. I was escorted onto a shuttle bus with the other morning visitors, mostly black and Latino moms with children in tow. I found a seat up front next to a large Latina with fresh ink covering fleshy arms.

"Where you headed?" she asked.

"Rose Singer Center? The women's jail."

"Rosie's, yeah, I been there, few years back." She shook her hair extensions at the memory. "These boys like to think they're all hard, up in here, but I tell you what, there some ladies over in Rosie's meaner than any dude in any of these hotels."

"What were you in for?"

"Some bullshit, the ex had a bunch of coke at our place, couple keys. I didn't even know about it, not that it mattered when they came crashing in. Carlos wasn't even there and guess who took the fall?"

Yeah, I'd seen that movie. Another conviction that solved nothing; punished the almost innocent.

"I did thirteen months here myself," I told her.

She raised an eyebrow. "You? What'd you do?"

"Used to deal some weed," I said.

"I feel you, yeah, I knew plenty of dudes went down for that bullshit. Little over a year, huh?"

It didn't seem like much, unless you'd done it. She had, and she knew what it meant for someone who looked like I did. "Bad times, weren't they?"

"Spent most of it in solitary," I said. "But not enough."

"Shit's fucked up when you'd rather be locked down in a hole, ain't it?"

I nodded, fought off the flash of repressed memory.

"So, who you going to see? Girlfriend got busted or something?"

"Something like that."

The shuttle bus pulled to a stop and the driver called out the Rose M. Singer Center. Stepping off, it occurred to me that I had more in common with these fine, suffering folks than the Juliette Cohens of the world, despite my delusions of still belonging to my original caste.

Inside Rosie's I was escorted into a brightly lit visitors' room with prisoners slouched before their spouses or lawyers or other loved ones. Guards stood watch around the perimeter, looking bored. The chair across from mine was empty. A few moments later a line of orange-clad women came shuffling out of a cellblock door. I saw Cass before she saw me. It was the first time the sight of her didn't produce a sexual pang. She saw me and tried to smile.

Sitting down, she said, "Well, orange will definitely never be the new black."

We frowned at each other, unable to break the ice.

"It's good to see you, Duck," she said at length.

"You too."

"Can you believe this shit?" she asked. "Eddie says he'll have me out soon."

"When's the last time you spoke with Lutelman?"

"Couple days ago, why?"

"He was attacked yesterday," I said. "I saw him wheeled into an ambulance."

"What? Is he gonna be okay?"

"Dunno. They were trying to get his heart restarted."

"You were there? Where, Duck? You gotta fill me in here."

"So do you, Cass."

"I don't know what that's supposed to mean, but could you please tell me what's happened to Eddie? If my lawyer is dead, that is going to be a serious problem."

"I was supposed to meet him," I said. "I contacted him after I got back from Miami. I figured you would have been in touch. He agreed to meet at the bar downstairs from his office."

I studied her face.

"And then?" she asked, impatient.

"And then someone attacked Lutelman outside the bar while I waited inside. Seems to be the same guy who's been creating havoc since you called. When I went out to see what was going on, Dr. James Crowley approached me in the crowd. You remember Crowley, don't you, Cass? He certainly remembers you. After the ambulance left, we went back inside and had a chat."

The crumbling of her face was worse than anticipated. It confirmed the lies.

"He told me about you two," I said.

"Duck . . ."

"He told me how you were cheating on Victor Wingate with him. You know, your dead love who was pushed to his death?"

I waited for her to interrupt, but she just looked back with weary, beaten eyes.

"I also met with Dr. Lipke," I said. "Down in Miami. And perhaps most important, I spent last night with Carl's widow, Uli . . . at your personal dungeon on Orchard Street. Seems you and Uli were quite close, until you killed both men."

Her face grew hard, a fierce glare appeared in her dark eyes. "So now you think you know me, is that it? You think you have it all figured out?"

"I don't know you at all," I said. "That appears to be the problem, doesn't it?"

"Duck, I can explain the rest, but right now you have to believe me. I did not kill anyone. I'm being set up. And now they got to my attorney. Fuck."

She shut her eyes, squeezed her fingers against them, shaking her head. I wished it stirred some sympathy, but I wasn't feeling so generous.

"You know, I can maybe see Wingate, you pushing him off that waterfall, a moment of impulsive madness. Calling me, insisting to the cops that it couldn't have been suicide, all very clever. That part I can see. I'm not happy about being used, but it makes a certain sense. But Carl Kruger, Cass? Did you have to kill him too?"

"I did not kill anyone," she said again.

"Your prints were on the murder weapon," I said. "Care to explain that part?"

"My prints were on that javelin because Carl handed it to me. He let me hold it the last time I saw him. He didn't let anyone touch it, ever, but we bonded and he let me."

"Uli told me that Carl didn't trust you. She said your foursome was like a family, except for the tension between you and her husband. She said he never warmed to you, and when he learned of your relationship with Crowley, he was outraged. Then when Wingate died, Uli said, he was convinced you did it."

"Uli said that?"

"She did. Care to explain why she might have that opinion?"

"I can't," she said. "I don't know why she would say that. Carl and I, we were friends. He was a good man."

"I'm not inclined to believe everything that comes out of your mouth at the moment."

"Then don't, Duck. Get up and walk away. Go home and pour yourself a nice big drink. Drink your whole life away and pretend nothing matters. You're good at that."

I almost did. Hands on my knees, my thighs tightened to stand. Instead I said, "Despite your lies I came out here this morning. You might want to remember that. Unless you have another slave lawyer ready to serve you, you might want to acknowledge that you need some help, and that I'm about the only one who can help you. Oh, and maybe you can also remember that *you* called *me*. You brought me into this shit, Cass. Don't forget that."

We looked at each other until her face softened and her eyes averted. It was the first time I could remember ever having the upper hand.

"Can I explain?" she asked.

"You'd better."

Chapter 32

By the time I returned to the free world, I was salivating for a drink. I wanted to believe her, I did. But life experience has not conditioned me to an instinct of trust in those you love. More likely, lies and disappointment and the worst being true . . .

Save it for the therapist.

Until her innocence could be established, I had a more pressing concern:

Oliver Lipke, "son" of Eberhard, unhinged henchman of Dr. Crowley, a live-wire meth-head who'd managed to track my movements since I left him humiliated on that Hell's Kitchen sidewalk. Every player, Cass included, appeared to be working hard at his or her own self-interest. Each insisted there was nothing to hide, beseeching me in various conversations to believe in their blamelessness. That is, all except Oliver, who seemed to be taking a sick pride in his spreading of mayhem, perhaps he was watching me now. I knew he wasn't through. There was still more suffering to inflict.

I needed to remember my aikido instincts. *Instead of resisting, receive. Accept the bad energy and aggression and use it against itself. Don't seek. Wait and respond.* I could do that, as long as I treated the accompanying anxiety.

Before I returned home, I stopped at the Old Town and washed down a tuna melt with a couple pints. There was a Mets game on the TV mounted high in the corner. A blond flamethrower known as Thor was pitching. I couldn't remember his real name, but the moniker suited him. He looked like a Nordic god up there on the mound. I watched him strike out the side, then stared at myself in the mirror behind the bottles while the ball game went to commercial. Many drunken days and nights spent looking in that mirror. The Old Town never let me down. It felt better than home. Beneath the high tin ceiling the bartenders were friendly and fast; they started to pour your pint before coming over. At the straight-backed booths the waitresses operated with unsmiling efficiency. It was a place you could picture Walt Whitman sauntering into a century and a half ago, a good-looking boy on his arm, a folded letter from Emerson in his pocket. The walls were lined with framed book covers, memorializing the writers who drank there. When I got up to piss, I reveled in the giant porcelain urinal, a masterpiece of the lavatory arts. The city was a fallen mess of bad taste and dumb wealth, but as long as the Old Town stayed open, all was not lost.

I came out of the men's room and felt almost optimistic. My back and ass were covered with welts, courtesy of Uli; my partner was locked away in Rikers; and I was being hunted by a dangerous addict with ties to power I couldn't comprehend, but I was feeling sick enough to be totally confident. I'd dealt with worse. Or perhaps not, but I'd gone deep enough to know there is no bottom. There is no worst. All one could do was rise or fall with the tides of evil.

I climbed back on my barstool and raised my arm for the bartender. The game was back on. Now the Viking was at bat. Syndergaard, that was his name. My phone buzzed as he took a ball low and away. Detective Miller, about damn time . . .

"Hello, Lea," I said. "Lovely to hear from you."

"Where are you, Duck?"

"Having a drink at the Old Town, care to join me?"

"Stay there."

"You coming?"

"Yes. You are not to leave, is that understood?"

"I didn't intend to, but now you're making me wonder. What's going on, Lea?"

"Stay where you are, Duck. I'm serious."

She hung up before I could tell her I didn't appreciate the tone. I watched Thor stroke a single through the gap. I swallowed the impulse to get the hell out of there. Her manner did not promise positive news forthcoming. But where should I go? Home? Let whatever was coming find me.

Receive. Accept. React.

Detective Lea Miller arrived ten minutes later, flanked by a pair of beefy officers in uniform. Both had hands on their weapons. Not a smile among the three. The other patrons stiffened over their drinks. When Detective Miller addressed me, I felt a palpable exhale from my fellow drinkers. It wasn't them they were after. I raised my beer, gulped it down, and turned to face her.

"There she is," I said. "What can I get you?"

She glanced at one of the uniforms and he stepped forward. "Lawrence Darley, you're under arrest."

"For what?" I asked. Then I remembered the pint glass broken over Crowley's head. "Oh, right, the glass . . ."

"Anything you say can and will be used against you," he continued.

I turned to Lea. "What does he have, a concussion?"

The arresting officers lifted me from my stool and forced

me around. I felt the cuffs lock around my wrists, heard them click shut.

"So I guess this means Crowley is pressing charges?" I asked.

"No, Duck," said Lea. "He's not. He's dead."

The bludgeoned body of Dr. James Crowley was found the night before in Stuyvesant Park by a neighbor walking his beagle. Killed by blunt-force trauma, by a lot more than a pint glass to the head. My apartment on East 17th Street was about two hundred yards from the spot where he was discovered under the trees. The police did not appreciate the proximity. Neither did I. But at least I had an alibi. So I waited patiently in an interrogation room, confident in the knowledge that I'd be out soon enough. After enough time to make a guilty man squirm, the door opened and in stepped Miller, along with another detective I didn't recognize.

"Where were you last night?" she asked.

"Aren't you going to introduce your friend?"

She glanced at him; he looked at me, offered a scowl. He was a tall, well-built cop, clean-shaven, with a bent, hooked nose.

"New partner?" I asked.

He said nothing, waited for Miller to take the lead.

"Duck, where were you last night?" she asked again.

"About time you guys got around to establishing my alibi," I said. "I was otherwise engaged last night, with a woman named Uli Kruger." When Lea's mouth tightened at the name, I added, "That's right, the widow of Carl Kruger. I was with her all night long, at her bar, and then, later, alone with her at an apartment on Orchard Street. You'll find she can verify my whereabouts from the moment I left Crowley at that bar—where I reported our altercation to you, Lea—until about three a.m. last night. May I assume that the murder occurred sometime before three?" I searched their faces for confirmation; the nameless partner began to chew his lower lip.

"So you spent the day and then the night with Ms. Kruger, is that correct?" asked Lea.

"Yes, like I said, I was with her for quite a while yesterday, from roughly two p.m. until three a.m. You might say we became close."

"Did you have sexual relations with this woman?" asked the partner.

"He speaks. Nice of you to join the party, Officer, what was your name again?"

"Did you have sex with Ms. Kruger?" he asked again.

"I did, yes."

"And she'll verify that?"

"If she won't, I'm pretty sure my DNA will."

"So, to clarify," said Lea, "your alibi in the death of James Crowley, a man you admit to assaulting in front of witnesses yesterday afternoon, who was then beaten to death in a park very close to your home—your alibi is that you were drinking with, and then having sex with, the widow of the man that your partner has been charged with murdering? Is that correct?"

" 'Tis."

Lea couldn't meet my eyes. "You're all class, Duck," she said.

She turned and left the room. Her partner lingered for a moment, looking down at me like he wanted to fire a jab over the table. I smiled up at him until he suppressed the urge and left me alone.

They took their time about it. I was transferred to a holding cell, where a junkie lay curled in the fetal position on the floor. Open sores were visible along his scarred arms. He closed his eyes, braced for withdrawal. Soon he was shaking and sweating on the cement. I felt better about myself by comparison. No easy task. Here I was, hours after a return to Rikers, back behind bars, facing a bogus murder charge. At least I knew Cass didn't do it. I would have asked for an attorney, but the only one I knew was Eddie Lutelman, and I wasn't sure if his heart was still beating. Whatever, I was confident that Uli would establish my innocence. I'd be released after they spoke to her.

I tried to imagine Crowley's movements after I broke that glass over his head. Had I knocked him out? Or did he shake it off? I knew he had a high tolerance for pain. Was he killed in Stuyvesant Park, or dumped there after? Within shouting distance of my front door, that wasn't an accident. What happened in the intervening hours? Did he go to the hospital for stitches, a possible concussion? Did he file a police report?

I could picture our spooked ginger waitress relating the whole encounter: "*It was a tense conversation, I was afraid to go near them and drop off their drinks. The older guy, he stayed pretty calm, but the other one, he was drinking heavily and sweating and really angry. Then when he got up, he grabbed his glass and smashed it over the other guy's head. My manager and I went outside after him, but he jumped in a cab and sped off. . . .*"

And what did the good doctor do next, after he washed the blood from his hair and treated his head wound? Crowley didn't strike me as the "official channels" sort. He had too much to hide himself. He would be less likely to file a report and press charges, and more likely to seek out Oliver. Where was that sneering Aryan?

Hours passed before I was summoned back to the interrogation room. Detective Miller and Detective No-Name joined me a minute later. He took a seat on the chair across from me and scooted in close. Lea lingered a few strides behind his shoulder.

"They say every good lie must have a grain of truth," he said. "You ever hear that one, Darley?"

I smiled back without a nod or shake of the head.

"It's true. You have to start with some truth, then you just shave it and convince yourself that this altered version is the actual memory. It's how so many guilty folks pass lie detectors. It's just a matter of convincing yourself of a new reality."

I kept smiling, offered nothing. Tried to slow the acceleration of my heart rate.

"So . . . here's the deal," he said. "We followed up on your alibi. We spoke to Uli Kruger and we confirmed that you were almost honest with us. But not entirely, my friend, and that is where we have a problem."

I looked over his head and made eye contact with Lea. "Is this clown going to get to the point?"

She stepped forward, pressed the tips of ten fingers on the table, and leaned in. "Uli Kruger says you arrived at her bar yesterday around two p.m., soon after you assaulted Crowley."

"As I told you."

"Ms. Kruger stated that you drank through the afternoon. She says that the bar emptied of other patrons around four thirty p.m., at which point the two of you began talking. She joined you for a drink, and the conversation became infused with sexual tension."

" 'Infused'? Was that Uli's word?" I asked. "I like that, *'infused.'* Good word."

"Miss Kruger confirmed that you did indeed have sexual relations in her bar bathroom soon after. When you emerged from this encounter, she reports that the bar began to fill again, and that you returned to your seat and continued to drink."

"All true," I said.

"But then we have a problem," said her partner. "The rest of your story is bullshit."

"Miss Kruger further reports that she chose to close the bar early last night, around ten p.m., after it emptied, leaving you as her only customer. At this point you had to be very intoxicated. Can we establish that you had been drinking for approximately nine hours straight?" Lea asked.

"No," I said.

"No?"

"I also had a half-dozen drinks at the Wheeltapper earlier, waiting for Crowley, and then while we talked."

"Okay, eleven hours then. You had been drinking for eleven consecutive hours at this point?"

"Give or take."

Detective No-Name snorted with disgust. I guessed a night out for him was two or three Michelob Ultras after a good sweaty workout with other sweaty men.

"So you left with Miss Kruger as she closed the bar, is that correct?" asked Lea.

"Yes."

"And outside, she mentioned, you had an altercation with some gentlemen while she locked the door?"

"A couple cokeheads that wanted to keep drinking," I said. "Some rude hipsters, we had words. That was it."

"And then you left?"

"Yes, with Uli. We went to Cass's apartment-cum-dungeon, a few blocks away on Orchard."

"I don't think so," said No-Name.

"I don't care what you think. What did Uli say?"

The detectives exchanged a look. Lea blinked, gave a

nod, let him deliver the blow. He turned with a crooked smile and said, "That's it, end of night, end of alibi. Uli Kruger reports that she said good-bye to you then. She says that you were drunk and belligerent, and she advised you to sleep it off. She returned to her apartment on Henry Street, while you walked off in the other direction, Uptown. I'm sure we can find the gentlemen you confronted to confirm the altercation. Uli says they're regulars."

"She didn't mention us going to Cass's place on Orchard?"

"No, Duck," said Lea. "She says she went home."

"James Crowley was killed approximately two hours later, around midnight," said her partner. "Do you have an alibi for those hours, after you left Uli Kruger?"

"I told you—"

"And she told us otherwise."

"I don't know why she would say that, but you can check the place on Orchard. We were there, together. There has to be evidence of that." But even as I said it, I was picturing the spotless décor of Cass's dungeon. It was wiped clean after every use. Uli saw me out, said she was going to clean up after us. She wouldn't have left so much as a thumbprint. I remembered the whipping she'd given me, the marks that must still be covering my back. I stood and turned. "Check it out," I said. "Pull up my shirt and take a look. Uli whipped me last night. You'll see the marks. Just look."

Lea stepped around the table and raised my t-shirt, then dropped it and shook her head at her partner. "There's nothing there," she said. "Looks clean."

"What the fuck? It still stings, you're telling me you can't see any marks?"

Detective No-Name was enjoying this. He stood and came around and had a look for himself. "Nothing there, partner, sorry," he said. "I heard you were messed up, but this is pretty twisted. Your partner, Cassandra Kimball, kills Carl Kruger, you screw his widow, and then you go off and kill this Crowley, and your alibi is that the widow was whipping you in your partner's dungeon at the time of death?"

"That's the truth," I said. Though I wasn't sure if I still believed it myself.

"We have another problem, Duck," said Lea.

I knew before she could get the words out. I remembered Uli's face, her averted eyes, when I said his name. The way she shushed me and took control when I probed further.

"Oliver," I said. "He's her son."

Miller nodded. "He confirms that his mother was home last night soon after ten p.m."

Chapter 33

Mothers and sons. Who among us can question that bond? Who would doubt what they are capable of doing for one another? Boys are born into the world and held by the one woman that will forever forgive them. Mothers never lose that image of their baby boy, helpless and pure, in their arms. Even as the boy grows with bad intentions, and a less than pure heart, the naughtiness is charming at first. As he becomes a teen, though, it becomes destructive—there's drugs, the fighting, the uncontainable anger. When he's a young man, there are arrests, escalating in severity. The boy's path looks like a hellbound train, but the mother doesn't see that. She continues to see her loving child. Sure, he can be a bit unruly, a little difficult at times, but underneath it all he's really a sweet boy.

And sons never lose that earliest image either, the Madonna who protects and loves without condition. Even as the mother ages with bitterness and poor decisions. Even as the drinking and the pills take over, and she stops caring for him as well as she should, as the men come and go, before she decides that one is more important than the boy and she chooses the man over the son. Even then, the boy remains convinced that beneath all the ugliness of life, there's the mother he can always return to, who will shield him from harm.

Or something like that.

But who was the father? Lipke indicated that he'd adopted Oliver and said he'd taken his name. Crowley said that was a recent development, and used quotes around the term "son." Biologically it couldn't be Carl Kruger, of course. Still, the presence of a child would not have been something he would hide. Carl wanted to share his story with the world. Wasn't that why he was collaborating with Victor Wingate on the book? I wondered if he even knew about the boy.

But Uli knew all about her son. What he became, what he was capable of, and now she was protecting him. Shielding him the way he always knew his mother would. How long had she been with Carl? It had to be three decades, since before the Wall came down in '89. It was a love story worthy of Hollywood. A pair of abused and doped athletes come together in the waning days of their failed country; escape to freedom; make a life together in a city of reinvention and tolerance. But left behind: a child, Uli's boy, to be raised motherless in a crumbling East.

I could see the resemblance now, too late: the strong Germanic nose and jaw, the intense, watchful eyes. They both moved with that athlete's grace.

Her boy was back with her now, and it looked like the mother was making amends. Helping to frame others for the murders her boy was committing. Could he have killed her love, her Carl? Would mother choose son over husband? And when had Oliver turned on Crowley, his one-time boss? Had mother instructed son to tie up this loose end, now that she had a drunken fall guy? It closed a circle and contained their sins, while Cass and I paid for them.

I tried to explain this theory to the detectives. One looked on with pity, the other with contempt. Detective

Miller asked her partner for a moment alone with me. His parting shot: "*We got you, loser.*" And maybe they did.

When he was gone, Lea took the chair across from me. Something like sympathy flashed in her eyes. I wondered if this was a bad time to ask for a second chance.

"Duck, have you ever heard of a condition called alcohol-induced psychosis?"

"Jesus Christ, Lea . . ."

"It's also known as pathologic intoxication. There's a growing body of literature that . . ."

"So you're telling me that I hallucinated that entire trip to Cass's dungeon, where I let Uli Kruger whip me? And meanwhile, I was actually in a blackout state where I went off and killed James Crowley? That's what we're going with here?"

"You'd been drinking for eleven straight hours, by your own admission," she said.

"Will you just check out Cass's place, please? I can tell you where it is. My prints must be there. Someone must have seen us coming or going. Please, Lea. This isn't some alcoholic hallucination. I did not kill James Crowley. I don't even know how to reach the guy."

"What's the address?" she asked.

"The what?"

"The address, to your partner's apartment on Orchard, what is her address?"

"I'm not sure. . . ."

"Fucking hell, Duck."

"Wait. It's just north of Canal, about halfway up the block, on the west side of the street. There's a blue sign that says 'Success' next door. It's a red door with a bench out front. Her place is on the first floor of a tenement, at the end of the hall, last door on the left."

"But you don't know her exact address?"

"That was my first time there!" I shouted. "That's the thing. I'd never seen her place before. Cass always guarded her privacy. She was part of my life, but I was never really a part of hers. Does that make sense?" Lea looked back without expression. So I added, "Ask her. Go ahead and ask, you know where to find her—at Rikers, where I'll be soon too. We're both being set up here, and I know who's behind it."

"Who's that, Duck?"

"Oliver! Oliver Lipke, Uli's son, adopted by the doctor who doped her back in Germany. They created each other's alibis last night. They'll swear they were together at home, a mother-and-son reunion, while in reality one was off killing his former boss, and the other was whipping me in Cass's dungeon."

"You need to talk to a lawyer, Duck. I think you should stop."

"Just listen to me, Lea. You know me. You know I didn't do this. Neither did Cass. Did either of us write that letter to Juliette Cohen, threatening her son? No way. It was Eberhard Lipke, Oliver's father, or whatever he is. They're behind all this. Uli's son, he was the one who warned me before I went to see Cass after Wingate died. He told me to walk away, said some things aren't worth it. While I was gone, he spray-painted a hate slogan on the front door of my apartment. He must have been the one who came in through the back of Kruger's Bar and knocked me out and then killed his stepfather. . . ."

"Duck. Stop."

"Just tell me my motive. Tell me Cass's motive. Why would we kill the people we're being accused of killing?"

"Talk to your lawyer. I'm serious. We're done here."

She left me there without looking back. I felt eyes watching me behind the dark glass. Felt them listening to everything I muttered alone in that room. I stared at my hands until a young officer came in and escorted me back to my cell. Lea was right—I needed a lawyer. I could try Lutelman, see if he was still breathing, and if so, would he be willing to represent me? I knew he'd fight for Cass, but I wondered if we were still a package deal. We were being charged with separate crimes, connected but not united. I'd need my own representation. And I had no one.

No, that wasn't true. There was one person I could call.

A day later she posted my bail. Maybe it was because I insisted I knew who threatened her son. I promised to track him down and take care of it. Regardless, Juliette was there for me. Soon enough I'd traded my cell and my junkie roommate for the deep leather seat of her Benz, with her tanned legs stretched out beside me. She wore a short white sundress. Her hair was down and glowed golden across her face. The scent of her, the rich clean smell of lavender and lotion, filled the space with promise. Everything would be taken care of, until our problems drifted away in the rearview. I gazed out the window as the sedan glided through the city. A shirtless homeless man was slumped on a stoop. We made eye contact while stopped at a light. He held an empty vodka bottle by the neck in one hand. The look on his ragged face said he was contemplating flinging it through our window. The light changed and he was gone.

"How's Stevie doing?" I asked.

"He's fine. He's taken a liking to Terrance. He loves hearing his stories."

"Sounds like I've been replaced."

She glanced over, but didn't reply. We drove a few more blocks in silence before she said, "So tell me how you're going to deal with this. How are you going to find this guy and prove he did it?"

"I'm working on it."

"You haven't got a clue, have you?"

"I said I'd take care of it."

"Well, at least you have strong incentive. It's your ass that's going down if you don't."

"Thanks for the reminder."

"Though you're probably more worried about saving your partner's ass than your own. You're so damn obsessed with her."

"Fuck her," I said. "You never had any need to be jealous, Juls."

She scoffed. "It wasn't jealousy. Don't flatter yourself. I am not threatened easily. But stop pretending. You are obsessed with that woman."

Now wasn't the time to bicker with the lady responsible for posting my bail. The judge had set it at one million—a down payment of a hundred grand to the bail bondsman, a good-sized check, even to Juliette.

"Can I see him?" I asked after a few more blocks.

"Who?"

"Stevie, I'd like to talk to him."

"I don't think that's a good idea."

"Why?"

"Because he's scared to death, Duck. He's eight years old and he's in danger. He's not stupid. He knows what's going on. He goes to school with an armed bodyguard. He already has anxiety and now he knows that someone wants to hurt him, for reasons he can't understand. All he knows is that you're responsible for it."

"That's why I'd like to see him, to reassure him. Please, Juls."

"No."

There was no sense arguing. Her cub was in danger and mama bear wasn't budging. Until I took Oliver off the board and proved he was behind it, the conditions of my release were clear. I was free only to continue my job. If I couldn't do that, Juliette would make sure I ended up back in jail. I was back in her employ. Now instead of those envelopes of cash on the nightstand, I was in debt, a hundred large and counting.

"Can I ask for one more favor?"

"What?"

"I need a lawyer," I said. "I'll follow up with Cass's guy, Eddie Lutelman, but I'm not sure he's alive, or if he is, if he'd be willing to help me."

"I'll find someone," she said. "I'll email you the details later tonight."

She drove the rest of the way in silence until we stopped in front of my building on East 17th. Juliette had never been to my place before. I didn't bother to ask how she knew where I lived. Cardboard still covered my tagged front door. I spotted old Mr. Petit peering out his parlor window as I climbed from the Benz. I glanced back at her sharp blond profile. She turned and said, "Get to work."

Chapter 34

I learned that Lutelman was still alive, and no, he was not interested in speaking with me. He'd suffered a heart attack on the sidewalk, but they managed to reboot it in the ambulance. He was taking an extended leave from his practice. That was all I could get from his secretary. I wondered if he would still be helping Cass. The loyalty of slaves is hard to overstate. Cass owned him in a way that no spouse ever could. My guess—as long as Eddie Lutelman was breathing, he would do Cass's bidding. But as for her partner, that guy could fend for himself.

I considered Oliver. He was staying with his mother, at least on the night of Crowley's murder. It appeared Uli lived around the corner from her bar. I thought about heading to Kruger's to confront her, but that would land me back behind bars in short order. I decided to lurk nearby unseen, wait for her to leave, and then follow her home. Maybe I'd get lucky and catch Oliver in the neighborhood. Maybe he was so damn brazen that he'd stop in for a beer at his mother's pub, sip it on the same spot he killed her husband. No, Uli may be complicit in her son's crimes, but I never doubted that she loved Carl. Her son would keep his distance from the scene of that particular crime. If he was indeed behind it . . . I remembered with a jolt that Crowley was killed half a block away, in the park across the street.

I finished the rest of my beer and headed back out.

The police tape was still up. Whoever bludgeoned him had done it in the prettiest spot in the park: under a centuries-old elm in sight of the statue of peg-legged Peter Stuyvesant. The usual assortment of students and muttering addicts were scattered along benches around the perimeter. A few dogs pulled at leashes. Their owners looked away as the dogs pissed over blooming tulip beds. I wondered if anyone was watching me. So typical—the accused posts bail and returns to the crime scene. Even if an officer wasn't assigned to my tail, there were cameras hidden in the trees. There are few public places in this city where you are not being filmed. Good luck getting away with a crime committed in the open. They must have footage of the night Crowley died, the night Detective Miller seemed to think I was in a murderous blackout state of alcohol psychosis.

Perhaps those telltale tree cameras didn't reveal much at all. A hoodie and a mask under a dark night would make any ID difficult. I wondered if I had any hoodies at home, anything that could function as a mask. Wondered about the reliability of my memory and whether or not I was going insane. Had Uli really taken me to Cass's dungeon— the home I'd been so curious about for so long? Had I submitted to her kinky torture, while her son stood in this park and beat his boss to death? I remembered limping home, feeling the sting of her lashes, but then why weren't there any marks? I closed my eyes, tried to imagine the scenario I was being accused of. Did I do it? Was Uli telling the truth?

I shook away that madness, swore my innocence. It couldn't have been me. I could trust myself. Couldn't I? I began to salivate for strong drink. Another muttering addict, just like the bums on those benches . . . I still had a roof over my head, I wasn't that far gone, but for how long? When would I fall through the floorboards? The poles of ruin and respectability were so much closer than anyone dared to admit. The billionaire on the sidewalk, waiting for the light, alongside a homeless smack addict, drooling over scarred skin—they were aliens to each other, two different species forced to share the same city. But wasn't I a testament to that cruel swinging pendulum? I began life inside the gilded homes of the rich, and now I was dangling my foot over the abyss, a few decisions from that bench, or another jail cell.

Back home I stared down the bottle of Bulleit on the counter. Lost again. I knew it wouldn't help matters, but sometimes a man needs his medicine. I poured four fingers and gulped it down before any guilt could rise. If I didn't care about myself, the least I could do was help the boy. Maybe Stevie was safe now after all. If Cass and I were taking the fall, then why would anyone bother to fulfill those threats? All I had to do was give up. Let come what may. Maybe Lutelman would get Cass off. Maybe Juliette would find a lawyer to help me too. Maybe I just needed to sit back and let the law handle this. At what point do you give in and stop searching?

Never.

The cops aren't there to help. Neither are the lawyers. They're there to clean up. The only one that can help you is you.

Come night I would travel down to East Broadway. I would do whatever it took to find Oliver and prove his guilt, but first I needed to do some homework. I reached for my cell and found the number for their offices in Coral Gables. She owed me. The girl sold me out to her boss.

*   *   *

"BioVida," chirped the receptionist. I pictured her, all peroxide and silicone and overdoses of vitamin D.

"Could I please speak to Natasha?" I asked.

"She's very busy, may I ask who's calling?"

"Tell her it's Duck," I said. "Tell her it's urgent."

"I don't, um . . . okay, just a second. Let me see. Hold, please."

I hummed along to Jimmy Buffett Muzak while I waited. "Changes in Latitudes . . ." It did not improve my attitude. I listened to the whole bastardized song before she came on.

"Let me call you back in ten minutes," she said.

"No, it's urgent. Listen . . ."

"Not here. I'll call you back."

Click.

I reached for the bourbon while I waited, then thought of Stevie and pushed it aside. Some, I would grant myself some, but not much. Strictly maintenance drinking from here on out, there'd be time to drown myself later. In my days at chez Cohen, playing mentor to the boy, lover to his mother, I had been teaching myself temperance. It seemed long ago now. I could relearn it. It was the only way.

My alcoholic ponderings were silenced when my phone rang ten minutes later, as promised.

"I heard," she said by way of hello.

"About Crowley? Or that I'm being accused of it?"

"Both. Are you okay?"

"Out on bail," I said.

"Have a good lawyer?"

"Working on it."

"Listen, Duck, about the last time I saw you, with Dr. Lipke . . ."

"You sold me out, darling, and now you can make it up to me."

"I can't help you. I shouldn't even be talking to you."

"You know I didn't kill Crowley, right?"

"No, I don't know that. I barely know you. I know you're a liar and that you had a hard-on for him, so who knows?"

"It was Oliver," I said. "Lipke's son."

"Eberhard doesn't have children," she said.

"Oliver's adopted. Considering his boy's outright racism, I'm not surprised he kept him away from the office."

"Duck . . ."

"Apparently, it's a recent thing, the adoption. That's what Crowley told me. I don't know what his relationship is to his so-called father, but he's a fucking lunatic. He's worked for them, in some capacity, as their muscle. He's a full-on neo-Nazi. He's also evidently on a meth bender. I think he's killed them all—Victor Wingate and his step-father, Carl Kruger. Then he hit the trifecta when he bashed in the skull of Crowley. And now his mother is covering for him."

"His mother?"

"Uli Kruger, Carl's widow. I'm guessing Lipke knew him as a kid, felt some responsibility about the demon he became."

I listened to her breathe, pictured the baking pavement down Ponce De Leon Boulevard. Finally she spoke: "She was upset about the book."

"Uli contacted BioVida?"

"A few months back. She spoke to Dr. Lipke. I heard she was distraught."

"Did he tell you that?"

"He did. He's an old man. He feels a lot of guilt for what happened back then. He never meant to hurt anyone."

"He hurt a lot of someones, and as far as I can tell, he never paid for it. What did he get, a small fine, some bull-shit slap on the wrist? And then he set up shop down in South Florida, where he could teach Americans how to cheat? I know you're not that naïve."

"What do you care? Why does anyone care? It's sports. That's what people do. I got no time for that high-and-mighty moral bullshit."

"We're talking about murder, Tasha. Three and counting—maybe ordered by your boss, a man who has both a past and a present to protect. And as for sports, it was child abuse back then. Those kids he doped, they were minors and they didn't have a choice. Lives were ruined, and—"

"You think this is *Scarface?* Somebody's putting out hits from down in Miami? Listen to yourself. Lipke's an aging queen who just wants to be left alone. As for this boy, Oliver, I'd remember if some racist Nazi came around the clinic. I never met the dude, but if he's Uli's son, my guess is that Eberhard was trying to look after him out of guilt."

"Maybe at first," I said. "But Lipke's no fool. He made a point of telling me how dangerous Oliver is. He probably has some kind of paramilitary training with hate groups. You send out a guy like that, on a mission with a head full of meth, on a case that involves the mother who abandoned him? You're asking for a horror show, and that's what we've got. So I need you to deliver a message to your boss from me. Tell him what I just told you. Tell him I know all about Oliver and his mother, Uli. Tell him that he's an accessory to murder. You tell him that, and then tell him to call me. Can you do that for me?"

"Okay, Duck. I can't promise he'll call you back, but I can tell him."

"If he doesn't, he'd better close up shop and fly somewhere far away, because his life in this country is over."

"Is that all?"

"That's all, Tasha."

She lingered on the line. I thought she must be remembering our time together in that hotel room, so I said, "When this is over, I'd like to see you again."

"Never gonna happen," she said, and hung up.

* * *

Lipke made me wait an hour. Enough time for a refill and some loud apropos music. *Hedwig and the Angry Inch* ... "Try and tear me down." I worked myself into a righteous lather. I thought of Carl Kruger pouring drinks and cranking his metal behind that bar, an inverse through-the-looking-glass reflection of Hedwig. I thought of all the poor souls robbed of youth by Lipke, and other abusers worse than him.

When my cell finally rang, I was not feeling charitable.

"You asked to hear from me," said Lipke.

"Goddamn right," I said.

"You seem to have things mistaken, Mr. Darley. I was very forthcoming with you when we spoke. I told you the truth. Now I hope you'll allow me to clarify some of your misconceptions."

"And I hope you'll listen closely, because if you fuck with me now, you'd better hope the cops reach you first."

"The threats again, I understand you're upset, so am I. . . ."

"So are you?" I shouted. "I'm being charged with murder, so is my partner. Murders that *you* had a hand in. Don't tell me you're upset."

"If you'd calm down, I'd like to explain."

"You do that. Now."

"I fear my son is in the midst of a psychotic episode. I'm very worried. It would be in all of our best interests if you could find him."

"That's funny, your partner told me the exact same thing . . . before your son killed him. Maybe your boy, Ollie, will decide to take care of you next."

"He won't do that."

"And why's that? Psychotic meth-heads are always so rational, I'm sure you can reason with him."

"Because we love one another," he said. "You have to

understand, this boy's mother abandoned him. She left her husband and left her son behind when she defected. Two years ago Oliver sought me out in Miami. I felt an obligation to him. I tried to keep him out of trouble. I'm afraid his birth father is no longer. He has no other family."

"Who was the father?" I asked.

"That is irrelevant."

"The law won't think so," I said. "Maybe you had a hand in his death too. For a man with nothing to hide, you have an awful lot of bodies to account for."

"Please, enough with the blind accusations. Oliver's father was a man named Hans Zesner. He was a former patient of mine, like Uli and Hilde. Hans was a member of our national swim team, alongside his future wife. They were part of our program in Leipzig, where I was the head doctor. That's how they met. Hans was a bit older than Uli, by six, seven years. She became pregnant at seventeen. It ruined her athletic career. But Hans was in love with her and insisted they marry. Uli resisted at first, and then consented."

"But then his wife fell for Carl Kruger . . ."

"Hilde. This was before . . . the change."

"I can't imagine that was a very popular romance back home."

"It was a terrible scandal. Oliver was just a toddler. His father won custody, Uli was unwelcome, and then she fled."

"And let her son be raised without a mother."

"Yes."

"I'm surprised she wasn't jailed and executed by your party."

"Mr. Darley, the DDR had its problems, but we are not talking about the Third Reich. Please don't sound so American."

"So Uli and Carl went and made a life in the States,

while this Hans raised the boy by himself. What happened to him?"

"Unfortunately, Hans Zesner was not up to the task. He struggled after Uli left, after his competitive days concluded. He drank. Mental illness emerged, much as it has in his boy. He coached at the institute for some time, but he was soon unemployable. And with the instability after the Wall came down, Hans could not cope. He was killed in a drunk-driving accident when Oliver was ten. Hans was the one drunk. Three others died with him. After that, Oliver was sent to a home. I'm afraid I lost track of him after I left the country."

"Until he tracked you down in South Florida."

"Two years ago, yes. It was quite a surprise when he turned up."

"Not every day a long-lost neo-Nazi comes knocking."

"Mr. Darley, I detest the way you think you can speak to me. What is it with this verbiage of yours? I've done everything I can. I've tried to be open with you and you insist on demonizing me."

"The thing is, Eberhard, I tend to believe in guilt by association. Your dead partner was a confirmed alt-right medicine man. Your son, or whatever he is, has a body covered in hate-filled tattoos. There's 1488 on his knuckles, the letters NSM on his forearm—I told you, I know what that stuff means. National Socialist Movement, it's the underground Nazi party. Don't tell me you didn't know that."

"I did not," he said. "I swear on my life, I did not know what his tattoos meant. Unlike you, and most decent people, I have never been in prison."

"Where you fucking deserve to be—"

"You are an ignorant, accusatory American, and I will not stand for your language any longer."

"Okay, Doc, let's say you're as clueless as you say. I'll

help you piece it together. Here's what I think happened. I think your boy, Oliver, drifted into some bad scenes after he was orphaned. He was a perfect recruit. No parents to set an example, adrift and angry, no future in a crumbling, failed country. He probably came under the influence of some far-right, racist groups. With his strong athletic genes, they must have found him very useful. Seduced by a time that never was, when there was order and dim white boys had the world at their feet."

"You are a disgrace to your race," said Lipke.

"From you, a high compliment," I said. "Thanks for confirming what I already knew."

"I have confirmed nothing. You know nothing of me, nothing at all. When Oliver came to me in Florida, he was looking for a fresh start. I gave it to him. I got him on the medication he needed, we cared deeply for each other."

"How deeply, Doc?"

"How dare you . . ."

"No, I'm serious. Your own dead partner put the word 'son' in quotes when I mentioned your relationship to him."

"This conversation is over, I'm hanging up. . . ."

"Then I suggest you head straight for the airport. The feds should be raiding you shortly."

I waited to hear him call my bluff and end the call. I listened to his breath. Then he decided to continue talking.

"Oliver learned of his mother's whereabouts," he said. "Uli contacted me. She did not want the story told any more than we did. She abandoned her son, tried to forget him completely. A selfish woman determined to keep her secrets. I tried to keep him from her, but my partner, my now-deceased partner, told him. It was an awful thing to do, but James was desperate. He thought he could manipulate Oliver. The bastard, I will never forgive him for that."

"You don't sound too heartbroken about his death."

"I am disheartened about each death, Mr. Darley, but as you see, I had nothing to do with any of them."

"Aside from setting it all in motion," I said.

"I do not see it that way."

"Have you heard from Oliver since he got to New York?"

He hesitated, said, "No, not yet, but when I do, I will encourage him to turn himself in."

"Because you know he murdered Wingate, then Kruger, then Crowley."

"I don't know that, no. All I know is that Oliver needs help. He is very confused right now. He needs me. I pray that he has not had a hand in these killings."

"Your gift for denial is impressive. You really don't grasp your guilt, do you?"

That was my last provocation. With a plaintive gasp he hung up.

Chapter 35

Kruger's was closed. Lights off, locked door, no sign of movement inside. I stood out front and searched my phone for listings for a Carl or Uli Kruger, C. or U. Kruger, anything in that wheelhouse. Came up empty. Like Cass and countless New Yorkers, they were probably living on someone else's sublease, with no landline, had all mail delivered to the bar. Home was an anonymous notion.

Detective Miller had their address, but that information would not be forthcoming, not for a murder suspect intent on pinning the rap on a son with a mother's alibi. I remembered Lea mentioning Henry Street and found it a block south of the bar. The street ran from the shadow of the Manhattan Bridge all the way to Grand Street, just before the East River. It reminded me of my home as a teenager on Pitt Street, after the fall. It was a graceless stretch of tenements and projects, public schools and blacktop playgrounds. The top of One World Trade could be seen across the island to the west, beaming in the night sky.

I wandered these blocks for a while. Examined the tired faces, the weary resignation of the have-nots in a city that had everything. I tried questioning a few without success. An older Chinese man broke into a run the moment I approached. A twentysomething hipster told me to fuck off and kept walking. I caught up to three teenaged black kids leaving a playground. The only ones with the courtesy to stop and answer my questions, but they claimed never to have seen the folks I described.

I was contemplating a drink when my phone buzzed. It was a 305 area code, Miami: Lipke, or maybe Tasha, calling back, I figured. I answered and heard inaudible background noise. The called ended. I texted the number and asked who it was. The ellipses popped up, announcing a reply being composed.

I received an emoticon of a smiling purple devil.

Countered with **WTF?**

Again the ellipses appeared. I sat on a nearby stoop and looked at the screen. When the reply arrived, I almost collapsed. It was a video clip. I recognized the image at once—Stevie's bedroom. I pressed PLAY. The camera scanned the boy's darkened room until it reached the bed. There he was asleep under the covers, seemingly unharmed. I waited for the person holding the phone to turn it on himself. I heard his low laugh. The clip ended.

I was in the street, arm waving, but it was cab-less. I almost accosted a passing Camry; I'd remove the driver with force if necessary. I maintained just enough wits to call a Lyft. Waited on the corner for three desperate minutes, scanning for lit cabs, until he rolled up. I gasped out the Cohens' address, told him it was an emergency, offered all the money in my wallet as a tip if he ignored all traffic laws.

The driver was a young African guy, dark as night, with bright, hard eyes. He glanced back, took my measure. "What's the emergency?" he asked.

"A kid's in trouble, an eight-year-old boy. I think an abduction's in progress."

He turned to face the road. "Keep your money," he said. "I get you there."

I was flung back against the seat by the force of his foot on the gas. We hit seventy weaving through traffic on Grand Street. He sped through a red light, then another. I didn't know what his visa status looked like, but he drove like a man with diplomatic immunity. We barreled up the Bowery, spun left on Houston, right on Lafayette, the city streaming by. On Fourth Avenue I tried to think it through. Where were Juliette's bodyguards, Terrance and his soldiers from Warrior Security? Where was Juliette? How had he gained access? Stevie, what had he done to the kid? My thoughts spun out of orbit. Questions roared past like a meteor shower. One direct hit and I'd explode.

We were approaching the Cohens' building when I saw the sirens spinning in front of the building. Two police cars out front, commotion already in motion. I wasn't the first one on the scene, wasn't the only call.

My driver plowed to a stop next to them. "Good luck," he said. "Go."

I tossed four twenties over the seat on his lap. He may not have wanted them, but the man had earned it. "Thank you," I called.

I approached a pack of cops and the doorman speaking with alarm. They did not acknowledge me.

"It was food delivery," Ernie was saying. "I smelled the Thai food. Ms. Cohen approved it, her security too, how was I to know . . ."

"What did he look like, sir? Was he Asian?" asked a cop.

"No, he was white. He was wearing a black sweatshirt, a black Yankees hat pulled low. I didn't get a good look at his face."

"White guy doing delivery for a Thai place, that didn't arouse any suspicion?" asked another cop.

"No, I mean yes, it does now. That's partly why I called. It's been twenty minutes since I let him up, too long for a delivery. I called upstairs to Ms. Cohen and there was no

answer. Her security always answers. There's been . . .
Well, something must be wrong, so I called you."

"What's going on out here?" asked a baritone behind us.
The group turned together to find Terrance, Juliette's
primary guard, standing over them. The doorman started
to speak; the cop talked over him.

"Who are you?" he asked.

"Terrance Jones, Warrior Security," he said. "In the employ of Juliette Cohen. Does this concern her?"

"Terrance, your partner, Paul, approved the delivery,"
the doorman burst in. "Juliette did too. How was I supposed . . ."

I caught his eye. "Darley," he said. "What's going on?"

"Get us up there," I said. "Where the fuck were you?"

"Dinner."

I handed him my phone, played the video, and watched
his face. "When did you get that?" he asked, moving fast.

"About ten minutes ago," I said. "Got here as fast as I
could, cops were already here."

"It's a 305 area code, Miami. Know who sent it?"

"Name's Oliver Lipke, pretty sure he's behind all the
murders. His father wrote the note," I added.

We were in the lobby now, the cops calling after us, Ernie
the doorman still babbling uselessly at the door. Terrance
waved his entry pass and took a back stairwell, taking the
steps three at a time. I followed. Behind us cops shouted to
freeze. We ignored them. His weapon was drawn as he positioned himself in front of the Cohens' door. "Stay down,"
he growled at me.

Then we were inside the apartment, searching and shouting for Stevie and Juliette. We found his partner, Paul, first.
Shot through the chest in the entry foyer. The bag of Thai
food sat at his feet. On the living-room floor Juliette lay in
a splash of blood. Terrance knelt and felt for a pulse.

"Alive," he said. "Help her."

He was off down the hall toward the kid's room.

Juliette was unconscious, her face smashed and bloody. It looked like she'd taken the butt of a gun to the nose. I shook her; she started to stir.

"Kid's gone!" shouted Terrance. "Fuck!"

I heard him searching every room, each door opening and slamming shut. Knew he wouldn't find anything. My mind raced with doom. My blood boiled with impotent rage. The cops charged in. They got me down on the floor, found Terrance and forced him into submission. We tried to explain. Juliette was beginning to regain consciousness when the doorman came rushing into the room.

"He's getting away!" Ernie cried. "He's taken the car, he's driving away with Stevie!"

Everyone reacted at once, but I got away first. I was up on my feet and moving for the stairs before anyone could stop me. I made it down the three flights and out the lobby doors in time to see Juliette's Benz turn left at the end of the block onto Fifth Avenue. I chased after it, turned the corner in time to see it turn left again onto 10th Street. By the time I raced those three blocks down, the car was gone. I kept running, searching in four directions at the intersection. It was a calm night without disruption. The car that sped past moments before hadn't even been noticed.

Stevie was gone.

I took out my phone, started to dial Terrance's number. A message popped up—the 305 number.

You or the boy, it read. **4 Henry Street. Now.**

I was back waving for empty cabs in the street. This time I found one idling in front of a deli on the corner of 9th and University. I dove into the back, called out the address. A bored Pakistani glanced back, his face full of falafel. "On break," he said through a mouthful.

"Not anymore," I said. "Drive!"

Such rudeness to city cabdrivers does not fly, but this time he seemed to grasp the urgency. Maybe it was the mania in my eyes, maybe I was just riding some good luck with drivers, or maybe he was another decent New Yorker who knew when it was time to lend a hand. For the second time that hour I was thrown back against the backseat as my driver sped through the city's streets.

"A kid's been abducted," I panted between the seats. "Sooner I get there, the better chance we have to save him."

"I get you there," said my driver.

His name was Ali and he drove like a champ. Ten minutes later, in a blur of Broadway, through the maze of lower Manhattan streets, and I was approaching the same spot I'd just left. The same block where I'd received that video of Stevie's bedroom—the stoop where I watched it was just a few doors down from 4 Henry Street.

Uli Kruger's apartment: the son was returning to the womb for his final reckoning. I looked up at the crumbling building. Same as all the others, same as the one that Cass hid from me for so long; same as my old apartment on Pitt Street, where my mother drowned drunk in the bathtub; same as ones that housed countless miseries in this miserable city without memory.

The smell of rotting fish filled the air. Graffiti covered the sides of a Chinese corner market. As I approached the red front door, my phone lit again. I glanced down at the text. **Apt 2**, it read. He was watching me, as he'd been doing all along. I pressed the buzzer, waited for admission, and up I went.

Chapter 36

He was waiting with the door open, Carl's Luger pointed at me, a look on his face that was pure mad-eyed meth. Oliver was shirtless now, with exposed scalp sweating, his hat and sweatshirt shed. His torso was scarred with more racist ink. There was a swastika tattooed across the left side of his chest, SS lightning bolts on his ripped stomach. His body was a monument to hatred and ignorance. I raised my hands, thought of Stevie in there.

"Inside," he said. "If you're not alone, I kill everyone right away."

"I'm alone."

"We'll see."

As I crossed the threshold, I saw the kid sitting terrified in the chair by the window. Uli sat across from him on the couch, her eyes down and her hands in her lap. She did not look up at my entrance. I felt the gun touch the back of my head. I took in the surroundings. It was a narrow railroad apartment, with the kitchen in the middle, the bedroom in back. On a small dining table there was a mound of white crystals, a razor, and a cut straw.

"Don't worry, buddy," I said to Stevie. "I'm here."

"You hear that," said Oliver. "He's here. Aren't you happy? Now you can watch him die."

"Hello, Uli," I said.

She pretended not to hear. Oliver shoved my back, pushed me over to the sofa. "Down," he said, "next to her."

Uli couldn't bring herself to look up as I lowered myself onto the cushion next to her. She looked lost in an abyss of regret; perhaps accounting for all the ways she might have prevented this moment. Had there been a point when she could have stopped her abandoned son? When had she learned the truth? Did she know it was her boy behind the murder of her husband right away? I found that unlikely. But by the time she had her way with me in Cass's dungeon, she'd made her decision. She was going to protect her son, even if it meant sacrificing the lives of innocent friends. I remembered her words that afternoon at the bar: *We are all atoning for something, I think.*

She looked up for the first time and regarded her shirtless, pacing son. "Oliver, please," she said.

He stopped in the center of the room, swung around to face her, the Luger dangling loose at this side. "Please what, mother? Please don't speak to me like a parent? How about that?"

"No one else needs to get hurt."

"I'll decide that," he said. "You lost the right long ago to tell me what to do."

"It's gone far enough," said Uli. "Please, not the boy. It's not too late."

Oliver strode to his mother and whacked her atop the head with the barrel of the gun. She winced, grabbed at her hair. Tears welled in her tired eyes.

"It's too late for you, I'll grant you that," he said. "Too late for your freak husband. And too late for this prick too." He looked over at me on the couch and raised the gun. "I've been waiting for this," he said. "I told you I was a fan."

"Fan of what?" I asked.

"Of insanity, of suffering, of fear—our specialties, right, Duck?"

"Why the kid, Oliver? Why didn't you kill me quick, like the others?"

He seemed to brighten at the question, eager to offer explanation for his madness. "Excuse me a moment," he said. "I'll be right with you."

He went to the two-seat table with his mound of drugs. He faced us, kept one hand around the Luger, as he bent and cut thin white lines with the other. He set the razor aside and reached for the straw. I thought about lunging for him in his moment of meth distraction, but Oliver raised the gun at me as he leaned down and snorted.

"*Ahh!*" he said. "That's bet-ter. Now where were we?"

He rubbed at his nose and went to Stevie in the chair by the window. "Don't do drugs," he said to him. "Anyone ever tell you that? No one told me. My mother abandoned me. My father was a user himself. How was I supposed to know?"

He reached out his tattooed fingers and rubbed his knuckles over Stevie's face. He crouched down to meet his eyes. "Are you scared?" he asked.

Stevie, God bless him, shook his head.

"No? Impressive, most little boys would have pissed themselves by now, but not this rich punk." He swung back around. "You teach him that, Duck? To be a little badass?"

"You didn't answer my question."

"Ah, yes, why not kill you quick? Why get this boy involved? That part, the letter, was Eberhard's idea. He thought it would be enough."

"Your daddy told me he hated threats," I said.

"My daddy?" he asked. "He told you that, yeah? Sweet daddy Ebi." He laughed. "In exchange for taking his name, he promised to take care of me, to leave me much of his fortune. In exchange for his name and a few other things . . ."

At that, Oliver thrust his hips lewdly. "All I had to do was close my eyes and let him lower my pants on occasion. No big deal, a mouth is a mouth, right? I was forced to do worse for less as a kid in that home." He turned and leered at Stevie. "Is that what your relationship is like with this guy?" he asked.

"Don't listen to him, buddy," I said. "He's crazy."

"I know," said Stevie, staring straight back at him.

Oliver took a step toward him. I stood. He leveled the gun at my chest and looked down at the boy. "It's easy to be brave when you've never been hurt." He took a step closer to Stevie.

"Don't you touch that boy, Oliver," said Uli.

He swiveled his shaved head to face her. "Maternal instincts kicking in? A little late, don't you think?"

"If you touch that child, we will both be on you," she said, glancing at me. "You can't shoot us both at once."

"This little shit really means more to you than your own blood?" he asked. "You never fail to disappoint."

"You took my husband, Oliver. Isn't that enough?"

"No, no," he said with a sick smile. "We killed him. It wasn't just me there that night. Who was it again that knocked out this clown coming out of the bathroom?"

Uli looked away, avoided my gaze. Oliver kept grinning. "Who was it again who told me to take the cash out of the register, and to grab that bottle, to make it look like a robbery gone wrong? I believe those were your words, mother, were they not?"

"You said you only wanted to speak to him," said Uli. "You promised me that you would reason with him, we both would. With Victor dead he just needed to give up on that story of his."

"You believed that?" he asked, full of what seemed genuine disbelief. "I finally get to confront the bastard who stole my mother, and you thought I'd just want to chat?"

When she didn't answer, I said, "You set us up, both of us. You were prepared to let Cass and me take the fall for murders your son committed."

"I had no choice," she said. "He would have killed me."

"I suspect he still will," I said.

Oliver liked that. He stepped away from Stevie and came over to me, rubbing the barrel of the gun against his cheek. "I wasn't lying, you know. I was a fan of your work. True crime is a passion of mine, ask Eberhard. I love those shows. I learned all about your last case. I really was excited to meet you."

"Like an autograph?"

His foot came up fast, too fast to catch, and connected with my mouth. My head rocked back. I tasted blood and loose fragments in my mouth. A few teeth—I spit them out at his feet. He came closer and delivered another kick to my stomach, blasted the breath out of me. "You were lucky the cops were there that day," he said. "You might have a few moves, but I would have cleaned the sidewalk with you."

I gasped for air, wiped the blood from my mouth, tried to straighten up for Stevie. "Four murders and counting," I said. "You're lucky New York doesn't have the death penalty."

Returning to the table of drugs, he said, "It's funny that you've already included yourself in the death count."

"I haven't."

"You said four?" He leaned down and snorted up another line. "So far I count only Kruger, Crowley, and that useless security guard at the kid's place."

"You're forgetting about Victor Wingate," I said.

"The writer, the bitch's boyfriend? I'm afraid you're

mistaken, not my work. I was still in Miami at the time of his death."

"Bullshit."

"He was," said Uli next to me. "Eberhard called to tell me they were coming. He was worried."

"See!" said Oliver. "Alibis galore. Besides, my plane ticket will confirm that I was on a flight here *after* that man was killed. That one looks like the doing of your partner."

"No way Cass pushed him."

"Really? You know she was screwing Doc Crowley, right? He liked to talk about what a fiend she was. He was sure she killed him. That was the reason for his visit—to cover his own ass. Crowley was worried he was being set up, and, of course, he was worried about that book. Eberhard asked me to join him."

"What are you going to do with her?" I asked, turning to Uli. "Are you going to kill your own mother too?"

"The act of giving birth does not make a mother," he said. "She is nothing to me. Until I followed you to her bar, I didn't even know what she looked like."

"And the kid?" I asked. "What's your play, to kill us all and make a run for it?"

"Life is cheap," he said. "Something that spoiled little shit is about to learn."

"Fuck you," said Stevie from across the room.

Oliver spun around. "What was that?"

"Fuck you," repeated the kid. "You're a druggy racist Nazi. The cops will probably be here any minute."

"Is that so?"

Oliver stepped toward him and raised the gun. Stevie's face crumpled after his reckless burst of bravery. Tears flooded down his cheeks. "I hate you," he said.

Uli and I exchanged a glance, a flash of connection that communicated life and death and action. We turned toward Oliver and leapt together at him. I caught his right arm holding the Luger and knocked it from his grip as it fired. Uli put her shoulder into the small of his back and sent him falling forward toward the boy. The three of us tumbled into the chair as Stevie dove out of the way. The gunshot rang through the small apartment, ripping through the plaster ceiling. Oliver roared and flung his limbs at us, fighting back in all his meth-fueled fury. His elbow met his mother's head and sent her flailing back. I kept hold of his right arm and twisted it behind his back, ignoring the pressure point limit and kept twisting until I heard it pop. But his raging survival adrenaline blocked out the broken bone and his fight increased. I went for his eyes next, tried to gouge them out and blind his assault. Like the broken arm, a blinded eye didn't slow him. He was stronger than I was. The dope pumping through his veins gave him superhuman ferocity. He managed to flip me over, freed an arm, and drove a fist through my face. All was a blur. My world spun, my limbs went limp.

Then a second shot rang out from the Luger.

Chapter 37

Stevie was holding the gun. He kept it raised with both hands, shaking steps away from us. We made eye contact. The Luger lowered and dropped from his grip and he burst into tears. I scrambled to my feet, stepped over Oliver's lifeless mass, and wrapped him in my arms.

"It's okay, it's okay, it's okay," I kept saying, over and over.

Uli stirred next to us, wiped blood splatter from her face. She pushed herself to her feet and went to her son. Dead on her floor, shot through the temple, back in his mother's life for the first and last time. I watched as she stared down at him. Her body was very still, all emotion contained in a shell of shock.

We heard sirens approaching.

Uli knelt before him and pulled a blanket from the turned-over chair. She covered his torso and face with it, sat back on her heels, and shut her eyes. "I'm sorry, Oliver," she whispered. "So very sorry."

"He killed your husband," I said behind her.

"And I killed him many years before that," she said without turning. "I chose myself over my son."

Stevie looked up at me, confused. I hugged him tighter.

The little hero had saved us all. I didn't want to contemplate all the psychic damage it cost him.

Moments later the room filled with cops and shouts and déjà vu. I was practiced at such aftermath and I tried to be as helpful as possible. Questions were answered; statements were taken; a body was wrapped and wheeled away. I could have directed the scene myself. The senior detective on site had less experience than I did with such madness. This time there were few exterior injuries among the survivors, nothing requiring hospitalization, just a few lost teeth and rattled heads. Psychiatric treatment would come later.

Inside the 5th Precinct, Uli recanted her story about going home after closing the bar the night Crowley was killed. She established that she was indeed with me inside Cass's apartment-cum-dungeon at the time. I couldn't have killed him. She said that her son and his former boss were headed to my apartment when Oliver struck the doctor in the park. She confirmed that he killed her husband, Carl Kruger, in her presence. She said she tried to stop him, but had been scared for her own life. Cass and I were expendable ways for her to save herself.

It was the culmination of decades of betrayal, beginning with pills and needles of steroids shot into the muscles of young German girls. It continued with an abandoned boy, an amoral doctor, a couple desperate for freedom. The perpetuation of sin never slows. It only collects more momentum as it builds toward another reckoning. Those naïve souls who believe in the inherent goodness of man have always confused me. How much more evidence could they need before accepting the obvious truth—that this race was born doomed. The righteous choice is seldom the first choice. It's a minority decision that must be celebrated for its rarity. Dishonesty and self-interest are our natural settings. How could anyone with open eyes disagree with such an observation?

But sometimes there are kids like Stevie Cohen, whose fearlessness shines through at the exact right moment, and helps rescue us all. It wasn't genetic. I couldn't give his mother credit for instilling that bravery, and certainly not his absentee father. Maybe it was something that existed in everyone, but was seldom pushed to the surface. Whatever it was, it could never be predicted. Better just to be thankful when it appeared.

My former partner, Cassandra Kimball, was another question. She seemed to be one of the infinite selfish souls who acted on dark impulse, and then tried to save herself after the fact. She must have pushed Victor Wingate after all. First thought, best thought; ignore the noise that comes later.

For now, she would stay inside Rikers. She'd be cleared in the murder of Carl Kruger, but one murder was enough for life without parole, and plenty of folks have been known to rot on that hopeless island for years before a trial and any justice is declared.

It was a day later that Susie Wingate surfaced on a tabloid news program called *Inside Edition*. She was chum in the water for those bottom-feeders. A wounded relative of scandal, a close spectator to a story full of sex and death—they probably tracked her down and convinced her to talk. A producer called and tried to persuade me to participate. He mentioned another private investigator turned talking head that the show had helped make famous. I hung up on him. But that night I made sure to tune in to Susie's segment.

They made her look like a grieving angel, with her interview shot in sun-kissed morning light on her front porch outside Woodstock. For B-roll the cameraman captured gorgeous scenes of the sylvan landscape. The shot moved through the woods, along the trail where Cass led me, to the spot where Victor Wingate went over those falls, where my former partner was alleged to have pushed him. They found footage from our previous case—of both of us being led into the backs of cop cars and ambulances. We were a damaged pair of moral-free New Yorkers, the sort the heartland could shake their heads at and mutter about Gomorrah. In her sound bites Susie accused the media of missing the real story: her brother's murder.

"I don't care about that freak show in the city," she said, weeping. "All that other stuff that happened later, the other deaths. I just miss my brother." Zoom on the tear-streaked cheek as she said, "I loved him so much."

I turned it off and took a shower. Hoped it was the last I saw of her. If she had any sense left, she'd sell that mountain home of her brother's and live frugally off the proceeds. Like my apartment it would need to be cleansed of its demons.

The next morning I awoke to a message from Detective Lea Miller, informing me that she'd be by my place at ten a.m. I checked my phone; it was a little after eight, enough time to wake with sufficient refreshments. I texted back **Okay,** didn't bother to ask why. After I dressed, I sat around opening bottles and reading the bad news of the day. Another mass shooting, another powerful pig accused of serial sexual harassment, another natural disaster that decimated an island nation. She knocked a few minutes after ten.

With a well-rested smile she said, "C'mon, we're going for a drive." Her Prius was parked in front of a hydrant with the back door open.

"Where we going?"

"Few hours north. You eaten?"

Did three Beck's and a coffee count?

I glanced over her shoulder at an overnight bag in the backseat. "Do I need to pack?"

"Up to you," she said. "I'm going to stay the night, get some fresh air. When we're done, you're welcome to take the bus back. The Department will pay the fare."

"Where are we going?" I asked again.

"Catskills," she said. "Should be about two and a half hours."

"Why?"

"Someone wants to talk to you."

"Who?"

"Victor Wingate's sister, Susie. Let's go, I'll explain more in the car. I said we'd be there by one."

So much for never seeing her face again . . . I grabbed my phone, wallet, keys, and took a book—Tosches's *Me and the Devil*—maybe I'd finally have a chance to finish it on the ride back. No way I was spending the night outside the city.

We made it up the FDR and over the George Washington Bridge without too much traffic or talk. I waited for Lea to share more, didn't push it. On the Palisades she glanced over and said, "So, aren't you curious what Susie wants?"

"Not really." I shrugged. "I saw her on *Inside Edition* last night. They made her look half sane."

"*Inside* what?"

"The show, that tabloid that what's his name used to host? Anyway, yeah, she was on it. They asked to interview me too. I declined."

"What did she say, on the show?"

"How heartbroken she is, how guilty Cass is. What you'd expect."

Lea was silent for a moment. "When did this air?" she asked.

"Last night, at eleven, why?"

"When did a producer call you for comment?"

"I don't know, sometime yesterday afternoon, what does it matter?"

"So they must have filmed her earlier in the day."

"You want to tell me why I should care?" I asked.

"Because there's been a . . . development. It appears Susie discovered something that may clear your partner."

"Which is?"

"I'm not totally sure. I just spoke to a local sheriff up there this morning. Wingate's death is their jurisdiction, but since your partner is being held in Rikers, it had to go through us."

"What did his sister find?"

"A letter," she said. "And she asked to speak with you specifically. That's all I know."

"What about Dr. Lipke?" I asked. "Has he been arrested in Miami yet?"

Lea shook her head. "Appears he's left the country. A flight to Moscow was booked on his credit card. There's an Interpol notice out for him, but Russia isn't exactly helpful in returning suspects to America."

"I'm sure they'll welcome a proven doping Doctor. He probably already has a job."

The rest of the ride passed in almost total silence. Neither of us reached for the radio. The windows stayed up. The AC hummed. I stared out the window at the rolling green landscape, thought of Cass's escape to these parts after our last case. It had soothed her then, until it didn't.

Lea got off the Thruway at Exit 19 and turned on her GPS. The disembodied female voice guided us from there down winding two-lane country roads toward Woodstock until we found Wild Rose Road. She turned and slowed and searched for the number on the mailbox. Finding it, we crunched over a gravel drive at ten minutes before one.

A state police car was parked in front of a sagging farm-house, a country pile in advanced disrepair.

Susie Wingate sat on a rocker on her front porch, clutch-ing a mug with two hands. It was a warm spring day, but her shoulders were wrapped in a woolen blanket. Her face was slack, her eyes looked turned in on themselves. Two officers leaned against their squad car. They straightened up at our approach. Lea parked behind them and we stepped out into the sun.

"Afternoon," said one.

The other tipped his hat and said, "Detective Miller, thank you for coming." Then to me, "And you must be Mr. Darley."

If Susie noticed our arrival, it didn't register. Drugged, I presumed, heavy meds for a heavy time. In her lap I no-ticed a torn envelope. We stepped closer. The cops waited awkwardly for someone else to begin. Without turning, Susie said, "I hate the mail, I hardly ever check it. Nothing ever comes but junk."

The older of the two officers cleared his throat. "Miss Wingate received a letter from her brother," he said. "It seems to have been sent on the day he died."

"But it wasn't discovered until yesterday afternoon," added his partner.

"I almost threw it out," said Susie. "Then I recognized his handwriting. It was like seeing a ghost in the night." She turned and looked at us for the first time. "There are ghosts here, you know? Lots."

"Susie, is that the letter in your lap?" asked Lea.

She glanced down at it, nodded. "I guess you'd like to see it."

Lea went to her with caution. Susie appeared to be in a state of catatonic madness, but the slightest fright was li-able to throw her into frenzy. Lea stepped onto the porch, lifted the letter from her lap, and backed away. The air felt suspended, breezeless. The bark of a far-off dog came through the woods.

She came back to me and slid the piece of paper from the torn envelope. It was written in blue ink on a plain piece of printer's paper. Over her shoulder, I read:

> *Dear Susie,*
> *Please forgive me. You and I, we've always struggled with the crazies upstairs, haven't we? Remember, that's what dad used to call it when the depression got to him too? The crazies upstairs, I always liked that.*
> *I take this final plunge because there is no other way. The woman I thought I loved betrayed me. The book that was consuming me now seems destined to bankrupt us, or worse. If I continued, I'd be sued for millions. I've been threatened. They threatened to hurt anyone close to me. The thought of anyone harming you for something I pursued is too much to bear.*
> *Sell my house. It was appraised for almost a million. You can live on that for a good long time. I love you, sis.*
>
> *Good-bye.*
> *Victor*

Lea looked up at me when we finished. Her eyes were moist.

"Cass didn't kill him," I said. "It was suicide after all."

"Appears so."

Lea refolded the letter, placed it back in the envelope, and returned it to Susie's lap. "I'm so sorry for your loss," she whispered. "Your brother sounds like a good man."

Susie looked past her to me. "I could have burned it, you know? I could have let your friend rot. She helped kill Victor, even if she didn't push him."

"Thank you," I said. "For showing us, and for reporting it."

"Miss Wingate," said the older cop. "As discussed, we've made copies of your brother's note and we may need you for further questioning. You've done a good thing, ma'am. You're helping to free an innocent woman."

Hearing those words, a fire seemed to light in Susie's drugged eyes. "That whore's not innocent," she said. "Now I want all of you off my property." When none of us moved, she stood and screamed, "Now! Get the fuck out of here, all of you!"

We did as we were told. The cops waited for us to pull out first, then followed us back down the gravel drive. Lea and I didn't speak until we reached the town center of Woodstock.

"The bus leaves every hour from here," she said. "Unless you'd like to stay for a bit?"

"No thanks," I said. "I'm going back to the city—to see my partner."

Author's Note

The facts behind this work of fiction bear mentioning. This book came about through two preoccupations that were consuming me as I wrote the first draft in 2016. The first was in researching the "birth of doping" for a documentary I worked on called *The Last Gold*. It told the story, in part, of the East German experiment, when a generation of young women was sacrificed at the altar of sport, forced to dope as part of a political program, officially known as State Plan 14.25. While athletes of both genders were subjected to these "supporting means," the focus was on young female athletes—whose bodies could be transformed more dramatically with heavy doses of Oral Turinabol and other steroids.

One such athlete deserves special mention. His name is Andreas Krieger, formerly Heidi Krieger, a world champion shot-putter at the 1986 World Championships. In 1997, Krieger underwent gender reassignment surgery and changed his name to Andreas. Krieger is married to a former East German swimmer named Ute Krause, also a victim of forced doping. Unlike the characters they inspired in this book, they are alive and well. All similarities end with the broad strokes of their doping history.

The second preoccupation was witnessing the rise of

overt and shameless white supremacy during the 2016 presidential election. This was a year before the events in Charlottesville, Virginia, in August 2017, when that ugly undercurrent appeared to burst into the mainstream. While racism has always been an ignorant and enduring legacy of America, its Original Sin, so to speak, it has never felt quite so unconcealed in my lifetime. As *Vanity Fair*'s Graydon Carter wrote in his October 2017 "Editor's Letter": *This may sound unkind, but why are supremacists invariably the worst specimens of the race they are claiming to defend?*

So, to any neo-Nazis or white supremacists I may have offended with my uncharitable characterizations in this book: good.